BIBLE
KIDVENTURES

OLD TESTAMENT STORIES

TYNDALE HOUSE PUBLISHERS, INC.
CAROL STREAM, ILLINOIS

Cover design by Jennifer Ghionzoli
Cover illustration © Andreas Schonberg

Cataloging-in-Publication Data for this book is available by contacting the Library of Congress at http://www.loc.gov/help/contact-general.html.

ISBN: 978-1-58997-728-0

Printed in the United States of America
1 2 3 4 5 6 7 8 9 / 19 18 17 16 15 14

For manufacturing information regarding this product, please call 1-800-323-9400.

CONTENTS

Trouble Times Ten

by Dave Lambert

To Faith, forever my youngest—
My Faith
My hope
My love

CHAPTER 1

The cool water closed over Ben's head, shocking him. He panicked for a moment, holding his breath as his arms flapped frantically. Then he felt strangely calm. Surely his parents saw him fall off the dock and would rush to lift him out of the river.

He looked up. The sun was there, high above him, a bright spot filtered by the wavering water. All Ben had to do was move toward the light. He expected to see his father's face beside the sun at any moment. Ben moved his arms and legs, trying to push himself upward, toward the sun, toward the air. But he'd never had to swim before and didn't know how.

Thrashing wildly now, Ben wanted to scream. But he was afraid to open his mouth. His lungs felt as if they were about to burst.

He felt mud beneath his feet, and hope surged through him—he could push himself toward the surface now. He bent his knees and pushed himself upward with all his strength. But his feet sank into the soft mud, and he floated upward only a short distance. Then his exhausted arms reached hopelessly toward the sun. He coughed out the air he had held in his lungs all this time and watched it shriek toward the surface in huge dancing bubbles. He gulped in the murky, bitter water of the Nile, and everything went slowly black around him, fading . . .

And then Ben gasped, unsure where he was. One hand groped around him for someone, something—

And what he found was his blanket. He touched the thing he was lying on. He tried to stop his loud gasping. He heard his father's snoring.

He wasn't in the Nile River, or even beside it. He was on his own sleeping mat on the floor of his family's home near Rameses, in Egypt.

He heard his mother stirring. "Ben?" she asked softly. "Are you all right?"

Ben opened his mouth to answer, but his throat tightened and he felt tears burn his eyes. No, he didn't want to cry after some little nightmare. Only babies cried about nightmares. He closed his eyes and concentrated on stifling the sobs that formed in his throat. Then he felt a movement near him and opened his eyes. His mother was settling onto his sleeping mat beside him. She held a dim oil lamp in one hand. Ben couldn't help it. He buried his face in her shoulder and cried.

When he finished crying, he leaned against her, enjoying the warmth of her hand on his back. His mother was plump and soft and not much taller than he was. They sat in a small circle of lamplight. Their floor was sand, covered in most places by rugs or sleeping mats. Ben could just make out the hunched form of his father across the room. From the small room next to theirs came the sleeping sounds of his grandparents.

"Was it the river dream again?" his mother asked softly. Her sweet voice calmed him, as always.

Ben nodded.

His mother was quiet for a while, then said, "It's all right to be frightened. It was a frightening thing. But you're ten years old now. All of that was long ago."

Yes. Ben remembered the young man who saved him. After Ben lost consciousness in the river, he awoke lying on a sandy bank. An Egyptian man, young, strong, and dripping wet, leaned over him. His expensive clothes, dark with water, were clinging to him.

When Ben began to cry, the serious expression on the man's face changed to relief. "He'll be all right," he said and then stood. Suddenly Ben's father, his face twisted with emotion, appeared and gathered Ben up in his arms. Ben hadn't seen that man again. But he would never forget his handsome face.

Ben's mother stretched and made herself more comfortable on the mat. "When Moses was a baby," she said, "his mother put him in the Nile in a basket to save him from Pharaoh's men, who were killing the young children of our people. The river saved his life." She smiled. "Do you think Moses would be afraid of the river?"

Ben sighed. No, Moses wouldn't be afraid. Moses wouldn't be afraid of anything. Every Israelite knew the story of Moses. He'd been raised in Pharaoh's own household, the adopted son of Pharaoh's daughter, who had found that basket floating in the rushes along the river. Every Israelite also knew how Moses had rebelled against the treatment his people received from the Egyptians. He had fought a cruel foreman who was beating Hebrew men. In his rage, Moses had killed that Egyptian and then fled for his life.

"But he won't stay away forever," Ben's father and the other men all said. "He's the only one strong enough to stand up to Pharaoh. He is a hero of the Israelites, like Abraham and Jacob and Joseph. He'll come back when we need him."

Yes, Moses would come back. And he wouldn't be afraid of Pharaoh.

No, Moses wouldn't be afraid.

But Ben was afraid of everything. Water. Rats. Bullies. The dark. Loud barking dogs. The list of things Ben was afraid of was long.

Why couldn't he be more like Moses?

Early the next morning, wiping sleep from his eyes, Ben stepped from his house. He blinked at the huge golden sun, still very low in the sky. The sun gleamed on the river a short distance from the village. It was one of many channels cut by the Nile River as it wandered across its flat, fertile delta on its way to the sea.

Away from the river, in the other direction, Ben could see the gleaming city of Rameses, where Pharaoh lived. North and east of Rameses stretched the land of Goshen, where for hundreds of years Ben's people, the Israelites, had lived. But the Israelites were no longer welcome in Egypt. Now they were little better than slaves.

Ben stepped out into the narrow, sandy street and walked away from the river. His mother had asked him to run to the marketplace for some dried fish. The shortest way to the marketplace was to walk down to the river and take the river path. But Ben decided to take the longer way so that he wouldn't have to walk near the water.

He'd been walking for only a few minutes when up ahead in a narrow passageway between two tall mud-brick buildings, he saw two dogs. They weren't big dogs. But they were circling each other, growling and showing their teeth. He stood waiting, watching. Maybe the dogs would chase each other somewhere else.

He stood too long. He felt something on his shoulder, and when he looked down, there was a scarab beetle, bright and green, crawling toward his neck! With a shriek, Ben brushed it away—and heard a sudden burst of laughter from behind him. Whirling around, he saw several of the neighborhood boys. One of them picked up the beetle and held it out toward Ben, a mischievous grin on his face. "Hey, you dropped your pet! Want him in your pocket?"

Ben backed away quickly.

"Come on—afraid of a little old *bug?*" One of the boys laughed. Then he flung something directly at Ben, who screeched and backed away. The thing dropped near him. Just a stick.

Because Ben was small for his age and not a fighter, he relied on his words and his wits to get him out of tight situations like this. With his heart still beating rapidly and his breath quick and shallow, he opened his mouth to say something—anything—and suddenly he was drenched with cold water!

Leaping in fear, sputtering, yelling, he spun around yet again. There was another boy from the village, still holding the dripping bucket he'd emptied over Ben's head.

"Why are you shaking, River Boy?" the boy asked, laughing. "The water too cold? Or are you just . . . *scared?*"

Of course I'm scared, Ben thought. *And all these boys know it. Why don't they just leave me alone?*

"How about this, River Boy? Want a bite?" One of the boys thrust a frog into Ben's face—a dry, tired, sick-looking frog that was obviously being squeezed way too tight.

"Hey, you're hurting him!" Ben protested, then reached out and took the frog.

Frogs were one of the few things Ben wasn't afraid of. He'd had frogs for pets, in fact, and he knew that this frog needed to get back into the water if he was to survive. Ben held it back out to the other boy. "Take him back to the river. He's going to die if he doesn't—"

"*You* take him back, River Boy!"

Ben hesitated. "No, I—"

"You're afraid, that's what! Just like you're afraid of bugs and snakes and dogs and cats—"

"I'm not afraid of cats!"

Ben wasn't quite sure why that sent the boys into fits of laughter.

"Oh, he's *not* afraid of cats! Did you hear that? There's something he's not afraid of!"

"Maybe that's because he's never met the right cat!"

"Leave him alone," said a quiet voice.

There was a second or two of quiet as the boys surrounding Ben turned to see who was speaking. It was Joel, with his older brother, Micah.

Joel was Ben's best friend. He was bigger than Ben—big enough that these boys wouldn't be quick to tease or bully him. He was stocky, rather than slender like Ben, and already starting to show muscles on his arms and shoulders, like his father. But now, as always, Joel's face was split in a grin, and his nose was peeling—Joel's fair skin sunburned easily and constantly.

"Ha, ha, ha! You guys are real funny," Joel said. "Now if you're through with my friend here, I need him."

The other boys stood uncertainly for a moment, looking at each other. Suddenly the one who'd given Ben the frog grinned and said, "Yeah, we're done with River Boy. After all, now we've got . . . Eggshell!" The boys snickered at Micah, then began to walk away. He looked back at them blankly.

Micah was . . . well, Micah was different. The boys called him Eggshell partly because of his egg-shaped head and partly because they claimed there was nothing in his head, as empty as an eggshell with the egg sucked out.

Micah couldn't talk; he simply made sounds of distress or anger or misery, as a baby would. And when he wasn't making those sounds, his jaw hung open, his lips slack. He was stick-thin and small for his age, smaller even than Ben, although Micah was two years older. He had Joel's unruly, straight-black hair, but that was where the family resemblance ended. All you had to do was look at his deep-set, not-quite-straight eyes to see that something was wrong with Micah.

"Can you go with me to the marketplace?" Joel asked Ben, still grinning. "I have to get some things for my mother, and you know how Micah is. If I'm looking at the vegetables, he's over pulling the candles out of the bin."

"Sure," Ben said. "But let's be quick because I need to leave soon, or I'll be late getting to the Red House."

Ben's father and grandfather, like most of the Israelite men, worked as laborers, making bricks from mud and straw to build monuments and pyramids. But Ben, like many of the women and children, worked in the royal city of Rameses as a house servant for a wealthy Egyptian family. They lived in a huge home that Ben called the Red House because it was made from a special kind of reddish sandstone brought from far away. Ben's master, the head of the home, was a high-ranking official in the court of Pharaoh.

At the marketplace, Ben quickly found the dried fish his mother needed, but by the time Joel had found everything on his list, the sun was high.

"Better get home," Joel said, looking at the sky. "Must be about time to leave for work. You want to—"

Both boys looked up suddenly and then looked at each other. There was a commotion at the other end of the marketplace. A voice was calling loudly, a crowd was gathering, and Ben could hear the sound of feet running. Joel grabbed Micah's hand and started toward the sound, with Micah protesting loudly all the way, pulling against him.

The boys jogged up to the edge of the large group of people.

"Tell us more!" people urged.

"That's all I know," a man's voice replied from somewhere in the middle of the crowd. "Moses has returned, and he has asked to talk to the elders. They've probably begun their council already."

A shock ran through Ben. Moses had returned?

"Now let me through, please!" the man's voice insisted. "I must spread the word to others. Please!" There was the sound of scuffling and then of feet running away.

Moses had returned!

Ben clutched at Joel. "We must see him!"

Joel nodded excitedly, ignoring Micah's wails of impatience.

Moses!

Trembling with excitement, the boys raced after the crowd that surged through the streets, all of them chattering and tense. Suddenly Ben slowed, and Joel looked back at him.

The crowd was heading toward the river.

It wasn't just that Ben didn't *like* to walk along the river. He *couldn't*. His fear paralyzed him. His body wouldn't do what he told it to do when he came near water. "I'm sorry," he said softly, looking up at Joel.

Understanding washed through Joel's eyes. "They're heading for the open square in front of the elders' hall. We'll cut behind the tanners' yard and come out on the side of the square away from the river. We can still see from there."

Ducking into a narrow alley, the boys raced past several low mud-brick buildings and emerged at the edge of a foul-smelling open yard filled with clay vats of dark liquid in which animal hides floated. Holding their hands over their noses and mouths, they ran along the edge of the yard to another alleyway, Micah protesting all the way. They emerged at the large open-air meeting place used when the elders needed to address everyone at once. The boys found a place along the base of a pillar. It was far from the elders, but at least they had a good view.

"Where's Moses?" Ben asked excitedly.

Joel quickly scanned the crowd. "I don't think he's here yet."

The elders were deep in conversation with two men dressed in travel-worn, patched clothes, with traveling staffs in their hands.

Surely neither of these men was Moses! He heard an elder call one of the men Aaron. Then, to Ben's amazement, the one named Aaron gestured toward the other man and used the name Moses.

Ben and Joel glanced at each other.

Moses was so . . . *old!* His hair was mostly gray; his beard was long and scraggly. And he didn't even do his own speaking. He stood back, leaning on his staff, while the other man spoke. Moses wasn't particularly big or strong-looking—certainly not the hero-warrior Ben had always imagined. He looked more like someone's grandfather.

Micah's squawking grew louder, and Joel hurriedly reached into his market bag and drew out a handful of dried beans for Micah to play with. "What did he say?" Joel asked. "I couldn't hear."

Ben smiled. Joel might be bigger and stronger than he was, but Ben had always had sharper ears. "The other man said that God has spoken to Moses and sent him to us to lead us out of this land to a better place—a place flowing with milk and honey."

"Flowing with *what?* What does that mean?"

"I don't know."

Micah began to loudly crunch the dried beans between his teeth.

"What are the elders saying?" Joel asked.

"If you'll hush, I can hear them," Ben said with annoyance. He listened. "They're asking how they can know that this is indeed Moses, and that all of this is true."

To Ben's surprise, some of those in the crowd began to shout out their doubts: "I remember Moses, and you're not him!" one old man shouted.

"The Egyptians will refuse to let us go—and then they'll whip us for rebelling!" another called.

As the elders and the crowd shouted their objections, Ben felt a growing sense of alarm. He saw something on Moses' face that he hadn't expected to see—something that frightened him. It got worse when quarrelsome men from the crowd drew nearer to Moses and Aaron. As the men from the village threatened and shouted, Ben wondered, *Was Mother wrong about Moses?*

The chief of the elders raised his hand, and the crowd grew quiet. The old man quietly asked again, "And how do we know that all of this is as you say?"

Aaron and Moses were both silent for a moment. Just as the crowd again began to grow restless, Moses raised his hand with his staff high above his head. When the crowd quieted again, Moses tossed the staff away from him onto the sandy ground.

And suddenly, where the staff had been, there was a large snake!

Ben gasped and shrank back against the pillar. The crowd, too, surged backward, away from the snake, away from Moses, shouting in surprise and fear. But Joel, clearly delighted, leaned forward. Despite his fear of snakes, Ben watched carefully. It was true—the staff was gone, and in its place was a snake, writhing, hissing!

"It's magic!" Joel whispered.

Ben shook his head. "It's a sign! God really has sent Moses to lead us to freedom!" He jumped to his feet and started away.

"Wait!" Joel called. "He may do more tricks! Let's stay and watch!"

Ben shouted over his shoulder at Joel. "I've got to go tell my mother that Moses has returned to lead us out of Egypt!" He pushed his way through the crowd and out into the street again.

But as he ran, Ben could think of only one thing—something he had seen clearly in Moses' face. Ben had seen something there he knew well.

His mother had been wrong. Moses wasn't brave. Maybe when he was younger, but not now.

Moses was afraid.

Just like Ben.

CHAPTER

4

The next day, Ben was again late getting to the Red House. He snuck in the back way, hoping that in the hustle and bustle of preparation for the feast to be held that night, no one would notice one small boy slipping quietly down the long hallway.

A strong hand clasped him by the back of his neck. Strong fingers turned his head until he was looking back at the stern face and dark eyes of Enoch, the older Israelite boy who supervised the younger ones. Enoch's face was hard—at first. But after a moment, it broke into a grin.

"You're late, Ben," the older boy said. "And there's much to do. Now hurry upstairs. You're to help her ladyship choose the linens." He gave Ben a gentle shove toward the stairway. Enoch was never resentful that Ben seemed to be a special favorite of those who lived in the Red House.

The reason Ben was late that day was that so many interesting things were happening in the village. Women, including his mother, had been huddled together in doorways or gathered in small groups in the streets, whispering excitedly, their shawl-covered heads close together. Old men sat in the marketplace arguing loudly, shouting back and forth to each other.

And it was all about Moses.

But Ben was puzzled. He was hearing as much doubt and complaining from the people in the village as excitement. "He's just another homeless troublemaker from the desert, as far as I'm concerned!" one sour-faced woman had told his mother shrilly. "No good will come of it, you'll see!"

Upstairs, her ladyship sat staring at several shelves of stacked linens for table coverings, napkins, and guest towels. Ben bowed slightly as he entered the room—blushing as she looked up, smiled, and winked at him to acknowledge his tardiness. "So glad you're here, Ben," she said teasingly. "We have much—"

Her eyes rose to the hallway behind Ben, and he turned to see his lordship come up the stairs with the slow dignity he always showed.

"Well, well," he said pleasantly. "Please, my dear, don't rise. And Ben, I'm glad you're here. I was hoping to speak to you. Enoch!" He shouted the older boy's name down the stairway, and Ben could hear Enoch pounding up the stairs. "Come in, come in." His lordship motioned for Ben and Enoch to stand beside his wife. "I was hoping you boys would both be here. I have something to say to you about what happened in Pharaoh's court this morning."

Ben and Enoch looked at each other with carefully guarded excitement.

"Moses, it seems, has returned." His lordship began to pace back and forth in the large room. "It's been forty years since he fled into the desert. Now he has returned and presumes to speak for your people. He asked Pharaoh . . ." His lordship paused as if thinking, looking out the window across the desert landscape. "It was ill-advised. He asked Pharaoh to let your people ignore their tasks and responsibilities for three days to go into the desert to have a festival to worship your God."

Ben looked at Enoch in confusion. Moses had asked only for three days in the desert? But last night hadn't he said—

"Moses should have known," his lordship said, shaking his head and turning back toward them. "He has lived in this court before. Pharaoh wasn't pleased." He lowered his voice and took on a stern expression, imitating Pharaoh. " 'I do not know your God, and I will not let Israel go.' Then he accused Moses and his brother of enticing your people away from their work. His lordship appeared apologetic. "So I'm afraid that Pharaoh has taken it into his head to make things difficult for your people. He has given orders that from this day on, the laborers from among your people are to be given no straw for their bricks. They must gather their own straw. But they are nevertheless expected to make their full quota of bricks."

"But—" Ben started to protest. A quick look from her ladyship silenced him.

"And, further, I'm afraid," his lordship continued, "that Pharaoh has encouraged his foremen to be, well . . . *harsh* with your laborers."

Enoch looked at Ben. Ben's father was at the brickyards making bricks for which he was being given no straw to mix with the mud. The men would be forced to scavenge for straw, which would slow their work, which would anger the Egyptian foremen.

Suddenly Ben couldn't wait to get home. But he couldn't leave. A morning and afternoon of work stretched ahead of him.

At dusk, released at last, Ben raced home through the narrow streets of his neighborhood. The sounds he heard alarmed him: women and children weeping, angry men shouting, other men groaning in pain.

"Was Moses there to gather straw for me today?" Ben heard one man yell. "Was Moses there to take my beating from the foreman when I fell behind?"

Ben covered the final few blocks at a sprint. He dashed through the doorway of his family's home. His father and grandfather sat on small stools, their backs bare. Ben turned away, unable to look at the welts and bruises on their skin.

Ben's mother and grandmother bent over their men, damp cloths in their hands. Ben's mother looked up. "Ben, fill our bowls with fresh, cool water from the cistern, please," she said quietly.

He did, then stood against the wall in front of his father. "I heard at the Red House," Ben said. "I came home as quickly as I could. Is there something I can do?"

His father looked up, his eyes dull, exhausted, and hopeless. "You're a good lad, Benjamin," he said. "There is something you can do. There is no way I can gather my straw and make my bricks all in a day, and if I fail, I'll be beaten again."

"As will I," croaked Ben's exhausted grandfather, too tired even to lift his head and look at Ben.

"So, lad, we'll need you to gather our straw for us each day, after you're done at the Red House."

Ben was confused. "But, Father, it's nearly dark."

"Yes. But we'll still need straw tomorrow—enough for me and for your grandfather."

Ben's face went cold with fear. He looked up at his mother.

"This isn't a time to give in to fear, son," Ben's father said, his voice firm but not harsh or unkind. "I have fears of my own, but still I must get up in the morning and go back to the same field where today they beat me till I couldn't stand. And so you too will have to ignore your fears and do what must be done." He smiled through his pain. "Tonight, perhaps it would be best if your mother went with you."

Ben shivered only a little less when he heard that he wouldn't have to go out into the dark alone. He would still be out in the dark.

And who knew what else would go wrong, as long as Moses was stirring up trouble?

CHAPTER 5

The next morning, Ben walked to the Red House to help clean up from the feast the night before. He still felt both sad and angry from watching his father get ready to leave for the brick-making yards. His father's bruises and welts looked even worse than they had the night before, and he was stiff and sore.

Ben couldn't escape the voices all around him as he walked the narrow streets, voices of people standing at the corners, voices drifting out from the open doors of houses.

"Moses and Aaron were waiting to meet us as we left the brickyards yesterday!" one huge black-bearded man said. "Can you believe it? After the trouble they caused?"

"What did you say to them?" an elderly man asked.

"It's a wonder we didn't lay hands on them and throw them out of Egypt," the big man growled. "The man next to me said to Moses and his brother, 'May the Lord look upon you and judge you! You have made us a stench to Pharaoh and his officials and have put a sword in their hands to kill us.' "

The other men in the group nodded their approval. "And what did Moses say?" the old man prodded.

"Ha! Moses? He said nothing. He looked frightened, as if he thought we might trounce him at any moment. We've placed our fate in the hands of the wrong man, I tell you. He's no savior. And he has no power over Pharaoh, that much is clear. We were better off before Moses came back."

"Come, Ben," the master of the Red House said to him that morning, smiling, as Ben helped gather the dirty bowls and cups strewn about the courtyard by the guests at the feast. "I need you for something else."

Ben followed his master into the house, where her ladyship held up some new white clothes. "For you, Ben," she said, smiling.

"Thank you," he stammered, embarrassed and happy and surprised. He touched the fine white cloth.

"Yes, I need you to look good this morning," his lordship said. "You're coming with me to court."

Ben felt a rush of excitement. This wasn't the first time he'd been to court with his master. In Pharaoh's court, it was customary for important people to have their hands free and to have servants follow them carrying everything they needed. On those trips, Ben was awed and amazed to see so many important people together in one place, talking, hurrying, getting important things done. And sometimes he even saw Pharaoh himself.

"I'm hoping to get Pharaoh's approval for plans I've been working on for months now," his master continued. "You're to carry this box." He held up a carefully carved ivory box. "It contains a small gift for our esteemed ruler. In appreciation."

A short time later, Ben followed two steps behind his master as they climbed the stairs to Pharaoh's palace. Ben wore his sparkling new white clothes and carried the ivory box.

Pharaoh's dwelling was a huge complex of buildings and courtyards and temples that stretched far in every direction. There were people scurrying everywhere, slaves cleaning, meals being served. But the most important business was always conducted in Pharaoh's court, where Ben headed, following his master. Pharaoh's massive throne sat at one end of the huge room. Groups of men stood around the edges of the room, awaiting their turn to present their cases—and their gifts—to Pharaoh.

As soon as Ben and his master entered the court, his lordship stopped so abruptly that Ben almost ran into the back of him. "What's this?" he grumbled. Ben peeked around him to see. It was Moses! He was standing before Pharaoh, Aaron at his side.

"It's that madman again," Ben's master said. "Well, that's sure to put Pharaoh in a bad mood. Not a good day to press for my plans. We'll wait. And I don't like waiting. Pharaoh is sure to throw Moses into prison now. The man is a murderer, after all."

Ben couldn't hear what was being said between Aaron and Pharaoh. But when he saw Moses lift his staff high in front of him, he knew what was coming next. Moses dropped the staff, and it immediately changed into a large snake. The crowd stirred and murmured.

"So, he's a magician too," said Ben's master. "Well, Pharaoh has magicians of his own."

And, indeed, Pharaoh turned to his own two magicians, who stood always by his throne. They whispered between themselves for a short time and then came to stand before Moses. They too raised their staffs, and when they dropped them, those two staffs also changed into snakes!

Ben was so disappointed he almost felt sick. When he'd seen Moses' staff turn into a snake back in the village that first night, he'd thought nothing but God's power could cause such a miracle. But now here were heathen magicians who didn't even know the God of Abraham, Isaac, and Jacob, and they too could turn their staffs into snakes. Was his master right? Was Moses nothing but a magician?

But as Ben continued to watch, a strange thing happened. The snakes slithered slowly toward each other on the floor, tasting the cold stone with their tongues. Then they seemed to get angry, coiling and striking at each other, fighting, throwing loops of their bodies around each other. And Moses' snake quickly won the fight. As the other snakes lay exhausted or injured, slowly writhing on the floor, Moses' snake began to swallow them headfirst, one at a time!

"Well, enough of this," his lordship said, turning and striding from the room. "We can hire our own magician to come to the house if we want to be entertained."

The next morning, Ben pulled his grandmother's cart cautiously nearer and nearer to the river. It was close to the bluff where the yearly floodwaters carved away the soil and revealed a rich band of heavy red clay. Staying as far away from the water as he could, he selected a part of the bluff along the river where the clay seemed dark and rich and free of pebbles and sticks.

It was this clay that his mother had sent him for. She needed it for making pottery.

Ben edged along the bluff, just a few feet from the river behind him, and began to gather handfuls of the moist, firm, heavy clay, then dropped them into the huge basket sitting in the cart.

Ben wished he were anywhere but here.

The other boys only tease me because they know I'm afraid of them, and this river—and everything else too. And the only way to make them stop bothering me is to stop being afraid.

As Ben had dressed and eaten that morning, he had thought and thought of ways to overcome his fears. But the only answer he came up with, over and over again, was the one that scared him most of all: To overcome his fears, he would have to face them squarely, head-on, and keep facing them until they stopped scaring him. To overcome his fear of bugs, he would have to find a bug and hold it until he was no longer afraid of it. To overcome his fear of dogs, he would have to find a dog, stand close to it, and pet it until he was no longer afraid of it. To overcome his fear of water—no, that would be too hard.

And yet there it is, Ben thought, *right behind me. If I ever wanted to face my fear of water, this is the time. There's nobody around to tease me if I panic. And there's nobody around to save me either. Just me and the river. I can stand on the bank, face my fear head-on, pick up my foot, and—*

Ben shuddered. *And what? Who am I fooling? I could never step into the water. I could never face that . . .*

But wait. A strange thought came to him. He could never face the river. But suppose he weren't facing it? Suppose he *backed* into the water?

He giggled. It was such a silly thought. And anyone who saw him would laugh.

But there was no one here to see. He was alone.

He thought again of the teasing boys.

He stopped gathering clay. He looked away from the water. Could he do it? Could he put his feet into the water if he weren't looking?

Ben gathered a few more handfuls of clay and pulled the cart away from the bluff. "Is that a frog? There, in the grass?" Ben asked himself, knowing there was no frog but needing to trick himself into coming closer to the water. "Maybe I'll take a closer look." He circled widely, walking sideways, until he was very near the river but with his back to it. "I can't see anything—maybe I need a different angle."

He took a small step backward. Then another.

Then he lifted his foot, sucked in a mouthful of air, squeezed his eyes shut—*This time I'll feel the river for sure!*—and put his foot down. "Ahh!" he yelled abruptly and then shook his head. No water. He hadn't backed into the river yet.

But it couldn't be far. He took one more step backward, hunching his shoulders and hissing through his teeth, feeling with his big toe—lower, lower—and yes, there it was! His toe was in the water!

He froze in position, unsure what was going to happen. Would he panic and run? Would a crocodile leap out of the river and devour him? He waited through one long, slow breath, then another, then a third— and nothing happened. He was still alive; he hadn't panicked. After all this time, he could do it! He wasn't over his fear, not yet, but if he had taken the first step, he knew he could take the next one.

Could he actually look at the water? He had touched it—why shouldn't he look at it too?

He would try it. He looked down from the sky toward the distant city on the horizon. Then down at the ground near his foot. Then back toward his toe that was dipped into the—

With a leap of terror, Ben hurtled away from the river, twisting about in the air to land on both feet facing the water.

The water that had now turned to blood.

Thick, red blood.

"The Nile seems better today," Enoch whispered a few days later as he and Ben worked shoulder to shoulder, scrubbing the tiles of the courtyard at the Red House. "Yesterday I noticed that the blood had mostly washed on down the river, along with most of the dead fish. Today the water looks almost normal, and the birds are beginning to hunt along the shore again. By tomorrow it will be normal."

That was good news. The truth was, in the days since Moses had turned the water to blood, Ben was beginning to wish he had never heard of Moses. Everyone, Egyptians and Israelites alike, had had to find some other source of water. They had found it by digging pits near the river's edge. But that was hard work. Besides, the fish had died in the bloody river and floated by the tens of thousands in the fouled water at the edge of the river, stinking horribly. Ben had dipped several jugs of water from a pit that morning himself—standing with his back to the river. After his experience on the day the water turned to blood, Ben was more afraid of the river than ever.

"Do you think Moses will leave Pharaoh alone now?" Ben asked. "His tricks are doing no good. Life has been worse for all of us."

Enoch scrubbed the stones silently for a moment, then playfully butted Ben's shoulder with his head. "You've lost faith in him already?"

Ben thought about the welts and bruises on his father's back—even more of them since the water had turned to blood. "Maybe it's Pharaoh I don't trust. Either way, I doubt that Moses' arguments will bring about our freedom."

More and more of the Israelites seemed to feel that way. Just that morning, as Ben had walked to the Red House, the talk on the streets of the village was all about Moses. "If he was going to curse Pharaoh and the Egyptians, why'd he curse us at the same time?" one old man had growled.

"Who asked him to help us, answer me that," his wrinkled companion had said, spitting into the sand. "We might not be rich here, but at least we didn't have trouble, not till Moses came."

"No, and all his tricks don't amount to much anyway. Pharaoh's magicians can turn their staffs to snakes too, just like Moses, and they can turn water to blood."

That, Ben had to admit, was true. He himself had seen the court magicians turn their staffs to snakes, and he'd heard that when Moses had turned the Nile to blood, Pharaoh had turned to his court magicians, who had likewise turned water to blood.

Enoch slopped some water over Ben's hand and chuckled when Ben drew his hand back in surprise. "Don't give up yet, Benjamin, my friend. I think Moses is doing something bigger than we understand. The day may come when we'll talk to our grandchildren of these days. They'll sit spellbound as we tell of the wonders God worked through Moses."

It was Ben's turn to chuckle. "Will our grandchildren be that interested in hearing us tell of scrubbing cobblestones?"

Enoch shrugged. "Who knows? How does anyone know, while he's trying to live through it, whether the days of his life are the stuff of great stories and tales that will be told throughout all time?"

Ben worked quietly, thinking about what Enoch had said, until Enoch sat back on his haunches and laughed. "And how about you, little one?" He reached to the side and picked up a small green frog. "Do you think we're living in days that will become legend? And where did you come from, anyway?"

Ben pointed with his scrub brush toward the courtyard wall. "He came with his friends." Two more frogs sat in the shade of a potted palm, one of them squatting on the foot of the statue of the frog god, Heket, in its little garden shrine.

"So he did," Enoch said. "It is odd, though. I haven't seen frogs in the—"

Suddenly there was a shriek from somewhere across the courtyard, and Ben and Enoch both jumped to their feet. Enoch tossed the frog into his bucket of water as they raced toward the sound.

The shriek sounded again, and now the boys could tell that it was coming from the kitchen. Enoch made it to the doorway first. Ben, right at his heels, burst into the kitchen and saw that Naomi, the Hebrew cook, was standing on a stool. Her flour-covered hands were over her mouth. She pointed toward her worktable. "Get them! Quickly! Please! I have no idea how they got in there!"

Enoch and Ben rushed to the worktable and peered into a huge bowl full of batter.

A half-dozen small grayish tree frogs slogged through the heavy batter or stumbled across its surface, their feet and legs so coated that they could barely move.

"Quickly! Get them out of here!" Naomi insisted shrilly.

But Enoch just glanced up at her, then looked at Ben, one eyebrow raised. "Well, I'd heard Moses had something else up his sleeve. I think we just discovered what it is."

Joel, Ben, and Micah stood in the street in front of Joel's house, looking for frogs. They had agreed the night before to get up early and search for the biggest frogs they could find to keep as pets. And there should have been plenty of them. The day before, by the time Enoch and Ben had helped Naomi get the frogs out of her batter, frogs had been everywhere. They were coming out of every hole in the ground and the walls and were swimming in every liquid. Frogs were climbing in every potted plant the mistress had placed around her home.

This morning, the three boys were surrounded by frogs—all dead. Every frog on the street was dead. And there were thousands if not millions of them. Tree frogs, toads, big green frogs, smaller brown frogs with yellowish legs—they all lay still, looking shrunken and dry.

"What happened to them?" Joel asked.

Ben shook his head. "I don't know. Do you suppose Pharaoh agreed to Moses' demands, and so Moses caused the frogs to die?"

Joel snorted, kicking at a pile of dead frogs. "Or else Pharaoh's magicians killed them. Didn't you hear that after Moses and Aaron caused the frogs to come out of the river, Pharaoh asked his magicians to make frogs come forth too—and they did? So far, every trick Moses has pulled, Pharaoh's court magicians have done the same thing!" Joel shook his head. "Why should we think Pharaoh will listen to him?"

Ben poked a stick among the dead frogs, hoping to find one still moving that he could revive with a little water. "All I hear is people saying they wish Moses would just go away so things could get back to normal." He waved his hand in front of his face, trying to clear away the cloud of gnats that arose from the frogs when he disturbed them.

"You boys!" someone yelled, and Ben and Joel looked up. One of the elders strode down the lane, holding part of his loose sleeve in front of his face. "Find something to use as a rake and begin pulling all of these dead frogs into big piles so they can be hauled away. They're starting to stink and to attract gnats. Quickly! Everyone must help!"

Ben and Joel looked at each other and shrugged. They weren't going to find any live frogs for pets anyway. And they couldn't disobey an elder.

By the time the frogs were raked up, the gnats had become worse than the stink of the rotting frogs—and it was obvious to everyone that the presence of the gnats wasn't natural. Moses had done it again.

Ben tossed aside the forked stick he'd been using as a rake and ran back home; it was time to gobble some food and hurry off to the Red House. His mother had a scarf tied across her face when he rushed into their house.

"Oh, Ben," she moaned. "These gnats! I'd rather have the frogs! At least you can pick up a frog and throw it away, but what can you do about gnats?" She brushed several of them away from her face, then handed Ben a bowl of porridge. "This isn't much, I know. I'm sorry. But with these gnats . . ."

Ben grabbed a piece of bread to dip into the porridge. Then he stopped. "There are gnats in it!" he cried.

"Well, scoop them out," his mother said wearily, sitting near him and pulling her head cloth closer around her face so that nothing but her eyes showed. "I'm sorry, but what can I do? They're everywhere."

Ben took a bite of his bread . . . and immediately spit it out. "*Pfah!* There are gnats in my mouth!" He looked at the piece of bread in his hand. Gnats swarmed all over it. He looked up at his mother to yell out his frustration. But when he opened his mouth to suck in a breath, he got more gnats than air and immediately choked. He tried swiping the gnats out of his mouth with his fingers, and he tried spitting them onto the ground. But in the end he swallowed most of them. Tears sprang into his eyes.

His mother pulled him close to her. "I don't understand this," she said. "Since Moses came, we've had nothing but more work, bruises, and mouthfuls of gnats. I just don't understand."

But that evening, as Ben and his family struggled to eat dinner without swallowing more gnats than food, they were all strangely excited. "The master was very upset this afternoon," Ben said gleefully, pulling aside the scarf that covered his mouth and nose. "This time Pharaoh's magicians *couldn't* make the gnats appear from the dust as Moses did! They even admitted to Pharaoh that they thought it was the hand of God that caused the gnats to appear, and that he'd better listen to Moses!"

Ben's father nodded, hungrily shoving into his mouth a piece of bread dipped in the meat-and-vegetables dish Ben's mother had prepared. There were gnats all over it, but his father didn't seem to care. "And while our Egyptian overseers were as cruel and impatient as ever," he mumbled around the mouthful of food, "they also seemed worried."

Ben's mother shook her head, still swathed in cloths to keep the gnats away. "We're fooling ourselves. Pharaoh won't listen. And besides, we're as bad off as the Egyptians. We have to suffer through the gnats too! If Pharaoh doesn't listen this time—which he won't—then what will Moses unleash on us next? If Moses is supposed to be our savior, then he's saving us to death!"

Ben was at the Red House two days later when he discovered just what it was Moses—and God—would unleash next.

Ben hadn't noticed much out of the ordinary at first—just a few more flies than usual—until the master rushed home early. "Enoch!" he yelled, sweeping into the house's main salon on the first floor and tearing off his cloak. "Gather everyone! I want every window covered, every door, every opening in the house! Pharaoh's court is already overrun, and they're moving this way!"

"What, sir?" Enoch asked, bursting breathlessly in from the courtyard.

"Flies," the master said impatiently, pointing at a few that were crawling along the wall near the window. "Don't just stand there! We'll soon be drowning in them if you don't move! Get everyone, the entire household! Find every sheet, every towel, and cover everything! Keep them out! *Move!*"

Everyone in Egypt knew that flies were more than just an annoyance; they often carried disease. Enoch barked out his orders, and Ben and the other servants in the household leaped into action. Soon, while the master and mistress and their children huddled in an inner room, Ben and the others were racing through the house with armloads of cloths pulled from every chest and cabinet in the house, trying their best to cover every opening to the outside, but it wasn't working. The flies were growing more numerous every minute.

Suddenly Ben heard his master's voice bellowing from the room where he and his family had taken refuge. "Ben!"

He rushed into the room. The entire family huddled on the floor in the middle of the room under an immense cotton cloth.

"Is no one taking care of the animals?" the master barked.

"No one, sir. You told us all to—"

"Take two others and go out to the pens. Bring all of the animals into the barn."

"Yes, sir," Ben said, then ran from the room.

Outside, the sheep and goats were running back and forth across their pens, trying to escape from the flies. "Azariah!" Ben yelled to the smaller of the two boys he'd brought with him. "Go into the barn and close all the doors and windows! We'll bring the animals to you!"

When the last sheep had been shoved into the barn, Ben said to the other boy, "Come on, Nathan, now the ducks and geese."

"What about them?" Nathan asked, sobbing, the tears striping his dirty cheeks. "Just leave the ducks and geese."

"We can't just leave them," Ben said, regardless of how badly he wanted to do just that. "The master said—"

"I don't care!" Nathan shouted, slapping violently at the back of his neck, at his shoulders, at his arms. "They're biting me *through* my clothes!" Then he turned and ran—not toward the Red House, but toward home.

Ben wanted desperately to follow him, but he was afraid of what his master would do to him if he disobeyed. "Azariah!" Ben yelled as he tried to brush away the flies crawling up his legs. "Are you all right?"

"I guess so," the younger boy answered, his voice shaking. "They're not quite as bad in here."

"I've got to go do something about the birds," Ben said. He ran around the barn and pushed through the gate into a wide pen dominated by a shallow pond. The ducks and geese inside were panicked. Rushing from side to side, their wings spread and flapping, they ran into the woven fence of the enclosure trying to escape from the flies.

Honk!

The sound was so sudden, so loud, and so hostile that Ben looked up in surprise, forgetting about the flies. There were three huge male geese, their eyes blood-red and angry, their oversized wings spread, their necks outstretched—and they were coming for *him!*

Ben turned and ran. He made it through the gate, but not before one of the geese had bitten him painfully on the calf. And as he dragged his leg through the opening, that gander came through the opening too before Ben could slam the gate shut behind him. The huge goose lunged forward, its beak snapping, grabbing Ben's clothes, trying to get to his face.

Ben turned and ran for home, yelling, slapping at his body and at the air around him. The goose still snapped at his heels. Ben swatted at the flies that bit and swarmed and crawled under his clothes and into his eyes . . .

Until suddenly the flies weren't crawling across his face anymore. Ben stopped in surprise, then quickly turned and looked behind him. No, the goose was gone too. Ben had been running for some time; he was already back to the edge of the Israelite village. He shook himself like a dog shedding water, getting the last of the flies off, and then looked around in wonder. A few flies here and there, but nothing unusual. A normal day.

Then he looked back toward the city of Rameses. It was too far away for him to see the flies themselves, but he could see cloudy patches in the air caused by the swarms of flies. And he could see people and animals running, slapping at something. Yes, the flies were still there.

But not here.

And then he remembered what his mother had said the night before: *We're as bad off as the Egyptians. We have to suffer through the gnats too!* Had Moses finally done something right—hurting Pharaoh and the Egyptians in a way that didn't also hurt the Israelites?

The breeze from the river brushed through Ben's hair, and he lifted his face to enjoy the lightly scented air, so free of flies or gnats.

Two days later, Ben spent a hard afternoon in the hot sun, a cloth tied across his face to fight the smell, helping the servants from the households in Rameses drag the bodies of goats, sheep, and other livestock to the edge of town, where they were piled and burned.

Hundreds of animal bodies.

Thousands.

Ben had been amazed when Joel had awakened him that morning, hissing from the doorway with the news: All of the animals owned by the Egyptians had died during the night. But all of the animals of the Israelites were still alive.

Actually, not *all* of the Egyptian animals had died. Moses had warned the Egyptians the day before that if they would take their animals out of the fields and put them in their barns, the animals would be spared. But Pharaoh had laughed at Moses' words and left his animals in the fields. And so of course the rest of the people of Rameses had done the same.

And only those few animals in the barns had survived whatever sudden sickness had killed the rest.

Even so, Pharaoh hadn't agreed to let the Israelites go into the desert to make their sacrifices and worship God.

As Ben walked through the streets of Rameses the next day on his way to the Red House, he was surprised to see no Egyptians on the streets, only Hebrew servants rushing on urgent errands. When he got to the Red

House, he found out why: His lordship and her ladyship and all of their children lay moaning and complaining in their soft beds, their skin bare because of painful boils that covered them everywhere.

The Israelite servants, none of whom were afflicted with boils, scurried back and forth between the bedrooms and the kitchen, hauling bowls of cool water into which Naomi had poured a little vinegar. Ben and Enoch and the others sponged the red, swollen skin of the Egyptian family with the vinegar-water, trying to bring some relief to them in the hot desert air.

Later, on their way to the kitchen for fresh water, Ben and Enoch stopped in the courtyard in the shade of a palm tree for a moment. "Have you heard of any of our people with boils at all?" Enoch asked.

Ben shook his head. "None. How did this happen?"

"Haven't you heard?" Enoch asked. "It's another of Moses' plagues. He and Aaron brought handfuls of soot to Pharaoh's court this morning and flung it into the air. The wind carried it high over the city and farther, over the whole land of Egypt. Then it rained down, and all of the Egyptians were suddenly stricken with painful boils. I heard that Pharaoh asked his magicians to copy Moses' feat—or better yet, make it go away." Enoch chuckled. "But they were in such pain from the boils that covered their bodies that they could do nothing."

Ben thought. "None of our livestock died yesterday, and none of our people have boils today. And the flies left us alone too. God has decided to spare us from the plagues He is visiting on the Egyptians."

Enoch nodded, then grinned. "I guess Moses is doing something right after all. Remember how little faith you had in him, my friend?"

Ben snorted. "Pharaoh hasn't let us go yet. Either he ignores Moses and the plagues or else he agrees to let us go and then changes his mind as soon as God removes the plague. And I don't hear many people in my village who want to go, anyway. They're afraid to go."

Enoch raised an eyebrow, and Ben blushed. Enoch knew, as did everyone else, of Ben's fears. But Enoch never teased him. "If it is God's will for us to leave Egypt," Enoch said, "then we should be afraid to stay."

By the third day, most Egyptians had recovered enough from the boils to tend to their business, although their skin was still tender.

Once again the sound of sheep, goats, and cattle echoed from the pens in back of the Red House. On the same day the plague had killed the Egyptians' animals, Ben's master had sent servants out to neighboring lands to buy more livestock and bring them back. Most of the other wealthy Egyptians had done the same. The first herds of animals had begun to arrive the day before.

Ben gathered up the linens that had been hung out to air that afternoon. He noticed Enoch talking quietly with another Israelite who served in the palace running errands. After the other servant had scurried away, Ben motioned Enoch over and asked, "Is there news?"

Enoch nodded. "Moses has promised a hailstorm, the worst storm ever to afflict Egypt. He has given Pharaoh and the Egyptians a day to bring their new livestock into the barns for protection. The storm will come tomorrow morning."

Ben was surprised. Hail? He'd heard of this ice that fell from the sky, but he'd never seen it. Even rain wasn't common in this part of Egypt; their water came from the river. "We'll see hail!" he said excitedly.

Enoch shook his head. "It's not likely to be fun—the whole purpose is to make Pharaoh and the Egyptians suffer because they won't listen to God. I wouldn't want to be caught out in it."

Ben nodded slowly. Yes, but . . . hail! Tomorrow he'd finally see it.

The next morning Ben and Joel and Micah went out into the fields to gather straw. The Egyptian taskmasters still expected the Hebrew men to provide their own straw for making bricks. And straw was becoming harder to find.

But today Ben didn't mind. And Joel felt the same. Out in the field was exactly where they wanted to be. "When is the hailstorm supposed to start?" Joel asked.

Ben shrugged. "This morning sometime. Look at those clouds." He pointed toward the dark, looming clouds piled high to the west.

Joel nodded. "It might be soon. And where do you suppose it will fall?"

"Where? What do you mean?"

"I mean the flies were bad throughout Egypt, or so we've heard—*except* where we Israelites live. The boils didn't affect us; our livestock didn't die when—"

"Ah," Ben said. "I see. So when the hail falls . . ."

"It will miss us and hit the Egyptians," said Joel. "So if we want to see the hail . . ."

Ben nodded. "You know, I think we might be able to gather more straw in the fields over toward the city of Rameses today. We haven't gathered there yet."

"Just what I was thinking," said Joel. He shouldered his bags for straw gathering, and Ben tugged his grandmother's cart behind him. Joel touched Micah's arm and motioned for him to follow.

They felt the first drops of rain before they had covered half the distance between their village and Rameses and looked up in surprise. The clouds that had been looming in the west were now overhead and moving rapidly. The rain increased, and the boys stopped to watch in wonder as the clouds sped across the sky, soon covering the sun. A cold wind blew across them, making their now-damp skin shiver. Micah gave a low, uneasy moan.

And then they saw their first hailstone.

It landed with a pebbly rattle in the wooden bed of Ben's cart. The boys didn't realize at first what had made the sound, and they gathered around the cart. There it was—a tiny ball of white about the size of a pea.

Joel picked it up, and a delighted smile spread over his face. "It's cold!" he said in awe. "*Very* cold!"

Ben held out his hand, and Joel dropped the hailstone into his palm. Ben pinched it between his thumb and forefinger. He had lived his entire life in the desert, so this tiny ball was the coldest thing he had ever felt.

And then one hit him on the head. He was surprised at how much it stung. When it bounced to the ground in front of him, he realized it was about twice the size of the one he'd held. Then another hit, and another, and soon hailstones were falling everywhere. They stung and they were cold, and the boys were getting thoroughly wet. But Ben and Joel grabbed each other's hands and danced and twirled and wrestled and ran, laughing with the sheer joy of this new thing they'd discovered.

But the size of the hailstones grew. From the size of beans, they grew to the size of almonds, then grapes.

"Ouch!" Joel said uneasily. "This hurts!"

Micah moaned again and crowded close to the boys.

Then one the size of an apricot hit Ben on the head, and it hit so hard, Ben felt with his hand to make sure he wasn't bleeding. "Come on!" he said. "Let's get under something!"

"What?" Joel said, looking all around. "Hey—those palm trees!"

A small group of palms grew a short distance away. Ben grabbed one side of the now-wailing Micah; Joel grabbed the other. The boys raced to the trees. They huddled in the middle of the small grove. But the hailstones—now the size of Ben's fist—shredded the fronds of the palms and fell on the boys almost as hard as when they'd been in the open.

"This is no good!" Joel said in a panicky voice, trying to tuck the frantic Micah under his body. "Come on—let's hide in that old furnace!"

Ben turned to look. It was a brick-making furnace, huge and abandoned. "Come on, then!" he yelled, and they rushed through the pounding hail, slipping and falling on the muddy ground. They dove, bruised and filthy, into the sooty, dark furnace.

Then they were safe. The furnace was covered except for a round chimney hole in the middle. The walls of the furnace were thick, made of heavy bricks, and although the hail made a horrible racket pounding on it, the boys knew that the furnace would stand.

A fist-sized hailstone rolled into the furnace, becoming covered with a layer of black soot. Micah picked it up and immediately began sucking on it. Joel knocked it from his hands. "Dirty, Micah! Leave it alone!"

Micah yelled in anger, then stepped outside into the storm, trying to catch another hailstone to suck. When he looked up, a large one exploded on his face, and he screamed. Ben and Joel wrestled him back inside, and Joel reached out to find a big clean hailstone for Micah to hold against his sore cheekbone. "Good thing it didn't hit his eye or his nose," Joel grumbled.

Then they stood quietly, just inside the furnace, looking out across a dark, obscured world rapidly turning into a wasteland.

"Ben," Joel said quietly. "Stop it. You're scaring Micah."

Ben turned and looked. Micah was looking at him with big, scared eyes and was beginning to moan in the way he did when he was frightened.

"Look normal," Joel whispered. "Your face is white; you're trembling..."

Ben took a deep breath, closed his eyes, and looked away from Micah, willing his legs and hands to stop trembling. He was as thoroughly frightened and miserable as he ever remembered being in his life.

"Come, Ben," his master said early one afternoon several days after the hailstorm, hurriedly pulling on his headdress. "I've just been summoned to Pharaoh's court. Moses has arrived and demanded—demanded, mind you—to speak to Pharaoh. I want you to come."

"Yes, your lordship. Is there something you wish me to bear for you?"

"Not this time, Ben," he said as they rushed out into the street. It had been growing warmer day by day and would soon be summer. "I simply want you to hear what Moses says so that you can report it back to your parents, to the others in your village. I doubt that your people understand how unreasonable Moses is, and how he threatens all Egypt with these plagues."

Ben didn't know about that, but he did know that there had been many rumors in his village lately: Moses and Aaron had been killed; Moses and Aaron had fled Egypt. Pharaoh had finally agreed to let the Israelites leave Egypt; Pharaoh had agreed, but then changed his mind and demanded that all Israelite men be jailed and beaten. Moses had announced a new plague—lions would prowl the streets of cities throughout Egypt. No one seemed to know what Moses was up to. Perhaps Ben could find out.

But even though they hurried, sweating in the hot sun, Ben and his master arrived too late. Moses and Aaron, looking stern and angry, were stalking out of the court. Right behind them came some of the court officials and even a few of Pharaoh's soldiers. They looked just as angry, muttering among themselves and pointing at the two departing Hebrew men.

"What is it, Horus?" Ben's master asked one of the officials.

The man spat on the ground. "Called down another plague. Moses said that locusts such as we have never seen before will cover all the land and devour everything the hail didn't destroy. Then they turned on their heels and walked out. Pharaoh never said a word. His advisors and magicians are with him right now, trying to convince him that he has to respond somehow. Moses has already shown that his God can send a powerful plague. If these locusts are as bad as he said they'd be . . ."

But Ben's master just shook his head. "No," he said quietly, almost as if he were talking to himself. "Pharaoh won't listen to reason. And he won't grant Moses' request. He will never let the Israelites go."

The locusts came the next day. Ben awoke before his father and grandfather had even left for the brick-making yards. He heard the muffled, anxious voices of people out in the streets. His mother and father looked at each other, but no one spoke. They all knew what Moses had foretold. Ben slipped out the door and joined the crowd gathering there.

A warm wind from the east ruffled Ben's hair. It was the same wind that had been blowing since the day before; he'd heard it rustling things outside all night long. People were gathered in groups everywhere, talking quietly and pointing at the sky. A few locusts crawled on the ground already, but most were high overhead. Clouds of them were coming from the east, riding that wind and creating a dark smudge across the whole sky.

By midmorning, the clouds of locusts were so thick, the sky was darkened. And on the ground they were everywhere—just as the frogs, the gnats, and the flies had been. But when they landed, they didn't just sit. They ate. Everything. Every green plant. Cloth, wood, leather, bread—anything their sharp, little mouths could chew. They left behind only dirt, brick, stone, and bone.

Instead of cowering inside, as he would have before, Ben walked away from the village, past the houses and out into the fields. *This is one more chance,* he thought, *to show myself—and everyone else too—that I'm not as frightened of things as they think.* He stopped brushing the locusts off his clothes—although he still brushed them from his face. He closed his eyes and stepped across the ruined field, feeling the crunch of locusts beneath his sandals. He could feel them crawling over his clothes, over his skin, across his hair. He wanted to scream, wanted to brush them off. But he forced himself to ignore them, to let them crawl.

Little, scratchy feet across his hands.

The whir of locust wings next to his ears.

Run! his fear screamed. *Shake them off, brush them off, stomp them off, and then run home where it's safe!*

But he didn't shake, didn't brush, didn't stomp, and he knew that home wouldn't be any safer anyway. He had watched his mother that morning, near panic as she and Ben's father tried to keep the locusts out, or at least kill all those that managed to get in.

Ben stopped walking. Slowly he opened his eyes. He looked down at his arms, his hands, his legs. Locusts everywhere—brown grasshoppers crawling all over him, chewing at his clothes. He fought the fear, the panic that screamed at him to run. He simply stood, trembling.

And when he looked up, there was Joel, covered with locusts.

Joel laughed. "Ben," he said, "I'm proud of you. Look at you! They're all over you—and you're not afraid!"

Ben managed an uneasy smile. "Well . . . I am afraid, really."

"Even better! I mean, I'm not afraid of locusts, so when I stand here like this, it doesn't mean I'm brave. But you're afraid of them, and when you stand here like this, that takes courage."

Ben was surprised. Yes. He'd never thought of it that way. It wasn't really that the other boys were braver than he was. They simply weren't afraid of the things he was. There was a difference.

"I just thought of something, Joel," Ben said.

Joel raised one eyebrow, his way of asking what Ben meant.

"Just think what kind of power it took for God to make all these things happen. All these locusts. The hailstorm. Turning the river to blood, and all the rest. A God who can do all those things can do anything. Anything!"

Joel nodded. "I suppose. But Pharaoh—"

Ben shook his head. "Pharaoh will lose, Joel."

Joel looked surprised. "You mean Moses will win?"

"Not Moses." Ben brushed away a locust that landed on his chin. "God. The Master of all. We've been thinking all along that this was some kind of contest between Pharaoh and Moses. But all Moses is doing is saying what God tells him to say. Pharaoh doesn't know it, but he's fighting against God. And Pharaoh can't beat God! He just hasn't realized it yet."

"If God has already won," Ben said in a low voice, "if He really is more powerful than Pharaoh, then why are we still here?"

He and Enoch walked side by side through the streets of Rameses. They leaned toward each other, Ben's shoulder rubbing Enoch's elbow, so that they could speak quietly and still be heard. It was early afternoon, several days after the locusts had all been blown away on a strong wind from the sea. And yet Pharaoh, to no one's surprise, had once again refused to let the Israelites leave.

"Why is God waiting for Pharaoh to change his mind and say we can go?" Ben continued.

"Shh," Enoch cautioned him, glancing around. "Everyone is upset. Just trust God and wait."

Ben almost laughed. "I do trust God, Enoch. But what is He—"

A fist-sized rock crashed off the building next to Ben and bounced into the street, leaving a white mark on the wall. Ben and Enoch both jumped and then glanced all around. Everywhere they looked they saw Egyptians with hostile faces. Any one of them could have thrown the stone. "Go away, Hebrews, and leave us in peace!" someone shouted. "Tell your Moses that your problems aren't our fault!"

"Come, Ben," Enoch whispered. "Hurry."

Only when they were safe in the courtyard of the Red House did Enoch pull Ben behind a palm tree and say quietly, "It isn't just that God is more powerful than Pharaoh. Of course He is. But He has also proven Himself to be more powerful than the gods of the Egyptians."

Ben was confused. "There are no other gods. There is only one God, the God of Abraham, Isaac—"

Enoch waved his hands impatiently. "I know that, Ben. Of course there is only one God. But don't you see? God is using these plagues to prove that to the Egyptians. What gods do the Egyptians worship?"

Ben shrugged. "They have so many gods, I can't keep them all straight. There is Hapi, the god of the Nile—"

Enoch grinned. "Yes, and what did God do to his water?"

Ben's eyes opened a little wider. "Turned it to blood."

"Could Hapi stop God from doing that?"

Ben shook his head.

"What other gods?"

Ben pointed toward the squatty statue in the bubbling fountain in the corner of the courtyard. "Heket. The frog god."

Enoch nodded, still grinning. "You see? What did the Master of all do with Heket's frogs? Neither Pharaoh nor his gods are a match for our God."

Ben nodded. "Yes, I said this same thing to Joel on the day the locusts came. And soon Pharaoh and the Egyptians too will know who is Master of all."

The boys sat quietly, thinking, watching a flock of geese fly high above. "What will God do next, then?" Ben asked. "Which Egyptian god will He embarrass next? And when? The Egyptians already hate us because of the plagues. Their crops and their livestock are gone. Even our own people are getting more and more angry and upset. My father and grandfather are being beaten worse than ever at the brickyards. If things get any worse—"

"They will get worse," Enoch said. "They have to if God is to prove Himself to the Egyptians." Then he shrugged. "I don't know what will happen next. But I believe this: Before we leave Egypt, God must show that He is more powerful than the highest Egyptian god of all."

Ben looked up into Enoch's earnest eyes and nodded. "Ra," he said. "The god of the sun."

No one was surprised, an hour later, when the wind from the southwest picked up. This was, after all, the time of year for the *khamsin,* the hot desert wind. And no one was surprised to see the sunlight begin to dim as vague clouds of reddish-brown sand and dust began to move across the sky from the southwest. The *khamsin* often carried such clouds of dust. But by midafternoon the sky was as dark as twilight, and the mistress ordered all the lamps lit in the Red House. People began casting worried looks outside and muttering to each other in low, serious voices. Never before had the sand carried by the *khamsin* made the sky so dark in the middle of the day.

The mistress walked into the storeroom where Ben was sorting and counting candles. "Have we enough?" she asked quietly.

"Yes," Ben said. "More than enough. Enough to last for many days."

She nodded, then counted the jars of oil. "I would like to have ten more jars of oil this size. Run over to the merchant's shop and tell him to bring ten more before nightfall."

"But we always have these dust storms this time of year, your ladyship."

She was so distracted she didn't even reprove him for arguing with her. "I fear that this one is different, Ben. I sense the hand of Moses in this darkness. And I expect the worst."

By the time Ben had placed the order for the oil and started back for the Red House, it was almost as black as night. And the air was thick with sand, so thick and dark that he couldn't see more than a few feet ahead. He walked with one hand trailing along the stone wall to his left so that he would know where he was. The other hand held a fold of the light cloak he wore across his nose and mouth, his eyes squeezed into slits.

Now and then huddled shapes would pass near him. Their feet shuffled along the gritty cobblestones of the sidewalk, their arms outstretched to keep them from bumping into something they couldn't see. Few people were out. No one spoke.

The wall to his left ended. To get back to the Red House, he would have to cross the street here. He turned and set his back directly against the corner of the wall so that he was heading—he hoped—straight across the street. He took a deep, gritty, choking breath and set out into the rapidly darkening murk. Now he could only see as far as his outstretched hand, and the wind drove the grains of sand against his skin with such force that they stung.

One step at a time, one foot in front of the other, short steps. How far had he come—maybe halfway across the street? There was no way to judge. But if he kept on as he was—

Ben cried out in a sudden rush of fear as something bumped hard and fast against his legs, and he spun, crashing to the ground with a thud. The air rushed out of his lungs, and he lay still, moaning, trying to catch his breath. What had it been? A dog? A goat?

He felt around him. He had no idea which direction he should move.

The darkness was complete now. He could see nothing, not even his hand in front of his face. Ben was so terrified by the darkness that he almost found it impossible to move. And then he realized why. This darkness, so thick with sand and dust, was closing over him just as the Nile had closed over his head when he'd fallen in years before. Cutting off all light, making it impossible to breathe, choking him . . .

He fought the fear. He had to move.

On his hands and knees, his cloak pulled over his head, Ben crawled for what seemed like hours, bumping into walls and then following them, with no idea which way he was heading. *God,* he prayed, *God of Abraham, Isaac, and Jacob, please hear my prayer. I know that You are sending this darkness to show Pharaoh and the Egyptians that You are the only God. But I am only an Israelite, caught in the middle of Your lesson. I want to go home!*

Tears dripped from his closed eyes. His hands and knees were raw and sore from crawling. But he kept going. Soon he realized that the ground over which he crawled was now rough and uneven, and softer. He was no longer on the street but on open, unpaved ground. Where was he? He tried to think of somewhere in the city that wasn't paved.

Then he began to climb a soft hill of sand—a dune. There were no sand dunes in the city. He had somehow crawled right out of the city.

After he had crawled over several dunes, scraping through scrubby desert bushes sometimes, he realized that the wind wasn't quite as loud. Then he noticed that there was actually a little light filtering through the cloak over his head. He pulled it aside slightly and peered out. Yes, the storm was letting up just a little.

At the top of the next dune, Ben stood carefully, bracing himself against the wind that remained, and cautiously looked out through his slitted eyes.

He knew where he was. He stood on the dunes that sat southwest of the village where he lived. He thought he could just make out his village in the valley below him. He began to walk down the dunes.

Something rustled in some scrubby bushes near him, then broke free and began running rapidly toward him. With a cry, Ben turned to run, tripped over a trailing end of his cloak, and fell face-first into the sand. He looked up in time to see a rabbit scurrying away.

A rabbit. Just a rabbit, and Ben's heart was beating as if he were about to die. Was there nothing he wasn't afraid of?

He had only been fooling himself when he had felt so triumphant about overcoming his fear of the locusts. So what? There would always be something else to frighten him. He would never be a man, strong and un-afraid like his father. A man? Ha! He would never even make a good boy, like Joel, who could do the things he wanted without having to worry first about his fears. Ben was more like a girl.

Ben sat in the small, sandy space behind his family's home, stroking the lamb tied there on a leather leash. He was waiting for Joel, but he was in no hurry. He liked the lamb. It pushed its head against his hand, enjoying the attention, bleating softly now and then. Ben wanted to name the lamb, to make it into a pet, but there was no point. The lamb would be dead before long, killed by Ben's grandfather.

"I'm sorry, little one," Ben said, nuzzling the lamb's soft wool. "You don't know what's coming." Then he chuckled. "None of us know what's coming, do we? We've surely learned that in these past months."

Pharaoh had once again refused to let the Israelites leave Egypt. The storm of darkness had terrified Ben, but it had not convinced Pharaoh.

"I'm sorry. I know that Moses is supposed to be one of us," Ben's grandfather said inside the house, and Ben could hear his feet in the sand as he paced back and forth across the room. "But he's never even lived among us! Raised in Pharaoh's palace! Then for forty years he lived in the desert—and even took a wife from the desert tribes. What does he know of God's chosen people?"

Ben heard a noise and looked up. Joel and Micah were coming, carrying their own spotless white lamb. *There will be a lot of sad children on the day these lambs are killed,* thought Ben. But then he remembered why the lambs were to be killed. There would be much sadness for other reasons too.

Ben thought about that sadness all week. And he was still thinking about it when, on an errand for his mistress one afternoon, he passed a strong-looking, richly dressed Egyptian man on the street. He was laughing and playing with his son, who was only a couple of years old. He would swing the boy up onto his shoulder and then tumble him down as the boy shrieked with laughter. The boy's long hair, bound in back with a cord of red and gold, swung as his father swept him through the air.

It wasn't until Ben had rounded the corner that he realized where he had seen that young nobleman before. His eyes shot open wide. He turned immediately and flew back down the street, looking for the man and his son. Finally he saw them crossing an open square near Pharaoh's palace. He ran until he pulled in front of them. He held up his hand, but he couldn't speak. He was out of breath.

The man stopped, his son perched on his shoulder. "What is it, boy?" he asked.

Panting deeply, Ben waved the hand he was holding up as a sign that the man should wait.

"I'm going to be late, boy. Now if you have something to say to me—"

"You saved my life!" Ben blurted between gasps.

The man looked at him curiously.

"Years ago," Ben said. "I fell into the Nile, and you saved me."

The man looked surprised. "So that was you," he said. "And you remember me? You weren't much older than my son." And he looked up at the boy on his shoulder. "Well, you seem to have recovered nicely."

Ben nodded. "I owe you my life."

The man chuckled. "Well, if your God keeps visiting us with these plagues, none of our lives will be worth much."

Ben looked deeply into the man's eyes and said, "There will be one more." And then he told the man what would happen, and what he must do for the sake of his son. Ben prayed that the man would listen and believe.

And then the time came. Once again Ben found himself sitting in the sand behind their home, petting the young lamb and listening as his parents and grandparents discussed what to do.

"None of this sounds like the traditions of our forefathers," Ben's father objected. "Blood on the doorposts, eating the feast with our sandals on—I can't believe that Moses has heard this from God!"

Ben heard his grandfather breathe deeply. "And yet this *is* the tradition of our forefathers, my son. Throughout history God has raised up men to lead us. Some were like Abraham, strong and wise and true. Some were like Jacob, crafty and weak. And we, God's people, followed them, even the weak leaders. Why? Because it was God we followed, the Master of all. We obeyed God. And if God is calling us to begin a new tradition tonight with this blood and this feast, then that is what we'll do, Moses or no Moses."

"We will perhaps be among the few who actually obey," Ben's father said. "I've heard many of the men at the brickyard scoffing at these new instructions from Moses and saying that they won't—"

Ben could just imagine Grandfather's response, shaking his head and raising one hand as if to hold off the words of Ben's father. "I know, I know. And no one has had more to say against Moses than I have." He paused. "But we will obey God. It is He who has turned the water to blood and loosed the hail and the darkness and the locusts on this land, not Moses. And it is He alone who has the power to save us."

When Grandfather had spoken, there was no more to be said. Ben heard the rattle of metal as his grandfather chose the knife. Then his father appeared beside Ben, holding out his arms for the lamb. Grandfather, holding the thin, sharp knife, stood behind him. Both men were grim-faced. Ben offered the lamb up to his father and then turned his head away as the lamb began to bleat in fear. And when the bleating suddenly stopped, Ben held his face against the warm mud brick of their home and cried.

Later, Ben's grandfather dipped a bunch of hyssop into the lamb's blood and slapped it against the doorposts of their home. Then Ben's mother and grandmother roasted the lamb's meat over an open fire, and they ate it, all of it. They ate it standing, wearing their sandals, with Ben's father and grandfather eating with one hand and holding their staffs with the other. It had been a strange feast. When Ben asked why, his father had simply said, "Because this is how God said it is to be done. It is the Lord's Passover."

Afterward, though, his mother had knelt beside him where he sat on his mat and said, "God is telling us that we are, finally, going to be leaving Egypt. And that when we do, we are to move in haste. That's why we stood and wore our sandals as we ate, and why Father and Grandfather held their staffs in their hands, with their cloaks tucked into their belts, as if they were getting ready for a long journey."

There was a sound of laughing, and of people moving past outside. Ben and his mother both crossed to the doorway and knelt there, peering out around the edges of the doorframe. Drunken men were dancing past, waving their own bunches of green, unbloodied hyssop over their heads, pointing and laughing at each doorway that had blood spread on it.

When they passed Ben's house, one of the men saw him peering out. With his eyes wide and a horrible grin gleaming through his dark beard, the man reached grasping fingers toward Ben and growled, "I am the Angel of Death! And I am coming for yoooouuu!" He stepped toward the door, and Ben shrank back into the room behind his mother. He could hear the laughter of the men as they continued down the street.

"I wonder if their wives think this is so funny," Ben's mother said quietly.

"Let's hope they have no sons," his grandmother said.

For this was to be the final plague: Tonight, the Angel of the Lord would sweep over Egypt, and in those homes where the blood of the lamb had not been shed and splashed against the doorposts, the firstborn son would die. Throughout the land of Egypt.

Even, Ben thought, his heart aching, *in the Red House.*

He stood. "I want to go see Joel, to make sure that his family has the blood splattered on the doorposts of their—"

"No!" his father shouted, moving toward him and holding out a hand. "You may not leave. None of us may leave this house until morning."

"But why?" Ben asked in a small voice. "I'm worried about—"

"Joel's father will do what needs to be done," Ben's grandfather said quietly. "Tonight, great harm will be done in Egypt. And our only protection against that harm is to do exactly what God says must be done. To the letter. Every jot and tittle. And so we will. He said none of us should leave this home until morning. We'll stay here."

Ben lay on his mat that night, in the darkness and the quiet, waiting. He could tell that his parents were both awake as well, and he was sure that, in the next room, his grandparents were also awake. All were waiting.

Before they had gone to their own mats, both of his parents and his grandparents as well had come to Ben to say good night, to touch his face, to close their eyes and mouth a silent prayer. And as he watched his mother's lips move silently, looking at the lines of worry on her face, it suddenly occurred to him that this was all for him. The lamb, the feast, the blood on the doorpost—all for him. Both his father and his grandfather had older brothers, still alive and living elsewhere—neither was a firstborn son. When the Angel of the Lord came this night, it was coming only for firstborn sons. And Ben was the only firstborn son in this home. All of this had been for him—all of the effort, all of the worry. The death of the lamb.

The night was surprisingly silent. And very dark. Ben huddled under his cloak, trembling. Had they made any mistakes? Forgotten anything that God had told them to do? Would he die because they'd done something wrong? Would the angel see the blood on their doorposts in this darkness?

From far down the street, a hideous wailing began. Ben's heart hammered in his chest. Was that the sound of the angel? No, that was a woman screaming out her grief—and suddenly Ben knew why. Her son had just

died. Her firstborn son. Just like him. Ben had to bite his lip to keep from
yelling out in fear. It had begun.

Ben heard a quiet, whispering sound and realized that it was his
mother, weeping quietly. She too was frightened. He felt a movement on
his mat and reached out his hand and found hers. She had reached across
to comfort him. Or perhaps to reassure herself that he was still alive. They
grasped each other's hands tightly. Ben could hear his parents whispering
but couldn't hear what they said.

Another wailing cry went up, closer now, only a house or two down
the street from them, and Ben's mother clutched Ben's hand so tightly
it hurt. This time it was the voices of a woman and a man, the parents,
no doubt, of a young firstborn son whose life had just been taken by the
angel.

The angel was getting closer! Their house would be next!

Ben's heart pounded so loudly it felt as if it would burst out of his
chest. And despite the wailing, he felt as if the night was perfectly still,
perfectly quiet, waiting, waiting . . .

*Lord, You protected me during the darkness. You brought me out of it to
my home. Did You save me then only to let me die now? Please, Lord God,
my father and grandfather have tried to obey You. Let me live now, to go with
them out of Egypt to . . . to wherever You're going to take us. Save my parents
from the grief of—*

And then a loud scream sounded in Ben's ears, so hideous that he
cried out. He feared that what he heard was the Angel of the Lord standing in the room with him, ready to steal his breath, to take away—

But no, that was no angel—that was a human scream. And it was
coming from a house on the *other* side of their house. The *other* side. The
Angel of the Lord had passed by. He had seen the blood on the doorpost
and had passed by. He wasn't going to take Ben. His father and grandfather had done everything right. "Every jot and tittle" as his grandfather
had said.

Ben's heart was still pounding. He was still trembling, and tears stung his eyes. He heard his mother's weeping increase in her relief, and he could tell by the muffled sound of it that she had buried her face in her husband's shoulder as she wept. Despite Ben's fear and confusion, he had to smile when he heard the almost identical faint sound of his grandmother weeping in the other room.

And still his mother clutched his hand, stroking his fingers tenderly with her thumb.

She wouldn't let go all night.

CHAPTER 12

Ben visited the Red House one last time the next morning. By the time he returned to his house—the house he and his family were just about to leave forever—his parents and grandparents had packed up all of their belongings. They had even wrapped up the bread dough his mother and grandmother had mixed that morning but had no time to bake. They would have to bake it later. Ben remembered the feast of the night before—eating with their sandals on. It had been true, just as God had said. They would leave in haste.

Runners had come through the village at the first light of dawn, spreading the news: Pharaoh had summoned Moses and Aaron in the middle of the night to tell them that all of the Israelites were to leave Egypt. Today. Now.

Despite the doubt and grumbling and disappointments they'd experienced in previous months, no one doubted this time—thanks to that horrible night none would forget. This was the day on which all of them would leave. Where they'd go, they didn't know. But today Moses would lead the Israelites out of Egypt.

Even his lordship at the Red House had agreed that it was best. Ben had stood with him in the room where the small, cloth-wrapped body of his young son lay. Candles and incense burned as they waited for the wagon to come take the body to be embalmed. In a voice hoarse with grief, his lordship had said, "Pharaoh should have agreed to Moses' demands months ago." He had gestured toward the white form of his son.

"No offense, Ben, but if your people don't leave now, there will soon be no one left alive in Egypt."

With tears in his eyes, Ben thought about that spoiled, affectionate, and gentle young boy who had run through the house with such energy. Now still.

Then her ladyship had given Ben a small packet of gifts to remember them by. Later, when Ben had looked inside, he had gasped in surprise. There was gold! Enough to help his family begin a new life in whatever place God led them to.

Ben thought about this now as he watched his family preparing to leave. His father and grandfather had found some boards from somewhere and enlarged his grandmother's little cart. It was still small, but their possessions were so few that it held them all.

And as they pulled it through the streets to the fields north of the village where the elders had instructed them to gather, Ben saw death even in their all-Hebrew village. In the doorway of one house—a house with no blood on the doorposts—lay the body of a man. His eyes were open but dead, and his mouth hung open, lips slack, through his black beard. With a shock, Ben realized that this was the man who had danced mockingly through the streets the night before, teasing Ben that he was the Angel of Death come to take him.

And Ben felt a shiver, much as he had felt during the night, fearing for his life. Woe to him who mocked God!

All that day, the Israelites came from Goshen and all over Egypt to gather in the wide fields near Ben's little village. The women built fires and baked the dough they had brought with them. And all day, Ben, Joel, and Micah—under strict orders from their parents not to stray out of sight—had watched the size of the crowd grow to fill the fields. Ben was amazed. He had had no idea that there were this many Israelites. There must have been more Israelites than Egyptians! No wonder the Egyptians were afraid of them!

And Ben was amazed too at the number of animals. Ben's family owned no animals. But some of the groups that came to the fields that day brought with them *herds* of animals, even cattle. Ben wondered how Moses would find food for all of these people and all of these animals. Most of the people he saw, like his own family, had brought little with them. They probably had food only for a few days, if that.

And then word came, called back and forth through the vast crowd: Moses had said it was time to begin. Belongings were quickly repacked, fires stomped out, babies picked up. And slowly, that immense body of people began to move. Ben and Joel and Micah kept together, almost trembling with excitement, avoiding the still-glowing embers of fires. Surrounded by the shouts of mothers to their children and the bawling of cattle and sheep, Ben and his friends and family walked away from Goshen. They were leaving the only home Ben had ever known, going toward—well, Ben had no idea where they were going.

"Where are we?" Ben asked his father one evening a few days later, when they stopped for the night.

His father pointed down a gentle, sandy slope toward a wide, still sea. "That's the Red Sea," he said. Then he looked back the other way. "I'm told Migdol is back there. I've never been this far from Rameses before."

"Are we still in Egypt?"

Ben's father shrugged. "I think so."

At least there was no reason to worry that they were lost. God had performed another wonder for His people. He had sent an immense pillar of cloud that moved ahead of them. All they had to do was follow it. Ben glanced up at the cloud now as it reddened and brightened with the sunset, and he felt reassured.

As they sat down to their food that night, word began to spread quickly and quietly among the many thousands of people camped there. It was just a rumor at first, quickly dismissed by most. But soon the voices grew louder:

"Pharaoh is coming after us!"

"Look! I see the dust from his army and his chariots!"

When Ben and the others stood to look, they saw it was true: There on the horizon, back toward Migdol, was a smudge of dust. Someone was pursuing them.

The Israelites left their dinners unfinished and crowded toward Moses. "Why did you bring us here to die?" some shouted. "We could have died back at our homes, or stayed slaves, which at least would have been better than dying in some forsaken corner of the desert none of us have ever seen before!"

Moses raised his staff for silence, and eventually the people quieted down.

"Don't be afraid!" Moses shouted. "Stand firm and you'll see the deliverance the Lord will bring you today. The Egyptians you see today you will never see again. The Lord will fight for you; you need only be still."

And then Moses gazed up into the sky, seemingly in prayer. And while he prayed, the pillar of cloud began to move. Ben watched, amazed, as it moved slowly from in front of the Israelites, then around the side. Finally it positioned itself right behind them, between them and the army of Pharaoh. They could no longer see Pharaoh's army—nor, Ben realized, could the soldiers see them.

Uneasily, the Israelites finished their meals and unrolled their mats on the sand. Ben lay under the stars that night, trying to sleep. He looked up at the thousands of bright stars in the clear desert sky as the wind picked up from the east. Stronger and stronger it blew, all night long. It was a warm wind, a desert wind. Ben sensed something in that wind—he didn't know what, but it was something God was doing to protect His people.

Yes, God is to be feared, Ben thought. *But He is also to be trusted.*

CHAPTER
13

Ben had thought that he would get no sleep that night, but before he knew it, Joel was shaking him awake. "Come quickly!" he said. "You've got to come see what Moses has done!"

The warm desert wind was still blowing strongly as Ben shook his head to clear the fog of sleep, rubbed his eyes, and struggled to his feet. Then Joel was off, running as fast as he could toward the Red Sea, and Ben tried unsuccessfully to keep up. It was still the time of first light, gray and dim. The sun wouldn't come up for a long time yet.

Even though there was little light, before they reached the water's edge, Ben stopped dead in his tracks, still surrounded by sleeping Israelites.

Before him, right across the middle of the wide sea, there stretched a path of dry sand. On either side of the dry path, the water of the sea was piled into high walls—with nothing to hold it back! The walls were high and steep. Ben thought that churning inside them, he could make out the shapes of fish and other water creatures.

Joel laughed and danced at the edge of the sea. "Look!" he cried. "God has given us a path to escape from Pharaoh!"

Ben shook his head dully. He didn't see escape in that path. All he could imagine was getting to the middle of the sea and then the water walls collapsing and all of the water rushing back in over his head. And then he would find himself once again deep under the water, looking up at the surface that he would never reach.

And what was to stop crocodiles and hippos from coming out of those water walls and attacking the Israelites as they crossed?

Around him, families were awakening and getting slowly to their feet, discovering the wonder that had happened during the night.

"Boys." It was Ben's father. He put a hand on Ben's shoulder, another on Joel's. But he wasn't looking at them. He was looking at the path across the sea, and his voice was quiet with wonder. "Come back. Have something to eat. We must get ready to leave."

All of them turned reluctantly and struggled through the growing crowd back to their campsite. Ben's mother handed them a simple breakfast of bread, cheese, and water. "Hurry and eat," she said. "I'm sure it's almost time to leave."

The boys gobbled their food, and then Ben's mother shooed Joel back to his own campsite. "Help now, Ben. We must get everything packed away and back into the cart." She began rolling up the mats the boys had been sitting on.

"Are we going to go . . . you know . . . across that path?" Ben asked fearfully.

His mother put her hands on his shoulders and looked into his eyes. "Yes, I'm sure we are, Ben. Who do you think opened that path through the water?"

"God did."

She nodded. "Yes. And if God has opened that path and told us to cross it, then we must obey Him. And we can trust Him not to harm us. We are His people. Would you rather face Pharaoh's army?"

That was a harder question than she knew. Ben wasn't sure which frightened him the most.

But she didn't wait for his answer. "Hurry now. Pack and load." She turned away.

Ben did manage to help pack, but he wasn't sure how. His mind was churning, and his hands were trembling. How could he step onto that path across the bottom of the sea, with those walls of water towering on either side?

In a few moments, Ben's father jogged up from wherever he'd been.

"Moses is telling us all to cross now," he panted. "Is everything ready?"

"Yes, son." Ben's grandmother chuckled. "While you've been off investigating these wonders, we've been working."

"Good." Ben's father nodded. "Let's begin." He lifted the front of the cart and began to pull.

Just then Ben heard a voice calling, "Ben!"

He looked around and saw Joel waving him over. "May I walk with Joel?" Ben asked.

Ben's mother looked across the crowd until she saw Joel's family and waved at Joel's mother. "All right," she said. "But stay right with Joel's family. Don't wander off, you and Joel." And then she turned and followed the rest of the family as they headed down the slope toward the sea.

Ben watched them go until other Israelite families, with their flocks of sheep and goats and cattle, got in the way and he couldn't see them anymore. When he turned back toward Joel's family, all he could see were several large cows, moving slowly. A couple of loud-mouthed girls were trying to drive them toward the sea and not having much luck. Ben tried to get behind them so that he could cross toward Joel's family, but after the cows came a long line of people pulling heavy carts, surrounded by families yelling to each other.

By the time Ben found a break in that line and rushed through to find Joel, he realized that he'd gotten turned around, and he had absolutely no idea where Joel and his family were. He was lost in a vast, noisy, crushing crowd of people and animals and carts and wagons.

Ben felt a rush of terror at being lost. But it didn't last long, and he knew why. If he'd found Joel and his family, he would have had to follow them down onto the path across the sea. Was he more afraid, as his mother had asked, of Pharaoh's army or of crossing the sea? He didn't know.

Maybe he wouldn't cross the sea at all.

But why are you still frightened? Ben asked himself. *Don't you remember that you promised yourself to get rid of these fears, to stop acting like a baby? There are little children already crossing on the path God has made—babies—and they're not afraid.*

But they had never almost drowned. They had never sunk to the bottom of the Nile River, looking up at the surface they could never reach. Ben was afraid, and that's all there was to it.

He thought of Enoch. Enoch was brave and wise. What would Enoch do?

He would pray.

All right, then, Ben would pray too.

He pushed through the crowd until he came to a small group of trees that formed a small space between their trunks. He crawled into that small space and lay down on his face, while all around him thousands of people and thousands of animals crowded noisily toward the Red Sea.

As he prayed, Ben remembered, one by one, the plagues God had sent to persuade Pharaoh to let the Israelites go.

Turning the water into blood.

The frogs.

The gnats.

The flies.

The death of the livestock.

The boils.

The hail.

The locusts.

The darkness.

And the last plague: the death of the firstborn sons.

And yet, through all of those things, Ben thought, *God somehow kept His people safe. Even those Egyptians who obeyed Him were saved from some of the plagues.*

So couldn't that same God be trusted to protect Ben now?

What about when I fell into the Nile? Why wasn't God protecting me then?

There was no use in denying it. Ben was terrified, still, of water and didn't want to go between those walls of water on that path, no matter who had created it or why.

Ben scrambled up into one of the trees so that he could see, straining his eyes in the still-dim light. On the seashore below him, the Israelites and their animals were stepping onto the path through the sea. Some moved slowly, fearfully, glancing at the walls of water. Some looked behind them toward Pharaoh's still-hidden army and ran quickly onto the path.

Ben watched carefully. Nothing reached out from the walls of water and pulled the people in. There were no crocodiles, no hippos, no hidden pools to fall into. In fact, as near as Ben could tell from this distance, no one was even getting wet. And yet Ben was—

"Papa!" cried a tearful voice. "Papa!"

Ben looked down. Near the trunk of the tree cowered a small boy, only a couple of years old. Tears streaked his face, and his nose was running. He was dressed in rich clothes. But he wasn't an Israelite; he was Egyptian. And his long hair was bound in back with a cord of red and gold.

The last time Ben had seen this boy, he had been sitting on his father's shoulders while Ben talked to his father in the city of Rameses.

This was the son of the man who had saved Ben's life.

And he was alive! Which meant that his father had listened to Ben and slapped lamb's blood on the doorposts of his home.

And he was here . . . but why? And what was going to happen to him now?

Ben crawled quickly down from the tree and knelt in front of the frightened boy, who stopped yelling and popped a thumb into his mouth. Ben wiped the boy's messy face on the hem of his tunic. "Can't find your papa?" Ben asked. The boy shook his head.

"Out of the way!" someone bellowed, and suddenly a herd of goats was all around them. Ben pulled the boy into the shelter of the trees. Then he looked down toward the water, searching for a tall Egyptian man. But in all of those thousands of people . . .

He looked back, only to find that they were now near the end of the crowd of Israelites. The tall pillar of cloud was growing nearer—with Pharaoh's army right behind it, no doubt.

The sun wouldn't be up for some time yet. Daybreak was just beginning to paint the clouds of the east in pale pink and orange, but the sky was light. Ben looked both directions one more time—ahead toward the path across the sea, back toward Egypt—and made the hardest choice he had ever had to make. Then he knelt in front of the boy again. "Come on," Ben said. "I'll help you find your papa." He took the boy's hand and stepped out of the trees into the churning, bawling mass of people and animals.

Ben had no time to look for the boy's father as they walked. He was too busy trying to keep himself and the boy from getting trampled by cattle or run over by heavily laden wagons. And before he knew it, he and the boy were at the edge of the Red Sea—although now, at least right here, it was dry.

Ben stopped, and the boy stopped right beside him. But before he could even think about what he was about to do, a fat woman bumped into him from behind. "Oh, sorry, sweetheart," she said. "But move along, please—hurry! There are many of us here waiting to get across!" She put her heavy hand on Ben's back and pushed him gently but surely ahead.

Ben stumbled forward a few steps . . . and then there he was, with the walls of water on either side of him. They weren't high here near the edge, where the sea was shallow—only as high as his ankles. He picked up the boy and held him in his arms, when a large ram appeared suddenly beside them. Then the fat woman's family crowded in behind, pushing them several steps farther ahead.

Ben glanced at the walls of water—as high as his waist now. He scurried out of the way of a large cart on the other side and scrambled to get around some rocks in the path. Without looking, he could tell that the walls of water were higher than his head. If they collapsed around him now, he would be underwater.

Don't look, Ben told himself. *Keep walking. Look straight ahead. Keep your eye on the shore.*

In the distance, Ben could see the thousands of Israelites—with his own family somewhere among them, and Joel's too. They'd already crossed and were now milling around on the opposite bank. *You'll be there soon.*

"Now, you see?" he said to the boy in his arms, who was starting to get heavy. "We'll be across in no time, and then we'll find your papa. You aren't afraid, are you?"

The boy looked back into Ben's eyes and shook his head. Then he put his head down on Ben's shoulder.

No, of course he's not afraid, Ben thought. *All he has to do is relax in my arms, because he thinks I can do anything.* He shifted the boy in his tired arms.

For the next few minutes, Ben had all he could do making sure the two of them didn't get run over by the crowd of people and animals. When he looked up again, he was amazed at how close they were now to the other side! While Ben had been dodging cattle and carts, they had crossed most of the sea! He moved faster, wanting to cover the rest of the distance as quickly as possible. The ground beneath his feet grew steeper as they climbed up from the sea bottom.

"My son! My son!" a voice cried, and the boy in Ben's arms lifted his head quickly. A tall, richly dressed man ran down the path toward them, dodging people and animals. The boy lifted his arms to him and began to wail.

Ben offered the boy up to him as the man reached them, and he clasped the crying boy tightly, his eyes closed in relief. But the crowd behind them didn't allow much time for the reunion. "Move it along now! There are still many behind us!" people shouted.

The man put his hand on Ben's shoulder and guided him quickly up the slope toward the bushes along the shore. "You have saved my son's life not once now but twice," the man said. "I listened to what you said and decided to obey the God of Abraham, Isaac, and Jacob—your God. And

God honored my obedience! The firstborn sons of all of my neighbors and friends died in the night, but not my son."

The man buried his face in the neck of his now-quiet child. "I've decided to follow your God wherever He leads me," the man continued. "What choice do I have? He is God. And I won't forget you, my young friend."

"Look! Pharaoh and his army!" someone yelled, and everyone looked back toward the distant opposite shore of the sea.

It was true. The pillar of cloud had lifted, and Ben could just make out the horses of Pharaoh's army rushing from side to side, and rows of chariots moving slowly toward the path. Ben could just imagine the surprise of the soldiers now that they could see the wonder God had wrought during the night. But that surprise didn't last long, and the army began to charge.

It was a magnificent sight, even though these soldiers were the enemies of Ben's people. Their armor and weapons flashed gold in the growing light, and even at this great distance, the tiny horses looked powerful and beautiful.

"Quickly!" People began to call to those still on the path. "Pharaoh is coming! Come quickly!"

Those few stragglers rushed to the shore, helped by those who had already made it, and in just a few minutes, all of the Israelites were out from between the walls of water.

But what now? Would Moses command them to flee across the hills? Ben looked back to where he stood, high on a rocky place behind them. He stood motionless, looking back across the sea.

And so they stood and watched as an odd thing happened to Pharaoh's army. When they got to the middle of the path, they seemed unable to go any farther. Maybe the chariots bogged down in the sand. Or maybe the wheels of the chariots came off. For whatever reason, the army stopped and was milling around in the middle of the sea.

Suddenly the sun rose above the ridge of hills to the east, flooding the valley with golden light. Everything seemed to glow—the massed Israelites with their animals on the shore of the sea, the sea itself, and the army of Egypt's Pharaoh, circling in confusion in the middle of the wide path God had made.

Ben looked back at Moses, silhouetted against the rising sun. And slowly Moses raised his staff, pointing out across the sea until his arm was high above his head.

And Ben looked back toward the water. Pharaoh's army, it appeared, had started to flee back toward the opposite shore. But it was too late. Starting on the far side, the shore toward which they fled, the walls of water began to collapse, to topple over. The path began to fill with water, slowly at first. Then it was faster, and so quick that horses, chariots, and soldiers were swept away by the force of it and disappeared under the water.

An entire army was disappearing beneath the roiling surface of this sea, and neither they nor their horses would ever make it to shore. People were dying right before Ben's eyes.

Then for some reason Ben tore his eyes away from that horrible drama and looked closer, where the walls of water still held, on the near side of the sea. And a shock of sudden fear washed over him. Because there, still standing down on the path that split the sea, out where the walls of water were high, was one Israelite everyone had forgotten about: Micah.

Clearly Micah had somehow gotten separated from his family as they had crossed the sea and had been distracted by the shining, shifting wall of water. He had always been fascinated by anything bright and shimmery. Now he stood, motionless, only a hand's breadth from the water, his nose nearly touching it.

Ben looked frantically around him. Where was Joel? Where was his family? But he saw only strangers.

Ben pushed through the crowd around him down to the edge of the path. "Micah!" he yelled. "Micah!" But of course Micah paid no attention. Maybe he couldn't even hear above the noise.

Again he looked around. "Joel!" he yelled. "Father! Mother!" No one answered. Wherever his family was, they couldn't hear him.

And then he saw familiar faces—the same boys who'd taken such pleasure in teasing him before the plagues began. He ran up to them, but they barely noticed him, still watching the waters closing over the army of Pharaoh. "Look!" he told them. "It's Micah—he's still out there!" And he pointed.

Their eyes reluctantly followed to where he pointed, but they didn't seem concerned. "Hey, it's Eggshell. He'd better get out of there," one boy said.

"But you know Micah," Ben protested. "Somebody has to go in there and get him."

They laughed. "Are you kidding? Why should we risk our lives to save a dummy? Forget it, River Boy."

"Hey," one of them said. "Why don't *you* go get him, River Boy?" They all laughed. "You like water so much, you won't care if you get a little wet saving a dummy."

Ben turned away and tried to get the attention of some of the adults gathered there near the edge of the sea. But there was so much noise—from the people, from the wind, from the crashing of the water as the walls collapsed. Some of the adults didn't hear him at all. Others looked as if they were in a trance.

There was no one to rescue Micah.

No one, that is, except Ben.

The boy who was afraid of everything. Especially water.

Ben stood a moment longer, watching the walls of water collapse over the rest of Pharaoh's army. The dry path the Israelites had just crossed now disappeared. The waves crashed together as the sea returned to its bed, closer to Micah, closer . . .

Thoughts raced through Ben's mind, seeming to take forever: first, the horrible memory of the day he nearly drowned, the water closing over his head, the mocking sun high above, wavering through the water. Then lying on his mat in his home back in Egypt, trembling in fear as the Angel of the Lord passed over his house. God had saved him then. Would He let Ben die now?

And then with a yell, without realizing that his feet had begun moving, Ben was racing down the slope onto the path between the walls of water. They had closed as far as the middle of the sea and were rapidly closing toward Micah, toward Ben, faster and faster . . .

Ben leaped over rocks. "Micah!" he yelled, but still Micah didn't respond. "Help me, God!" Ben yelled, shouting for God's help, screaming to make sure God heard. "Hold back the waters until we are safe, God, please!"

All Ben could see beyond Micah was the crashing together of the walls of water. Whirling in the waves, he could see a helmet from one of Pharaoh's soldiers, a spear, the saddle blanket from someone's horse.

And then he was there. Ben grabbed Micah, who began to wail and fight him off. But Ben wasted no time or effort trying to comfort Micah or ward off his blows. He simply dragged the screaming boy behind him toward shore.

Micah tripped and fell, sprawling face-first into the sand. Ben, holding tight, fell with him. Gritty sand filled Ben's mouth, and his eyes stung as sand flew into them too. Spitting the sand out of his mouth, he dragged Micah to his feet and pulled him steadily toward the shore. The walls of water were still more than head high on either side, and another scene flashed through Ben's mind: the way the sun had looked as he sank toward the bottom of the river years before.

He looked up to see how far they still had to go. So far! They would never make it. The shore was lined now with people calling out to them to hurry, reaching out to help pull them to shore—but still much too far away.

Micah rained blows on Ben, screaming in anger and fear. But Ben hardly felt them, so intent was he on getting himself and Micah to that line of shouting people who lined the shore.

Ben was vaguely aware that the walls of water seemed lower now, perhaps no higher than his head. Then Micah fell once more, and Ben grabbed him around the waist with both arms and pulled him up.

Even louder than Micah's yells was the crashing of the water, sounding as if it was right at their heels, the sound of the seagulls wheeling overhead, the shouts of the people on the shore.

And then Ben was scrambling up the steeper slope at the shore; arms were reaching out to him. Someone grabbed him powerfully by his upper arms and yanked him the rest of the way.

He felt Micah being pulled from his grasp. Suddenly Ben was in someone's arms, safe on shore just as the water came together with a crash behind him. Waves from the collision of the walls of water splashed up onto the shore, getting everyone there wet. But now they all laughed.

Yes, even Ben found himself laughing, though he was also trembling so hard he had to concentrate to keep his legs from collapsing under him. He'd just gotten splashed, water soaking him from head to foot. But he didn't feel that surge of fear he'd always felt whenever water covered him. Instead, he felt only relief and thankfulness.

He turned and looked back over the water. Clear across the Red Sea, from the churning at their feet to the distant shore, stretched a path of disturbed water. It sloshed back and forth, covered with foam over which seagulls swooped and called.

Just then someone grabbed Ben tightly from behind, and Ben heard his father's voice in his ear: "Benjamin! Oh, Benjamin! We couldn't find you, and then we heard people shouting, and we looked back toward the water . . ."

And then his mother was there as well, and Ben also saw Joel's father scoop up Micah in his arms, and for once Micah didn't resist.

"This one saved the other boy's life," someone said, patting Ben's shoulder. "Ran back out onto the path across the sea just as the water was collapsing. Nobody else would go, but he did."

Joel's father, his eyes filled with tears, reached across and ruffled Ben's hair. "We thought we'd lost Micah," he said, nodding. "He got separated from us somehow in the confusion. Ah, but Ben, my lad, you found him. What can I say? How can I ever thank you?"

Ben felt embarrassed and hid his face in his father's side for a moment.

God didn't take away the danger, Ben thought. *The water still crashed behind me. And I was still afraid. But God helped me do what I needed to do anyway.*

You did it, didn't You, Master of all? You sent the Egyptian man to save me when I fell into the water and couldn't help myself. Then You showed Pharaoh and the Egyptians that You are mightier than any of their gods—that You are the only God. And then You saved us from Pharaoh's army, and saved Micah and me from the water. You did it all! Master of all, I love You.

Ben heard someone running up and skidding to a stop right beside him. "What happened?" he heard Joel call out.

Joel's father laughed. "Your friend Ben saved Micah's life, that's what happened. He would have drowned."

Ben turned and looked at Joel.

"You . . . you went back into the sea—after Micah?" Joel asked quietly. "But you could have been . . . You had to . . ."

"But I wasn't," Ben said.

"Weren't you afraid?"

Ben nodded.

Joel looked at his friend quietly. "But you went anyway." He grinned. "And look at you! You're soaked!"

The two boys laughed. "I guess I lived through it," Ben said.

Joel looked over Ben's shoulder, then smiled and pointed. Ben looked behind him, and there stood the boys who liked to tease him. But they weren't teasing now. And Ben suddenly realized they wouldn't be able to tease him again—not about his fears, anyway. The boys stood quietly, simply watching him. Those faces that so often had looked at him with contempt now wore expressions of respect and interest.

Ben and Joel looked at each other and grinned. Joel leaned toward Ben and whispered in his ear, "If they call you River Boy now, it'll mean something entirely different! They'll be thinking of the time you risked your own life to save someone else. That's something they'd never have been brave enough to do."

The crowd around Ben and Joel began to murmur, and soon they heard someone say, "Moses is beginning to sing! It's a celebration!"

"What's he singing?" someone else asked.

Ben's father still had his arm around his son. They turned toward the hill behind them, where Moses stood high on the rocks above them.

"It's a new song, I think," Ben's father said. "But I can't quite hear the words."

Soon they could hear them, though, as all the people began to catch on, singing with Moses.

> I will sing to the Lord,
> for he is highly exalted.
> The Lord is my strength and my song . . .

Ben looked at the joy on the faces of the people around him as they raised their hands toward heaven, faces turned upward.

> *The Lord is a warrior . . .*
> *Pharaoh's chariots and his army*
> *he has hurled into the sea. . . .*
> *The deep waters have covered them;*
> *they sank to the depths like a stone.*

High on the hill, near Moses' rock, Ben saw an older woman, about the age of his grandmother, begin to dance, swaying back and forth with a tambourine in her hand.

"It's Moses' sister, Miriam," someone said.

> *By the blast of your nostrils*
> *the waters piled up.*
> *The surging waters stood firm like a wall . . .*

To Ben's surprise, even his mother and grandmother began to dance along with Miriam. So did all the other women, clapping their hands, singing, taking small steps. Ben looked up at his father, and his father looked back down at him, squeezed his shoulder, and laughed as he sang.

And suddenly, as much as Ben was enjoying the song, the dance, the memory of what had just happened, he began to feel something else. He could hardly contain his excitement to begin this journey—to wherever God would lead them.

> *Who among the gods is like you, O Lord?*
> *Who is like you—*
> *majestic in holiness,*
> *awesome in glory . . .*

LETTERS FROM OUR READERS

Which story is true? This one or *The Prince of Egypt* one? (Faith L., Grand Rapids, Michigan)

Neither is totally true. Each story is based on the book of Exodus, chapters 4–15 in the Old Testament of the Bible. Both our story and the movie *The Prince of Egypt* are an attempt to show people what it must have been like to live then and experience those amazing and scary events. *The Prince of Egypt* looks at the events from the eyes of Moses, while *Trouble Times Ten* looks at the events from the eyes of a child.

The most important part of the story is the real part: about God being the one and only true God. We can trust that God has us in His hands even when everything else seems to tell us the opposite.

I never thought about the plagues that much. Were they really that bad? (Rob D., Sellersville, Pennsylvania)

Yes, they really were that bad. We ran out of room in telling this story, so we couldn't fully describe what it must have been like. We think the scenes that tell about the gnats and the locusts were probably the most accurate.

I'm glad I didn't live back then. (Eric A., Atlanta, Georgia)

We're glad we didn't either, Eric. Bees who attack picnics in the summer are bad enough.

God seems so mean. He hurt everybody. (Devyn S., Lincoln, Nebraska)

God had to show all of Egypt and all of Israel that He was all-powerful. We think the plagues were meant to show the people of Israel that He was the one calling them out of Egypt—and to show the people of Egypt that He was more powerful than all the gods they worshipped. Moses wasn't the star of this show. It was God. He wanted to make sure the Israelites knew they had to trust Him completely. There were hard times ahead for the Israelites, and they needed to be sure about God. These plagues taught them that they could trust God.

Throughout the Bible you'll find passages in which God seems to be mean. Honestly, no one can always understand God. We must trust that God is ultimately good even while He is allowing death and destruction. He is holy and uses everything to teach us, to lead us, and to build strength of character in us. He can be scary, but He can be trusted.

Where was the Red Sea? (Angie I., Canton, Ohio)

There are many opinions about the actual location of the body of water called the Red Sea in Exodus. Was it a lake? Was it part of the present-day Suez Canal? No one is really sure. And frankly, it doesn't make much difference. It would be best not to get bogged down in minor details and lose sight of what's really important—God's hand working among the people of Israel.

I heard there wasn't really a miracle parting the Red Sea at all. The Israelites just crossed a shallow lake. (John B., Mobile, Alabama)

There have been many suggestions about what happened in Exodus 14. Some believe that it was a natural event every year—the strong winds blew, and the waters would move aside on the lake bed.

Others have suggested, as you did, that the Red Sea was actually a very shallow body of water, and the people waded across.

Even if it happened either of these ways, it was still a miracle. If the dry land appeared naturally in the sea every year, it was still a miracle that it happened at the precise moment the Israelites needed to cross the water. It was also a miracle that the wind ceased or shifted direction at the precise moment when Pharaoh's army was in the middle of the sea. And it would have been a miracle if an entire army drowned in a shallow body of water, but none of the Israelites did! Also, the Bible account is very clear that the people crossed "on dry land." It doesn't say they waded.

ABOUT THE AUTHOR

DAVE LAMBERT is author or coauthor of ten books, six of them for kids, both fiction and nonfiction. Dave is also an editor of books and magazines. He has six kids and eight grandkids, and lives in the woods in Michigan. He's editorial director for Somersault, a company that explores new opportunities in publishing.

Ruled Out
by Randy Southern

To Ann, Amy, and Brady

C*RRRR-AAA-CK! B-RRRR-UMMMMM!*

Lightning exploded overhead, but the blinding flash was quickly swallowed by the thick, dark clouds that covered the top of Mount Sinai. The thunder that followed made its way down the mountain with a low, grumbling sound, shaking rocks loose and sending them tumbling after it.

The ground under Ethan's sandals vibrated with the rumble. *Good one*, he thought. He grinned and held his stomach, which was doing some tumbling of its own. Nobody liked lightning more than Ethan did, and this was *super*lightning.

He glanced around impatiently. Melki was missing all this. *Where is he, anyway? He was supposed to meet me at the boundary marker.*

Ethan started walking up the path again, picking his way through the brambles that had overgrown it. Every so often he lifted his head to stare at the mountain in front of him—a tower that rose suddenly from the flat desert floor, its granite as dark brown and rough and wrinkled-looking as an old man's face. He tried to imagine climbing the sheer cliffs, hand over hand, but the path was the only way up the mountain as far as he could see. Narrowing between two large rocks, it twisted and turned up the side until it disappeared into the clouds that had settled on the peak.

Lightning flashed again, and the thunder clapped a few seconds later. *Close*, Ethan thought, *but not close enough*. He wanted to see the white-hot bolts, the spiky fingers reaching down from the sky. What else was there to do when you were stuck in the middle of a miserable desert, having to follow a bunch of stupid—

"You there!" It was a man's voice, calling from somewhere up the path. Ethan dropped his gaze from the mountaintop and saw a muscular-looking, gray-robed Israelite pop from behind a boulder. "What's your business here?" the man said, scratching his tangle of a beard.

Ethan swallowed. He swallowed again when he saw that the man had a bow in his hand and a quiver of arrows slung on his back.

"I said, what's your business?" the man repeated. "You should be back in camp, boy."

Another man, taller and skinnier than the first, stepped from behind the boulder. He seemed more curious than angry, but Ethan noticed he was armed with bow and arrows too. "A visitor?" the second man asked.

"Some kid," the first man growled. "The last thing we need."

Ethan glanced back over his shoulder, toward camp. He could see rows and rows of tents, and knots of people here and there, braving the desert sun. But he didn't see Melki.

He groaned. Melki was good at stuff like this, standing up to adults and speaking his mind. It usually got Melki into trouble, but maybe getting in trouble was better than being a meek little sheep. Lately Ethan was getting tired of being a sheep.

He cleared his throat, which felt as rough and dry as the mountain in front of him looked. "Is—is the boundary around here?" he asked.

The first man raised his bow and pointed it farther up the path. Ethan could see a pile of a dozen or so large stones stacked on top of each other. "That's the marker," the man said gruffly.

Ethan wrinkled his nose. *Not exactly what I expected.* The adults had made such a big deal of the boundary, he'd almost thought the marker would look like one of the giant stone archways they'd left back in Egypt, guarded by statues of weird-looking animals or dead pharaohs. But it was just a pile of rocks.

"You've gone as far as you need to go, boy," the first man warned.

The taller man looked at Ethan, giving him an "aren't you a cute child" smile that made Ethan wince. "In case you haven't heard, son, God has told Moses that no one is to go up the mountain."

I heard, Ethan thought. *Everybody who hasn't been in a cave for the past week has heard.*

"So you're . . . guarding the boundary?" Ethan ventured.

"That's the general idea," said the first man, reaching back over his shoulder and pulling an arrow from the quiver. He fitted the arrow to the bowstring and narrowed his eyes at Ethan.

Ethan gulped.

The taller man frowned at his companion. "Come on," he scolded. "You're gonna scare him. He's just a boy." He turned toward Ethan. "How old are you, son? Eight?"

Ethan felt his cheeks turn red. "Nine and a half," he mumbled.

"Well, I'm sure your family has chores for you to do. Run along, now. Got to follow the rules, you know."

Ethan clenched his teeth at the word. Rules. *That's all we have anymore.* Kicking a stone off the path, he turned and slowly started walking back toward camp.

He hadn't gone far when another lightning flash lit up the sky. He turned to the mountain but couldn't see anything through the clouds. Disappointed, he stood there as the thunder echoed in his ears.

"Hey," came a sudden voice from behind him. "Guess I'm a little late, huh?"

Whirling, Ethan saw Melki standing in the middle of the path. "A *little* late?" Ethan cried. "I had to stand up to the boundary guards myself. They have bows and arrows and—"

Melki snorted. "Oooh, I'm scared. What are they, a couple of guys who used to make bricks in Egypt? Not exactly soldiers. They probably couldn't hit the broad side of a pyramid with their arrows."

Ethan looked up at the sky, searching in vain for more lightning. "Maybe not. But they won't let us get any closer. We'll have to watch from here."

Melki sighed long and loud but found a broad, flat rock where they could sit. They waited in silence for a minute or so, until lightning flared again behind the clouds.

After the thunder faded, Ethan glanced over at his best friend, who was poking a stick into a crack in the rock. "Could you see it *that* time?"

"Just barely," Melki answered, obviously unimpressed. "I'm telling you, we need to get closer if we *really* want to see."

"We can't *get* any closer!" Ethan said. "The boundary marker's right up there. It's just a pile of rocks, but—"

Melki shook his head. "A pile of rocks!" He picked up a handful of sand and threw it toward the mountain. "All we have to do is walk *around* it." He pointed to a small plateau several hundred feet up the mountainside. "That's where we need to go. We could lie on our backs and stare up through the bottom of the clouds. We'd be able to see *everything!*"

Ethan looked over at his friend. *Wish I could be more like Melki,* he thought. It wasn't just that Melki seemed older, even though they were the same age and almost the same height. It wasn't just that Melki's dark hair was curly and wild, as if someone had spilled it on top of his head, and Ethan's was straight and neatly groomed and boring. It wasn't just that Melki was broad and muscular, like his father, and Ethan was thin and wiry, like *his* father.

It was the fact that Melki didn't have to worry about . . . rules.

"You know we're not supposed to go past the marker," Ethan said and then made a sour face. He didn't like the words that were coming out of his mouth. And he *especially* didn't like saying them to Melki. "We have to stay off the mountain until the Lord talks to Moses. You know the rules."

"Rules!" Melki roared with laughter. "Do you know who you're starting to sound like?" He lifted his head as high as he could, puffed his chest out, and started stroking an imaginary beard. "Ethan, you know the rules," he said in a deep, stern voice. "You can't eat manna that other families have collected. You can't leave our tent area on the Sabbath. And you can't go to the bathroom after sundown."

Ethan snickered and then lowered his head to hide his smile. Melki's imitation of Father was perfect, but it didn't seem right to encourage him. "You know my father doesn't have a rule about going to the bathroom."

"Maybe not yet," Melki answered. "But give him time. He has rules for everything else—you said so yourself."

Ethan sighed. "Yeah, but the rule about the mountain didn't come from my father. It came from Moses." He glanced up to see the end of a lightning flash and then looked down again. "He said we can't set foot on it because God is there, and God is holy. Besides, even if we wanted to climb the mountain, we couldn't. *They* wouldn't let us." He pointed back over his shoulder toward the guards. "That path is the only way up this side of the mountain, and there's no way we could get past them without getting caught."

"We could if we did it at night," Melki whispered. "There's a lot more to see here at night anyway."

"How do you know?" Ethan demanded.

"I snuck out of our tent last night and came over here," Melki answered. He gave Ethan a sly smile.

Ethan looked up and down the path to make sure no one was coming or going. "Are you crazy?" he asked, keeping his voice low even though no one else was in sight. "Did you—"

"*No*, I didn't go on the mountain," Melki finished. "But I could have. There was only one guard by the boundary marker, and I think he was asleep. But I knew you would want to go with me, so I decided to wait until you were there."

Well, that's kind of nice, Ethan thought, sitting a little taller. *Melki never waits for anything. Kind of like Leah—*

Leah! he thought, suddenly remembering. "Uh-oh," he said. "My sister's probably waiting for me." He got up from the rock. "I'm supposed to meet her by the dead tree, near the stream."

Melki rolled his eyes but got up too. "Let's go," he said. "Wouldn't want to keep Leah the Law Lover waiting."

Sweat was trickling down Ethan's neck and into the scratchy collar of his robe by the time they reached the northern border of the camp. It was nearing the hottest part of the day, and the clouds around Mount Sinai didn't reach far enough to block the sun. At least being skinny made it easy for Ethan to wind his way through the tight maze of tents, cooking fires, and people. Melki followed, mumbling about the heat and how it had never seemed this hot back in Egypt.

Ethan looked around at the tents, row after row of goatskin shelters in various shades of tan and gray. None of them flapped even a little in the breezeless air. He was glad the Israelites had been in the Sinai Valley for only a few days—not long enough for the camp to take on the sharp, stomach-turning odor of sweat, boiling manna, and animal waste mingled together. But he knew that smell would come soon enough. It always did.

The sun was directly overhead now. Ethan could feel it baking his scalp. "Leah's going to be mad," he said. "She told me not to be late, because she didn't have time to wait for me today."

Melki snorted again. "Oh, then we'd better hurry," he said and proceeded to plop himself down right in the middle of the path to the dead tree.

Ethan's heart seemed to squeeze in his chest. "What are you doing?" he asked, looking around to make sure no one was coming. "Get up!"

"No," Melki said. "Leah may be *your* master, but she's not mine."

"What are you talking about?" Ethan snapped. He could feel his face turning red. "Leah's not my master."

Melki rolled his eyes and shook his head. "*Everybody's* your master," he said with a laugh. "Your father, your mother, your sister, and everyone else who tells you what to do. They say, 'Do this,' and you do it. They say, 'Don't do this,' and you don't do it. It's like you're still a slave."

"I'm as free as you are," Ethan said. He wanted it to sound like a challenge, but it came out sounding more like a question.

Melki stood up and took a step toward him. "Have you ever told your father how much you hate it out here in the desert, or that you wish you'd never left Egypt?" he asked.

"No," Ethan answered, looking down at the sand. "Have you?"

Melki laughed. "My father and I talk about it all the time. He hates the wilderness as much as I do! My mother does too."

"Yeah, but I can't talk to *my* family about things like that," Ethan muttered.

"Why not?" Melki asked. "Because you're afraid of getting beaten or yelled at, like when you were a slave in Egypt?"

"No," Ethan answered. He knew his parents would never beat him, and they rarely raised their voices. But that didn't mean he was free to break the rules, did it?

"A free person can do whatever he wants—including climbing that mountain," Melki explained. "A slave does what he's told and follows other people's rules. So does that make you a free person or a slave?"

Ethan saw a quick vision of himself being led around by three chains—one held by his father, one by his mother, and one by his sister. He closed his eyes and shook his head, trying to erase the image from his mind. "Just drop it, okay?" he told Melki.

Melki laughed again and grabbed Ethan's arm. "Come on, slave. Your master—I mean, your sister—is waiting."

Ethan dug his sandal into the path and then kicked sand in Melki's direction. *He's right,* Ethan thought. *I'm not just mad because he said I'm a slave. I'm mad because he's right.*

Long before they reached the dead tree, Ethan could see Leah waiting. There was her profile—the nose that stuck out a little too far, the chin that didn't stick out far enough. She was squinting the way she usually did. Altogether she reminded Ethan of some homely, nearsighted bird.

No wonder nobody likes her, he thought. *And she just makes it worse with the way she acts.*

The closer they got, the more clearly Ethan could see his frowning sister scouring the horizon for a sign of him. Finally her squint settled on the two boys, and her frown deepened. She shook her head as they approached.

Don't give me a lecture in front of Melki, Ethan warned silently. *And don't tell me how disappointed you are. You're not my mother.*

Sometimes it was hard to remember that himself. Even though Leah was only two years older than he was, Ethan often felt as if he had three parents—the shortest of whom constantly lectured him about rules. The fact that Leah looked a lot like their mother, with her almond-shaped eyes and wavy black hair, didn't help.

"You promised you would be here *before* midday," Leah said, her voice nasal and piercing. "Remember Father's rule. When you make a promise to someone, you must always keep it."

Ethan bit his tongue and tried not to look at Melki. He could feel himself blushing again.

Leah picked up a bundle of bone-white clothes from the ground and threw it at Ethan. He lurched to catch it, but it fell to the sand.

"What's that?" Melki asked.

Leah looked at Melki as if a locust were crawling out of his nose. "It's Ethan's Sabbath outfit," she explained. "We're on our way to the stream to make our clothes clean—like Moses told us to do."

Melki snickered. "My father said we didn't have to clean *our* clothes again, since we just washed them a week ago."

Leah ignored him and turned to Ethan. "We have to go *now*. Mother and Father are already at the stream waiting for us." She shook her head at Melki and started off toward the stream.

Melki just grinned at her. "Leah the Law Lover," he said. "She's got you trained, that's for sure."

Ethan set his jaw and bent down to pick up the clothes. "I'll see you later," he said. "Come by our tent after supper tonight." He started to follow Leah, but Melki grabbed his arm.

"Don't be a slave your whole life," Melki whispered. "Do something *you* want to do." Then he pointed to the mountain and smiled.

Just then the lightning flashed. "I'll think about it," Ethan replied as he started off after Leah. "You can count on that."

When he caught up with Leah, Ethan fell into step beside her—but said nothing. Suddenly she turned to him with a big smile on her face, and he got a sinking feeling in the pit of his stomach. Anything that could make her smile like that was bound to be bad news for him.

"I almost forgot to tell you what Father said," she announced. She said it so loudly and so excitedly that an old man who was nursing a lamb's injured leg nearby looked up from his work.

"What?" Ethan asked, grabbing her arm to keep her moving.

"He said the Lord is going to give Moses a whole new set of rules for us to follow!" She grinned at him expectantly, as if she thought he might do a little celebration dance.

Ethan stopped dead in his tracks, startling an old woman who was boiling manna near the path. "*More* rules?" He spat out each word as though it were a bad taste in his mouth. "We don't *need* more rules. We have too many rules *now!*"

"You won't think that way after you learn to follow them," Leah said, looking down her nose at him.

"Don't you ever feel like you're a slave to rules?" For a moment Ethan wasn't sure whether he'd asked the question out loud or just thought it. Then he saw Leah's eyebrows bunch together in confusion.

"What are you *talking* about?" she asked.

Ethan's grip tightened on the bundle of clothes in his hands. "Don't you ever get tired of doing what you're told?" he asked. "Don't you ever feel like thinking for yourself?"

She frowned. "Are you saying you're wiser than Moses? Wiser than God? That you can come up with better rules on your own?"

He stared at the mountain in the distance. "I could come up with *fewer* rules, that's for sure."

Leah folded her arms across her chest. "I suppose you liked it better in Egypt. Some people do, I hear. Maybe you liked the Egyptians' rules better, and their false gods."

You just don't get it, do you? he thought. Ethan waved his arm around at the rows and rows of tents. "Don't you ever wish you were back there? I mean, look! This is the desert! We live in tents! Don't you remember what it was like in Egypt? We had actual *furniture!* Real food, not just manna that we have to scrape off the ground every day! Sure, it tastes kind of like honey, but anybody would get sick of honey after a while . . ."

"Don't *you* remember what it was like in Egypt?" she shot back. "We were *slaves* there!"

"And we're *still* slaves," Ethan said. "Slaves to rules. And where have the rules gotten us? To the middle of nowhere, with nothing to do but . . . sweat and argue."

"Well, you should know," Leah said, making a face. "Those are the two things you do best." She turned and headed down the path toward the stream.

Shaking his head, Ethan followed. "Just forget it," he mumbled, disgusted. "You wouldn't understand anyway."

The stream was barely a trickle, at least compared with what Ethan remembered of the Nile River in Egypt. This water was no more than eight feet wide at any point and barely rose above the ankles of the people who stood in it, washing their clothes.

Ethan saw his mother standing in the middle of the stream, smiling and waving her arms over her head to get his attention. He took off his sandals and left them on the bank. He could hear Leah splashing along behind him as he made his way into the rippling, sun-warmed water.

His bare feet sank in the wet sand as he passed at least a half-dozen families who were washing their clothes together. It seemed strange to see men, women, and children washing side by side. Usually only the women cleaned clothes.

Ethan's mother cupped a handful of water and gave him a playful splash when he got close. Behind her, his father grunted and strained as he rubbed his grayish cloak on a rock in the stream. Sweat poured from his dark hair down the side of his long, thin face. He seemed to be concentrating hard and didn't look up.

It's a good thing he doesn't wash clothes very often, Ethan thought. *He'd rub holes in everything.*

Ethan walked over and knelt in the water next to his father. After scrubbing his robe against the rock for a few seconds, Ethan broke the silence. "Uh . . . there sure is a lot of lightning on the mountain today," he said.

His father kept rubbing his own cloak against the rock, seeming not to hear.

Ethan tried again. "Father, how dangerous is the mountain?"

Finally his father looked up and seemed to notice Ethan for the first time. "Hmm? The mountain?" He turned toward Mount Sinai. "It's only dangerous to those who don't follow the Lord's commands."

It was the kind of thing Ethan had heard him say many times. Ethan wasn't surprised when Leah came splashing over to listen, either.

"Think of it as a scorpion," his father continued. "If you treat it with respect and keep your distance, it isn't dangerous."

Ethan nodded and slapped his robe against the rock. The coarse material felt even rougher when it was wet, and the folded edges scratched his hands and forearms.

His father watched for a few moments and then spoke. "Ethan, you need to put more effort into your work. Your clothes should be cleaner than they were the day you first wore them."

"Tell him *why*, Father," Leah urged. For a moment Ethan wanted to slap *her* against the rock.

"The Lord Himself has come to meet with Moses," his father explained. "He wants us to be ready for Him. The way we make ourselves look on the *outside* will show how much we care on the *inside.*"

Ethan stopped washing and stood up straight. "Melki's father said *his* family didn't have to wash their clothes again, since they washed them last week."

His father drew himself up too—in a way that always made him look about a foot taller than he actually was. He began stroking his beard. Ethan thought of Melki's impression and tried not to smile.

"Did Melki's father change Pharaoh's heart and convince him to let our people leave Egypt?" Father asked.

"No," Ethan answered.

"Did Melki's father lead us in battle against the Amalekites?"

"No."

"Did Melki's father hold back the waters of the Red Sea so that we could cross over on dry ground?"

"No."

His father took a step toward Ethan and leaned in close—so close that their noses were almost touching. "That's why *my* family is going to listen to the *Lord,* and not to *Melki's father,*" he said.

His voice was so intense, it seemed to bore a hole between Ethan's eyes. Without another word, his father went back to his cloak washing.

In the distance, thunder rumbled from the top of Mount Sinai. Ethan turned toward the cloud-covered peak and stared. The longer he looked at the mountain, the more he wanted to be there.

He replayed Melki's words in his head: *Do something* you *want to do.*

"Do you want to be a slave your entire life?" his best friend had asked.

No, Ethan told himself. *One way or another, I'm going to be free.*

The next morning after breakfast, Ethan stood by his family's tent. He could still taste the manna in his mouth. *Yuck,* he thought. *Will I be eating this every day for the rest of my life?* He longed for the bread they'd had back in Egypt—puffy, golden loaves made with oil and poked full of holes, sending out a rich, fresh smell when his mother slid them from the brick oven. Even flatbread would taste good now, thin and chewy with a piece of roast lamb tucked inside . . .

Shaking his head and trying to forget, Ethan gazed at the mountain. There was something different about the lightning today. The flashes seemed to come more often. He could imagine himself with Melki, looking up through those clouds. *We could see everything up close,* he thought.

He turned to his father, who was shaking sand from one of the sleeping mats. "Do you think we'll be allowed on the mountain after today?" Ethan asked. He tried to keep his voice casual, as though the question had just popped into his head. Picking up a rock, he tossed it on the sloped part of the tent roof and caught it when it rolled down.

His father tossed the mat inside the tent and then straightened up. "Why are you so curious about the mountain?" he asked. "Three times now I've told you that Mount Sinai is forbidden ground, yet you still ask me about it. What do you have in mind, son?"

Ethan froze. What could he say? He hated to lie to his father. But if he told him the truth about what he and Melki were planning, there would be a different kind of lightning storm to worry about.

"I was just—" Ethan started, but suddenly his words were drowned out by a sound unlike any that had ever met his ears.

It was a blare, a blast that seemed to come from the top of Mount Sinai. At first he thought it was thunder, but the noise was too shrill and high-pitched, a sort of squeal but more powerful. It echoed crazily throughout the valley, making it seem as though it were coming from ten directions at once.

"That's it!" his father said excitedly. "Moses said a trumpet blast would be our signal." He reached toward the rest of the family. "It's time to go to the mountain! Stay together!"

A trumpet? Ethan wondered. *What kind of trumpet makes a sound like that?* It didn't sound like any ram's horn he'd ever heard.

But it didn't matter. What counted was that he was going to the mountain. Maybe he could get closer this time. Maybe when it was over, he could go farther up the path, even to the plateau with Melki.

The walk to the mountain was too long, too slow. No one else seemed to be in a hurry. Most of the people acted nervous, even scared, as they made their way toward Sinai. Ethan had to match their trudging pace.

Worst of all, he wasn't anywhere near the front of the crowd. *I'll never get to hear Moses,* he thought. It was always like this when he was at the back of the crowd on the way to an important camp meeting. With about two million people in front of him, he could never tell what was going on.

Just as he'd feared, the journey ended about a quarter mile from the base of the mountain, near a small foothill. This was as close as they were going to get to Mount Sinai.

Ethan scrambled to the top of the foothill and looked around. Even though the hill was no more than eight feet high, he could see quite a distance across the Sinai Valley.

Not bad, he thought. *I wonder if Melki can see me up here.* He waved at the crowd around him, just in case Melki was watching. *I hope so. He'd be so jealous.*

People were pouring into the valley from all directions. The way they moved reminded Ethan of the waves on the Red Sea. "The Israelite Sea," he said to himself.

"The Israelites see *what*?" came a voice right behind him. It was Leah.

"What are *you* doing up here?" Ethan cried. "This is *my* spot!"

"Father told us to stay together," she explained. "That's the rule, so that's what I'm doing!"

Ethan gritted his teeth when he heard the word *rule*. For a moment he could see himself giving Leah a shove and watching her roll down the hill. Sure, there would be a couple million witnesses—but if they knew what Leah was like, he thought, they would probably cheer him on.

Just then he noticed that his sister was staring at something in the sky behind him. When he turned back toward the mountain, it took his brain a few seconds to register what he was seeing.

The clouds on top of Mount Sinai appeared to be . . . *melting*.

Dark wisps drifted slowly down the mountainside like a creeping fog. Even in the heat a chill ran down Ethan's spine, and he felt the hair on the back of his neck begin to rise.

Soon he saw that the dark fog wasn't a cloud at all—it was smoke. Within a minute it had blanketed the entire mountain in blackness.

The trumpet blasted again, this time so loudly his ears hurt. From his perch on the hill, Ethan noticed a ripple of movement at the front of the crowd. He guessed that people were trying to back away from the mountain. *Cowards,* he thought and then noticed that his own palms were getting sweaty.

In the midst of the smoke, just barely visible through the dark billows, he saw an orange glow and flickering yellow lights. It was as if the dead rock of the mountain had caught fire.

How can that be? Ethan wondered. *And what does all this have to do with God coming down?*

His head started to swim. The weird sights and sounds were starting to come a little too fast. He could hear Leah gasping behind him.

Trying to calm down, he looked away from the mountain and spotted movement out of the corner of his eye. About one hundred paces to the east, a lone figure stepped out of the crowd and walked toward the smoky mountain. Ethan's breath caught in his throat as he recognized the long silver beard and the white cloak with up-and-down purple stripes.

"It's Moses!" he called down to his parents.

"Moses?" a woman in the crowd asked. "What's he doing?"

"He's walking toward the mountain," Ethan called out. "Now he's standing still, looking up."

The people around the foothill murmured expectantly. Ethan stood taller, proud to be the bearer of such important news. He'd never gotten closer than fifty feet to Moses, but this was almost as good as seeing him face-to-face.

Just then a new sound roared from the mountain, louder than the trumpet. It seemed to come from the fire at the middle of Mount Sinai. It started as a *whoosh* of wind, like the one Ethan remembered hearing when the waters of the Red Sea parted. Then came quick bursts of thunder like the pounding of giant drums. Each burst rattled the mountainside and shook the ground under Ethan's feet. His knees started to buckle.

"The voice of God!" someone cried out. "The Lord is speaking to Moses!"

Ethan's heart thumped wildly in his chest. Was it really God's voice? For months his father had been telling him that the Lord was leading the Israelites across the wilderness. But Ethan had never seen the Lord nor heard Him speak.

The booming sound echoed throughout the valley. Ethan squeezed his eyes shut, straining to make out anything that might sound like words. But before he could, the sound stopped just as abruptly as it had started.

Opening his eyes, Ethan watched as the black smoke that encircled Mount Sinai rose like a curtain. Soon it vanished into the dark clouds on top of the mountain.

A lightning flash lit up the whole valley. Ethan could see that Moses was now facing the crowd, gesturing broadly.

Feeling dizzy, Ethan took a deep breath. "I think Moses is saying something," he called down to the crowd below. But he was too far away to hear what Moses was saying. They would all have to wait for the message to be relayed back to them.

Whatever Moses said, it didn't take very long. After a couple of minutes, he turned back toward the mountain and knelt. Ethan couldn't tell for sure, but it looked like Moses was adjusting his sandals.

Leah grabbed Ethan's arm. "Look," she said, "the people closest to the mountain are starting to pass Moses' message back." Ethan watched as the message made its way through the crowd. As soon as one section of people heard it, a dozen or so of them would spread out to share it with other parts of the crowd.

Finally, after what seemed like hours, a short, chubby teenage boy in a green robe elbowed his way through the crowd to the foothill where Ethan and Leah were standing. Huffing and puffing his way to the top, the young man held out his hands for silence.

"This is what the Lord says," he began in a high, raspy voice. "'Be careful that you do not go up the mountain or touch the foot of it. Whoever touches the mountain shall surely be put to death. He shall surely be stoned or shot with arrows; not a hand is to be laid on him. Whether man or animal, he shall not be permitted to live.'"

Ethan frowned, remembering the guards at the boundary. *Stoned or shot with arrows—just for setting foot on the mountain!* he protested silently. *It's not fair!*

Wondering how Melki was taking the news, he turned and noticed Leah whispering to herself: "Not a hand is to be laid on him . . . whether man or animal . . . not permitted to live."

He groaned. She was memorizing the new rule the same way she memorized *every* new rule that God or Moses or Father or anyone else came up with. Before long she'd be reciting this new rule to him every time he walked within three hundred paces of Mount Sinai.

The teenage messenger finished his speech with one last piece of news: "The Lord has called his servant Moses to the top of the mountain."

Ethan heard someone at the bottom of the foothill gasp, and he wondered why. *I'd love to climb the mountain!* he thought. *Just think of all the great stuff Moses will get to see.*

The young messenger brushed past Ethan and Leah and then hurried down the hill to spread the news to another part of camp.

Ethan turned back toward the mountain just in time to see Moses head slowly up the path. Ethan remembered Melki's words about the boundary marker: "All we have to do is walk *around* it."

Only if your name is Moses, Ethan thought, digging the front end of his sandal in the dirt.

A crash of thunder echoed across the valley. When the echo faded, Ethan heard the people around him talking. They sounded scared.

"Moses is an old man," a woman said. "What if something happens to him on the mountain?"

"What if he gets struck by lightning?" a man asked. "Who would lead us then?"

"Where would we go?" another man joined in. "Back to Egypt? We would all be killed."

Ethan looked around for his father, expecting him to say something comforting like, "The Lord will protect us." But his father was gone.

Leah must have noticed him looking around. "Father went to tell the people behind us about the Lord's new rule," she said, putting extra emphasis on the last two words.

Ethan looked back at the jagged cliffs and steep slopes of Mount Sinai. *Maybe those grown-ups are right,* he thought. *I'll bet there are a lot of places where an old man could fall and hurt himself.* He glanced around at the adults' worried faces. *What if something happens to Moses up there? If no one else is allowed on the mountain, he'd just lie there until he died.*

The more Ethan thought about it, the more his stomach knotted. *What if Moses* does *die? How will anyone know it? How long will we wait for him to come down? Until* we *all die of hunger or thirst?*

He pictured himself lying at the base of Mount Sinai, too weak from hunger to move, his tongue swollen and dry in his mouth, while scorpions crawled over his sun-blistered body.

Why did God have to send us out here? he wondered. *And why did He take away the only person who can get us out of the desert alive?*

Then another thought struck him. *Maybe it's all because of those stupid rules. Maybe God is like Leah. Maybe He cares more about rules than He does about people.*

"I hope you make it back, Moses," Ethan said under his breath. "You're all we've got, and I'm too young to die."

"Come on, Ethan, use your strength," his father encouraged. "Pull harder!"

Ethan grunted, wishing there were something more fun to do than adjust the tent after last night's sandstorm. Two weeks had passed since Moses' climb up the mountain, and the whole camp seemed to be marking time with busywork, anxiously waiting to see whether the Israelite leader would return.

Ethan gritted his teeth, dug his heels into the sandy ground, and tugged at the goatskin strap as hard as he could. The tent flap barely budged. A trickle of sweat rolled down his forehead and into his eye.

The tent peg was right there. If he could just . . . stretch . . . the flap . . . a little . . . farther . . .

The muscles in his arms quivered, begging him to stop. He relaxed just for a second and then yanked backward with a loud "Aaauuuggghhh!"

The back of his hand brushed past the wooden ground peg. He fumbled to get the strap around it. Once, twice, three times he wrapped the strap around the peg and then tied it off with a double knot, just as his father had shown him.

"How's that?" Ethan panted, looking up.

His father knelt next to the tent peg and gave the strap a couple of hard tugs. "No sandstorm is going to blow *this* knot apart," he said with a smile.

A warm feeling grew in Ethan's chest. "Now all we need to do is clear out the sand that blew in last night," he said. He expected a surprised look from his father and got it. Ethan volunteered to do extra work about as often as he asked for second helpings of manna—which was almost never. But today was different. Today his father had given him a man's job to do—busywork or not—and Ethan had done it. He tried to stop himself from grinning, but he couldn't.

His father looked at him and then started to grin too. "If you're that anxious to work, you can help me find a piece of wood to use for a new tent peg, something we can carve into a point." He paused and looked at the tent. "But let's get some water first. I think you've earned it."

Ethan jumped to get the pitcher, but his father stopped him. "Stay there—I'll get it." It was Ethan's turn to be surprised. His father fetched water about as often as Ethan volunteered for extra work.

"You have a lot of strength, Ethan," his father called from inside the tent. Ethan looked down at his arms. He'd always thought they were scrawny, but the more he looked at them now, the more muscular they seemed.

His father returned with a clay pitcher and a cup made from a hollowed-out piece of driftwood, a souvenir from the Red Sea. He poured water into the cup and handed it to Ethan. Ethan wanted to gulp it down as quickly as he could, but instead he sipped it slowly, the way his father did.

"Your strength isn't all in your arms, though," his father continued. "It's here." He touched Ethan's forehead. "And here." He pointed to Ethan's heart. "Moses has been on the mountain for two weeks now, and people are starting to get restless. Some might try to tell you what to think or do. Don't let them. Use the strength inside you to resist them."

Ethan nodded his head—not because he understood exactly what his father was saying, but because he knew it was the response his father wanted.

"The only guidance you need is the Lord's commands," his father finished.

Ethan stiffened. He knew "the Lord's commands" was a fancy way of referring to the rules that made him feel like a slave. But this time he resisted the urge to roll his eyes and sigh. If his father was going to treat him like a young man, the least Ethan could do was act like one.

"I need to tell you something." The words were out of Ethan's mouth before he knew they were coming.

"What's that?" his father asked.

I'm tired of doing what other people tell me to do, so Melki and I are going to climb up Mount Sinai, even though Moses said not to. I'm going to sneak out of our tent some night and meet Melki at the boundary marker. Then the two of us are going to follow the path up the mountain until we get high enough to see the lightning.

Those were the words that were coming. Ethan could feel them.

Melki's going to kill me, he thought.

"Melki and I—" Ethan started.

"Father! Father!" Leah came running around the side of the tent. Her face was red, and she had little beads of perspiration on her upper lip. She struggled to spit out her message between gasps of breath. "Elizah the Judge . . . sent me to find you. . . . He said there's going to be . . . trouble at the boundary marker. . . . He wants you . . . to meet him there."

Ethan jumped to his feet. Trouble at the boundary marker? It had to be Melki. *I'll bet he tried to climb the mountain without me and got caught,* Ethan thought.

His father handed the clay pitcher to Leah and then hurried off toward Mount Sinai without a word. Leah gave Ethan an excited smile and said, "I feel so honored. Elizah said he was giving *me* the message because he knew I could be trusted to deliver it."

Ethan snorted but didn't bother coming up with a reply. All he could think of was Melki being held prisoner by a mob of angry Israelites.

He shoved his water cup into Leah's hand. "Hold this," he said. "I've got to get to the boundary marker."

He jogged after his father—not fast enough to catch up with him, but fast enough to keep him in sight. He was afraid that if his father saw him, he'd send him home. And Ethan *had* to know what was happening at the foot of Mount Sinai.

"Don't get in trouble!" Leah called out behind him.

Don't tell me what to do, Ethan thought. *You're not my master.*

Keeping one eye on his father and one on the mountain, he made his way through camp. As he'd done for two weeks, he studied each cliff and rock for a sign of Moses. As always, he saw nothing. Dark gray clouds still covered the peak; thunder still rumbled, growing louder as he got closer.

The scene at the foot of Mount Sinai was not what he'd expected. There was no angry mob holding Melki, or anyone else, prisoner—just a group of about forty men talking in low voices. Some looked excited, as though they couldn't wait for whatever was about to happen. Others looked angry.

Ethan saw his father talking to a couple of men who had scowls on their faces. One was a small, white-haired man who kept pointing to the mountain with one hand and shaking his fist with the other. *Must be Elizah the Judge,* Ethan decided. His father was nodding in agreement with whatever the old man was saying.

Ethan crept forward as far as he dared, being careful to stay behind large rocks as he moved. Just as he got close enough to hear what the men were saying, they all stopped talking.

His eyes widened. *They spotted me!* he thought. Flattening his body against a rock, he tried to will himself to become invisible.

"Men of Israel," a voice boomed out, "I stand before you today with unpleasant news."

Ethan peeked around the rock and breathed a sigh of relief when he saw that no one was looking at him. Instead, all had turned their attention to the speaker, a tall man in a fancy blue robe who was standing next to the boundary marker.

Ethan noticed the man's clean-shaven face. *Uh-oh, he's an Egyptianite,* Ethan thought. *Father's definitely not going to like him.* "Egyptianite" was the name Ethan's father used to describe Israelites who he thought tried to look and act like Egyptians.

"It's time to choose a new leader!" the man continued. "Moses has been on the mountain for over two weeks now—and for what? More rules? We have more than enough rules already! What we need is food and drink—and the land that was promised to us!"

Ethan gasped and then held his breath. *He's reading my mind!* he thought.

"Moses speaks for the Lord," called a voice from the crowd. "*He* is our leader." Ethan couldn't tell who had spoken, but from the way people turned toward the white-haired man, he assumed it had been Elizah.

The blue-robed man next to the boundary seemed to expect that response. "How do we *know* Moses speaks for the Lord?" he asked. "We all heard the same sound when the cloud came down the mountain, but only Moses understood it. Or should I say, only Moses *pretended* to understand it."

Pretended to understand?

Ethan blinked, trying to make sense of the words. Was that what had happened? Was Moses . . . a fake?

But if Moses was only *pretending* to understand what the Lord was saying, how could he know for sure where to lead the Israelites? Ethan looked down at the dry desert sand. *Maybe this isn't where we're supposed to be.* That thought made his stomach seem to fall, fast. All of a sudden he felt very lost.

Hey, wait a minute! he thought. *If Moses isn't really speaking for the Lord, then the laws he gave us weren't really from God. If they weren't from God, there's no reason to follow them. That would mean I've been a slave to rules for nothing! I'm free to do whatever I want!*

Lightning lit up the sky overhead. *What if he's right?* Ethan thought as he watched the man talk.

"The laws Moses has given us make no sense," the man was telling the crowd. "He has us scared of this mountain for no reason. *Nothing* is going to happen if we cross this boundary line."

The man took a step toward the mountain. Ethan watched, openmouthed. From where he stood, the man appeared to be no more than a few inches away from the boundary line.

"Do not cross that boundary, Jeru!" This time Ethan saw that it *was* Elizah who spoke. "The Lord has given us His commands, and we will obey. If you cross that line, *you will be stoned to death*." The tone of the judge's voice made it clear that he wasn't bluffing.

Jeru's eyebrows rose. He turned slowly back to the crowd and glanced at a group of men on his left. They gave him some kind of hand signal that Ethan couldn't see very well. Jeru nodded and then turned to where Elizah and Ethan's father were standing.

"You are a respected elder, Elizah," Jeru said with a smile that made Ethan think he didn't really mean it. "So I will honor your request today. But since you are one of the leaders of our people, I will ask you to consider what I have said."

Elizah said nothing. Ethan couldn't see the old man's face, but he could picture the judge staring angrily at Jeru. The Egyptianite stared back for a moment or two and then threw up his hands and walked away with six or seven men from the crowd. The rest of the group watched in silence before starting home themselves.

Ethan leaned back against the stone, his mind racing. *What if Jeru is right? Are we following rules we don't have to? Would the men really have stoned Jeru to death just for crossing the boundary line?*

Ethan heard footsteps approaching and hunkered down. "This is just the first battle, Amon," Elizah said on the other side of the rock. Ethan peered out just in time to see his father and the judge walk past. "I'm afraid things are only going to get worse around here until Moses returns."

You mean if *he returns*, Ethan thought.

He watched as his father walked toward the camp. The back of his tunic was soaked with sweat, probably from running to meet Elizah.

In his hand, his father held a large, round rock.

When Ethan realized what the rock had been meant for, he shivered.

CHAPTER

5

"How big of a piece are we looking for?" Melki asked. He picked up a chunk of tree bark and threw it at Ethan.

Ethan caught the bark with one hand and chucked it back at Melki. "I don't know—big enough to carve a tent peg from." He brushed sand away from the end of a buried branch.

"Well, if we can't find it here, I don't think we'll find it anywhere," Melki said. "This is probably the only dead tree within a hundred miles."

Ethan looked around. Melki was right. There was plenty of mountain and sand to go around, but wood was pretty scarce in the desert. "I think I found something here," he said as he tried to wedge his fingers under the buried branch. "Give me a hand."

"What happens if we don't find the right piece of wood? Is your father going to *stone* us to death?"

Ethan looked up so quickly, he almost lost his balance. Melki was staring at him with a sarcastic gleam in his eye.

"How do you know about that?" Ethan asked. "It just happened yesterday."

"Word travels fast in this camp," Melki answered.

"How did you find out?" Ethan demanded.

"Calm down, son," Melki said as he knelt next to Ethan and started digging out the other side of the branch. "If you must know, Jeru told my father about it."

"Your father knows *Jeru?*" After Ethan asked the question, he realized how harsh it sounded.

Melki lifted his chin defiantly. "Yeah, he knows Jeru! They grew up together in Egypt. Is that any worse than your father knowing people like Elizah, who would stone someone to death just for saying what's on his mind?"

"Jeru was getting ready to cross the boundary line," Ethan said. "I was there—I saw it."

"Aren't *we* getting ready to cross the boundary line?" Melki asked. "Do you think *we* deserve to die if we go through with our plan?"

Ethan looked down, watching his fingers dig in the sand. He wasn't sure what to say. The mountain was as inviting as ever, and not just because of the lightning. Each day it seemed more like a symbol of what he wanted more than anything else—to be free of rules, free of this awful desert.

"I don't know *what* to think anymore," Ethan finally said. "When Jeru said we have too many rules, I agreed with him. But then when my father says that rules are important, I believe him too."

"What about when Leah says rules are important?" Melki asked.

"I want to punch her in the face," Ethan said.

Melki fell face-first into the sand, his body shaking with laughter. Ethan couldn't help laughing too, even though he hated it when people laughed at their own jokes.

"Come on," Ethan said between chuckles. "Help me get this branch out."

Melki wiped the tears from his eyes, pulled himself up, and grabbed the end of the branch Ethan was holding. "One, two, three—pull," Ethan grunted, yanking back as hard as he could.

The branch slid out of the sand more easily than Ethan had expected. Melki let go in time, but Ethan tumbled backward, pulling the branch, some sand, and a weird-looking black thing about three inches long with him.

The branch flew over his head, the sand rained down on his face and chest, and the black thing landed at his feet. Then it started crawling toward him.

"Look out! It's a scorpion!" Melki yelled.

The large, crablike creature seemed stunned by its short flight and hard landing. It moved from side to side as it walked and slapped its stinger tail wildly in the sand.

Ethan tried to scream, but it came out sounding like a whimper. He kicked his feet and tried to back away from the deadly pest, but he couldn't get a foothold in the ground. All he managed to do was throw a cloud of sand in the air.

The scorpion moved so fast that Ethan didn't have time to kick twice. It scampered across the strap of his sandal and up his leg. Ethan's flesh tingled as he felt the scorpion's hard-shelled body crawling over his ankle and shin. The creature stopped just above Ethan's knee and slowly waved its stinger in the air.

"Don't move!" Melki shouted.

Ethan closed his eyes tightly and tried to control the shiver that was running through his body. He felt the scorpion shift its weight on his leg and knew without looking what was coming. He braced himself for the sting.

Thwack!

Ethan opened his eyes and saw Melki standing over him with the tree branch in his hand. Melki pointed to a spot about twenty feet away where the scorpion was lying on its back, writhing and twisting its body as it tried to flip over.

"Thanks," Ethan said weakly, "for not hitting my leg when you swung that thing."

Melki grabbed him by the hand and pulled him up. "Come on," he said, "let's go have some fun."

Still too shaken to move, Ethan watched Melki creep toward the injured scorpion. Melki poked the scorpion with the branch and flipped it over. The creature tried to crawl away, but Melki was too quick for it. With a flick of the branch, he turned it back over. "These things aren't as dangerous as everybody says," Melki explained.

Watching Melki roll the helpless scorpion on the ground, Ethan remembered what his father had told him a few days earlier—that Mount Sinai was like a dangerous scorpion that should be treated with respect. He looked toward Mount Sinai. The dark clouds were still there, along with the thunder and lightning. But the mountain didn't seem quite as scary as it had before. It seemed almost . . . climbable.

"I'm bored," Melki announced, giving the scorpion a final swat. "Let's go explore those hills out beyond the camp over there." He pointed to the area just west of Mount Sinai.

"Okay, but we can't go too far," Ethan said.

"Why, will your father stone us?" Melki asked.

"Stop saying that," Ethan complained. "It's not funny."

"All right, all right," Melki said. "Here, catch." He tossed the tree branch to Ethan. "If you can't make a tent peg out of it, you can save it as a souvenir of your first battle with a scorpion. Now, let's go."

Ethan stared at the ground in front of him as they walked, making sure there were no more scorpions around. Melki stared at the mountain. Neither of them spoke for fifteen minutes or so. Finally Ethan broke the silence. "What are you looking for over there?" he asked.

"Some other way up the mountain," Melki answered. "If there's another path somewhere, we won't have to worry about getting past the guards at the boundary marker."

"Do you see anything?" Ethan asked.

"No, it's too steep on this side," Melki answered.

Ethan saw he was right. The west side of Mount Sinai was a sheer wall that rose at least 150 feet straight up before receding into more rugged, and slightly more horizontal, terrain. "There's no way we could—"

"Shhhh," Melki interrupted, holding up his hand for silence. "Did you hear that?"

Ethan halted, listening. Noises that sounded like a scuffle came from behind a large sand dune to his left. Then he heard a series of boys' voices:

"You will all bow down before Anubis, the god of the dead!"

"No one is greater than Sobek, the crocodile god!"

"I am Geb, the earth god, and this ground is mine!"

"Ptah is ruler over all!"

These strange announcements were followed by more sounds of fighting, groaning, and grunting.

Ethan looked at Melki and shrugged. Melki put his finger to his lips and motioned for Ethan to follow him. Ethan tried to make his way to the sand dune as quietly as possible, but the strap on his sandal was loose and it slapped against his foot each time he took a step. The scuffling sounds stopped.

Ahead of him, Melki was on his hands and knees, peering as far as he could around the dune. Melki's body froze just for a moment, and Ethan had a sudden urge to run away. But then Melki stood up and brushed the sand off his legs.

Ethan stepped forward and saw four boys about his age, maybe a little older, standing on top of a small hill. They were looking down at him and Melki with their arms folded across their chests.

"We're playing Mountain of the Gods," one of them explained. "If you want to play, choose a god and try to knock us off the mountain."

"Choose a god?" Ethan asked.

"Yeah," he replied. "I'm Anubis, he's Sobek, he's Geb, and he's Ptah."

Ethan glanced at the players. "Anubis," the one doing the talking, was about Ethan's size and had a front tooth missing. "Sobek" and "Geb" were obviously twins. The only difference between them was that Geb's nose was bleeding. "Ptah" was the biggest of the four by far. He was even bigger than Melki. He had a scratch on his face that ran from the middle of his forehead to the side of his left cheek.

Ethan had never seen any of them before. *Probably from the southern part of camp,* he thought. From the looks of them, he guessed they liked to play rough.

"Okay, I'll be Osiris," Melki announced. Ethan stared at him in shock—not just because he was willing to play, but also because he was able to name an Egyptian god so quickly.

"What about you?" Ptah asked, pointing at Ethan.

Ethan cleared his throat nervously. "Those are all . . . Egyptian gods, aren't they?" he asked.

"Yeah. So what?" Ptah replied. He started down the hill toward Ethan and Melki.

"Um . . . uh . . ." Ethan fumbled. Then he remembered his father's words: *You have a lot of strength, Ethan. . . . It's here and here.* Ethan recalled how his father had touched his head and his chest. He took a deep breath and announced, "Moses said that the God of Israel is the only true God."

Ptah grinned and looked around at his three friends. "Look, it's one of Moses' sheep!"

"I'm not a sheep," Ethan said.

"Baaaaa! I will follow you wherever you go, Moses," the bloody-nosed twin said in a mocking voice. "Baaaaa, I will do whatever you say."

"Baaaaa! Your mother's calling you, little lamb!" his brother added.

"I'm not a lamb!" Ethan yelled.

"Go back to your shepherd, sheep!" Ptah said. Suddenly he charged, his arms straight out and pointed at Ethan's chest.

"*Oof!*" Ethan grunted as the air was shoved out of his lungs. Losing his balance, he found himself tumbling backward into the sand.

"Go back to your shepherd, if you can *find* your shepherd," Ptah declared. "If he's still alive, he's somewhere up there." He pointed to the top of the mountain.

"Let's show him what we do to Moses' sheep in our part of camp," Anubis suggested with a cackle that made Ethan dread what was coming next.

Ptah reached down and grabbed the front of Ethan's tunic.

"Leave him alone," Melki said. His voice sounded firm but calm. Ptah let go of Ethan's tunic and turned toward Melki. Ethan scrambled to his feet.

"We've got five players already," Melki said with a friendly smile. "We don't need him. If he doesn't want to play, let him go."

Ptah looked at his three friends and then nodded at Ethan. "Okay, little sheep, we'll let you run along home. But if we see you out wandering around again—"

"We're going to sacrifice you!" Anubis finished. All four of them burst out laughing.

His cheeks burning, Ethan looked to Melki for help. Melki just looked away and started up the hill.

The laughter followed Ethan as he walked away. He clenched his fists and tried to hold back tears. He couldn't decide whether to be grateful to Melki for saving him from a pummeling or to be mad at him for staying behind to play. Ethan's throat seemed to get tighter and tighter as he made his way back to camp.

That's what I get for trying to obey Moses' rules, he thought, staring at the sand in front of his feet. *Now all I have is enemies.*

He glanced over his shoulder at the mountain. If he was ever going to be free now, it looked like he'd have to do it himself.

CHAPTER 6

I'm trapped, Ethan thought.

Sitting on a rock in front of his family's tent, he kept thinking about Anubis's warning from the day before: *If we see you out wandering around again, we're going to sacrifice you.*

Ethan stopped sharpening the stick he'd found and looked at the flint knife his father had given him. He wished the chipped edge were sharper. This cutting was taking forever.

Just then his mother and Leah returned from washing clothes. His mother looked surprised when she saw him. "Ethan, what are you doing home? I thought you would be out playing with Melki."

He sighed, not wanting to admit that Melki had abandoned him yesterday. "Uh . . . I was going to. But I . . . uh . . . thought I would get started on carving the new tent peg that Father wanted."

He could feel Leah giving him a suspicious look, so he kept his gaze on the knife blade.

"Well, I'm glad you're here," his mother said. "You can go to the stream with Leah to get water while I stay here and prepare supper."

Ethan's heart skipped a beat. "I can't leave this area!" he blurted without thinking.

"Why on earth not?" his mom demanded.

"Because . . . Father *really* wants me to finish this tent peg." It was a lame answer, but it was all he could come up with off the top of his head.

"Well, you can finish it when you get back," his mother said as she draped the clothes in her basket over the tent cords to dry.

Leah grabbed the small clay pitcher and started toward the stream, leaving Ethan the larger—and much heavier—washing basin to carry. He picked it up and hurried after her, looking around nervously.

"Let's take the shortcut!" he called. If Ptah and his friends—whatever their real names were—were out looking for him, they'd probably be on the main path that ran through the middle of camp. The shortcut—a trail that wound around people's tents and through their cooking areas—was inconvenient but fairly well hidden.

"Father said we're not allowed to take the shortcut anymore," Leah replied without turning around or slowing down. "He said it bothers too many people."

"Come on, just this once," Ethan pleaded, struggling to get a good grip on the basin and catch up with her at the same time. "Let's stay off the main path."

"No!" Leah said firmly. "You know the rule—no shortcuts. You need to learn to obey."

"And *you* need to learn to be a real person!" Ethan snapped back. "It's no wonder you don't have any friends. You're always trying to be like Father. It's really annoying—and it makes you boring to be around."

Leah stopped dead in her tracks.

Aw, no, Ethan thought. *Now she's going to tell Father what I said.* He took a step toward Leah. "Uh, sorry," he mumbled. "I didn't mean—"

"That's Aaron in front of us!" Leah interrupted.

Ethan looked up and saw several dozen people gathered around a tall bald man who had a bushy white beard. "Aaron?" Ethan asked. "You mean Moses' brother? What would he be doing in this part of camp?"

"Let's go find out," Leah said as she hurried toward the group. Ethan paused to look around for potential attackers and then followed.

One of the men in the crowd pointed angrily at Aaron. "This is your responsibility now, Aaron!" he shouted. "Moses is gone, and his God has deserted us. We need a new god to lead us out of this desert!"

"He's right!" a woman called.

Ethan glanced back and forth as the heads around him nodded in agreement.

"Can you believe they're saying such things to *Aaron?*" Leah whispered. She looked surprised and a little scared.

Ethan shook his head. He *couldn't* believe it. Talking about other gods in front of a powerful leader like Aaron seemed like, well, suicide. If people like Father were ready to stone someone for crossing a boundary line, just think of what they would do to a person who asked for a new god!

Aaron held up his hand for silence. *Uh-oh . . . here it comes,* Ethan thought.

"I have discussed this matter with several elders in the camp," Aaron said. He seemed tired and a little sad as he fingered the waist cord of his rust-colored robe. "We have decided to honor your request."

All at once the crowd began to cheer and yell. A couple of women hugged each other.

What's the request? Ethan wondered. He looked at Leah, who was staring back at him with her mouth wide open.

Aaron held up his hand again, and the crowd quieted. "Gather your gold earrings and bring them to the foot of the mountain."

Leah brushed past Ethan and ran back toward the main path. Ethan tried to follow, but the surging crowd got in the way. By the time he reached the path, Leah was out of sight.

Ethan hurried down the path, his grip on the basin making his fingers ache. All the way to the stream he thought about Aaron's words, but none of them made sense.

When he got to the stream, Leah wasn't there. He looked around to make sure Ptah and his friends weren't nearby; then he dipped the basin in the water and filled it almost to the top.

Ethan made the journey back to the tent with small, painful steps. Filled with water, the basin was almost too heavy to carry. At one point Ethan wished Ptah and his friends *would* jump out at him, giving him an excuse to drop the basin and run. But they didn't.

When he finally got back to the tent, Leah and his mother and father were standing out front. Ethan set the washing basin down with a heavy grunt.

"Are you *sure* that's what Aaron said?" his father was asking.

"I'm *positive*, Father," Leah answered. "Ethan was there; he heard it too."

His father looked at him, and Ethan nodded.

"Mother, will we have to give up our gold earrings?" Leah asked.

"No, you won't," their father answered, anger in his voice. "Because this is a *very* bad idea."

"*What's* a bad idea?" Ethan asked. "What are the earrings for?"

"It sounds like Aaron is going to use the gold in the earrings to make some sort of idol," his father explained. "And this family will have no part of any idol. The God of Israel is our God!"

That night, Ethan lay awake on his mat while the rest of the family slept. He was thinking about earrings and idols, new gods and the God of Israel, Melki and Mount Sinai.

Then he heard the noise.

Mmmbrmmbmmmbrmm.

He sat up and looked around. Someone was outside the tent!

The vague mumble of low voices grew clearer. Three, four, five sets of footsteps approached the front of the tent. *It's Ptah and his friends coming to pound me!* Ethan thought, holding his breath. He looked at the goatskin flap that covered the tent entrance and wished it were a lot more solid.

"Amon!" came a shout from outside, and Ethan jumped. "We're here for your gold!"

Ethan could hear his father stirring. "Who disturbs my family at such a late hour?" Father asked.

Three men burst through the tent flap. Leah screamed. Ethan could see the flame of a small torch that one man carried. The other two grabbed Ethan's father and pulled him to his feet.

Ethan wanted to help his father, but his legs wouldn't move. He could feel himself shaking all over.

"We're here to collect your gold earrings!" one of the men declared. "Aaron needs them."

"What Aaron *needs* is to remember which God led us out of Egypt!" Father growled, pulling himself free of the men's grasp.

"The God of Moses has deserted us," the man said, sounding almost as if he were pleading. "If Aaron doesn't make a new god to lead us, we'll all die in the desert!"

"Enough talk!" the torch bearer yelled. "Give us your earrings or you *and* your family will be hurt!" He took a step toward Ethan, but Ethan still couldn't move. He watched as the man's face twisted into a frightening sneer.

"Here!" Ethan's mother screamed. She hurled something at the torch bearer's feet. "Take our earrings and leave us alone!"

With a grunt the torch bearer bent over and picked up the jewelry. The other two men hurried out of the tent. As he left, the torch bearer said, "In time you'll be glad you helped us."

No one spoke after the men left. Ethan's mother and sister huddled in the corner, sobbing quietly. His father stood in the middle of the tent muttering to himself, with his arms at his sides and his fists clenched.

Still trembling, Ethan rolled over on his side, facing away from his family. He stared at the hairy goatskin of the tent. One question kept repeating over and over in his mind: *Where was the God of Moses just now, when we needed Him?*

Maybe He really has deserted us, Ethan thought.

For the next week Ethan stuck close to his family's tent. His father helped him carve three new ground pegs from the tree branch he and Melki had found. Then father and son dug up the old pegs, anchored the new ones with rocks, and repacked the dirt on top.

His father never mentioned the nighttime intrusion, so Ethan didn't say anything about it either. What was there to say? Aaron had the earrings and was using them to make an idol. There was nothing anyone could do about it.

There's nothing I can do about anything, Ethan thought, slumping in front of the tent with his knife in one hand and a leftover piece of tree branch in the other. *I can't climb the mountain. I can't play with Melki anymore. I can't go exploring 'cause I might run into Ptah and those guys.*

I'll never be free, he thought. *I'm more of a slave than ever.*

All he could do was try to carve this stupid chunk of wood. He held it up and looked at it from different angles, trying to picture a shape he could turn it into. A goose? No, too hard. A fish, maybe?

He sighed. Fish made him think of water. He looked around at the flat, broiling desert and shook his head.

Suddenly his mother emerged from the tent, carrying a pitcher. "I'm going to take some water over to Nathiel. She's been sick for the past couple of days and needs some help. Your father's still at his meeting, and your sister's taking a nap. Will you be okay here by yourself?"

"Sure," Ethan said. But he swallowed and looked around for Ptah and his gang.

Noticing that most of the tents seemed deserted, he shifted nervously. "Where *is* everybody, anyway?"

"Probably at the dedication ceremony for the idol," his mother answered. Her large brown eyes looked sad, but there was an angry edge in her voice.

Ethan sat up, surprised. "The idol is finished already?"

"They've had people working on it night and day," his mother said, staring off toward the mountain. "I heard they melted down the gold and then hammered it into sheets and put those around a piece of wood they carved."

Ethan looked down at the chunk of branch in his hand. For a second he wanted to hide it but wasn't sure why.

There was a pause, and finally his mother spoke. "They asked your father to speak at the dedication." Her voice was little more than a whisper. "Your father told Elizah no."

"Elizah the *Judge?*" Ethan asked. "*He's* helping with the idol?"

His mother nodded.

Then why aren't we *helping?* Ethan wanted to ask. *If people like Aaron and Elizah think the idol is a good idea, why can't we just accept it? Why does our family always have to be the outcasts? How long are we going to be slaves to God's rules?*

But he knew those questions would hurt his mother. So all he asked was, "Then what are we going to do?"

She looked as if she was trying to smile, but it wasn't working. "That's what your father's meeting with four of the elders is about." She hoisted the water pitcher to her shoulder. "I'd better go see Nathiel. Don't cut off your finger with that knife while I'm gone, all right?" she said.

"All right," Ethan repeated. He couldn't think of anything else to say as she turned and started the long trek to the southern part of camp.

As soon as she was gone, Ethan heard a rustling sound behind him. *Ptah!* he thought, and his stomach grabbed. But when he turned, all he saw was Leah poking her head out of the tent.

"I thought you were taking a nap," he mumbled.

"No time to talk," she said loftily, stepping outside and heading for the main path.

"Where are you going?" Ethan called.

"For a walk!" she called back.

Thunder rumbled from the top of the mountain. "No, you're not!" he yelled. "You're going to see the idol!"

She stopped walking.

Aha! he thought. *I was right!* Throwing down the knife and wood, he ran after her. "You're going to get in trouble!" he said. "I never thought I'd get to say this to *you*, but you're breaking the rules!"

"No, I'm not!" she cried, putting her hands on her hips. "Father never said I couldn't go."

"Then I'm coming with you," he said. "If it's not wrong for you, it's not wrong for me." *And besides,* he thought, *I don't want to stay here all by myself and get pounded.*

"Do what you please," she said, sounding disgusted. "You always do." She started toward the mountain again, and Ethan followed.

The dedication site was only about fifty paces in front of the boundary marker. A huge crowd had gathered, but no one seemed to know whether to stand or sit. Ethan squeezed his way to a spot near the front and then groaned when he noticed Leah still at his side.

Aaron, dressed in a fancy yellow robe, stood on a platform that was about five feet high. The only other thing on the platform was a wooden altar about half the size of a family tent, covered by a red cloth. Ethan guessed that the idol was under the cloth.

Aaron, his voice deep but a bit shaky, said a few words about "new beginnings" and "showing us the way out of this wilderness." Ethan only half listened, concentrating instead on looking around for Melki and his Mountain-of-the-Gods friends.

When Ethan glanced back at the platform, he noticed that Aaron was praying. Leah didn't have her head bowed or her eyes closed, so Ethan didn't do those things either.

After the prayer, Aaron walked over to the altar and pulled the cloth away. A cheer went up from the crowd, though Ethan and Leah didn't join in.

The sun, reflecting off the idol's gold surface, shot a blinding glare into Ethan's eyes. He squinted and tried to shield his face, but it didn't work. "What is it, a mountain lion?" he asked Leah.

"A *mountain lion?*" a nearby woman said with more than a little scorn. "It's a calf!"

"How is a *cow* going to help us get out of the desert?" Leah asked. She didn't seem to be talking to anyone in particular but spoke loudly enough for everyone around them to hear.

Ethan nudged her with his elbow and gave her a look that he hoped would shut her up.

"It's a *calf*," the woman repeated.

"Oh, *excuse* me," Leah said. "How is a *baby* cow going to get us out of the desert?"

Ethan began to perspire, and it wasn't just the heat. "Come on, Leah," he whispered, pulling at her elbow. "Don't cause a scene."

"I'm not making a scene!" she cried, loudly enough to make Ethan grimace. "I just want to know how a *cow* that's made out of my *earrings* is going to *save* us!"

Two men in front of them turned and stared at Leah. Neither of them looked happy.

Ethan tried to smile at them. "Uh . . . don't listen to her," he said. "She . . . uh . . . hit her head on the way here, and she's not thinking clearly."

"Then get her out of here!" one of the men barked.

"Yes, sir!" Ethan said quickly. His hands were trembling as he grabbed her arm. "Come on, Leah, you heard the man. Let's go home and put you to bed. You need your rest."

He pulled her away. She didn't fight as they made their way back through the crowd—but she didn't go quietly either. "This is *wrong*, and you all know it!" she shouted.

Ethan didn't turn around to see how many people heard her. He didn't really want to know.

When they got to the main path, Leah looked over at him, her nostrils flaring. "Why didn't *you* stand up for what you believe back there?" she asked.

"How do you know what I believe?" he shot back.

"Do *you* think those people are doing the right thing?" Her tone made him think that if he said yes, she might pick up a rock and try to stone him on the spot.

He threw up his hands. "I don't know what to think!" he cried. "All I know is that we've had a God who gave us rule after rule—and look where it's gotten us." He paused, waiting for the first rock to be thrown. "What if this new god doesn't give us as many rules, and things get better around here?"

Leah looked at him with an expression he couldn't name. It wasn't anger or sadness or disappointment, but a mix of all three.

She didn't say a word the rest of the way home.

And that made Ethan nervous—very nervous.

CHAPTER

8

I've gotta get out of here, Ethan thought later that evening. He was sitting in front of the tent again, carving a small half-moon wedge from the bottom of his chunk of wood, shaping the area around it into four legs.

The problem was that all the passersby seemed to be staring at his family. Laughing and talking excitedly about tomorrow's Festival of the Golden Calf, the strangers paraded up and down the path—except when they paused to look down their noses at Ethan and his family. One man even stopped for a moment to spit on the ground at the edge of their campsite.

Ethan felt like a leper with oozing sores, rejected by everyone. *I wish I was going with them tomorrow,* he thought. *They have a new god now. They're free to do what they want. The only freedom I have is to be miserable.*

Just then Ethan's father made things worse. Looking up from the sandal he'd been fixing, he announced loudly, "The God of Israel is the *only* God!" Some of the passersby glared at him.

His mother chimed in, setting down the dishes she'd been cleaning. "What will Moses say when he returns?" she asked loudly.

"He will wonder why our people have become so impatient!" his father said in a booming voice. "He will be angry that we allowed our fears to overtake us and that we couldn't remain faithful until he returned. He will come to us with words from the God of Israel—the only One who can lead us out of this desert!"

Leah, sitting in the doorway of the tent, grinned. She seemed to not care about the disgust and anger on the strangers' faces.

Ethan, however, ducked his head. He wanted to crawl under a rock, bury himself in the sand—anything to escape the stares. *Even running into Ptah and his gang would be better than this,* he thought.

Finally he could stand it no longer. Dropping his knife and wood, he got up. "I . . . uh . . . need to stretch my legs a little," he said to no one in particular. "Is it okay if I take a walk?"

His father looked around as if he'd just been awakened from a deep sleep. "A walk? Uh . . . yes, that's fine. Just make sure you head toward the stream and not the mountain."

I'd head toward the middle of the desert if it were the only way out of here, Ethan thought. He could feel his family's eyes on him as he walked down the path.

He made his way around a group of women who were twirling and waving scarves. Two small children ran past, singing a song they'd obviously made up themselves about the golden calf.

When he was sure his family could no longer see him, he started running. He thought of the way that man had spat on the ground, and he ran faster. He thought of the men bursting into his family's tent in the middle of the night, and he ran faster still. He thought of all the rules he'd been obeying for so long, and—

He tripped over the foot someone had stuck in front of him.

As if in a dream, Ethan noticed that his arms and legs were still moving in a running motion as he sailed headfirst across the path. He tried to tuck his shoulder under himself, but it was too late. He landed face-first in a pile of sand just off the path.

"Oww," he moaned as his brain scrambled to make sense of what had just happened. He heard cackling laughter behind him and then felt a sinking feeling in the pit of his stomach.

Rolling over, he brushed the sand from his face. Melki and the four Mountain-of-the-Gods players were standing over him. None of them seemed worried about whether he was hurt. All of them had big grins on their faces.

"You should be more careful, running around like that," one of the twins said. He held up his foot. "There are a lot of things you might trip on."

"We saw you coming down the path," his brother explained.

"You were running like one of Moses' little lambs," the biggest boy—Ptah—said. He grabbed Ethan by the front of his robe and pulled him to his feet. "And we told you what was going to happen if we saw you out wandering around."

"It's time for a *sacrifice!*" the fourth boy yelled. Ethan couldn't remember which god he had been.

Melki didn't say anything. But he didn't move to help Ethan either. He just stood there, watching.

"Let's take him down to the stream and give him a bath!" one of the twins suggested.

"Yeah!" the rest of the boys—even Melki—agreed. Ethan glared at Melki, who seemed not to notice.

Ptah and one of the twins gave Ethan a shove in the direction of the stream. Ethan looked for a place to run, but he knew he wasn't quick enough to get away from all five of them.

I'm dead, he thought.

"You said you were just taking a walk!" The voice came from the path behind them. Ethan turned to see Leah standing there.

Oh, great, he thought.

Leah didn't seem to realize what was going on. She pushed her way past Melki and the big guy and stood right in front of Ethan.

"Why are you hanging around with these *rebels?*" Leah asked Ethan in a scornful voice. She looked at Melki. "Your father helped make the idol, didn't he?"

"Yeah, so what?" Melki answered. "It's more than *your* father has done for our people!"

Leah gave Ethan a disapproving look. "What would Father say if he knew you were here with these guys?" she continued. "What do you think *Moses* would say if—"

For a moment Ethan forgot where he was and who was around. He forgot about everything except the look on Leah's face—and he couldn't take it anymore.

"Moses is *dead!*" he yelled.

Leah stepped back and looked at him with wide eyes and a wider mouth.

Ethan let fly the words he'd been holding back for weeks, and they felt like little arrows shooting out of his mouth. "He was an old man, and he tried to climb the mountain by himself! His body is probably splattered all over a bunch of rocks at the bottom of a cliff somewhere. And since Moses is gone, his God is gone too. But who cares? The only thing Moses' God has done for us since we crossed the Red Sea is lead us deeper into the desert and give us more rules to follow. And I'm sick of following rules! I'm not a slave!"

For a moment he thought she might start crying or slap him. But after looking around the group, she started to say something but stopped. Then she shook her head and walked away.

Now I'm really dead, he thought, his heart beating double time. *These guys are going to beat me up, and Leah's going to tell Father what I said.*

But when he looked around, he saw that the other boys were all smiling.

"You really told her off!" Melki said with a touch of admiration in his voice.

"That was pretty good, what you said about Moses," one of the twins declared.

"I liked what you said about rules," his brother added.

The big guy stepped forward, and Ethan flinched. But instead of hitting him or grabbing his clothes, the boy put his arm around Ethan's shoulders. "I guess you're not one of Moses' sheep, after all," he said.

Ethan was too stunned to say anything. He'd been preparing himself for pain, not compliments.

"Hey!" Melki said. "Do you want to head over toward the mountain with us?" The other boys nodded.

"Huh?" Ethan said. *I can't believe they're inviting me to join them—just because I yelled at Leah!*

"We've got a little game we like to play near the idol," one of the twins explained.

For a moment Ethan thought about what his father would say. *What does it matter?* he finally decided. *I'm already in trouble. What's a little more going to hurt?*

"Let's go," he said with a grin.

On the way to the mountain, Ethan found out from Melki that the twins' names were Orek and Patek. The big guy's name was Uli; the other guy's name was Tovar.

"Shhh!" Tovar hissed when they got close to the dedication platform. He pointed to a group of boulders about twenty paces from where the idol stood. Then he got down on his hands and knees and crawled over to them. Ethan and the others followed.

Peering out from behind the rocks, Ethan could see four large torches on the platform, one on each corner. The altar was covered with the red cloth again, and Ethan recognized the outline of the idol underneath.

In the torchlight Ethan saw one man on the platform, another in front of it, and a third to the left of it. He guessed there were also men on the right and behind the platform, but he couldn't see them.

The guard on the platform was holding a sword and walking slowly around the altar. The others stared intently into the darkness.

Uli reached into his pocket and pulled out a handful of small rocks. "Everybody take one," he whispered. "The one who comes closest to the guard in front is the winner."

Ethan grabbed his rock quickly so the others wouldn't notice that his hands were shaking. *I wonder how many rules I'm breaking right now?* he thought.

"I'll go first," one of the twins whispered. Ethan wasn't sure whether it was Orek or Patek—he couldn't really tell them apart. The boy stood up, threw his rock, and then fell to his knees in one quick motion.

Ethan listened for the rock to land but didn't hear anything. "Too far to the right," Orek or Patek admitted.

"My turn," the other twin said. He stood and threw his rock with the same quick motion his brother had used. Ethan heard it land, but it sounded well short of the target.

"I'll show you how it's done," Melki whispered. He leaned out as far as he could and flung his rock with a quick sideways motion. Ethan watched as the front guard jumped and started looking around at the ground in front of him.

Ethan snorted and tried to keep from laughing. The rest of the guys were holding their hands over their mouths and shaking silently.

After a minute or so, Uli said, "Now it's *my* turn." He stood up and took aim, not seeming worried about whether anyone saw him. After a quick windup, he let the rock go.

Ethan heard the sound of the rock hitting the sand, followed by a loud "Ow!"

"What happened?" the man on the platform yelled.

"Something hit me!" the front guard answered. "I think it was a rock."

"You must have hit him on the bounce," Tovar whispered to Uli.

"Where did it come from?" the platform guard yelled.

Ethan peeked out from behind the rock and saw the front guard looking all around. "I'm not sure!" the guard yelled back.

Uli gave Ethan a lopsided smile. "Your turn," he said.

Ethan nodded and took a step back from the boulder. He brought his hand all the way down to his knee and heaved the stone in a high arc. But as soon as he let it go, he knew he'd thrown it too hard.

CLANK!

"You hit the golden calf!" Melki hissed. His eyes were as wide as his smile. The other four guys were grinning too.

The guard on the platform yelled something Ethan didn't catch. Whatever it was, it scared the other boys enough to send them running in five different directions.

His heart in his throat, Ethan sprang up and ran too. He could hear the guards yelling behind him. He ran as fast as he could all the way to the main path.

When he got there, he stopped and looked around, panting. A lot of people were standing outside their tents, talking and laughing, but none seemed to be paying attention to him. He let out a deep sigh. After a few moments he headed home with a big smile on his face.

Now that's *what freedom is like,* he told himself.

His father, mother, and sister were all in bed when he got back to the tent. In the dark Ethan couldn't tell whether they were asleep. But no one said anything as he made his way to his mat at the back of the tent.

I guess we'll talk about things in the morning.

It was not a comforting thought.

E than got up the next morning and helped his family gather manna, just like every other morning except the Sabbath. He knelt with his family in the middle of their tent while his father prayed, just like every other morning. He ate a bowl of manna that his mother cooked, just like every other morning.

But to Ethan, it didn't *feel* like every other morning. This morning felt different. *He* felt different, though he couldn't tell exactly what the difference was.

After breakfast, he scooped up his mat and started to head outside to shake the sand from it. His father met him at the tent entrance.

"Put that down and take a seat," his father said. His voice was calm, but the tight lines around his mouth showed anger.

Ethan put the mat down, took a deep breath, and sat cross-legged. *Stay calm,* he told himself. *Just explain that you're tired of being a slave to—*

"What is this?" his father asked, holding out the piece of wood Ethan had been carving.

Ethan swallowed. "Uh . . . It's the piece of wood we used to make—"

"I *know* it's a piece of wood!" his father said. "I'm asking you what you're carving it into!"

Ethan's heart dropped to his stomach. He covered his eyes with his hand so that he wouldn't see his father's reaction. "It's a calf," he said quietly.

"A calf like the one at the foot of the mountain," his father said. Ethan couldn't tell whether it was a question or an observation, so he just nodded.

"Do you know what an idol is, Ethan?" his father asked.

"Yeah, it's a god," Ethan answered.

Reaching down, his father gently lifted Ethan's chin so that they were looking each other straight in the eyes. "No," his father said in a quiet but very firm voice. "An idol is a *pretend* god. It has no power. It's nothing but an ugly statue. The God of—"

"I know what you're going to say," Ethan interrupted. He closed his eyes and took a deep breath, trying to force the next sentence out of his mouth. "The God of rules is the only God."

He opened his eyes and saw that his father's upper lip was beginning to tremble. *"The God of rules?"* his father cried. "This is how you refer to the Lord? Who taught you to be so disrespectful? Your new friends? The ones who laughed when you said those things to your sister last night? Did they teach you to hate the Lord's rules?"

"No!" Ethan protested, his heart hammering. "I've felt this way for a long time! You always talk about the good things the Lord has done, but you never mention how hard He makes our lives with His rules. I feel like I'm still a . . . slave." A bead of sweat rolled down his cheek.

His father stared at him for a moment with sorrow in his eyes. "Rules are like family members, Ethan," he finally said. "You don't know how important they are until they're gone. I don't expect you to understand that now, and I pray that you will never have to find out for yourself."

If obeying rules is so important, Ethan thought, *why does it feel so much better to break them?* His mind drifted back to last night's adventure. He couldn't help but grin as he recalled the look on Melki's face when that rock hit the golden calf—

"Is this *funny* to you?" His father's angry voice brought Ethan back to reality. "This camp is being torn apart by people who don't want to obey God's rules. I will not let *you* become one of them!" His father gave him one more stern look and walked out of the tent.

Exhaling loudly, Ethan flopped back on his mat and looked up at the patched tent ceiling. *If Father only knew how fun it is to be free of rules, he'd probably change his mind.* He lay there for what seemed like a long time, remembering the night before and snickering softly.

Finally he left the tent and looked around for his family. *Probably went to wash their clothes,* he thought. *I guess they don't want me around right now.*

Thunder from the top of Mount Sinai echoed through the camp. *If I head toward the mountain,* Ethan thought, *I might find Melki and the rest of the guys. We could laugh about last night—and plan more fun stuff.*

He scanned the empty campsite. "Well, my family deserted me," he said aloud. "I think I'll desert *them* for a while." He started walking toward the mountain.

On the way he passed several people who looked like they were dressed for the evening festival. Some had already begun celebrating. They were laughing and dancing in front of their tents. A few were drinking from long leather wine pouches. Ethan smiled and waved as he passed by. *That's how free people live,* he thought. *Look how much fun they're having.*

The scene at the foot of the mountain had changed since last night. In place of the guards, dozens of men waited near the platform. Some held birds, others held lambs, and at least two held goats. None of the animals were moving. *They're offering burnt sacrifices,* Ethan thought, *just like we used to do for Moses' God.*

The golden calf now rested on a stand at the back of the platform. The altar, with a fire burning on top of it, sat just in front of the idol. Aaron stood before the altar, dressed in the same fancy yellow robe he'd worn at the dedication ceremony.

At the edge of the crowd, not far from last night's hiding place, Ethan found a flat rock. He sat on it, glad he could see everything that was going on.

You shouldn't be here, a little voice in his head told him.

Ethan ignored it.

One at a time each man in line carried his dead animal to the platform and handed it to Aaron. Aaron cut each animal's body into four pieces and threw them into the fire. Aaron worked quickly, Ethan noticed—much less carefully than the priests who offered sacrifices to Moses' God.

Ethan thought about the first time his father had let him watch a burnt-offering ceremony. He remembered the thrill of sneaking away to one of the slave quarters in Egypt, where a secret altar had been set up. He also remembered the warm, peaceful feeling he had as he watched the priest pray over the offering and ask the Lord to receive it. "This sacrifice is the way we receive forgiveness for our sins," his father had explained.

A pang of guilt stabbed at Ethan's stomach. *There probably aren't enough animals in the whole camp to make up for all the rules I've broken.* But then he reminded himself: *If I'm free from rules, I don't have to worry about breaking them.*

Looking up, he noticed that the next man on the platform with Aaron wasn't holding an animal. He was holding a wineskin. Aaron shook his head and held out his hands to stop the man. But the man just pushed him away and danced around the platform for a minute or so with the wineskin over his head, while Aaron shook his head and watched. Then the man walked over to the altar and poured his wine in the fire.

Whoosh! The flames shot at least ten feet into the air. The crowd oohed and aahed; some people clapped. The man then jumped off the platform and started dancing in front of it.

Another man climbed onto the platform and took off his robe. Dressed only in a loincloth, he started tearing the robe apart and throwing the pieces in the fire. Meanwhile, the men who were waiting to offer *real* sacrifices seemed to be getting impatient. Two of them tried to get on the platform at the same time and then started yelling and shoving each other. Finally one man pushed the other off the platform to the ground below, and the crowd clapped and cheered.

Ethan's stomach churned. *Why are they acting this way?* he wondered. *This is supposed to be a serious ceremony.*

Suddenly he felt someone grab the back of his shirt. Looking up, he

saw a man holding a wineskin over his head. "Our new god has commanded you to drink!" the man said, slurring his words. Before Ethan
could move, purple wetness came raining down, splashing his forehead,
soaking his hair.

Gasping, Ethan yanked himself free and stood up. Wine dripped
from his hair into his face. The smell reminded him of rotting manna,
and the churning in his stomach grew worse.

The man looked at Ethan and started laughing. Losing his balance,
the man fell hard on his rear end—but the laughter didn't stop.

Trembling, Ethan backed away. All around him he saw dozens, maybe
hundreds of people, joining the celebration. "Hail to our new god!" someone yelled. A man was on his knees, arms stretched over his head, eyes
closed, swaying from side to side. A woman wearing a pink veil over her
face was dancing around him.

Ethan took a couple of steps to his left and bumped into a large, beefy
man who had a neatly trimmed black beard. "Why aren't you worshipping, boy?" the man growled.

Ethan tried to say something but couldn't. All he could think about
were the purple stripes painted on the man's face and neck.

"I . . . I . . . just want to go home," Ethan stammered.

He turned and ran as fast as he could back toward the main path. He
glanced behind him a couple of times to make sure no one was following
him, but all the people he saw were heading *toward* the mountain, not
away from it. Gulping air, he ran all the way home.

When he got there, panting and wincing at the pain in his side, his
family's campsite still seemed deserted. *Where could they be?* he wondered,
bending over to catch his breath.

Just then he heard noises coming from inside the tent. Was it somebody moaning? Crying? Afraid of what he might find, he walked slowly
to the open flap and looked in.

He gasped. His father was lying on his back in the middle of the tent, a large bump in the center of his forehead and a dark bruise near his temple. His eyes were swollen shut, his upper lip split almost to his nose. Blood was matted in his hair, dried on his cheek, dripping from his ear.

His mother was kneeling over his father, gently wiping his face with a wet cloth. Her head and shoulders were shaking, and Ethan could hear her quiet sobs.

"W-what happened?" Ethan asked. His eyes began to water so much that his father's face looked blurry.

His mother turned toward him. "Three men attacked him on the way to the stream," she said, wiping the tears from her cheeks. "They beat him with clubs and kicked him."

Ethan felt his jaw clench. *"Why?"*

"They said he was a traitor. They said if he didn't change his mind about Aaron's idol, the whole camp was in danger. They warned him to stop worrying about commands that didn't matter anymore."

Ethan looked down at the ground. He could feel the tears in his eyes start to spill over.

Blinking, he brushed his cheeks with the back of his hand and looked around the tent. "Where's Leah?" he asked hoarsely.

"She went to find you," his mother answered. "She said she knew where you would be."

He froze. Leah was walking by herself through that mob in front of the mountain? The thought made him sick to his stomach.

And it's my fault that she's there, looking for me, he thought.

"I've got to go find her," he said as he ran out of the tent.

*R*ules are like family members, Ethan. You don't know how important they are until they're gone.

His father's words had sounded so ridiculous this morning. So why were they rattling around in his head now, while he was half walking, half running to find his sister?

Leah's not gone, he told himself. *She's at the mountain, probably making fun of someone for worshipping a cow.* He pictured her, with her fake grown-up voice and know-it-all expression, arguing with someone three times her age about obeying the Lord's rules. And for the first time he could remember, that image didn't make him want to punch her.

Please, God, help her to be okay.

"Moses and his God are dead!"

Ethan stopped to see where the shouting was coming from. Two men ran from a tent just ahead of him. "Long live the new god of Israel!" one of them yelled. He kicked over a large boiling pot in front of the tent and sent water running everywhere.

"What are you looking at?" the second man shouted. He was holding a club and staring at Ethan.

Ethan felt his palms get sweaty. "I was just—"

He stopped. There was blood dripping from the end of the club.

Shuddering, Ethan started down the path again. *I've seen enough blood for one day,* he thought.

A long rumble of thunder rolled from the top of Mount Sinai. All at once Ethan pictured someone at the festival pulling out a club and beating Leah bloody for speaking out against the golden calf.

His heart skipped a beat. *It's your fault she's there,* he told himself. *She's looking for you.*

He started running and felt the pain immediately. The muscles in his legs cramped, and his lungs felt as if they were on fire. *I wish I hadn't run all the way home,* he thought. But he didn't slow down. He couldn't.

Out of the corner of his eye, he spotted something moving on the mountain, about halfway between the bottom of the clouds and the ground. Whatever it was disappeared behind a ridge. A mountain lion, he guessed. *Better not let Father see it—he might try to stone it to death for being on the mountain.*

For a second he smiled. But then he remembered the blood dripping from his father's ear, and he ran faster.

If I were Leah, where would I look for me? he wondered. He flinched at the thought of actually *being* Leah—doing nothing but cleaning clothes, washing dishes, and fetching water all day. *No wonder she thinks about rules all the time. Maybe they're the only things that make her life interesting.*

Ethan's legs were aching so much, he had to slow down. Soon he had to walk anyway because the path was clogged with people. In the distance he could hear trumpet blasts and screaming festival-goers. The sounds reminded him of celebrations in Egypt—the ones his father always pulled him away from. "People who worship strange gods do strange things," his father would say. "Things you should never see."

Ethan gazed around, shaking his head. Those Egyptian festivals couldn't have been any stranger than what he was seeing now. To his right, two men were dancing together. To his left, a group of women were throwing themselves, face-first, onto the sandy ground.

In the distance, shadows of the mountain were creeping across the Sinai Valley. The platform was already in the shade. *It's getting late,* he realized. *It's going to be dark soon.* His heart raced. *There's no way I'll be able to find her in the dark!*

Desperate for just a glimpse of her, Ethan clambered to the top of one of the boulders that he and the other boys had hidden behind. Moments later he looked out over the entire crowd. But where was Leah?

He glanced at the sky. The sun was getting lower and lower. "What am I going to do?" he murmured. "I'm running out of time. There's no way—"

"Eeeethaaan! Eeeethaaan!"

His eyes widened. Leah's voice!

"Eeeethaaan! Eeeethaaan!" Her voice didn't sound as loud this time. She was getting farther away!

He scanned the crowd as quickly as he could, looking for anyone who seemed to be out of place. He started on the right side of the mob, slowly working his eyes across the middle. When he got all the way to the left side, he started back on the right. Once, twice, three times he repeated the process—but without success.

His heart was in his throat as he turned his head to the right for a fourth time. Just then he caught a glimpse of a girl about Leah's height. She walked slowly on the left fringe of the crowd. Her head kept moving from side to side, as though she were looking for someone. Ethan saw her cup both hands around her mouth.

"Eeeethaaan! Eeeethaaan!"

"Leah!" he yelled. He jumped up and waved his arms even though she was walking away from him. She didn't turn around. He looked again to make sure it really was her.

"Le—" This time the word stuck in his throat.

From his perch on the rock, Ethan watched as five boys sneaked up behind Leah. He didn't need to see their faces to know who they were.

"Leah, look out!" he yelled. He stepped to the edge of the boulder. It was a long way down, but he'd have to jump anyway. Holding his breath, he leaped—and felt the back of his robe brush the rock as he fell, and fell, and fell.

"*Ooomph!*" He landed on his feet, crouching. *Ow!* he thought. The sandy ground was harder than it looked. His knees and ankles tingled as he tried to stand up.

"Nice jump, boy!" a man in the crowd yelled.

"Do it again!" a woman added.

A huge crash of thunder shook the valley. Ethan noticed that the clouds on top of the mountain were much darker than he'd ever seen them. They rolled over and around each other as though stirred by a giant, invisible hand. Even though the sun hadn't set, it looked like late evening in the valley, and the glow of burning torches on the platform caught Ethan's eye.

Jolts of pain shot through his ankles as he started to run in Leah's direction. He tried to shift his weight back and forth as he ran, and that seemed to ease the pain a little.

I must look pretty strange to these people, he thought as he half galloped, half waddled his way through the crowd. A woman who looked to be about his mother's age fell to her knees in front of him and began waving her arms in the air. "Save us, save us," she chanted.

Okay, maybe I don't look strange to these people, he thought, making a wide circle around her.

When he finally reached the edge of the crowd, he heard Leah's voice above the singing and shouting.

"Let go of me, Melki! What are you guys doing?"

Ethan breathed a short sigh of relief. She sounded more annoyed than worried.

He pushed his way through the last few people in the crowd, out into the open, and looked around. Uli, Melki, Orek, Patek, Tovar, and Leah were standing less than ten paces away on his right. Uli and Melki were holding Leah's arms.

Melki smiled and motioned for Ethan to come closer. "Look what we found wandering around," he said.

"I can't believe you're in on this!" Leah said when she saw Ethan. "I thought you'd stopped wasting your time with these rebels."

I came to rescue you! he wanted to yell. *I nearly broke both of my ankles jumping off a boulder to get here in time!* But he didn't say anything. He just stared at her, trying to think of a plan to get them both home safely.

Finally he asked, "What are you guys doing?" His hands and legs were shaking, but he tried to keep his voice calm.

"We're going to play Mountain of the Gods again," Uli answered. He had a smile on his face, but his voice sounded mean. "Only this time we're going to use a *real* mountain."

"Melki told us about your plan to climb the mountain and get a closer look at the lightning," Tovar explained. "It sounded like a good idea."

"We heard the boundary guards are gone," Melki said. "Now that Moses is out of the picture, nobody cares who crosses it anymore." He glanced at the struggling Leah and snickered. "Well, almost nobody."

"A rule is a rule!" Leah said through gritted teeth. "God will punish anyone who crosses that boundary. Maybe He'll even strike them with lightning."

Melki laughed. "Yeah, right. You'd like that, wouldn't you, Leah the Law Lover?"

Uli grinned. "Well, there's only one way to find out. Let's test your theory, Law Lover."

Ethan's mouth went dry. "What do you mean, *test* it?" he asked.

"Let's take your sister over the boundary and see what happens," Uli replied.

"No!" Leah yelled. She tried to jerk her arms free, but Uli and Melki held them tight. She looked at Ethan. "This isn't funny," she said. "You shouldn't even joke about things like that."

"Who's joking?" said one of the twins.

"Come on, Ethan," Melki said. "She's been making our lives miserable since we left Egypt. Let's show her what happens when she breaks one of Moses' precious rules."

"Yeah," said the other twin. "*Nothing* happens."

Melki and Uli started dragging Leah up the path toward the boundary marker. Her eyes got wide and her mouth dropped open. She twisted her body and tried to fall to the ground, but Melki and Uli wouldn't let go.

"Noooooooo!" she cried.

You've got to do something! Ethan told himself. *Now!*

"Let her go!" he screamed.

Melki and Uli stopped and stared at Ethan. Tovar and the twins stared too.

"Ethan!" Melki said, sounding exasperated. "I thought you were with *us!*"

Ethan swallowed. "So did I."

"You're sick of rules, remember?" Melki said. "You said so yourself about a million times."

Ethan lowered his gaze to the path. "That was before I saw what happens when the rules are gone," he said so softly he could barely hear himself. In his mind he saw his father lying in the tent bleeding.

He looked up to see Uli's angry face. "Hold her," Uli told Tovar. "Make sure she doesn't get away."

Tovar grabbed Leah's arm. She didn't try to escape. She didn't even look at Ethan.

She's probably praying, Ethan thought. He glanced up at the storm clouds on the mountain and thought again about the invisible hand that seemed to be stirring them. *Lord, if You are still up there, please—*

Before he could finish, Uli grabbed him by the front of his robe and swung him toward the ground. Ethan tried to catch himself but couldn't. He landed on his back with a spine-rattling jolt. Uli planted his fists firmly on Ethan's chest.

"I *knew* you were one of Moses' sheep," Uli growled.

"It's . . . . better than being . . . one of Aaron's donkeys," Ethan managed. With Uli pressing down on his chest, the words came out muffled and breathless. But Uli heard them, and tiny splotches of red appeared on his cheeks and forehead, spreading until his entire face looked sunburned.

"Get up," Uli snarled, grabbing a handful of Ethan's hair and giving it a yank.

"Oww!" Ethan yelled. He grabbed Uli's left arm, the one that was clutching his hair, and managed to pull himself up to a standing position. His eyes watered and his scalp tingled.

He looked over at the adults who were dancing and chanting less than twenty feet away. A couple of them watched his struggle with smiles on their faces. *Why don't they do something?* Ethan wondered.

"Help!" he yelled. "They're going to—"

Uli grabbed Ethan's right arm and twisted it behind his back so that Ethan's knuckles were almost touching his shoulder.

His shoulder felt as if it had burst into flame. He tried to groan, but no sound came out. The burning sensation shot down his arm to his elbow and then back up to his wrist. He still couldn't make a sound, but he couldn't stop the tears from rolling down his cheeks either.

"Let's take *both* of them to the mountain!" one of the twins yelled.

Ethan looked up and saw a jagged bolt of lightning explode through the clouds and disappear behind the mountain.

"Maybe the next one is coming for *you*," Uli whispered in his ear.

CHAPTER 11

Thunder rolled like boulders from the mountain, the deep sounds seeming to find their target in Ethan's chest. As Uli pushed him up the path, he could see bright bolts of lightning striking faster and more furiously than ever.

Ethan could barely breathe, but now it wasn't from excitement. *A few days ago, this was the only place in the world I wanted to be,* he thought. *Now it's the last place in the world I want to be.*

He tried to laugh, but it came out as a sob.

"I think he's crying!" Uli announced.

Ethan could hear Tovar and the twins laughing behind him. He wondered what Melki and Leah were thinking.

Leah, Ethan thought. *If it weren't for her, I might have a chance. I could try to fight my way out or at least try to run away and get lost in the crowd. But as long as they have her—*

He had to think of something, and fast. Something that would get the other boys to let Leah go.

His heart pounded as they neared the boundary marker. *No guards,* he thought, looking around. The men had been a pain when he'd wanted to go up the mountain, but now he wished they were still there.

The flashes of lightning were coming even faster, flooding the landscape in blue-white brightness. *Maybe we won't get hit,* he told himself. *Moses never said we'd be struck by lightning if we crossed the line.* But Ethan felt another tear trickle down his cheek anyway.

I wish I were braver, he thought. Suddenly that gave him an idea.

"Hey, Tovar," he called out. "Has Uli always been a coward?"

"Coward?" Uli yelled. He pushed up on Ethan's arm, still bent behind his back. A hot pain shot through the entire right side of Ethan's body.

"Yeah . . . a . . . coward," Ethan groaned. "You're afraid to go up the mountain yourself, so you're making a girl do it for you."

Uli let go of Ethan's arm and spun him around so that they were face-to-face. Ethan breathed a silent sigh of relief and wiggled his arm, trying to get the blood flowing again.

"I'll show you who's a coward," Uli said. He gave Ethan a shove and then stepped toward him. Ethan looked back and saw that the boundary marker was only about fifteen feet away.

"Let her go!" Uli yelled back over his shoulder. "Otherwise he might start crying again. I'll go up the mountain with him. I'm not afraid of Moses' God."

Melki and Tovar glanced at each other, shrugged, and let go of Leah's arms. She just stood there, staring at Ethan, looking scared and confused.

"Run, Leah!" Ethan yelled. "Run home! Don't stop until you get there!" The tone of his voice seemed to snap Leah out of her trance. She looked at Ethan one last time and then pushed Tovar out of her way and ran back toward the festival crowd.

"Ow!" cried Ethan as Uli shoved him in the chest again. Ethan stumbled backward, but kept his balance.

The boundary marker was now almost close enough to touch. Ethan noticed that Melki, Tovar, and the twins stayed where they were.

"Listen, Uli," Ethan said, gazing worriedly at the stack of stones. "Something bad's going to happen if we cross that boundary. We might not get struck by lightning, but if someone sees us, they might take us out and stone us."

Uli snorted. "Who's the donkey now?" He pointed to the festival crowd. "Do you think anyone down there is going to care if we cross this stupid line? Look at them! We have a new god. We don't have to worry about Moses' rules anymore."

More thunder rumbled overhead. "I am looking at them," Ethan said, starting to feel dizzy. "The whole camp is a mess. Maybe God gives rules for a reason. Maybe He doesn't want us on the mountain because He's holy, and—"

Before he could say anything else, Uli turned and gave him one more shove. Instead of stumbling backward this time, Ethan fell to the ground. He stuck his rear end out to absorb most of the impact and managed to get his elbows behind him in time to keep from hitting his head on the ground.

In an instant Uli was on top of him, straddling his stomach. Ethan squinted at the boundary marker and saw that his shoulders were even with the back of the stone pile. His heart jumped. *If my head touches the ground—*

Uli looked over at the boundary marker and smiled. He put his left arm on Ethan's chest and his right hand on Ethan's forehead. "Here we go, Sheep Boy!" he said.

"Don't . . . do it!" Ethan grunted. He could feel the veins in his neck standing out as he strained to keep his head off the ground. "Whatever happens to me is going to happen to—"

CR-RRR-AAAAAAA-CK!

Ethan felt the explosion in the pit of his stomach before the sound of it reached his ears. The noise was so sharp, so clear, and so loud that it made the hair on his arms and neck stand on end.

The ground below his shoulders rattled. Small chunks of rock, dirt, and sand pelted the side of his face.

Screaming, Uli tried to cover his head with his arms. Ethan couldn't tell if the boy had been hit or not.

Using every bit of strength he had left, Ethan lifted his hips and flipped himself over. Uli lost his balance and fell onto his left shoulder. Ethan expected him to get up and charge again, but Uli just lay there with his arms still covering his head and his knees drawn up to his chest.

Get away from the mountain! a voice in Ethan's head shouted. He tried to lift himself, but his arms felt like loose tent straps. He collapsed face-first back into the sand.

A deep roll of thunder started overhead. *Oh no,* he thought, *here comes more lightning!* He squeezed his eyes tight, covered his head with his hands, and braced himself.

But nothing happened.

Ethan lifted his face from the sand and listened. Everything was quiet. The singing and dancing had stopped.

He looked back at Melki, Tovar, and the twins. None of them were moving. They stared in Ethan's direction with their mouths open.

What's wrong? he wondered. *Am I on fire?* He reached back and patted his robe but didn't feel any flames.

All at once he realized they weren't staring at him. They were staring at something behind him. He turned slowly to look, not sure he wanted to see what was there.

"Moses!"

Only after the word was out of his mouth did Ethan realize he had said it.

The old man looked down at Ethan and then back at the crowd. He was standing about fifteen feet past the boundary marker. The long silver beard looked longer than ever. The white cloak with the up-and-down purple stripes was dusty and wrinkled. He was still as a statue—except for his nostrils, which flared like an angry bull's, and his eyes, which seemed to move from person to person in the crowd.

Ethan lowered his head and noticed something on the ground at Moses' feet. At first it just looked like rocks, but then he realized they were pieces of a whole. The whole was a flat rock carved with some kind of writing. It reminded him of stone tablets he'd seen in Egypt, the ones chiseled with symbols like eyes and birds and names of pharaohs.

Are those God's new rules? he wondered.

All at once he realized what had happened. *That must have been the crash we heard. It wasn't lightning striking—it was stone breaking. Moses must have dropped the tablets—or thrown them down—when he saw the idol!*

Out of the corner of his eye, Ethan saw a wobbly Uli stand up, look around, and sneak off—away from Moses and the crowd. Melki and the other boys just watched him go.

A moment later Ethan realized he was still lying on the ground. Standing stiffly, he brushed the sand from the front of his robe. He heard someone in the crowd murmur and saw that Moses was coming toward the boundary marker.

Backing away from the pile of rocks, Ethan gave Moses room to pass. *He moves fast for an old man,* Ethan thought numbly. *Especially one who's spent the last forty days mountain climbing.*

The old man didn't seem to notice him. Ethan fell in step behind Moses, figuring that if Melki or the others had anything planned, the safest place to be was in the Israelite leader's shadow.

But as Ethan passed the other boys, the way they all looked down at their sandals made him think he wouldn't have to worry about them any longer.

The crowd at the foot of the mountain backed away as Moses got closer. Ethan couldn't tell whether they were angry because their festival was over or were afraid of what was going to happen to them.

As the crowd fell back, Ethan saw Leah waiting for him with a grin on her face.

"I thought I told you to run home," he said.

"I didn't know that was a rule," Leah replied. "Otherwise, I would have obeyed you." Her smile faded. "The reason I came looking for you was to tell you that something's happened to Father. He—"

"Father! I almost forgot! I know what happened," Ethan said. "We've got to get back there—now!"

CHAPTER 12

It was nearly dark by the time Ethan and Leah got back to the tent. Ethan paused at the tent entrance and took a deep breath.

What if he's dead? he thought. He looked over at Leah. She shook her head as though she knew what he was thinking.

The air inside the tent was sour, like the smell of traveling clothes that hadn't been washed for a week. His father lay on his mat just across from the entrance. His mother lay on the ground next to him. Judging by the drag marks on the floor, Ethan guessed that his mother had moved his father by herself.

"I'm . . . so glad you two are home," his mother mumbled. She sounded more asleep than awake. "We've been worried sick about you."

"How's Father?" Leah whispered.

"The bleeding's stopped," his mother said wearily. "He needs rest. We all do. We'll talk about it in the morning."

Ethan limped over to his mat and plopped down on his back. His ankles were throbbing, his shoulder was stiff, and the skin on the back of his head was still tingling. He couldn't help letting out a groan.

"Are you okay?" Leah whispered, kneeling at the foot of his mat.

"Yeah, I think so," Ethan said.

"I . . . uh . . . just wanted to say thanks for coming to help me," Leah said. She kept her eyes on the ground in front of her while she talked.

"It's okay," he whispered, wincing at a pain in his arm. "After all, family members are like rules—you don't know how important they are until they're gone."

"Huh?" she said.

"Never mind. We'd better stop talking so Father can sleep. I'll see you in the morning."

"Right."

Ethan closed his eyes. In the distance he heard a sharp crack of thunder. *It's not over yet,* he thought, and a shiver ran down his spine.

The next morning Ethan woke to the sound of voices outside the tent. He glanced around and saw that everyone else was up already. Bright sunlight flooded the tent through the open flaps.

Father! he remembered. He tried to get up quickly, but his ankles and shoulder wouldn't let him. After a couple of tries he managed to pull himself up using one of the tent posts for support. He hobbled over to the entrance, trying to adjust his eyes to the brightness.

Outside, his father was sitting on a rock. He still had some scabs and bruises on his face, but most of the swelling was gone. Leah was wiping his face with a wet cloth. Ethan's mother was standing over the cooking pot, stirring. The smell of fresh manna made Ethan's stomach rumble.

I guess manna's not so bad, he thought. *Better than sand, anyway.*

His father noticed him in the doorway and tried to smile, but the muscles in his face seemed frozen. "Leah told me what happened," he said. "I'm proud of you, son." Only one side of his mouth moved when he talked.

Ethan's eyes filled with tears. "It's not right," he said. "It's not right what they did to you."

His father looked into the distance and shook his head. "I wouldn't want to be in their place," he said. "They will pay a high price for disobeying the God of Israel."

There was a long pause, and Leah finally spoke. "Some of the elders came by this morning to see Father," she told Ethan. "They said that after we left, Moses threw the golden calf in the fire. He told Aaron and his followers that they're going to be punished for what they did."

Ethan stared at Leah. For once she didn't sound glad that the rule breakers would be punished. In fact, she sounded sad.

"I know Melki was your friend, Ethan," she said. "I'm sorry."

Ethan looked at the flames of the cooking fire. He thought about Uli and Tovar, Orek and Patek, Elizah the Judge and the man with the stripes painted on his face. But mostly he thought about Melki and his family.

I came close to being one of them, he thought.

None of them said anything for a long time. At last Ethan cleared his throat. "Will it always be like this?" he asked. "Will we always wander in the desert? Won't we ever have a real home?"

His father turned toward him, and his eyes shone. "Someday," he said. "Someday, Ethan. A land flowing with milk and honey. That's the Lord's promise."

Ethan lifted his eyes toward Mount Sinai. *Maybe if God can bring Moses back after that long on the mountain, He can take us to the Promised Land too. Maybe.*

"And the new rules?" he asked. "What will they be like?"

"I don't know," his father said. "But I do know they'll be for our good."

Ethan nodded slightly, remembering the chaos in the camp. *I wanted to be free, like those people,* he thought. *But they weren't free at all.*

He sighed. This was going to take time, learning how to be free. But he had the feeling the answer had something to do with following the God of Israel—not running away from Him.

"Speaking of rules," his mother said, handing Ethan a bowl of cooked manna. "This morning the men said Moses is going back up the mountain. He broke the tablets that the rules were written on, so the Lord is going to give him new ones."

Ethan remembered the shattered tablets he'd seen. *So those* were *the new rules.*

Leah spoke up. "And I promise not to nag you about them," she said. "After last night, I can see you don't need my help to obey."

"Of course I don't," Ethan said, grinning. "As long as there aren't too many new rules."

His father chuckled. "And how many is too many?" he asked.

Ethan thought for a moment. "Oh . . . as long as it's less than ten, I should be okay," he said.

"Not even *ten* commandments?" his mother said with a smile. "We'll see, Ethan. We'll see."

LETTERS FROM OUR READERS

Which parts of this story really happened? (Pam C., Nashville, Tennessee)

You'll find the true story of this time in the book of Exodus, chapters 19, 20, and 32. The Israelites, having been freed from slavery in Egypt, had been in the wilderness for about three months when Moses went up the mountain to receive new laws from God. People aren't sure now which mountain was Mount Sinai, though tradition favors a peak called Jebel Musa in the southern Sinai Desert.

The people prepared to meet with God by washing their clothes, as in this story. They saw the lightning, clouds, and smoke and heard the thunder and trumpet blast and God's voice. Because God had come to the mountain, it was holy—which was why everyone except Moses was banned from climbing it. The penalty was being stoned to death or shot with arrows. As in the story, most of the Israelites rebelled while Moses was gone. They worshipped the golden calf Aaron had made. Moses reacted by smashing the stone tablets. Except for Moses and Aaron, the characters in the story are fictional. Ethan's family represents those who stayed loyal to God. Melki and the other boys reflect the attitudes of those who turned away from the Lord.

What was manna, anyway? (Brady S., Red Deer, Alberta, Canada)

God provided food so the Israelites wouldn't starve in the desert. This food was manna, a white, flaky substance that appeared on the ground in the morning and melted away in the heat of the day. The people collected manna, ground it up, and boiled it or baked it into cakes. The flavor was like wafers made with honey (Exodus 16:31) and like something made with olive oil (Numbers 11:8). There were rules about gathering manna. Each morning, people were to pick up only what they needed for the day—about three quarts per person. If they gathered too much and saved it for the next day, it would go bad, getting smelly and full of worms. The only exception was the sixth day of the week, when people were to gather twice as much as usual and save half so they wouldn't have to collect it on the Sabbath, a day of rest. God did provide quail to eat when the Israelites complained about their manna diet (Exodus 16:13), but they ate manna for forty years!

What rules were on the stone tablets? (Chris D. and Jon D., Flushing, New York)

God gave Moses many commands (see Exodus 21–31), but it's generally thought that those on the tablets were the Ten Commandments (Exodus 20). The custom at the time was to make two copies of legal agreements, so each tablet would have contained all of the commandments, written on the front and back by God Himself (Exodus 32:15-16). Writing on stone tablets wasn't unusual in those days. The ancient Code of Hammurabi, a Babylonian ruler, included a seven-foot slab recording more than 280 laws!

What happened to families like Melki's who rebelled against God? (Wesley W., Wheaton, Illinois)

After Moses smashed the stone tablets, he burned the golden calf, ground it to powder, sprinkled the powder on the water, and made the people drink it (Exodus 32:19-20). When some of the Israelites remained out of control, Moses stood at the camp entrance and called, "Whoever is for the LORD, come to me" (Exodus 32:26). Men from the Levite tribe responded, and Moses told them to take up swords and kill those who were still rebelling. About three thousand people died that day. Later the Lord struck the people with a plague—a disease—as punishment for worshipping the idol (Exodus 32:35). What happened to families like Melki's may depend on whether they continued to disobey God. The punishments may seem harsh, but the sin was very serious. Worshipping the idol was rejecting God. If He hadn't dealt firmly with the rebellion, it probably would have spread, ruining the whole nation's chances of ever being His people and living in the land He had promised them.

Did families like Ethan's ever get out of the desert? (Kurt B., Colorado Springs, Colorado)

Yes and no. The Israelites continued to wander in the desert for forty years, often grumbling and disobeying God. God may have let them do this because they weren't ready to enter the homeland He'd promised. Most of the people who had left Egypt as grown-ups must have died before the desert days were over. Kids like Ethan could have survived to see the "land flowing with milk and honey" (Exodus 3:8). God used these hard years to teach the Israelites many things, just as He sometimes uses our hard times to help us learn to depend on and obey Him.

ABOUT THE AUTHOR

RANDY SOUTHERN has written dozens of books, articles, and curricula on parenting and child development. Many of the principles in his work are drawn from his experiences as a single parent raising three children after the death of his wife. Books he has authored or co-authored include *Raising Highly Capable Kids, The World's Easiest Guide to Family Relationships,* and *Mind Over Media.* A graduate of Taylor University, Randy lives with his family in Fishers, Indiana.

Galen and Goliath
by Lee Roddy

To Jim Miller,
fifth-grade teacher at Forest Lake Christian School,
Auburn, California

Panting hard and ignoring the shouted insults of the watching Philistine soldiers, ten-year-old Galen quickly raised his small round shield. It blocked the blow from the tree branch that Leander thrust at him. Instantly Galen struck with his own branch, catching the older, heavier boy high on the chest above his shield.

A wild cheer of approval from the boys on Galen's team mingled with groans of those supporting Leander. The soldiers shouted encouragement to both boys as Leander landed a strong counterblow to Galen's arm just above where he gripped his branch.

Galen winced, but the pain was nothing compared to what he had suffered from the recent, unexpected deaths of his parents and only brother.

Leander's muddy brown eyes glittered with joy. He puffed. "I told you that you'll never beat me! So quit before I have to hurt you!"

"No!" The word erupted from between Galen's clenched teeth. "You're bigger, but I'm going to carry Goliath's shield!"

Leander laughed nastily and faked a thrust at Galen's face. As Galen ducked behind his shield, he heard his adversary growl, "I'm already doing that, and no little lizard like you will ever take it from me! This is your last chance! Quit now!"

Galen didn't reply. But in his frustration and pain, he knew his only hope for any future meant impressing the others in this round of mock battle. He opened his mouth wide, yelled loudly, and began wildly slashing with his branch as he rushed upon his adversary.

This was so unexpected that Leander took two quick steps backward and tripped over his own feet. He fell to the sand. Laughter erupted from the men, and Galen's friends shouted joyously.

Panting, Galen stood over his fallen foe. "Give up?"

"No!" Leander quickly swung his right leg up to hook his foot behind Galen's left knee. With a quick pull of his foot, Leander forced Galen's knee to buckle. Galen dropped heavily to the sand. Leander promptly kicked away Galen's shield and branch and then jumped onto Galen's chest.

This brought roars of approval and loud applause from the soldiers, but Galen's friends groaned in unison.

The older, heavier boy leaned forward and thrust his dark face close to Galen's. Through clenched teeth, Leander growled, "If you're ever going to be a big enough Philistine to carry Goliath's shield, you've got to win, no matter what! That's what I do—while you lose!" Leander's crushing weight kept Galen from replying.

Galen was aware of a sudden silence from the spectators. A shadow fell across him. He squinted against the sun as Leander leaped to his feet and stood at attention.

Galen's light brown eyes focused on the shadow maker. "Goliath!" the boy whispered, surging upright at the sight of the giant, who stood more than nine feet tall.

Even though Galen had performed menial chores for Goliath, the boy was always overwhelmed at the sight of the Philistine army's greatest warrior. He wore a bronze helmet with the distinctive featherlike crown that made him look twice as tall as Galen. Goliath wore his 125-pound coat of mail and the bronze shin armor on his legs as if they were as light as the desert air.

His deep voice mocked, "An ant tries to fell a bear." He laughed, a great booming sound of power.

Galen knew that if he was ever going to become the giant's shield bearer, he should offer some defense for his unfortunate position. Yet he couldn't think of what to say.

Goliath's mocking continued. "Galen the *healer* fights Leander the *lion-man*, and this is what happens."

Leander drew himself up proudly and threw out his chest at the giant's praise. Galen wished the ground would open up and swallow him before he was further humiliated.

Goliath boomed again. "Galen, do you think a reed can fell a tree? You're nothing and you never will be anything!"

Galen's shame deepened as the great warrior turned to Leander. "Galen fights like an Israelite. Isn't that right?"

Emboldened, Leander exclaimed, "Yes! He punches the air as if it had breath, stabbing everywhere but the target!"

Goliath threw back his huge head and laughed deep in his throat. "Very good, Leander!" The giant gently placed a massive hand on Leander's shoulder before adding, "Come to my tent and help me prepare to again insult those Israelite dogs yapping across the valley! Maybe this evening one of them will finally have the courage to accept my challenge."

Galen closed his eyelids tightly to stop the tears that threatened to slide out. He stood there in misery, hearing the soldiers and Leander's followers drifting away while hurling scornful remarks over their shoulders.

Galen heard the ground crunch under a sandal next to him. He cautiously opened his eyes to see one of his friends anxiously looking at him.

"You all right?" Ziklag asked, lightly touching Galen's wrist where angry red welts were rising from Leander's hard blow.

Not sure he could trust himself to speak without his voice quavering, Galen only nodded. He was tempted to wipe away the tear that escaped down his right cheek, but he pretended it didn't exist.

"You could have beaten him," Ziklag declared with stout loyalty. "He's two years older, he's taller, and he outweighs you by thirty pounds, but you're brave and smart and quick. You had him down, fair and square, but he didn't fight fair. Otherwise, you would have won."

Galen found his voice. He bitterly exclaimed, "Goliath doesn't think so!"

"He missed seeing you take Leander down. Goliath only stepped from between the tents just before Leander tripped you."

Galen shrugged. "It doesn't make any difference, Zik. Goliath thinks I'm only a tiny ant, or a reed growing by the water." Galen's voice began to rise in anger. "But he's wrong! I'm a good fighter, and I'm not afraid! I have a good head for thinking! I'll grow stronger, and I'll become a good warrior! You'll see!"

Zik protested, "You don't have to convince me! You're really strong for your age. More than that, I know from what you've been through that you're strong inside where it really counts. Next time you'll beat Leander."

"I thought I had him today, but I was wrong," Galen sadly admitted. He bent and retrieved his shield but ignored the fallen branch. "Somehow," he mused, hefting the small round shield, "I've got to trade this in for the right to carry Goliath's shield."

Zik's eyes opened wide. "His shield? Have you ever tried to lift it?"

"No, but I can."

"I'm not so sure," Ziklag said uncertainly. "One time when Goliath was eating and drinking with the other soldiers, I slipped into his tent and picked up his bronze spear. The iron head alone must weigh between fifteen and twenty-five pounds. So think how much heavier his shield has to be!"

"I don't care!" Galen said stubbornly. "Everything important in the world has been taken from me: my parents, my brother, my home. But when I carry Goliath's shield ahead of him into battle, all of our soldiers and even the Israelites will know I am somebody!"

"I hope you're right, Galen," his friend said sincerely. "But how are you going to do that?"

Pondering that question, Galen silently looked across the Valley of Elah. Soon the Israelite army would gather there, as it did every morning and evening. It had done this for more than a month while Goliath shouted insults and vainly called for the Israelites to send out one warrior to fight him man-to-man.

But the poorly armed Israelites had refused, knowing that if they sent a champion who lost to Goliath, all the others would become Philistine slaves.

Zik broke into Galen's musings to repeat his question. "So how are you going to do that?"

Galen firmly declared, "I don't know, but somehow I'll find a way. I must!"

CHAPTER
2

All through the heat of the desert afternoon, Galen and Ziklag sat in the shelter of the Philistine tents and stared thoughtfully across the Valley of Elah. The boys had exhausted all ideas of how to change Goliath's mocking insults into such admiration for Galen that he would be allowed to carry the giant's shield. In the cool of the evening, when both armies had gathered on their hillsides, facing each other, Goliath would again shout his taunts across to the Israelites.

Zik changed his position as the sun erased his shady spot. Lowering his voice, he said, "I don't blame the Israelites for not accepting Goliath's challenge. The Israelites only have wooden weapons, while our people use iron and bronze. So we're not only the best warriors anywhere, but we're equipped with the finest weapons in the world."

Galen nodded absently, his eyes sweeping the small valley, with its famous terebinth trees and seasonal wildflowers. A shimmering silver string along the valley floor marked a small stream. Galen shifted his gaze to the right, where the Israelite camp showed movement.

Galen mused, "I think they're getting ready to eat. When they finish, they'll come out and form up as they always do when they know Goliath is about to make his usual challenge."

"Then we'd better go to my tent," Ziklag replied, standing up. "You know how my mother likes to have us show up on time when she's ready to serve the meal."

A heavy sigh escaped Galen as the memory of his own mother flooded his aching heart. He was grateful that Zik's family had taken him in and had been kind to him after his parents and brother died. Still, nothing would ease the pain of having lost his entire family when disease carried them away. Galen still sometimes felt guilty because he alone had recovered.

As the evening cooled, Galen and Zik approached Goliath's tent. Inside, Goliath's armor bearer had already laid out the giant's coat of mail, helmet, greaves, spear, and javelin. The armor bearer's job was to follow after Goliath on the battlefield and finish off anyone he cut down. Leander looked up from where he was carefully oiling Goliath's huge shield.

From his great height, Goliath looked down at Galen and Zik and laughed. "So, the ant dares show up in spite of the inglorious spectacle he made of himself earlier today!"

Galen pretended he didn't hear Goliath's mocking tone or see the smirk on Leander's face. "I came," Galen began, taking a quick breath, "to ask to be your shield bearer for this evening."

Galen heard a surprised snort of derision from Leander, but Goliath narrowed his eyes. He thoughtfully regarded Galen for a few seconds before answering. Then he shrugged his mighty shoulders. "Why not?"

Leander made a startled, choking sound. Goliath half turned toward him and winked. Galen knew he wasn't supposed to have seen that, but it didn't matter. He had something to prove to both Goliath and Leander, and it was only natural they would see him as a pest.

The giant turned back to Galen and raised a huge arm that rippled with oversized muscles. "Yes, why not?" he repeated. "Those fools across the valley won't fight. They will continue to cower like women."

Behind him, Zik whispered so softly that only Galen could hear. "He's saying that to mock you again."

Galen acknowledged his friend's warning with the barest nod. Galen knew it was a sad victory for him because Goliath didn't think him worthy to go anywhere near a fight. Yet his determination made him risk even more ridicule.

"Thank you," he told the giant, but his eyes shifted to the great shield. It was metallic and circular-shaped, with leather-wrapped wooden handles inside to hold it. For a fleeting moment, fear surged through Galen and instantly dried his mouth like the desert sand.

Goliath motioned with a hand as large as Galen's head. "Pick it up," the giant rumbled.

Unconsciously licking his lips, Galen nodded and crouched beside the shield. He heard suppressed laughter from Leander, but Galen concentrated on the job before him. Flexing his fingers, he slid his right arm through the leather straps. His eyes confirmed what he had been told. Shields were commonly made from a wood or wicker frame and covered with oiled leather. But Goliath's circular shield was of wood and polished leather covered with bronze and reinforced with metal at the edges, making it very heavy.

Galen lifted one end so that he could better grasp a wooden and leather handle designed to give greater control. Even that small effort alarmed Galen because he realized that the shield weighed more than he had expected. He hesitated.

With a curse, Goliath rumbled, "Go on! Pick it up!"

Galen braced his legs and back to provide maximum power. He had better control with the leather-wrapped wooden handle, so he closed his fingers firmly and jerked hard.

He was astonished at how the massive weight threatened to throw him off balance while he struggled to lift the edge of the shield from the floor.

Leander exclaimed with obvious delight in his tone, "All the way! Lift it all the way off the floor!"

Straining every muscle and with great determination, Galen desperately tried to tilt the shield on edge to support it before setting it fully upright. It was useless. The dead weight threw him off balance.

He released his grip on the handle, but it was too late. The shield thudded back onto the ground, and Galen fell awkwardly on top of it.

Goliath laughed so hard that Galen felt the shield vibrate beneath him. The giant taunted, "Galen, why don't you go join the women?"

"Yes!" Leander added through his laughter. "Join the women, because you'll never be man enough to become a warrior!"

His face flaming with embarrassment, Galen blindly staggered out of the tent, with Zik following. Mocking laughter chased after them.

It wasn't long before Goliath and his shield bearer, followed by his armor bearer, walked out in front of the assembled Philistine soldiers to issue his nightly challenge to the Israelites. Galen believed everyone had heard of his humiliation with the shield.

He chose to sit at the back edge of the crowd, where he hoped to have some degree of freedom from the scornful laughter and jeering insults. He would have preferred to be alone in his misery, but Zik joined him in silent support.

Goliath, his full armor and helmet flashing, grandly strode out in front of the assembled Philistines. He cupped his huge hands around his mouth and shouted across to the opposite hillside, where the Israelites were gathered, as usual.

"Why do you come out and line up for battle?" Goliath's words echoed across the valley and then faded away.

He took a deep breath and called out again in his great booming voice, "Am I not a Philistine, and are you not the servants of Saul? Choose a man and have him come down to me. If he is able to fight and kill me, we will become your subjects. But if I kill him, then you will become our subjects and serve us."

Zik whispered, "I've heard him say that so many times, but it still stirs my blood to hear it again. Listen. Now he's going to say something more."

Goliath shouted across the valley. "This day I defy the ranks of Israel! Give me a man and let us fight each other!"

Again, the giant's words echoed across the valley and faded into silence. There was no answer from the Israelites. The stillness became so strong that Galen thought he could hear his own blood pounding against his eardrums. He was still sick at heart because of his inability to lift Goliath's shield.

I've got to show Goliath I'm going to be a man and a great warrior! Galen thought in despair. *But how can I prove that to him?*

The answer came as silently as a thought, but with the power of a blow from Goliath's great arm. Galen suddenly reached out and clutched Zik's arm. "Come on! I know what I can do!"

CHAPTER 3

Galen quickly led Ziklag away behind the Philistine tents while everyone in camp still focused their attention on the Israelites across the valley.

Zik complained, "Are you going to walk all the way to the Great Sea before you tell me your idea?"

"I want to make sure nobody hears us," Galen replied over his shoulder.

Galen passed the final tent and stopped, his eyes bright with excitement. "Zik, I know how to make Goliath change his mind about me!"

"Oh? How?"

Lowering his voice, Galen explained, "I'll sneak over to the Israelite camp and spy on them! I'll come back and report to Goliath how many men they have—"

"No!" Zik interrupted, throwing up his skinny arms in protest. "They'll catch you and you'll get killed!"

"No, they won't!" Galen exclaimed. "I'll be very careful. I'll wait until after dark—"

"I still say no!" Zik broke in again, his thin voice rising in concern. "It's too dangerous!"

A voice from behind the tent asked, "What is?"

"Oh no!" Galen muttered under his breath as a stout boy of about twelve stepped into sight, followed by four other boys. "It's Gath and the other Philistine lords! They must have seen us slip away and followed us."

Zik didn't reply because the other boys were close enough to overhear.

They swaggered proudly, pretending they were the young lords of the five main Philistine towns of Gaza, Ekron, Ashdod, Ashkelon, and Gath. From these communities, five adult male lords now ruled all Philistines. Each of the five boys had chosen to drop his given name to be known among friends by a town name. Gath had chosen his name because Goliath came from there.

"What's too dangerous?" Gath repeated, stopping and folding his arms in front of Galen and Zik. Two young Philistine lords flanked Gath on both sides and imitated his stance. Gath was the oldest in the group and a close friend of Leander.

Zik whispered, "Tell him, or they'll beat us up!"

The five young lords overheard and grinned without humor. Their hands curled into hard fists.

Galen knew that Zik spoke the truth, but his insides lurched at the thought of sharing his grand plan with Gath and the others. Galen sadly recalled other times when the lords had either laughed at one of his ideas or stolen it.

Gath would also tell Leander, and that made Galen's stomach twist painfully. He imagined those boys going on the spying mission by themselves, leaving Galen behind.

Ashdod, the heaviest of the young lords, broke into Galen's thoughts. "Maybe you need us to give you a couple of good punches to make you talk!"

Gaza and Ekron sneered and started to say something, but Gath cut them off. "I'll handle this," he snapped.

The four other lords fell silent.

Gulping, Galen thought of a risky possibility. "All right, but on one condition. It's my idea. If you don't like it, you must promise not to tell anyone until it's over. And if you do like it, then you must all promise that none of you will claim it was your idea."

Galen started to add, "And I'll be the leader," but decided against it.

Maybe, he told himself, *they'll be afraid and not want to go into the enemy camp.*

Gath sneered, "We don't have to promise anything."

Galen shrugged. "Fine with me. Come on, Zik. Let's go work out the details."

Zik's eyes widened in surprise as Galen turned and started to walk away. Then, apparently realizing that the five bigger boys would force him to tell if he stayed, he called, "Wait, Galen! I'm coming!"

Galen stopped and waited until Zik reached him. As they walked off together, Galen heard the Philistine lords whispering to each other.

Under his breath, Galen whispered to Zik, "That's a bad sign! I don't want them to know anything about this, but I'm afraid—"

Gath interrupted with a resigned expression. "You win, Galen! We all promise!"

Galen groaned in disappointment as the other lords nodded in agreement. Now he had to reveal his plan or else the five boys would spread word all over the camp that he and Zik were up to something.

"All right," Galen replied. "Gather around close so nobody hears, and I'll tell you."

Right away Galen was sorry he had disclosed his plan. The five would-be lords whooped with joy at the idea and insisted on going along with Galen to spy on the Israelites. He protested vigorously, pointing out that one person had a better chance of succeeding in the mission than a small group. An argument erupted, so Gath declared that they would ask Goliath's opinion.

Galen's mind was in turmoil. What if Goliath didn't like the idea? Or if he did, what if he approved of Gath's suggestion that all the boys go? Galen had planned to tell no one except Zik, and then to venture alone into the enemy camp. Galen's dreams of impressing the giant were starting to shred by the time the seven boys approached Goliath and his Philistine warriors.

The soldiers, with Leander on the edge of the group, sat on the hillside, laughing and talking. Shadows had filled the Valley of Elah. On the opposite hill, the black goat-hair tents of the Israelites were barely visible in the light from their campfires.

Goliath had taken off his armor. Leander silently polished the giant's helmet as Gath jerked his thumb toward Galen. Before Galen could speak, Gath said, "He has a plan we thought you might like to hear about."

Galen resented Gath's use of "we," but he had to be content that Gath had kept his word and given credit for the idea to Galen. He briefly explained the plan as the camp firelight chased shadows across Goliath's broad face.

When Galen finished, the other boys and all the warriors silently waited for cues from Goliath on how to react to the proposal.

"So," the giant's voice reverberated from his massive chest, "the little ant wants to be a flat-tailed scorpion and sting the Israelites in the night!"

Seeing a chance to salvage his original idea, Galen hastily added, "I'll go alone, so nobody else will be in danger."

"No!" Gath exclaimed. "We all go, even little Zik!"

A chorus of agreement came from all the other boys, except Zik. He remained silent.

Leander dropped one of the giant's shin guards. "Me too!" he exclaimed. "I want to go!"

Galen's heart seemed to sink with disappointment and anger. Desperately he explained to Goliath, "This plan will work best if there's only me—"

The giant interrupted. "You want to be a warrior worthy of carrying my shield," he said thoughtfully. "No one gets to be a warrior by hiding in tents. You may not have done well this afternoon with my shield, Galen, but here's your chance to grow up a little. Go, spy out the enemy!"

Galen's misgivings vanished. "Thank you!" he cried, imagining the praise from Goliath the next morning when he heard the good report that Galen would bring him. "I'll make you proud," he added heartily.

"Maybe," Goliath agreed, "but after your failure this afternoon, I think you'd better have company. So, all of these boys will go with you, except Leander!"

"But—" Galen's disappointed protest was lost in the roar of approval from all except Leander and Zik.

There was only a sliver of moon by the time the boys had each packed their small images of Dagon, the chief Philistine god. These wood carvings of a figure with a man's head, face, and upper body had a fish for the lower half and fins instead of feet. Dagon was supposed to protect the boys as they crossed the Valley of Elah.

Gath tried to take the lead, but Galen hurried ahead of him and stubbornly set a fast pace to keep his place. His heart thumped hard against his chest, but he wasn't sure if it was from the fast but silent walking or the fear. At first Galen hadn't been frightened, especially when all the others were bragging about what they would do to the Israelites if they were older. But as they neared the enemy camp, fear crept into Galen's mind.

The stillness of the night and the deep shadows of trees and brush on the hillside where the enemy camped caused Galen some doubts. Twice he turned and hissed warnings to the young lords about making too much noise. They walked carefully, making a wide arc before coming up on the back side of the enemy's hillside camp. There Galen stopped in the dark shelter of some trees.

While the others caught their breath, Galen whispered final instructions. "Remember what each of you is to do. Be very, very quiet. All our lives, we've been trained in warrior skills, so use them well. Count the tents in your section and try to see how many men sleep in each. Keep an eye out for any good weapons in sight, watch out for sentries, don't get seen or caught, and then meet back here as fast as you can."

Zik asked with a slight tremor in his voice, "What if any of us do get taken prisoner?"

Before Galen could reply, Gath spoke. "You heard what Goliath and the other warriors said. We're on our own. If anything goes wrong, they'll claim they didn't know anything about this trip. That way nobody gets blamed but us. But I intend to succeed!"

Galen reached out in the darkness and laid a comforting hand on Zik's skinny arm. "Don't think about what Goliath said. Nobody's going to get caught."

Zik protested, "But what if we're seen?"

Gath made a disgusted sound in the night. "Where were you when that was discussed awhile ago? We all scatter and run. Take care of yourself as best you can."

"But you're all bigger and can run faster than I can!" Zik said.

Gath's mocking laugh came out of the darkness. "Zik, you're afraid of everything! So maybe you should go back before you get us all in trouble."

"I make the decisions here!" Galen said sternly, refusing to release his role as leader and the honor Goliath would give him when the mission was a success. "We all go forward."

"Uh," one of the young Philistine lords said hesitantly, "I could take Zik back if he's scared."

Galen recognized Ekron's voice. He sounded as if he was frightened too but was trying to hide his fear by offering to help Zik.

"We all stay," Galen said softly but firmly. "Zik, I could use an extra pair of eyes with me. Come help me out. Everyone else, spread out and be careful!"

Galen heard a disgusted snort from Gath, who no doubt resented taking orders from Galen. But Gath didn't say anything as everyone silently moved off in preassigned directions.

In moments, again moving as quietly as possible, Galen and Zik stealthily approached the back of the first row of Israelite tents. These were faintly visible from the glow of the campfires, which had burned low.

Galen wasn't afraid because he was so determined to be a hero. That would have been easier if only he had been there alone. Now he would have to share the glory with the other boys.

Unless, he thought, *I can do something so special that it'll stand out far above what Gath or any of the others do.*

He felt the reassuring weight of Dagon in his tunic as he stealthily crouched low, rounded the first tent, and peered inside. Two men snored loudly.

Easing away from that tent, he glanced around to see that Zik was doing the same with the tent in the opposite row. Gliding on away from his friend, silent as a serpent, Galen heard only his racing blood thumping against his eardrums and the snoring of Israelite men.

Galen tried to think of something spectacular he could do to impress Goliath. *Maybe I can get inside a tent and take a spear from beside an Israelite!*

Barely breathing from excitement, Galen paused in the shadows of the nearest tent and secretly surveyed the whole camp.

There was no sign of the other boys, no unusual sound to give them away. Galen thought he glimpsed a shadowy figure dart from between some tents three rows over. A campfire there flared up briefly as the figure moved. Galen wasn't sure he had actually seen anyone.

He turned his attention back to the next tent in line. He was now deep inside the camp and far away from the trees and safety.

He noted the number of sleeping warriors and the types of weapons within easy reach of each man: poorly made bows and arrows and crude spears. Fearful the Israelite in front of him would awaken and catch him, Galen bent cautiously and gently felt the spear point.

Just as I thought, he told himself with satisfaction. *It's all wood—even the point. It's been hardened in the fire, but it's still very inferior to our Philistine ones of iron or bron—*

His thoughts snapped off as the sleeping man stopped snoring and rolled over toward Galen. He froze, holding his breath. His heart tried to beat a hole in his chest.

After agonizing seconds, the soldier began snoring again. Galen still held his breath until he slipped outside the tent, his mouth so dry he couldn't swallow.

That was close! he thought, glancing around. *I didn't dare risk taking his spear or drinking water. I still need something like that, but not from just any tent! Maybe their leader's! What's his name? Saul? Yes, King Saul! His tent must be marked in some special way.*

Galen crouched down and probed the rows of tents with eager eyes. For safety reasons, the leader often pitched his tent in the middle of the others.

There! By the dying light of a campfire, Galen glimpsed a pennant flying from a staff in front of a tent three rows away. *That must be his! Now if I can just take something from beside his head.*

Galen took a careful step and then froze again as someone moved outside the next tent. With a wildly racing heart, Galen waited until the other person passed a campfire. *It's Gath!*

Without realizing it, Galen had sucked in his breath when he glimpsed the other boy. In thoughtless relief, he exhaled in a soft rush.

The sound made Gath spin around and leap back. He fell over the dying campfire and involuntarily cried out. He leaped up, frantically beating at flames licking at his clothes. Galen could hear the Israelites in the nearby tents jump up and shout in alarm.

"Philistines! They're everywhere! Get them!"

Israelites poured out of their tents, weapons in hand, while the alarm cry of "Philistines!" echoed from other areas of the camp.

Trailing smoke but not fire, Gath darted wildly through the tents, racing for his life toward the valley.

Galen knew the other boys were also running, but he fought the temptation. He was farthest from the valley, so he forced himself to stand between the tents while all their occupants chased the fugitives. Galen, frozen with fright, was unnoticed in the darkness.

He recognized Zik's voice shouting, "Wait for me!"

Galen knew his friend was vainly trying to catch up with the older boys, but they wouldn't wait for him.

In moments, the entire camp had been emptied as the men pursued shadowy fugitives off the hillside and into the valley now wrapped in the black of night. All alone, Galen felt his heart hammering in fear. Goosebumps rippled down his arms, and his mouth instantly went dry. Trying to control his fright, he started to turn and head uphill into the trees. He planned to circle wide, enter the valley some distance away, and return to his own camp.

Then he stopped and looked back. The king's flag was still visible in the glow of the campfire.

Galen took a quick breath and sprinted to the tent. He didn't even break stride as he snatched the staff from the ground. He rounded the tent and raced between the rows, triumphantly heading back for the trees with the trophy in his hand!

For two hours Galen crouched in the trees behind the Israelites' camp, clutching his prize. He felt confident that Goliath would be impressed when he saw the king's flag. But it was too risky to move because the Hebrew soldiers were as agitated as bees in a disturbed beehive.

Galen cautiously peered over the top of a log as fuel was added to the campfires. In the bright blaze of the fires, he could see the Israelite warriors spread out, searching for the night invaders. Galen's rapidly beating heart and ragged breathing settled down only when the troops finally drifted back to the fires.

He saw that none of his companions was among them. The Israelites didn't return to their tents but stood around talking angrily. Their tones confirmed that they'd failed to catch anyone, not even Zik. Even if only one boy had been captured, they would have been celebrating.

When the excitement and campfires died down, full darkness slowly returned. Galen knew he had to start his dash for safety across the Valley of Elah's open, nearly treeless plain before daylight. He clutched the pennant, bent nearly double, and circled away from the camp. When he thought it was safe, he cut back toward the valley. Breathing hard, and still crouched low, he paused at the edge of the plain. He looked around one last time before starting his run.

That's when he saw the sentry coming toward him.

If Galen hadn't been bent down, he wouldn't have seen the silhouette of the Israelite against the faint light of the horizon. Silently laying down the banner, Galen dropped flat on his stomach. Gripping the banner, he crept under a bush by a little brook. The water made pleasant sounds as it passed over small stones. Galen hoped it covered the swishing sound of the disturbed bush and the noise of his labored breathing.

He had lost sight of the sentry, but he could hear the sound of a spear being thrust experimentally into the bushes as the sentry slowly moved toward him.

Stifling a groan, Galen lay perfectly still. He was terribly frightened, alone, and in mortal danger. Even if the sentry didn't find him, others must also be on guard in the night, watching and listening.

I have to get across the valley before daylight! he repeatedly reminded himself. He dared not try crossing when he could easily be seen. He couldn't outrun an arrow or spear—not even ones made of inferior wood.

Galen's ears followed the slow, deliberate approach of the Israelite sentry. In moments he would be at the dense bush where Galen lay. Galen's heart raced and his mouth was dry as only terror could make it.

He realized that his breathing had increased so sharply, it made a rasping sound. He tried holding it as the sound of the sentry's footsteps stopped at his bush. He flinched as the spear plunged into the foliage over his head. He flattened his body against the ground and pressed his face into the dirt, turning his head only enough to breathe.

Hold your breath! Galen sternly warned himself. *Don't move!* His skin crawled as he remembered the fire-hardened spear points he had seen in the Israelite camp. One of those fearsome weapons was now being thrust, seemingly at random, into the high portion of the bush.

His imagination brought the spear point closer and closer toward him. Closer . . . closer.

He stoutly held back the tears that threatened to leak out from his tightly shut eyelids. After all, he was ten, and Philistine boys were taught from an early age to be warriors and bear up under all circumstances. Besides, Galen intended to win Goliath's favor and be honored by carrying his shield. But in the black of night, cut off from his people, Galen was also a little boy with a deadly problem. Except for seizing the king's pennant, almost everything had gone wrong with Galen's plan to do a daring deed all by himself. And now this.

He could only wait, hearing the sentry's spear sliding in and out of the bush inches from his body as the soldier tried to make sure no one was hiding there. It was all Galen could do to not leap up and make a wild dash for the valley as the spear point struck the ground between his right arm and chest. But he knew that was futile, so he stayed frozen as the spear was withdrawn.

He willed himself not to think about it. He tried to cheer himself by remembering that the other six boys had escaped. Just when Galen couldn't hold his breath any longer, the sentry moved on.

Exhaling as quietly as possible, he took another quick breath and held it until he was sure the sentry was still moving away. Satisfied, Galen released the pennant staff and tried to relax. But he couldn't. Gloom seeped into his mind and heart. He had escaped this time, but if he moved now, the sentry would surely hear him. He had no choice but to wait where he was for a while.

He wondered where the other sentries were and how far away this sentinel would walk before he turned back. For now, Galen was safe, but what would happen when dawn came?

I have to do something! he sternly reminded himself. *But what? Stay here and risk being caught? Or try to crawl into the valley and hope they don't see me until I'm out of bow shot?*

As he debated, he shifted his cramped position to ease his aching muscles. Beside him, he felt the staff with the pennant that he had snatched from outside the Israelite king's tent. But what good would that do if Galen didn't return to triumphantly show it to everyone?

He reached into his tunic and gently touched the image of Dagon. Galen hoped to feel some comfort as he fingered the carving of the half man, half fish.

He had often heard his Philistine family speak of this god. Dagon was the principal god worshipped in the two Philistine cities of Gaza and Ashdod. Galen's father had come from Gaza; his mother from Ashdod.

Mother, he thought, closing his eyes and resting his forehead on his forearms, where he lay flat on the ground. His mind escaped the terrible reality of the moment by retreating to comforting memories. He could see her, hear her voice, feel her touch . . .

He realized he was getting sleepy, but there was such comfort in the memories that he kept his eyes closed and sorted through recollections. She was holding him, her voice soft and tender as she sang to him. He had often gone to sleep in her arms, secure in her love.

Then death had taken her, taken her suddenly, followed by her husband and their other son.

"No!" Galen whispered aloud, startling himself. He realized with a start that he had dozed and dreamed.

Frightened again, he quickly but quietly pushed the foliage aside. There was no sign of the sentry. Galen strained to hear until he could feel the blood throbbing in his eardrums, but there was no sound of nearby sentries.

Relieved, he wearily dropped his head and tried to recall more memories about his mother when he was younger. She held him by the hand. She had done that the first time she had led him through the marketplace with its strange smells and sights and sounds. He had looked up apprehensively, but she smiled reassuringly. It was almost as good a feeling as being hugged closely . . .

I was dreaming again! The knowledge hit him hard as he lifted his head and blinked; then he frowned. The sun probed slender, warm fingers through the bush where the spear had broken some limbs. *Daylight!* That realization struck him even harder. With trembling fingers, he pushed the leaves aside from his hiding place.

There was a great stillness, a silence so profound that it puzzled him. His eyes wildly skimmed the Israelite tents. There wasn't a soldier in sight.

With sudden hope, Galen twisted to look at the small Valley of Elah. It was wide open, friendly, almost seeming to call him. He started to get to his feet, but his entire body was stiff from inactivity.

An urge to dash across the narrow valley toward his people seized him. But where were the Israelites? How close? He couldn't see them. He listened and heard faint voices from beyond a hill past the camp. Puzzled, he darted a look across the valley, and then he knew.

The Philistine warriors were slowly gathering on the side of the hill in preparation for Goliath's morning challenge. That meant the Israelites were also assembling just out of Galen's sight, beyond the hill, where they could see the giant when he appeared again.

Galen's hopes leaped like a wild stag, and then crashed. He realized he couldn't cross the valley now. Both sides would see him. His people might try to come to his aid, but the Israelites were so close they would run him down or fill him with arrows and spears before he got very far.

I've caused a lot of grief for everyone, he chided himself. *Now what should I do?*

He didn't know, but he was keenly aware that he was very thirsty. He checked to make sure that no Israelite soldier was around. Then he crawled out of his hiding place and down to the brook. He cupped his hands together and gulped the fresh, cool water.

It felt so good that he closed his eyes and splashed another double handful of water on his face. It was so wonderful that he gave himself totally to the joy of repeating the process.

A footstep sounded behind him. His eyes popped open. A shadow fell across him.

Shocked, Galen started to scramble to his feet, horrified that he had been careless—something no aspiring Philistine warrior should do. But Galen knew it was too late to escape.

He glanced up and glimpsed an Israelite standing just three feet away!

With a racing heart, Galen tried to crawl away but was stopped by the bush where he had hidden all night. Trapped, he again glanced up and realized that the shadow was cast by an Israelite boy about his own age. He had dark eyes and hair but didn't look too strong, although he carried empty water skins.

Galen told himself, *I can handle him!* He stood up but remained alert, glancing around to make sure no other Israelites were near.

"Hello," the strange boy said calmly, lowering the water skins from his shoulder. "Don't you have a brook on your side of the valley?"

"Um . . . well, uh, yes." Galen quickly looked around, fearful that some adult Israelite would see him. He was relieved that there was no one in sight except the boy.

The boy took an empty skin and plunged it into the stream before asking, "Then what are you doing here?"

Galen hesitated. It would be dangerous to tell all the facts. After all, this was an Israelite boy and an enemy of the Philistines. Galen tried to think how to tell the truth without revealing all of it. "Uh . . ." he finally replied, "some friends and I were out . . . uh . . . exploring. They, well, they ran off and left me."

His excuse sounded a little lame to his own ears, but he felt that he had been truthful enough.

The other boy lifted the filled water skin from the brook. He observed, "You're a long way from your people."

Galen bristled and went on the offensive. It seemed logical since the stranger showed no signs of aggression. Galen spread his feet and scowled, demanding firmly, "Are you saying I'm a liar?"

The other boy shrugged. "No. I was just commenting, that's all."

Satisfied that his aggressive attitude seemed to be working, Galen added, "Well, it's a good thing you didn't call me a liar!"

Again, the Israelite boy took no offense. He thrust the next skin under the water. It bubbled as the air in it was displaced. He said, "My name's Reuben."

Galen automatically answered, "I'm Galen."

Reuben grinned up at him. "I've heard the name a few times. It means 'healer' in Greek."

Galen replied, "I like my name."

Reuben nodded. "No doubt you were named for some of your Philistine ancestors who originated in the Greek Isles before settling on the coast of the Great Sea."

Surprised and annoyed that the boy knew this, Galen felt it was necessary to say something he figured Reuben wouldn't know about the Philistines. Proudly, he announced, "We're called the Sea People, and we're great warriors."

"I've heard that said," Reuben admitted. He lifted the filled skin from the brook before adding, "But you must have heard how my ancestors defeated all the kings of tribes that used to live in this land."

"Rumors!" Galen scoffed. "The only great warriors are us Philistines! You Israelites have inferior weapons, and your men are farmers pretending to be soldiers. But we Philistines have the finest weapons and the most organized and well-trained soldiers anywhere. Right now, they're gathering on the hillside across the valley, waiting for Goliath to challenge one of your warriors to come fight him." Throwing out his chest, Galen added, "Someday, I will carry Goliath's shield!"

Reuben didn't seem impressed, so Galen quickly continued. "No Israelite will face Goliath, because if your people sent a challenger, he'd be defeated, and all the rest of you would become our slaves."

"My forefathers were slaves in Egypt a long time ago," Reuben replied, standing and drying his hands on his tunic. "We are free now, and this is all going to be our land." He slowly turned and swept his arms in a wide circle. "All of it," he added.

Galen bristled again. "You're wrong! You're saying the Israelites will defeat my people, yet not one man in your army will even answer Goliath's challenge, let alone fight him!"

"Our God fights for us," Reuben replied calmly.

"Your god?" Galen laughed shortly. "I've heard about him. He can't even be seen because he doesn't exist!" Galen reached under his cloak and brought out the small replica of his fish-man god and silently held it up.

Reuben asked, "What's that?"

Galen exclaimed in disbelief, "You don't know who Dagon is?"

Reuben laughed. "That's Dagon? That silly little thing is your god who you think can help you?"

Offended, Galen cried, "And who helps you? You have only one god, and you can't even *see* Him! What kind of god is that?"

Reuben opened his mouth to answer as Goliath's daily morning challenge echoed across the Valley of Elah.

Galen puffed with pride. "That's Goliath!" Pointing across the plain, he continued. "See him standing out there in front of our warriors? Twice a day he does that, and nobody from your side even answers him because your invisible God is no match for Dagon and Goliath!"

Reuben shrugged. "Our God will prove you're wrong."

Laughing, Galen challenged, "When? How?"

"I don't know, but it's not up to me to know such things," Reuben replied calmly. "But when it happens, I want to be there to see it, so I watch twice a day."

He placed the last water skin on the bank, turned around, and pointed. "I go up on that little hill where I can see everything. You want to come with me?"

Fearful of being seen, Galen shook his head.

"Too bad," Reuben said. "Everyone's gone to watch the soldiers, so nobody's around here to see you. But from up on the hill, we could see both my people's warriors and yours without anyone seeing us. Sure you don't want to come with me?"

Galen glanced longingly at the open plain but knew that his flight would take him within view of the Israelites. They wouldn't let him cross. He would have to wait for a better opportunity.

"Well," he said, "maybe just for a minute."

Galen followed Reuben up to a small rock outcropping on top of the hill. It had an opening wide enough for two boys to lie on their stomachs. Only their heads showed.

Galen's heart swelled with pride. Across the valley, Goliath stood like a mighty stone pillar in front of the assembled Philistine army. The morning sun reflected off the soldiers' iron and bronze weapons. They looked invincible as Goliath cupped his hands and once again roared his challenge.

Dropping his gaze to the Israelite army on their side of the valley, Galen almost sneered. "They're nothing but sheepherders and farmers! They don't even look like soldiers! And their weapons—why, the branches my friends and I play with are better than what your soldiers have."

"Looks aren't what counts," Reuben declared. "In fact, it wouldn't matter if your entire Philistine army was filled with Goliaths. All true might and power come from God."

Galen laughed. "That's the most stupid thing I've ever heard!"

For the first time, Galen's barbed words caused Reuben to react angrily. "You take that back!"

"No! I said it and I meant it!"

"Look, Galen, I've taken your insults about my people, but I won't let you dishonor my God!"

For a moment, the boys glared at each other, and then the fear and frustration that had engulfed Galen all night suddenly exploded. Yelling, he leaped on top of Reuben.

The boys scuffled on the hillside, panting and tumbling over each other while struggling to gain the upper hand. Galen was surprised at how strong Reuben was. But he reminded himself that he was a Philistine, and Reuben was only an Israelite, so naturally the Israelite had to lose.

Reuben obviously didn't know that, because he rapidly rolled aside when Galen tried to pin him on his back. Galen was startled to find Reuben suddenly sitting on his chest.

Looking down at Galen, Reuben puffed, "Had enough?"

"No!" With a mighty effort, Galen squirmed free and tried to leap to his feet. They flew out from under him. He fell onto his back and started sliding downhill. He instinctively reached out to grab something to hold on to. His fingers clamped down hard on Reuben's ankle, pulling him down. The boys tumbled together down the hillside.

They were stopped at the bottom by rolling into a small shrub that slashed them with sharp thorns.

Yelping in pain, they hastily freed themselves while they tried to catch their breath. Galen felt small wounds on his hands and face from the rough ride and the shrub's stickers. Reuben's right cheek was scratched and his tunic was torn.

Galen managed to puff, "Now have you had enough?"

Reuben hesitated and then said, "I have if you have."

Galen pounced on that. He wasn't so sure now that he could triumph over the Israelite, but he didn't want to give Reuben that impression.

"Well," Galen replied, still trying to catch his breath, "I guess I'll let you go."

Reuben surprised him by grinning. "I was going to say the same thing."

In spite of himself, Galen returned the grin before changing the subject. "Do you suppose any of your people answered Goliath's challenge?"

Reuben glanced up the hill. "Let's go see."

The boys climbed to the top of the hill, but they were too late. The giant's challenge had gone unanswered once again, and the humiliated Israelites were slowly returning to their camps with downcast eyes.

The stark reality of Galen's situation hit him hard. He still couldn't safely leave until nightfall, so he would have to return to his hiding place by the brook. He hadn't eaten since the night before, yet he dared not risk foraging in daylight. He certainly wasn't going to ask an enemy of his people to bring him something.

When Galen was again safely hidden, Reuben shouldered his filled water skins and departed. This left Galen with another concern. *What if he tells his people where I am?*

In spite of the shade under the bush, the morning sun soon made Galen uncomfortably hot. He tried to ignore his annoyance and minor pains by dozing off.

He slept fitfully, dreaming that his mother was preparing all kinds of good things to eat. That included his favorite: fresh bread and cheese. It really smelled wonderful, but when he reached for it, it vanished. He moaned in his sleep.

When he awoke, the good fragrance still lingered in his nostrils. He sniffed, his stomach growling in hunger. The scent persisted. He lifted his head and looked in the direction from which it seemed to come. Through the foliage, he saw a cut of cheese and two small loaves under the outside branches.

Hardly daring to believe what he saw, he squirmed around under the bush and touched the food. It was real!

Reuben! he thought. He quickly pulled the cheese and loaves into his shelter. He gobbled the delicious meal, marveling at what his people's enemy had done for him.

It was the longest, most tension-filled day of Galen's life. From time to time, Israelite soldiers walked past his hiding place. Older boys, too young to fight but eager to be helpful, periodically hurried past on errands for the warriors. Once, Galen held his breath as a youth briefly paused by his bush to drink from the brook. But no one noticed Galen.

Still, it was a huge relief when the sun dipped low. Galen consoled himself with the thought that it would soon be dark, and he could slip back to his own camp.

As Galen eagerly anticipated rejoining his own people, Reuben returned with his water skins.

Stiff and sore from the long-enforced inactivity and the cuts and bruises of the morning, Galen slid out from under his hiding place. He stood up but stayed close to the bush so others couldn't see him.

He felt awkward about expressing his gratitude to an enemy of his people, but he felt he must. "Those were really good loaves and cheese," he said.

Reuben lowered the water skins to the brook side. "Glad you liked them. Will your mother be worried because you didn't get back to your camp last night?"

Galen sadly lowered his head. "She's dead. So's my father and my brother. I'm living with—" His voice started to break, and he turned away to hide the unwelcome tears that suddenly misted his vision.

Reuben didn't say anything but reached out and gave Galen a quick pat on the shoulder.

Galen sniffed loudly and turned back to face the other boy. "I don't care! What is a family anyway? Warriors are tough and don't need families."

"Well, my family is mighty important to me," Reuben replied. "We're farmers, like many Hebrews. All Israel is really one big family, so I'm a part of that too. But in my own family, I'm the oldest son, so father lets me help the soldiers, like filling the water skins twice a day."

Hesitating, Reuben added, "Would you like to hear a couple of stories about my family?"

Galen wasn't going anywhere until full nightfall, and he was lonely, so he nodded and listened. Galen's memory of his own brother suddenly overwhelmed him, and he turned away again.

Reuben surprised him by saying, "I think you really do care about your family."

Fighting to maintain control, Galen suddenly jumped up. "Let's have a play fight!" He wasn't sure that was a safe thing to do, but he'd said it, so he glanced around and was relieved to see that nobody was in sight. He spotted a couple of dry branches that had fallen off a nearby tree. "Here," he said, "let's use these."

The boys grabbed them and stripped off all small twigs, leaving only four-foot-long sticks. They began flailing at each other, but not hard. No matter how Galen tried to thrust, Reuben blocked him. They fought for several minutes with the sticks banging together, but not a single blow landed on either boy.

"I'm wearing you down!" Galen cried, trying to convince with words what he wasn't doing with force.

"You're wrong!" Reuben replied, just as Goliath's challenge echoed across the valley. Instantly stepping back out of Galen's reach, Reuben said, "Listen!"

Galen was glad for an excuse to stop the mock battle. He strained to hear and then nodded.

"Good!" Reuben exclaimed. "Nobody will see you because they've all gone to see Goliath. So let's go watch!"

"That's fine with me, but I won," Galen replied proudly. He believed that and felt very good about it. However, he was disappointed to see that Reuben wasn't even distressed as he casually turned toward the hill.

Galen dropped his stick and followed, puzzled. Winning was important to him, even in play, but it didn't seem to trouble Reuben.

From their hiding place in the rock cleft at the top of the hill, Galen gazed down on the backs of the silent Israelite soldiers. He could tell from the slump of their shoulders and the way they kept looking down that they were discouraged as Goliath again called his challenge.

Without looking at Reuben, Galen asked, "How can your people stand there like sheep while Goliath insults them day after day?"

"Like our leader, King Saul, they're all waiting."

Reuben's calm, assured reply made Galen turn toward him. "Waiting for what?"

"For God to send someone to defeat Goliath."

Galen laughed loudly. "A puny Israelite defeat Goliath? That's not possible. Why, I've seen him in many battles, and he's always won."

When Reuben didn't answer, Galen added proudly, "And someday I will also be a great Philistine warrior! I'll be as feared and as well known as Goliath!"

Reuben smiled but didn't mock Galen. "You may be a great warrior, but before then, God will defeat Goliath in His own way."

The confident words troubled Galen, but he couldn't be sure why. He blustered, "We'll see about that! Why, there isn't a man alive—"

Reuben suddenly gripped Galen's arm and hissed, "Don't move! A soldier's coming this way!"

Both boys froze. Only their eyes followed the Israelite sentry patrolling along the brook at the base of the hill where the boys hid. Suddenly the soldier stopped and bent over.

"He's found my water skins!" Reuben whispered. "He'll probably start looking around to see who left them."

Without waiting for Galen's response, Reuben stood up. "You stay here and don't move until I get him to leave! I hope you make it safely back to your camp tonight!"

Galen stayed dead still as he watched the Israelite boy approach the sentry. Then Reuben bent down and casually filled the water skins. He and the sentry talked until the skins were full, and then they walked off together. Galen wondered if he would have done the same for Reuben.

Three hours passed slowly before it was totally dark and the Israelites' campfires had burned low. Sentries were some distance away. Galen gripped the banner he had taken from the Israelite commander's tent the night before. He hoped he was right that it had been King Saul's. He decided he would tell Goliath that it certainly was Saul's. This news would surely make the giant treat him with respect.

Preparing to return to his camp, Galen silently slid out from under the bush where he had spent the day. He wrapped the banner around the staff and held it in his left hand. He crawled on hands and knees into the Valley of Elah until he was too far for an arrow to reach. Then he stood up and ran hard into the night.

He could just imagine the astonished looks on his friends' faces when he showed them the prize. But he was most eager to impress Goliath. *He'll never forget what a brave thing I did*, Galen assured himself. *When I'm older and stronger, he'll let me carry his shield because of this deed!*

As Galen neared his camp, a Philistine sentry challenged him. Galen identified himself and was promptly escorted to the officer in charge of the sentries.

Galen was disappointed because he had expected to be taken directly to Goliath. But instead, the officer started asking questions. "How did you escape? All those boys with you claimed you were captured."

Galen repeated what had happened to him and then proudly unwrapped the flag from around the staff. "I took it from inside King Saul's tent," Galen declared, waving the banner and feeling his little addition to the facts wasn't really lying.

He added, "He never heard or saw me," and then immediately felt guilty even though this was true, because Saul had already left the tent.

The officer was more interested in knowing about the Israelites than about how the boy got the flag. He asked Galen, "How many warriors do they have? How well equipped are they? What weapons do they carry? Do they have anything except wooden spears and javelins?"

Galen answered as best he could but omitted any mention of Reuben. As he spoke, he vainly hoped that Goliath would arrive to hear his story. But when the officer finally dismissed Galen, he stepped outside the tent and was greeted by most of the small male civilian population and walking-wounded soldiers, who had heard about his return.

He was pleased to see Ziklag and the other boys who'd gone on the raid with him. But they were forced to stay in the background while the men bombarded him with more questions.

All the men heartily congratulated Galen on his escape and begged to hear details of his adventure. He obliged, almost strutting with pride. He showed his captured pennant and declared that he had snatched it from inside King Saul's own tent. The exclamations at this news encouraged Galen to tell them about hiding under the bush until it was safe to return. Again, he chose not to mention Reuben.

Unlike the mostly factual account of his experience he'd given to the officer, this version was embellished. Galen made it sound much more exciting and dangerous than it had really been. This brought loud exclamations of admiration from his audience.

Finally the older people allowed the younger ones to take their turn asking questions. By the light of the built-up campfires, Galen saw that the five young lords who had fled from the enemy camp now regarded him with open envy. However, Zik's eyes were different. Galen saw signs of tears in them.

Zik exclaimed in a trembling tone, "I thought you were dead!"

Galen lightly punched Zik on his shoulder. "I can take care of myself!"

Zik asked, "Weren't you scared?"

"Not even for a moment!" The second he said it, Galen felt another twinge of guilt. *I shouldn't have lied to Zik*, he told himself.

A young soldier pushed through the ring of admirers. "Galen," he announced, "Goliath sent me to say he wants to see you first thing tomorrow morning."

Galen was so proud that he felt he could almost float. He whispered to Zik, "Maybe Goliath wants to tell me that I can start training to be his shield bearer."

"Could be," Zik replied before adding, "We'd better get some sleep so you'll be at your best before him tomorrow."

Galen was reluctant to leave his admirers, but he nodded and followed his friend to the family tent.

The sun had not yet risen when Galen took the captured Israelite banner and appeared with it at the giant's tent. Goliath's tent was much higher, longer, and wider than any other tent in camp. A young soldier stationed outside said Goliath was expecting him.

Galen stepped in, expecting well-deserved praise and perhaps the coveted offer to someday be the giant's shield bearer. However, one look at Goliath made Galen feel unsure.

Even sitting down and without his armor, the Philistines' champion looked huge. He had no neck, Galen decided. The great head seemed to rest on massive shoulders above biceps that rippled with powerful muscles. He didn't speak but belched crudely and fixed Galen with bloodshot eyes.

That surprised Galen who had expected at least a look of appreciation. He asked, "You sent for me?"

Slowly the giant stood up, towering impressively above the boy whom he regarded with cold, hard eyes. "Where were you yesterday?" the giant rumbled.

Galen blinked in surprise and tipped his head far back to look up at the famous warrior. "I was in the Israelite camp," he explained and then added quickly, "I thought you must have heard—"

"I heard," Goliath interrupted. He seemed bored as he scratched himself and asked, "Did you kill anyone?"

Galen was shocked. He was only ten and had been on an adventure filled with danger and excitement, but he hadn't thought of killing anyone. Realizing that he wasn't about to receive the praise he expected, Galen answered in a low, quiet voice. "Uh . . . no, I didn't."

Goliath's lip curled in a sneer. "You were in the enemy's camp all that time, and you didn't kill a single person? What did you do—hide like an old woman?"

Galen licked suddenly dry lips, unsure what to say.

The giant's deep voice reverberated from his massive chest when he spoke again. "You want to someday carry my shield and become a Philistine soldier, but you don't seem to know what a real soldier does."

Towering over the boy, Goliath declared, "Soldiers kill. That's their purpose in war. Those Israelite dogs are our enemies! You must have had a chance to strike at least one, so why didn't you?"

Trembling with sudden alarm, Galen gulped, thought of Reuben, and stuttered, "I-I—well—"

The giant interrupted in a voice that boomed like distant thunder. "The very least you could have done is to have harmed someone! That would have made you a man, and much more so if you had struck down some Israelite and brought back his possessions—at least a sword or a spear."

Galen tried not to tremble at the giant's growing rage. Goliath scoffed, "Instead, Galen, you brought us a stick with a rag on it." He motioned toward Galen's trophy and added, "I doubt your story. I don't think you really risked your life for this. My guess is that you waited until all the Israelites were out of camp and you were alone when you picked it up."

Galen cringed at the scornful words. He found himself having trouble breathing. He thought of saying he was sorry but decided to remain mute while Goliath glared at him.

Finally the giant asked harshly, "You really want to someday carry my shield and become a Philistine warrior?"

Suddenly hopeful again, Galen exclaimed, "Oh, yes!"

"Good!" The giant clapped an enormous hand on the boy's shoulder. "The only way to ever do that is to return to the enemy camp and at least hurt someone, if not kill him. So do it tonight, and bring proof! Do you understand?"

Galen felt numb. He wanted to protest but knew he must not. Slowly, sick at heart, he managed to mumble, "Yes, I understand."

The giant's heavy hand lifted from Galen's shoulder and came down with a resounding smack on his backside. "Good! Tell the sentry outside my tent to give you a stout club to take with you. Bring me proof that you've earned the right to be a Philistine soldier!"

All the joy and excitement of Galen's Israelite adventure had drained out of him at the giant's terrible assignment. Galen was too ashamed to even confide his problem to Zik. All day he avoided other people and walked alone on the hillside overlooking the Valley of Elah. In his pain and anger,

Galen desperately ached for the comfort his parents had always given him when he hurt. But they were long cold in their graves. Then Galen vainly caressed Dagon, his fish-man god, and sought guidance from it. But it felt cold and lifeless, a piece of wood carved by someone's hands. He wondered how Reuben called on his invisible God when he needed Him, and if He answered better than Dagon.

As the sun eased toward the western horizon, Galen heard some older boys playing at being warriors. At first he ignored them. Then he realized they were watching him and whispering. They knew what Goliath had required Galen to do. Everyone in camp must have known by now. The only good thing was that Galen realized the boys were pretending to be him, and they thought he was brave.

They repeatedly acted out his striking down an Israelite so he could be a Philistine warrior and carry Goliath's shield. The boys carried on their mock battles until Goliath's evening challenge sent them running to see if an Israelite dog would dare meet the giant in one-on-one combat. Galen didn't move but stayed alone in anguish.

Before the stars sprinkled the darkness with tiny points of light, Galen had reduced his choices to the absolute basics. He could either stay in camp and be disgraced and treated with contempt, or he could return to the Israelite camp and carry out Goliath's order.

Galen knew he might be killed. But wasn't it worth the risk if he succeeded and became a Philistine warrior worthy of carrying the great Goliath's shield?

With a heavy sigh, Galen made his choice. He picked up the heavy club Goliath's sentry had given him and made sure that Dagon's image was in his tunic. Setting his jaw in firm determination, Galen slipped unseen away from the Philistine encampment and headed across the valley toward the Israelite camp.

He would watch for a lone Israelite and then strike quickly and hard before losing his nerve. Then he would grab up whatever possessions the Israelite had and vanish into the night.

It was a terrible thing for a ten-year-old boy to do, but Galen reminded himself that he was a Philistine, taught from early childhood to be a mighty warrior. He mentally prepared himself for what he must do.

Using the faint light of the Israelite campfires, Galen found his way across the valley and back to the brook with the bush where he'd hidden the night before. He barely heard the brook's murmur when his heart leaped at the sight of a lone figure standing there. The firelight was too faint to show his features, but that didn't matter. *It's probably better that way*, Galen thought.

Taking a deep breath and holding the club low so it wouldn't be seen, Galen quietly started toward the figure.

It turned toward him and spoke. "Hello, Galen. Why did you come back?"

CHAPTER

8

Shocked, Galen automatically drew back the club in the darkness and then hesitated. "Reuben!" Galen exclaimed, keeping his voice low so the Israelite sentries wouldn't hear him. "I didn't expect to see you!"

"I'm very late getting the water skins filled, and I'm very surprised to see you too!"

"I see." Galen quickly lowered the club, hoping Reuben hadn't seen it.

Reuben apparently hadn't because he asked, "Didn't you get safely back to your camp last night?"

"Yes. I had to come back to . . . to . . ." He let his voice trail off.

Reuben prompted, "To what?"

"Uh . . ." Galen muttered, trying to think fast. He couldn't tell Reuben that Goliath had instructed him to hit an Israelite over the head and bring back proof that it hurt. Yet in the same instant, Galen felt the weight of the club in his hand and realized that this was his opportunity.

He could strike the unsuspecting boy before him, take something personal from his fallen body, and vanish back into the valley. It would take only seconds, and then Galen could quietly return in triumph to show Goliath. That would earn the giant's respect and prove that Galen could be a good Philistine soldier who would someday carry Goliath's shield ahead of him into battle.

But the thought of hitting Reuben sickened Galen. He knew that would be wrong.

"Well?" Reuben asked. "Why did you come back?"

"I . . . uh . . ." Galen stammered while his mind spun with possible excuses he might offer.

He told himself, *My tribe is threatening his people, but he and I aren't at war. It would be wrong to harm someone—especially Reuben—just to prove something to Goliath.*

Reuben stepped closer, saying, "What's the matter? Why can't you tell me?"

Galen didn't reply while his mind wildly plunged on. *I feel so helpless! If I go back without doing something to an Israelite, Goliath will laugh at me! I'll never get to be a man and carry his shield! Besides, everyone else will think I'm a coward, and I'll be disgraced forever!*

Reuben turned so that his face was faintly visible in the reflected light of the distant campfires. Smiling, he said, "You don't have to tell me if you don't want. We can just talk."

Galen nodded, greatly relieved at the reprieve. He knew his problem wasn't solved, but maybe he could think of a way to handle it. Still, he was so upset that he didn't feel like talking. He needed action.

"Or we could have another play fight," he countered, realizing that instead of wanting to harm Reuben, he wanted to be friends.

"Too dark," Reuben replied. "We might hurt each other. But we could play war. One of us can hide while the other tries to find him. You know, like a spy sneaking up on a sentry. All right?"

Galen agreed. "You want to be the sentry or the spy?"

"Sentry," Reuben promptly replied.

"Good!" Galen replied. "Just stay away from the campfire lights. I don't want anyone to see me." Galen turned to face the valley's darkness but listened to the soft rustling sounds as Reuben ran to hide.

Galen was dismayed when another thought popped into his head. *This would be the perfect opportunity to make Goliath proud of me! I could—*

"Stop it!" he muttered aloud. He silently added, *I couldn't do something so terrible!*

A little voice inside his head taunted him, *Are you sure? Maybe you'll change your mind! Isn't that better than being thought of as a coward?* Galen shook his head and began looking for Reuben.

Galen's nighttime search involved sneaking up on bushes, large rocks, and a few trees where the "sentry" might be watching for the infiltrating "spy." Galen, trained to become a Philistine warrior from his youngest years, had learned one way to find someone in darkness.

He dropped down low to quickly scan the horizon. Against its faint light, he barely discerned Reuben's form pressed up against a tree trunk.

Using all the stealth skills he had learned, Galen tiptoed in back of Reuben. Silent as a shadow, with the club in his hands, Galen rose up just behind the unsuspecting boy.

It would be so easy! Galen realized, and then, disgusted with himself, he threw the club down.

The sound made Reuben jump and whirl around. "You're good, Galen!" he admitted with a nervous laugh. "I didn't hear or see you!"

Galen felt around in the darkness and retrieved his club. "Thanks, but I don't like this game. Let's just talk."

"Fine! You can give me some tips on how you sneaked up on me like that."

Galen headed toward the sound of the brook. "I'd rather talk about something else."

"Like what?"

Galen didn't answer until they were back beside the water skins, where the murmur of running water helped to cover their voices. "Tell me about your family." It wasn't what Galen really wanted to know, but he didn't feel like coming out directly with what he did want.

"I already told you just about everything. Except I don't think I mentioned that my parents adopted two little foreign kids after their mother and father died near our camp."

Galen asked, "Why did they do that? And why did you bring me food instead of turning me in to your soldiers?"

"Well, a long, long time ago," Reuben began, "my people were slaves in Egypt. Our God led us out of slavery and gave us this land where we are now. In the book of the law, He told us that we were not to do wrong to a stranger, because we had been strangers in Egypt."

Those were curious ideas to Galen. Dagon, his god, had never told anyone anything, as far as Galen knew. He asked Reuben, "Is that why you brought me food and didn't turn me in even though our people are enemies?"

"Our God trusts us," Reuben explained, "and He welcomes anyone who trusts in Him. I did that with you."

"Oh!" Ashamed, Galen eased the club head to the ground and opened his fingers to let it fall. He heard a light splash where it landed in the brook.

Galen took several seconds to ponder something before he spoke again. "Can your God make men?"

Laughing softly, Reuben spoke with assurance. "Of course! He created everyone, including you and me, and He will help both of us grow up to be good men."

Galen turned those words over and over in his mind as he said good-bye to Reuben and started across the Valley of Elah under cover of darkness. He didn't know how he could explain to Goliath why he hadn't struck an Israelite and brought back proof.

Maybe Dagon . . . he started to think and lightly touched the carved image snuggled against his side. The national god of the Philistines hadn't ever given instructions to be nice to strangers. In fact, from what Galen knew, Dagon was primarily believed to be responsible for growing grain and other crops. How could a carved image help a boy become a real man?

Galen's thoughts were momentarily interrupted as he imagined what Goliath would say when he reported on his second experience inside Israelite lines. The thought scared him so that he suddenly shivered. He flinched as he visualized Goliath's fury turning from angry words to powerful slaps with immense hands.

With an effort, Galen forced his mind back to more pleasant thoughts about the God of Reuben. Crossing the Valley of Elah under a star-splattered sky, Galen looked up. He wondered if Reuben's God was truly the most powerful of all gods, or even if there *were* any other gods.

Galen whispered, "The God of Reuben's people, if You are the only God, and I find out that You have all power and might, I will follow You. And I want You to make me a man."

He paused and then added silently, *And I can't really wait until I grow up, because tomorrow Goliath is going to make me wish I had never been born!*

CHAPTER

9

Passing out of the valley in the darkness, Galen approached his people's camp with sharply different feelings fighting inside him. A sense of peace over his decision was almost overwhelmed by the dread of facing Goliath. That reluctance and lack of courage made Galen fight to not run away in panic. Knowing he really had no choice, he answered the Philistine night sentry's challenge and entered the camp.

Without mentioning his adventure to the sentry, Galen walked through the sleeping encampment toward Ziklag's family tent. Glancing up at the midnight sky, he desperately wished his parents and his brother were alive so he could share the conflicts raging in his mind.

Hearing snoring from inside Zik's shelter, Galen removed his sandals to slip inside without awakening anyone. As he reached for the tent flap, Zik stepped outside.

He took Galen's arm, pulled him away from the tent, and demanded in a hoarse whisper, "Where have you been?"

Galen thought fast as they moved far enough away so that nobody could overhear. He had to talk to somebody, and he liked and trusted Zik. After swearing him to secrecy, Galen told him everything.

Zik sank down beside a dying campfire that made his face glow and his eyes shine brightly. He exclaimed in disbelief, "You talked to this god of the Israelites?"

"Well, sort of, I guess," Galen admitted, hurt that his confession seemed to have shocked Zik.

Galen watched the firelight playing on his friend's face before adding,

"But I feel good about it." He touched the Dagon in his tunic. "And I also feel bad."

"But," Zik pointed out, "you can't even see this Israelite god, so how can you know what he thinks?"

"Well," Galen replied, "He left instructions in something called the book of the law."

"Tell that to Goliath!" Zik whispered. "Or are you really going to tell him everything you've just told me?"

Thoughtfully, Galen admitted, "I don't think so. He's going to be angry enough that I had a chance to use my club on an Israelite but didn't."

Sighing heavily, Zik remarked, "I think you've lost all your chances with Goliath. I doubt he'll ever, ever let you carry his shield. But you can be sure he's going to have something terrible to say about you becoming a man and a warrior. In fact, the whole camp will probably hear him when he curses you as only he can."

Galen shivered, recalling how vile-mouthed the giant had often been to anyone who aggravated him. It seemed to Galen that all he had ever wanted was forever lost.

Zik continued, "You can see Dagon, Baal, and our other Philistine gods as easily as you can see Goliath. After all, he's the most powerful champion who ever was! My father says Goliath was sent by our Philistine gods to defeat the weak, foolish Israelites across the valley."

Galen protested rather lamely, "Reuben says that the God of the Israelites will defeat Goliath."

Zik snorted. "Why would a powerful god choose such cowardly people as the Israelites, who won't even send one man to fight Goliath? Why would a powerful god give his people poor wooden weapons and no iron or bronze ones? It doesn't make sense!"

Zik's voice began to rise, but he ignored Galen's warning to speak softly. "Them defeat Goliath?" Zik cried. "That's impossible! For nearly forty days, morning and evening, Goliath has challenged the Israelites to send somebody to fight him. No one has come."

Galen replied, "Reuben says that when it's the right time, their God will send someone to—"

"It won't happen!" Zik interrupted. "The Israelites won't ever send anyone to meet Goliath. They don't want to become our slaves when Goliath beats their champion. They sit over there on their hillside and shake with fear, but they won't fight! Some god they have!"

On that triumphant note, Zik declared that he was going to bed. Galen stayed outside to think, but he was now in more mental anguish and uncertainty than before. In spite of his determination to be a good Philistine, tears won. They continued for a long time. It was nearly dawn before he wearily crawled into the tent and slept.

Galen was awakened by Zik shaking him by the shoulders. "Wake up, Galen! Something seems to be happening on the Israelite side of the valley!"

Galen rolled over and muttered sleepily, "What?"

"You slept through Goliath's morning call for the Israelites to send someone to fight him. Today their soldiers are moving around excitedly instead of just standing around as usual."

Galen sat upright. "What does that mean?"

"Goliath thinks they may finally be going to send someone to fight him, so he's giving them a few minutes. Then he's going to challenge them again! If he's right, there's going to be a wonderful sight to see! So get up!"

Galen quickly obeyed, wondering if Reuben could possibly be right about the Israelite God sending someone to accept Goliath's challenge.

Moments later Galen and Zik pushed their way forward through the crowd until they were past everyone except the Philistine soldiers. Unable to see through the massed ranks, the boys ran off to one side. They stopped where there was a clear view of Goliath below them on the hillside and the Israelites on the opposite hill.

Zik spoke excitedly. "They're moving around like a swarm of bees, so they must have found a champion to fight ours! Do you suppose he's as big as Goliath?"

"I don't know," Galen admitted, feeling himself getting caught up in the excitement. He vainly looked for Reuben and wondered if Reuben could see him. "But," Galen told Zik, "whoever the Israelites plan to send against Goliath must really be a great warrior."

Galen dropped his gaze to his own people. As usual, the mighty Goliath and his shield bearer stood in front of his troops, facing the Israelites. Goliath made a splendid sight, towering more than nine feet tall in his 125-pound coat of bronze armor. He looked even larger in his helmet and shin guards, which were bronze too.

A bronze javelin was slung across his massive shoulders. At his side a great sword rested in its scabbard. His spear, as large as a weaver's rod with a 15-pound iron point, seemed tiny in Goliath's huge hands.

A few feet in front of him, Goliath's shield bearer waited, resting the giant's heavy buckler on the ground. Behind Goliath stood a warrior with a sword and a spear. Galen had seen all the weapons in use before. He knew that the armor bearer with the sword and spear would follow Goliath and deliver a death blow after the giant felled his adversary.

None of that was different to Galen. Neither was the usual mass of Philistine warriors and civilians. They'd gathered morning and evening for forty days to see Goliath shout across the small valley for the Israelites to send out a champion to meet him in mortal combat.

What was different, Galen saw at once, was that on the hillside across the valley, the Israelites were no longer standing around with heads down and shoulders slumped. Instead, they ran back and forth, talking among themselves and often looking behind them.

Zik asked, "What do you think they see back there?"

"All I can see are officers' tents," Galen replied, shading his eyes to see better. "I think they're expecting someone to come from that direction. Yes! See? The troops are parting right in the middle, making room for someone to pass through them!"

"You're right!" Zik exclaimed. "Now I can hear them shouting something, but I can't make out their words."

"Neither can I," Galen admitted. "They're looking back and starting to cheer! Listen to them!"

A great roar erupted from the throats of the assembled Israelites. They shook their inferior bows and spears in the air and jumped up and down, straining to see whoever was moving through the human path behind them.

Zik cried, "No doubt about it! They've found a champion!"

"I see him!" Galen declared. "There! Just stepping out from—oh no!"

He stared in disbelief. Across the valley, a boy not much older than Galen stepped out of the Israelites' ranks. He wore no armor, only shepherd's clothing. He carried a staff and sling but no shield or weapon.

"Who's he?" Galen asked in surprise as the Israelites' cheers became a mighty and continuous roar.

"Probably a messenger," Zik guessed. "Maybe he's being sent to say the Israelites have found a champion who needs a few more minutes to put on his armor. So this boy's going to ask if Goliath will wait."

Galen disagreed. "I don't think so. From the cheering of the Israelites and the way our warriors are laughing, I think that boy's going to challenge Goliath!"

"No! That can't be!" Zik exclaimed.

Galen and Zik studied the youth with sudden new interest as he stopped at the brook and slowly picked up some stones from beside it.

He was a handsome kid, Galen had to admit. And unusual. Not as dark-skinned as most Israelites, he had a ruddy complexion. Galen thought from this distance that the boy might even have red hair.

Galen watched as the youth bent to pick up another stone, which he then placed in the pouch of his shepherd's bag. Four times he repeated the action and then straightened up. Then calmly and confidently, he left the stream and deliberately began walking toward Goliath.

"Yes!" Galen cried in disbelief. "That *is* their champion! That shepherd boy is going to fight Goliath with just a sling and some stones!"

CHAPTER
10

The Philistines also seemed to realize that this mere puppy of a youth was going to accept Goliath's challenge. His warriors laughed in contempt and shouted insults at the lone shepherd boy purposefully striding forward.

Zik exclaimed, "I just can't believe this! Those Israelites are actually sending a boy against Goliath!"

Galen breathlessly watched the young man approach. He briefly wondered if Reuben was also watching.

Galen told Zik, "I don't think Goliath believes it either. He probably feels insulted!"

When the opponents came within speaking distance, the cheering from the Israelite army and laughter from the Philistines slowly died down. The silence was broken only by the sound of Goliath's scale armor as he followed his shield bearer onto the valley floor.

Galen couldn't see the giant's face, but the sun shone directly on his youthful opponent's. Galen had a clear, sharp view of the handsome, ruddy shepherd. A beardless face proved that he was too young to be an experienced soldier.

The challenger didn't seem frightened. In fact, Galen thought he appeared calm and confident even though he was facing a warrior almost twice as tall as he. Galen wished he knew the youth's name.

The crowds on both sides of the valley became very quiet. Soon there was such a stillness that Galen could clearly hear Goliath's sneering words to the youth.

"Am I a dog that you come at me with sticks?"

Galen noticed the scorn and contempt in the giant's tone and knew he despised the boy facing him. That was confirmed when Goliath began cursing the youth by the giant's gods Dagon and Baal.

Zik whispered, "He's not even scaring that boy!"

Galen nodded, aware that the youthful stranger's countenance remained serene.

Goliath told him, "Come here, and I'll give your flesh to the birds of the air and the beasts of the field."

The youth replied, "You come against me with sword and spear and javelin, but I come against you in the name of the Lord Almighty, the God of the armies of Israel, whom you have defied!"

Galen blinked, recalling how Reuben had said that the Israelites' invisible God was going to send someone to defeat Goliath.

The shepherd continued, "This day the Lord will hand you over to me, and I'll strike you down and cut off your head! Today I will give the carcasses of the Philistine army to the birds of the air and the beasts of the earth, and the whole world will know that there is a God in Israel!"

Galen gasped, astonished that anyone dared to talk that way to Goliath, plus all the Philistine warriors.

The youthful challenger added, "All those gathered here will know that it is not by sword or spear that the Lord saves; for the battle is the Lord's, and He will give all of you into our hands!"

Galen watched Goliath move closer to attack the youth, who ran quickly to meet him.

Zik exclaimed, "I can't believe he's doing that!"

Galen didn't reply because he was intrigued by what the stranger did next.

The boy reached into his bag and took out one of the five stones he had picked up from the brook. Fitting the rock into his sling, the youth swung it rapidly above his head and then released it.

Galen could barely follow its flight but saw it clearly just before it struck the giant's forehead. Galen heard it hit. He saw the giant falter and then slowly topple like a great tree before an ax. Goliath crashed facedown on the ground.

Galen barely heard the collective cry of astonishment from the Philistines lined up on the hillside. Leaping back in shock, he cried aloud, "God of the Israelites, save me!"

He trembled with fear and excitement as the youth with the sling darted toward the fallen giant.

Goliath's shield bearer, standing in shock in front of the giant, spun round and started running away, still carrying the great shield. As he drew even with Galen, he dropped it with a dull thud.

Galen's eyes flickered back to the stricken Goliath, and he again recalled Reuben's prophetic words about his God sending someone to overcome the giant.

Moments before, Goliath had been a man nine feet tall, fully dressed head to toe in protective scale armor made of bronze. Now, sprawled facedown on the ground, he was still huge compared to the youth standing over him. Yet somehow Goliath looked small and insignificant to Galen.

The victorious youth who had toppled the giant reached down and pulled big Goliath's sword from its scabbard. The sunlight glittered on the blade as he swung it high above Goliath's head. Galen quickly turned away and saw the looks of absolute disbelief on the Philistine warriors' faces.

They shrieked in a second collective howl of hysterical anguish as the sword flashed down. Instantly, Israelite soldiers triumphantly yelled and then charged across the valley, carrying axes and ox goads. A few had crude wooden spears or bows and arrows. Others carried slings.

The panicked Philistines turned and ran away from the onrushing army. Galen glanced toward Zik and saw him already frantically dashing after them.

Galen's mind told him to run for his life, but his feet wouldn't obey. Terror had frozen him where he stood, trancelike, watching the swarm of

Israelite soldiers surging across the narrow valley. They were covering the distance in an amazingly short time.

Galen's eyes were drawn back to the conquering shepherd boy as he lifted high his grisly trophy.

This horrific sight broke Galen's hypnotic trance.

He turned and started to run after his fleeing tribesmen, but he had waited too long. He couldn't catch up with them.

Frantically looking around for somewhere to hide, he saw only one possibility: Goliath's great shield that his bearer had dropped in his flight.

Even though Galen had once struggled to lift it, fear gave him strength. With the dreaded shouts of the oncoming Israelites in his ears, Galen lifted an edge of the shield high enough to squirm headfirst under it.

Just before the shield fell protectively over him, he had a final glimpse of the foremost Israelites now rushing upon the scene.

Trembling in terror, Galen hoped no one could see him as he hid under Goliath's abandoned shield. His eyes quickly adjusted from the bright daylight to the shadow under the shield. His drumming heart seemed as if it might burst through his ribs as he waited for the onrushing Israelites.

At first he heard only their war cries and the fading shrieks of the terrorized Philistine warriors as they tried to escape the pursuing Israelites.

It had all happened so fast that Galen had a hard time believing what he had just seen. Goliath the giant was dead, brought down by a shepherd boy armed only with a sling and a stone. The Philistine soldiers, who'd just witnessed their champion's defeat, were running away in panic. Galen hadn't dreamed that the Israelites with their inferior weapons would chase mighty warriors with their iron and bronze ones. But it was happening just as Reuben had predicted.

Galen heard the thud of countless running feet rushing toward his hiding place. The ground trembled where he lay facedown, helpless and alone. A dreadful thought exploded in his brain: *What if one of those Israelites stops and picks up this shield?*

The idea was so frightening that Galen cried out to the God of the shepherd boy, to the God of Reuben. He called to the God whose name he didn't know but in whose power and might he now believed. "Save me!"

It was all he could think to do as the first wave of Israelite soldiers flowed around Goliath's fallen shield. Galen pressed his face against the earth and tried to hold his breath as the horde of victorious, shouting Israelites thundered past him.

He could hear the distinctive twang of bowstrings as they released their arrows at the fleeing Philistines. He caught the short grunt of exertion as Israelites hurled spears and javelins.

The shriek of wounded and dying men mingled with the noise of wooden spears being splintered by bronze and iron swords. This told Galen that hand-to-hand combat had begun between the foremost Israelites and the Philistine stragglers.

In a vain effort to shut out the awful clash of battle and the shouts of victor and victim, Galen clapped both hands over his ears and prayed he would survive.

He didn't know how long he stayed that way, but gradually he became aware that the battle sounds were fading into the distance. He took both hands from his ears, cocked his head, and listened.

There was no doubt; the noise of battle was getting fainter as the Israelites hotly pursued the Philistines. Scarcely daring to believe he had been spared, he felt his racing pulse slow as apprehension ebbed away. For the first time he thought of Zik and his other friends. Had they survived? Or were they sprawled out there on the bloody ground?

Slowly, carefully, with great effort, Galen lifted the edge of Goliath's shield up and allowed a sliver of light into his shelter. The combatants had all vanished beyond a small hill, but dropped weapons and human casualties littered the area where the Philistine camp had been. The sight caused a wave of nausea to wash over Galen. He closed his eyes until the feeling passed.

When he opened them again, he saw nobody left standing. With a heavy sigh, Galen started to push up on the heavy shield so he could slide out. But then he stopped. Off to his right, where he hadn't looked before, two Israelite soldiers were heading straight toward his hiding place!

Galen sucked in his breath and dropped the edge of the shield. The welcoming soft darkness quickly engulfed him as his heart again started racing. He curled up in a tight little ball and suppressed a moan.

While the Israelite soldiers were still some distance away, Galen heard one speak in a deep voice.

"I can hardly wait to take whatever valuables Goliath has on him."

Galen swallowed hard as the two voices passed him some distance away. He heard the second soldier speak.

"I still don't think we should be doing this. We'll be in big trouble if our commander finds out we slipped away to strip the slain before the fight was over."

Galen noticed that this soldier spoke in a thin voice that suggested he might be a much younger man.

"Stop complaining!" the one with the deep voice growled. "Just be thankful we've got first pick of all these bronze and iron weapons. There! See that sword? Take it for yourself."

Galen had to strain to catch the other man's reply as both soldiers moved away from the fallen shield.

"Maybe I will. I can also use that bronze javelin over there, and that spear with the iron point."

His friend laughed. "You'll be so loaded down, you'll hardly be able to walk. Remember, we have to carry all this somewhere and hide it until it's safe to come back. I'm going to wait for whatever Goliath's got on him."

Galen strained hard to hear what else was said, but he guessed the men had come to where the giant had fallen. He heard the faint clink of Goliath's mail armor and the murmur of the scavengers' voices. Galen wondered if he dared try to slip away but decided it was too risky. He couldn't outrun a thrown spear or an arrow.

Moments later Galen regretted that decision when he heard the men walking back toward him. He began to tremble as they drew close enough for him to understand their words.

The younger man asked, "Where do you think we can hide all this for a while?"

"Over there looks like a good place."

Over where? Galen wondered, hoping they weren't going to come anywhere near him. But when the deep-voiced man spoke again, Galen knew his hope was in vain. The man was definitely coming toward where he was hiding.

The same man said, "We deserved getting first choice of these things because it's the only reward we'll get. Well, except for Goliath falling into our hands."

The younger man laughed. "*Our* hands? For forty days you and I stood and quaked with fright just as all the rest of our people did before David came along."

David? Galen thought from under the shield. *Could that be the name of the shepherd who killed Goliath?*

"That boy was a real surprise," the older man agreed with a chuckle. "You should have seen him when he came into camp with some roasted grain and loaves of bread for our commander. That was just shortly before Goliath shouted his usual challenge."

Galen licked his lips, realizing that the man's voice was now much closer than before. Galen guessed the men were slowly moving his way, still looting the slain. *They'll want Goliath's shield if they see it!* Galen thought, and his trembling increased. If the Israelites picked up the shield, would they strike him down or make him a slave?

The younger man said doubtfully, "I heard that David had come to see his brothers, who are in our unit."

"Yes, he did," the Israelite soldier answered. "I was standing near him when he greeted his brothers. That was when our people began shouting war cries and calling for us to form our lines facing Goliath, who had come out to taunt us."

"I wish I'd seen that part," the young soldier replied wistfully.

"If you had, you would never have forgotten it," his comrade answered. "Goliath shouted as usual, and our men turned and ran from him in fear. Well, of course I didn't. I've seen too many battles to do that."

Galen listened in fascination and yet with dread, because the Israelites were now definitely drawing closer to his hiding place.

The deep-voiced man continued, "David watched Goliath shout across the valley, and then he turned to me and some others standing there. He asked who was this Philistine that he should defy the armies of the living God? Just at that moment, David's older brother Eliab walked up and heard him. He was angry and accused David of coming to see the battle."

"Is that when he was taken to see King Saul?"

"No, not right then, because David protested and said that wasn't why he had come. But someone overheard him and ran to tell Saul. I followed along and was present when David told the king that he would go and fight Goliath."

Galen cringed as the sound of footsteps neared. He swallowed hard and felt his mouth go dry with fear.

"So I heard," the younger soldier replied. "But is it true that finally Saul agreed and put his own armor on David?"

"Oh, that's true. You know that Saul stands a head taller than all the rest of us, so it was really comical to see David trying to walk with all of Saul's armor on, including his bronze helmet. Anyway, David took it all off and even handed back Saul's sword. Then he went down to the brook and picked up some stones."

"I saw him do that," the younger man declared. "But why did he take five stones? He only needed one—"

Galen stiffened in alarm as the speaker suddenly broke off his sentence. *What happened?* he wondered.

"What are you looking at?" the man with the deep voice asked.

"That's Goliath's shield!" the younger soldier cried.

"It *was* his," his friend replied. "Now it's mine!"

Galen's skin crawled at the sound of a few hurried footsteps and then the sight of large fingers slipping under the edge of the shield just inches from his face!

Galen thought his heart would burst from sheer fright as the soldier's fingers started to lift the edge of Goliath's shield. Galen drew his feet under him in the vain hope that he might surprise the men so much, he could jump up and run out of range of either an arrow or spear before they could react.

"Wait!" he heard the younger man exclaim. "I saw it first, so that shield is mine!"

The deep-voiced man angrily growled, "Who do you think you're talking to?"

"You, that's who! I want his shield!"

Galen heard the older man growl again, "So do I, so you can't have it! Now leave me alone before—"

He broke off as Galen heard the distinctive sound of a sword being pulled from its scabbard. The fingers disappeared from the edge of the shield. It fell heavily, again leaving Galen in semidarkness. He caught the sound of a second sword being swiftly drawn from its scabbard.

The older man roared, "Pull a blade on me, will you? You fool! Now I'll take both the shield and your life!"

The ring of swords striking each other confirmed to Galen that the two soldiers were attacking each other. With furious shouts and loud panting, they pressed their assaults. Galen didn't know whether to crawl out from under the shield and try to run away or wait to learn what happened.

He remained still, listening to the clash of the life-or-death struggle that surged back and forth around his hiding place. Slowly, numb with fright, Galen realized that the fight was moving away from him.

After taking a minute longer to be sure, with sudden hope he risked raising the edge of the great shield. The two men were so involved in their fight that all their attention was on each other.

Still, Galen hesitated, debating what to do. If he ran, they might see him, stop their combat, and bring him down with a javelin or arrow. But if he stayed hidden, what then? Surely the victor would come to claim the shield. He would be discovered, and a soldier who had just fought to the death with one of his own kind would surely not spare an enemy Philistine boy.

He took another rapid peek at the combatants. They had dropped their swords and were rolling around on the ground, too busy to notice him.

Once again Galen called out to Reuben's invisible God. "Save me!"

At the same time, he strained to lift the edge of Goliath's shield farthest away from the men. Frantic to escape, Galen wiggled out into the open and quickly got to his feet. Bending low, he ran awkwardly toward the darkening shadows of the Valley of Elah.

The shouting and cursing of the two combatants told Galen that they still hadn't seen him. He didn't look back but felt his shoulder muscles tighten at the thought of an arrow striking him. He fled at his greatest possible speed across the valley toward the Israelite camp. Galen's lungs were on fire, and his breathing was so tortured it came in rasping gasps before he decided he was out of bow-shot range.

He slowed his desperate pace and looked back. There were no shouts of anyone chasing him. Greatly relieved, he took a moment to catch his breath. He had left one danger behind, but another loomed ahead.

Nervously, his eyes swept the Israelite camp. He was relieved to see that no soldiers had returned. There weren't even any young men, just old men and boys.

When none of them seemed to notice him, he started walking again. He was surprised that he staggered from exhaustion. He was aware of a painful stitch in his side that he hadn't noticed before. Cautiously, trying to control his suddenly wobbly legs, he walked on while his eyes flickered ahead in hopes of seeing Reuben.

Galen encouraged himself by thinking, *If I can just reach him, I'll be all right. I'll ask him to go with me to his parents. He said they had taken in other orphans; maybe they'll take me in too. I'll work hard for—*

He was jerked out of his musings by a shout from the Israelite camp. "Philistine! Philistine coming!"

A boy pointed toward him, screaming his warning over and over. Other boys ran to see too. They joined in shouting, "Philistine!"

In moments a crowd had almost miraculously formed, facing him. A few older boys arrived late and pushed their way to the front of the crowd. These teenagers were armed with sticks, stones, and slings. Some elderly men, moving slowly with age, arrived with farmers' sickles, forks, and axes.

Now so exhausted that he could barely stay on his feet, Galen lurched toward the Israelites. They were silent, their faces grim as they gripped their stones and weapons.

Galen frantically scanned the growing crowd for Reuben but didn't see him. Intimidated, he hesitated, his hands dropping wearily to his sides.

In his excitement, he had forgotten the image of Dagon carried in his tunic. Plunging his hand inside, Galen held up the carving of the Philistines' national deity. For a moment he studied the carving of half-man, half-fish and recalled Reuben's laughing remarks when he had first seen it by the brook.

That's Dagon? That silly little thing is your god who you think can help you?

The words silently echoed in Galen's memory, along with what Reuben had said about the God of the Israelites sending someone to defeat Goliath.

Reuben was right, Galen admitted to himself. He gazed thoughtfully down at Dagon's image. This visible Philistine god hadn't helped him, not a bit. Abruptly, mustering his remaining strength, Galen drew back his arm and hurled the object into the Valley of Elah.

Raising his eyes to the sky, Galen confessed his fears and hopes to Reuben's invisible but powerful God, who had sent a shepherd boy to overcome Goliath.

Galen whispered hoarsely, "Reuben's God, hear me! I'm afraid these people lined up over there will kill me because I'm a Philistine, but I have no place else to go! I was wrong about Dagon, and Reuben was right. You are the true Source of power!"

Pausing, Galen added, "It doesn't matter anymore that Goliath thought I wasn't strong or that he would never be proud of me. It doesn't matter that I couldn't even lift his shield off the ground. Now I know that carrying Goliath's shield and killing people aren't what make a man; it's what he is inside. You used Reuben, a boy like me, to show that You are the only true God. If You're willing to use me, I'm ready and I'm willing. I want to be in Your family, to serve You and grow up to be a man that You'll be proud of! But I can't if these people stone me! I need help!"

A voice called from the crowd of Israelites, "Galen? Is that you?"

"Reuben!" Galen joyfully exclaimed and forced his weary legs to run toward his friend.

Reuben raced to meet him, threw his arms around him, and exclaimed with a happy grin, "Welcome, Galen!"

Galen's weariness seemed to melt away in his joyous reunion. He thumped Reuben on the back and fought back tears of happiness. He couldn't stop the tremor in his voice as he blurted out his thoughts from a full heart.

"I've never been so glad to see anyone in my life! I threw away Dagon and asked your God to let me serve Him! I want to be a part of His family. I was afraid of those people watching me, but I told your God that I trusted Him because you said He would send someone to overcome

Goliath. So now I can't go back over there," he pointed across the Valley of Elah. "I have no one but you to turn to!"

Reuben grinned and grabbed Galen's arm, saying, "Come with me." He turned away, pulling on Galen.

"Where are we going?" Galen asked, glancing doubtfully at the Israelites watching the boys as they moved through the camp.

Over his shoulder Reuben explained, "To see my father. He'll welcome you—and so will my mother when we get home."

Galen exclaimed, "Really?"

Reuben stopped and smiled reassuringly. "Really!"

Staring, Galen cried, "You mean you think they'll take me in and give me a real home?"

Reuben's arm slid across Galen's shoulders. "I know they will. Not only that, but you'll be my brother!"

Laughing happily, the boys broke into a run.

LETTERS FROM OUR READERS

Where can I find this story in the Bible? (Lauren S., Anderson, Indiana)

You can find the story of David and Goliath in 1 Samuel 17. You won't find any mention of Galen or Reuben, though. When we hear the Bible story in Sunday school, we see the events from the Israelites' point of view. But the author wondered how a Philistine would see the story. What would it be like for a Philistine boy to see his people's hero defeated by an Israelite teen not much older than himself? And what would happen if this boy realized that his Philistine god Dagon couldn't help him? How could he learn about the one true God?

That's why the author imagined the boys Galen and Reuben—to help you see what it was like to live then and watch this amazing event in Israel's history. Of course, while the part about Galen, Reuben, and the other boys is imagined, the part about David, Goliath, King Saul, and the armies is true.

Who were the Philistines and where did they come from? (Jon E., Tallahassee, Florida)

The Philistines were a people from the area around the Aegean Sea or perhaps from the island of Crete (nobody knows for sure). They settled along the coast of Canaan before the time of Abraham. If you look at a map in your Bible, you can locate some major Philistine cities that are mentioned in the story: Gaza, Ashkelon, Ashdod, Gath, and Ekron. (Look west of Jerusalem, along the coast of the Mediterranean Sea.)

The Philistines manufactured iron tools and weapons, which gave them military superiority over the Israelites. They were at the height of their power during the reigns of King Saul (when this story takes place) and King David. After a while, though, their civilization disappeared.

Why did the Philistines worship a god carved out of wood or stone? Didn't they know it didn't have any power to help them? (Justin V., Kansas City, Kansas)

There's a yearning in every person's heart to know God, and if people cannot find the one true God, they will create a substitute. (Sometimes people know about the one true God but refuse to follow Him.)

The Bible is filled with stories about people who worshipped false gods (called heathens), as well as stern warnings to the Israelites to stay away from heathen religions. But even King Solomon, a man to whom God granted great wisdom, was enticed by false gods through his heathen wives (see 1 Kings 11:1-3).

Today, people are still worshipping false gods. If you look around at our culture, you'll see evidence of this every day. But the Bible still warns us to have nothing to do with heathen religions or idols (see Leviticus 26:1; 1 Corinthians 10:14; 1 John 5:21).

Why were there women and children in the Philistine camp in this story? (Emma C., Cookeville, Tennessee)

Some reference books say that the Philistines took their families along when they went to war. The families remained in camp while the men went into battle. Although the Israelites didn't do this, David's father did send him to take food to his older brothers and bring back a report about them (see 1 Samuel 17:17-18).

Was Goliath *really* over nine feet tall? (Randy J., Pocatello, Idaho)

Yes! No wonder the Israelites didn't want to fight him. Not only was he much larger than any of the Israelite soldiers, but he also had better armor and weapons. (See 1 Samuel 17:4-7 for a description of Goliath and his armor.) But David wasn't fighting Goliath in his own strength—he knew that only God could defeat Goliath. He made sure everyone understood that God would help him win the battle against the giant (1 Samuel 17:45-47).

ABOUT THE AUTHOR

LEE RODDY accepted Christ at seventeen after his first short stories were published. He later wrote radio dramas in Hollywood but switched to novels. His credits now total seventy books, including forty-four juvenile novels which have sold a few million copies. Most have four- or five-star reader ratings. A reviewer declared, "Lee Roddy is the grand master of exciting books for young readers." Lee, his wife, son, daughter, and two grandsons live in California.

The Prophet's Kid

by Jim Ware

For Al, Lissa, John, and Kathy,
who helped make it happen

In the great hall of Ahaz the King, all was festive and bright. Cups clattered. The voices of the guests echoed off the cedar-paneled walls and danced around the huge stone pillars. Jewels flashed in the ladies' headdresses. Brightly colored robes, fringed in gold and cinched up with long, striped sashes, swished across the marble floor. Earrings dangled. Ankle chains jingled. Ezra could see it all from his hiding place under the table that bore the silver wine cups.

Suddenly a sharp pain shot through his hand and up his arm. "Ow!" he cried. "Shub! You're on my little finger!"

"Sorry," said Shear-Jeshub, shifting his weight. Shub, as his friends called him, was tall for an eleven-year-old—nearly a span taller than Ezra, even though Ezra was more than two months older. It was a trait Shub had inherited from his father, the prophet Isaiah, but it didn't suit him as well as his famous parent. At least Ezra didn't think so. Isaiah was an imposing, daunting figure. Shub, on the other hand, was just gangly and clumsy—surprisingly so for an intelligent boy who played the harp and amused himself by writing poetry.

As Shub leaned to one side to remove his knee from Ezra's finger, his head jerked upward and bumped the underside of the table. *Bang!* The table shook. There was a light chime of ringing silver cups overhead.

"That was smart!" whispered Hezekiah, a stocky, ruddy-faced boy of ten. He was a boy who, in Ezra's opinion, spent too much time thinking and took everything way too seriously. Hezekiah could definitely be a pain. Still, he *was* the crown prince of Judah, son of King Ahaz, and he *did* look up to the two older boys—especially Ezra. So he was worth keeping around.

"I was afraid of this," Hezekiah went on, glancing nervously at Ezra. "Now they'll catch us for sure!" He darted a deadly look at Shub.

Shub shrugged apologetically. "Sorry," he whispered. "I'm a musician, not a thief or a spy."

Afraid, thought Ezra. *Hezekiah is always afraid!* Well, maybe he had a good reason to be afraid. After all, if they *were* caught, their little game—secretly "crashing" a state dinner party and stuffing themselves with as much stolen food as possible—probably wouldn't go over very well with King Ahaz. And Ezra would be in no end of trouble if his father, Tola, ever found out. Tola was Isaiah's right-hand man, a dignified statesman and staunch believer in the Lord. Tola had helped Isaiah set up the Remnant, a righteous community of "true disciples" of Yahweh, the God of Israel.

Not to mention the fact that Tola was considered to be a prophet himself—one who spoke for Yahweh. It was a lot for a kid like Ezra to live down.

While these thoughts were passing through Ezra's head, the ringing of the cups died away. The sandaled feet of the adults who stood clustered near the table shuffled this way and that over the polished marble floor. A conversation just beyond the fringe of the tablecloth began to gather steam. Apparently no one had noticed the bump. Ezra heard Hezekiah breathe a sigh of relief.

"No, absolutely not!" said a gravel-throated man who was standing not more than two arm's lengths away from the boys' hiding place. "I wouldn't hesitate to say it to his face."

"The prophet Isaiah himself?" The second speaker sounded much older. "I take it you've never met him. Why, he literally thunders when he speaks of the penalty Judah will pay for the sin of chasing after other gods."

"Ha!" laughed the first man. "And what have all his thunderings come

to? Things have never been better, I tell you. Turned my biggest profit
ever in the copper trade this year. Ahaz knew what he was doing when he
rebuilt the high places and introduced the Syrian and Assyrian gods into
the city."

"Don't count on it," said the older man. "Just look at Israel's history.
Decisions like this have always led to . . . *unpleasant* consequences."

That's when Ezra saw his chance.

"Come on," he whispered, pointing to a long side table that stood
over against the cedar-paneled west wall. "The really *good* stuff is over
there."

Then, with a swift, sudden motion, he pulled the tablecloth aside and
dashed into the open. The two other boys scuttled after him, crossing the
marble floor on hands and knees. Ezra fixed his eyes firmly on their goal:
a sideboard loaded with all kinds of delicious-looking appetizers. There
were bowls of moist dates, platters of raisin cakes, pomegranates, small
loaves of sweet bread, pressed figs, olives, and juicy little squares of hot,
roasted lamb. He could almost taste it. Past the wine vat . . . just a little
farther and . . .

Bang! Scrape! Inwardly, Ezra groaned. *Not again!* he thought.

But it was true. When he turned and looked over his shoulder, there
sat poor Shub, the latch of his sandal caught on one of the claw-shaped
feet of the huge silver wine vat. As Shub struggled to free himself, the vast
container shuddered slightly. A few drops of deep red liquid spilled at the
feet of a stout, important-looking man who was dipping out a measure of
wine into a fashionable lady's silver cup.

"Wait! Let me do it," whispered Ezra. He grabbed his friend's foot
and began fumbling with the leather sandal latch. All the while Ezra kept
a nervous eye on the stout man and fashionable lady. Fortunately, they
seemed absorbed in their conversation. That was when it hit him.

Mother! Why hadn't he recognized her before? Her hair, perhaps . . . piled high on top of her head and wrapped with ribbons and
chains of tiny gold rings. Ezra knew that his mother frequented affairs of

this sort, but he really hadn't expected to see her at this one. Father hadn't said a word about it. He wondered if Father even knew. To make matters worse, the man filling his mother's cup was none other than King Ahaz himself! Ezra ducked, hoping to avoid being seen.

"It's regrettable, Jehudith," the king was saying in his golden voice, "that the gods should have given a charming woman like you such an undeserving husband."

Jehudith bent her head slightly and batted her long-lashed eyes. Her dangling gold earrings sparkled in the lamplight.

"'Undeserving . . . a very apt choice of words, Your Majesty," said another man, stepping up to join the conversation. He was a darkly handsome man with a trim black beard, and he wore a robe of white linen and a scarlet turban. Ezra saw him lay a hand on his mother's arm and smile pleasantly into her face. "I might have used the term *dense* myself."

Dense? My father? thought Ezra as he tugged and tugged at the leather thong. He didn't particularly like the sound of that, but there was no time to think about it now.

"Oh, Tola is a very intelligent man, Hanun," Ahaz went on. "Like his fellow prophet, Isaiah. But they are also both exceedingly stubborn. I say we can learn much from the Assyrians. Their gods have obviously been a great help to them. Surely they can help us too."

One last pull, and the sandal latch came loose. "Got it!" whispered Ezra.

"My thoughts exactly, Your Majesty," said Hanun. "Why limit ourselves to *one* god? That's so—so *narrow*. Don't you agree, my dear Jehudith?"

"All right, Shub—*now!*" Ezra ordered.

"An astute observation, Hanun," Ezra heard the king say as he and Shub crept away. "Why, I'm even of the opinion that the Assyrian gods may be the key to ridding us of the Assyrians themselves *and* their bothersome tribute. The fire of Molech's altar is especially powerful, as *I* have good reason to know . . ."

As the king's voice droned on, the boys reached the side table, seized a handful of dates apiece, and plunged to safety beneath the embroidered blue tablecloth. There they sat, feasting on stolen fruit and talking in hushed voices.

"Whew!" said Ezra, munching a date and readjusting the leather headband he always kept bound around his black curls. "That was a close one."

"I *told* you," Shub said. "This kind of thing is a little out of my field. I'm much better off at home with my *kinnor*. Playing that little harp isn't nearly so dangerous." He smiled and took a bite out of a particularly plump date.

That's when Ezra caught sight of Hezekiah's face. He thought the king's son was looking strangely pale. "What's wrong with *you*?" he asked.

Hezekiah shut his eyes. "I couldn't help hearing what my father just said. About . . . *Molech*."

"What about it?"

Hezekiah just shivered and shook his head. "And that other man back there. Did you hear what *he* said? About the prophet and . . . *unpleasant consequences*?"

"Consequences?" asked Ezra, laughing.

"Yes, Ezra," said Hezekiah. His cheeks were red, and he had a very serious look on his face. He paused, as if a fog were lifting from his eyes. "I'm afraid we're going to get in big trouble for doing this, in spite of what you say. Don't you think so, Shub?"

Shub chewed thoughtfully. "It's possible. There are several ways of looking at it. On the one hand, as my father always says . . ."

"Your father!" snorted Ezra. "He's a fanatic, that's all. *Shear-Jeshub*— 'A Remnant Shall Return.' Come on! Who would name a kid something like that?"

"*Your* dad would," answered Shub with an ironic smile. "*Ezra-Elohenu*— 'A Help Is Our God.' "

"Don't remind me."

"But what if they're right?" Hezekiah managed to break into the conversation. "I mean, about God's law and consequences and all that. Maybe there really *is* a price to be paid for . . . for worshipping idols and . . . well, swiping food and stuff."

Ezra swallowed hard and scowled. "Do you *really* think that?"

"Don't you?"

"I'll tell you what *I* think. *I* think a kid can get away with *anything* if he's smart enough!" Then, smiling as if he had a sudden inspiration, Ezra added, "Watch this."

"Wait!" said Hezekiah. "Where are you going?"

But Ezra had already slipped out from under the table. Reaching up, he seized a pair of big red pomegranates from a white ceramic bowl and headed back toward the wine vat. Dropping to his knees in front of the huge silver vessel, he cracked the hard red rinds of the fruit against the floor. After prying the pomegranates open, he crushed the tiny juice-filled beads inside against the marble tiles.

It was done in a moment. The next instant he was back in his hiding place, gulping down a mouthful of honey-raisin cake.

"What was that all about?" asked Hezekiah.

Ezra glanced at him out of the corner of his eye. "Just watch," he said with a grin.

They did. It wasn't long before Ahaz's chief cupbearer approached to replenish the guests' supply of drink. He was a stiff, dignified-looking man. His white tunic was smart and crisp. His gray head was held high. He carried a golden tray of silver cups on his uplifted palm. Ezra saw him smile at Ahaz, Jehudith, and Hanun as he passed their small discussion group.

In the next moment the cupbearer's smile gave way to a look of horror. That was when his left foot landed in the middle of the mass of crushed pomegranate and shot out from under him with all the swiftness of lightning. It was followed just as suddenly by his right foot. Ezra choked down a laugh as the man's entire body flew forward feetfirst. Cups sailed in one

direction, the tray in another. The tray bounced off Hanun's richly tur-
baned head and landed with a bang as it went skidding across the floor.
There was a terrific splash, and before anyone knew what had happened,
the dignified cupbearer was sitting in the wine vat, dripping with red
liquid. Wine and pomegranate juice flowed across the white marble floor,
staining the hems of the guests' robes a deep shade of reddish purple.

Everyone stared. For a brief moment silence reigned. Ezra fought to
hold back his laughter. And then, from across the room—from the dripping wine vat—the angry cupbearer suddenly found a gap in the blue tablecloth. The man scowled at Ezra, who crouched hidden with his mouth
full of roasted lamb.

"I told you so," moaned Hezekiah. "He sees us. Now we're caught for
sure!"

"Just wait," whispered Ezra with a confident smile. "It's not over yet.
I can talk my way out of *anything!*"

"Your Majesty!" shouted the cupbearer. "Look! Under the table against
the wall. It's your son and that hooligan of a troublemaker, Tola's boy!"

Instantly the entire party was in an uproar. Guards in brassy armor
and pointed helmets descended upon the sideboard and dragged the boys
from their shadowy hiding place. Everything became a blur as Ezra was
pulled to his feet and shoved in the direction of the king. When he came
to a stop, he found himself standing in front of the king and Jehudith.
Beside him were Hezekiah and Shub.

"Better make it good!" whispered Hezekiah through clenched teeth.

"Well, well!" said the king as a hush descended over the great hall.
"What have we here?" He paused to hiccup and then bent down and
stared sternly into the boys' faces one by one. "Hezekiah?" he went on,
glaring angrily at his son. "What is the meaning of this? What were you
boys doing under that table? And who made this mess all over the floor?
Hmmm?"

"Father, I—I—" stammered the prince.

"Hezekiah, perhaps *you* can answer my question," the king growled.

Quickly Ezra sized up the situation. This was a tight spot for sure. His status as a hero was hanging in the balance. His theory was about to be disproved. Worst of all, his friend was about to be blamed for something *he* had done. Well, he'd told Hezekiah that he could talk his way out of anything, and if ever there was a time to start talking, it was now. So he blurted out the first thing that came into his head.

"Please don't blame him, Your Majesty," he said. "It's not his fault."

Ahaz frowned. "Not his fault? Well, then whose fault *is* it?"

"Mine."

Ezra saw his mother turn pale. It was a bold stroke, but he had his reasons for believing that it just might work. Hezekiah turned and stared at him in disbelief. Shub looked at his feet and scratched his nose.

"*Your* fault?" said Ahaz, eyeing the boy narrowly. He hiccuped again. "Hmmm. Tola's boy, isn't it?"

"Yes, Your Majesty."

"Son of our sweet Jehudith, here?"

"The same, Your Majesty."

A murmur arose and wafted around the hall. Ezra sensed that every eye in the place was fixed upon him. He trembled inside, wondering if he had miscalculated. And then, slowly—ever so slowly—a lopsided smile broke across Ahaz's face.

"Well," said the king with a chuckle, "I see no reason to make any more of this affair than it warrants. Boys will be boys, eh? And now I think you boys had better leave us . . . before something worse happens, hmm?" He hiccuped again and waved them off.

"Yes, Your Majesty," said Ezra. Then grabbing his two friends by their sleeves, he hurried from the hall as fast as he could go.

"Like the way I handled that?" said Ezra triumphantly when they were standing together at the palace gate. "I told you guys!"

Shub scratched his ear. "I'm still not sure how you did that," he said.

"Easy. The king's had too much to drink, and an honest confession was the last thing he was expecting. It's the old element of surprise. I *knew* it would work."

Hezekiah looked up at his friend with a confused frown. "I guess I owe you one, Ezra. But I still can't help thinking that your tricks are going to catch up with you one of these days."

"Even after what just happened? *Aauughh!* What does it take to convince some people?"

Shub looked amused.

"I'm sorry," said the prince, staring down at his sandals. "I keep thinking about the prophet and . . . what that man said."

Ezra heaved a frustrated sigh. "Looks like it's time I got serious with you, Hezekiah."

"Serious?"

"That's right. Time we started your education in earnest."

"Education?"

"Mm-hm." Ezra relaxed, smiled, leaned his shoulder against the wall, and straightened his headband. "You just wait. By the time we get through, you'll see that all this grown-up talk about gods and rules and judgment and consequences is just a big joke. You'll *know* I'm right. If a kid is smart enough and lucky enough, he can get away with *anything*. You'll see!"

It wasn't far from the palace to the house of Tola ben Abihu. Even so, it took Ezra nearly an hour to get home that evening. He had a long, aimless walk through the gathering darkness. After all, there was no reason to hurry. He wasn't exactly sure what to expect when he got to his father's door, but he was pretty certain it wouldn't be pleasant. Mother was at the king's dinner, he knew that. That meant Father would be in a mood. Even prophets, messengers of God, could get into a mood. And *that* meant Ezra would probably have to listen to a lecture about idolatry and the warnings of the prophet Isaiah. No wonder he felt like dawdling.

The sun had gone down in the softly glowing distance beyond Jerusalem's western wall, and the first stars were just winking out of the deepening blue overhead. Clay oil lamps were being lit and set into niches in the walls of the houses that lined the winding cobbled lanes. Ezra could see their tiny flames blinking through the latticework shutters over the windows as he passed by.

Ezra sighed, straightened his leather headband, and kicked a big rock that lay in his path. He *had* wanted to look for some fun in the streets with the others before going home, but Hezekiah had turned him down. Said he wasn't in the mood. *That Hezekiah!* thought Ezra. As for Shub, he had told Ezra that his parents and younger brother were holding another meeting of the Remnant somewhere in the neighborhood that night. So Shub wanted to go home and practice his harp while he had the house to himself. "They don't always appreciate my music," he had explained.

So Ezra was left alone. He kicked the rock again and shuffled on.

When at last he could see the flickering lamplight in the window of his own house, he brought his feet to a stop, folded his arms, and leaned up against the wall of a house. As he eased his back against the stones, bits of loose mortar crumbled and fell to the ground, making a skittering sound on the pavement.

Consequences, Ezra thought. *"Your tricks are going to catch up with you one of these days."* Remembering what Hezekiah had said, Ezra laughed to himself. *What's the big deal? What does it matter, anyway? Can't a kid have a little fun without everybody jumping down his throat?* He stooped down, picked up a rock, and with an angry grimace, heaved it into the darkness.

"*Ai!* Ow!" came the voice of an elderly woman through the gloom. Ezra froze at the sound. The blood rushed into his face. He hadn't meant to *hit* anyone with the rock. He hadn't even realized that anyone was *there*.

The voice cried out again: "Who did that? Come out, you young ruffians!"

Ezra took to his heels, darted down a narrow side alley, and came to the door of his house by a roundabout back way.

He wasn't expecting what he found there. The doorway was jammed with people. Ezra knew at once what it was: The meeting of the Remnant that Shub had mentioned was taking place at *his* house! And it was just adjourning. His father, Tola, a short, bulky man, stood in front of the house at the edge of the street, taking leave of his guests.

Ezra knew them all by sight. There, for instance, was Shub's goody-goody younger brother, Maher-Shalal-Hash-Baz, talking with Tola for all the world as if he were some kind of miniature adult. *Maher-Shalal-Hash-Baz*— "Quick to the Plunder, Swift to the Spoil." And *some* people thought *Ezra-Elohenu* was a strange name. At nine years old, Maher was already almost as big a pain in the neck as his father. A junior prophet in the making. Maher made Hezekiah look like a wild and crazy troublemaker. Always talking about "the Lord" this and "the Lord" that and "the Son of David." It was enough to make a kid want to run off and join the Assyrian army.

Then there was Shub and Maher's mother, Abigail—a petite, energetic, frizzy-haired woman who stood in the doorway just behind her boy. Most men called their wives things like *shoshanna* (lily flower) or *yonah* (dove) or *yephath-mareh* (fair one), but Isaiah referred to *her* as *nebiah*— "the prophetess." It was all just a little too weird for Ezra.

He watched the guests emerge from the house one by one and wondered what he ought to do. After weighing his options he decided that the best thing would be to try to slip inside as the members of the Remnant crowded *out*. That way his father would be too busy saying good-bye to notice him. Having made his decision, Ezra closed in on the house.

Closer and closer he edged. He could see his father listening intently to an elderly woman who was weeping and gesturing angrily and talking rapidly about something. *Now or never!* he thought. And with that he made a sudden attempt to duck behind the woman and push his way inside. But just as he thought he was home free, he found himself looking up into the face of a tall, imposing figure: the prophet Isaiah himself.

"Well. Hello, Ezra," said the prophet. His long, dark beard, streaked with strands of silver-gray, swept down over his chest as he bent to smile at the boy. "We missed you tonight!"

Ezra gulped. He tried to look cool and collected as he gazed up into the prophet's deep-set eyes. But his heart was pounding as if it would jump up out of his chest at any moment. "Ah . . . yes. Hello . . . *adoni* Isaiah . . . sir . . ."

Just then Ezra felt the grip of a thick hand on his left shoulder. He turned to see his father's nose an inch away from his own.

"Ezra," said Tola in a frighteningly low and controlled tone, "let's go inside for a little chat."

Ezra was caught without a comeback.

Tola clamped his other hand down on his son's right shoulder and turned to the prophet. "I'm sorry, Isaiah. We'll speak again tomorrow."

"Certainly, Tola. Good night," said the prophet. Gradually, the smile on his face gave way to a sober expression made up of gathering wrinkles and creases. "Come, Abigail, Maher." Isaiah took his shawl-clad wife by the arm. Then, followed by their son, they turned and disappeared into the night.

Meanwhile, Tola hadn't released his grip on Ezra. As soon as the prophet and his family were gone, he gently guided the boy into the house and shut the door.

"Sit," he said, still in the same carefully controlled tone. He pointed to a leather-covered stool that stood in the corner of the small, stone-floored entry hall that led to the main part of the house.

Now what? thought Ezra. Assuming a nonchalant, unhurried air, he sauntered over to the stool and sat down.

"Ezra, have you been throwing rocks again?" asked his father.

"Rocks?"

"Old Hephzibah was just hit on the arm by a rock. A big one. Near our house. I can't tell for sure, but she acts as if she's badly hurt."

Ezra was beginning to tremble. "Father! You think *I* would do a thing like that?"

"What I *think* isn't the question. Did you do it?"

"I didn't do anything!" said Ezra, assuming an angry, offended air. "I didn't throw any rock at anybody." This was true in Ezra's mind, since he hadn't meant to throw the rock *at* anyone.

Tola cocked an eyebrow and looked at his son. "I see. Well, then, why don't we move on to another subject. Perhaps you wouldn't mind telling me what happened at the king's dinner party tonight?"

Ezra felt the blood rush to his heart. *How can he know about that?* "What dinner party?"

"You know very well what dinner party," replied Tola.

Ezra could see his father's round cheeks coloring above his gray-streaked beard. He could hear the hint of a tremor in his father's voice. How it had happened he didn't know, but he'd been caught. The realization turned him sullen and resentful.

"What do *you* know about any old dinner party?" he said, casting his eyes down at the floor and readjusting his headband.

"Enough. Elisabeth, one of the king's maidservants, joined the meeting of the Remnant when her evening chores were completed." Tola bent down and gave his son a piercing stare. "She took me aside and told me everything."

"So? What do you care?"

That was when his father's anger suddenly burst its carefully set boundaries. His voice rose and swelled. "What do I *care*?" he shouted. "Am I not to care about my own son's actions? Actions that bring shame upon his father's household?"

"That's all that matters to you, isn't it, Father," said Ezra without looking up. "*Your* shame. *Your* reputation. Like I'm just some kind of an extension of *you*. Well, I'm not! I'm myself!"

"Have you no respect, Ezra?" Tola went on as if he hadn't heard the boy. "If not for the king, then for Isaiah and the Remnant and everything they represent? Elisabeth said you made a shambles of the party with your antics. How can you do this to me? What a way for Tola's son to behave." He bowed his head and passed a hand over his eyes. "As if your mother's unfaithfulness to the Lord weren't enough," he added quietly.

"Leave Mother out of it," said Ezra bitterly, looking up into his father's face at last. "She can do what she likes. Why do you think that everybody has to be just like you? Even the name you gave me is about *your* beliefs, not mine."

"Ezra," said Tola, his voice dropping again, "it is not a question of *my* beliefs or *your* beliefs. It is a question of hearing and obeying the Holy One of Israel. It is a question of *truth*. Of knowing the true and living God! 'Hear, O Israel: The Lord our God, the Lord is one!' There will be terrible consequences for those who forsake the Lord and follow false gods. Haven't you heard what happened to Aaron's sons Nadab and Abihu when they offered up strange fire in the desert of Sinai? The prophet said it again as he was teaching tonight. ' "This is what you shall receive from my hand," says the Lord. "You will lie down in torment!" ' "

Ezra jumped to his feet. "Then what about King Ahaz? *He* believes in the other gods. Don't *you* have any respect for *him*?"

"Of course I respect him—as my king. But he is wrong, Ezra. Sadly and tragically wrong. He will pay a heavy price for his sins one day." Tola shook his head and added, "Perhaps he already has."

"Yeah, right. Isaiah has been saying that for as long as I can remember. And nothing bad has *ever* happened to King Ahaz."

"Believe me, my son," said Tola sadly. "The day will come. The Lord's timing is not as our own. Nor is He a man that He should delay to strike the wicked in—"

But Ezra didn't want to hear any more. "I've had enough of consequences and judgments and all that stuff about the Remnant! And nothing bad is going to happen to Mother just because she went to the king's dinner party. Why can't you just lighten up a little bit?" With that he turned and stormed out of the entry hall.

"Ezra!" shouted his father as he went. "You're not to leave this house for a week!"

But Ezra wasn't listening. He could almost feel the skin of his face steaming with frustration and anger as he ran through the house. He ducked under the low arch that led to his room, pushed through the dark-blue curtain that hung over the doorway, and flung himself down on the reed sleeping mat in the corner. He didn't bother to light a lamp but lay there staring up into the darkness, breathing heavily, his hands behind his head.

The events of the evening ran through his head scene by scene: Hezekiah's sober, serious face under the table. His mother and the king and Hanun, their heads bent together in conversation about the Assyrian gods. The pomegranates and the spilled wine and the eyes of the crowd. King Ahaz's indulgent smile. A rock flying through the darkness. Isaiah's bearded face. His father's weighty words.

Suddenly Ezra laughed. "Consequences," he said to himself aloud, getting up and going over to the little window. There he stood, staring out at the darkened city through one of the spaces in the lattice. *I'll show them. I'll show them all! Nothing bad is going to happen to Mother or me or the king or anybody else. I meant what I said to Hezekiah, and I'm going to prove it. They haven't seen anything yet.*

"Why, Jehudith?" said Tola. "*Why* must you go out again?"

It was the following evening, and Ezra was listening to his parents go through the same old tired argument. The timing couldn't have been worse. He'd made secret arrangements to meet Shub and Hezekiah after dark, and the evening was wearing away.

"This is your home," Ezra's father went on, twisting the edge of his brown robe between his hands. "Your family is here—your son, the husband who loves you. *Why* are you never content to remain at home with us?"

Tola stood in the small entry hall at the front of the house, pleading with his wife, a look of desperation on his face. Jehudith was wrapped and veiled in a cloak of midnight blue bordered with a stripe of Tyrian purple. In her right hand she held a small pitcher-shaped clay lamp. Her left hand rested on the door latch. Gold bracelets with silver baubles jingled at her wrists. Matching earrings dangled at each side of her face—a surprisingly young and pretty face for a woman of middle age.

Ezra hung back in the shadows, beyond the circle of the lamplight. He hated it when his parents fought like this. The edge in his father's voice cut him like the edge of a knife. He didn't like to hear his father speak to his mother in that tone. After all, Mother had a right do as she pleased— that's what Ezra always said. But then he had to admit that he too hated it when she went out, as she did almost every other night. Somehow it always gave him a hollow, sick feeling in the pit of his stomach to see her leave. And yet he knew that there could never be a moment's peace in the house as long as she was there.

"I really don't see why it concerns you, Tola," said Jehudith in a cold and distant voice.

Ezra could see the light of the lamp gleaming on her white teeth and glinting off her shiny red lips from within the folds of her veil. "I should think you'd be too busy with the Remnant to notice or care whether I stay or go. And I *will* go, for I want to experience new things. I want to taste the gifts of the gods. Ahaz is a brilliant, forward-thinking king. He's done wonders for Judah. I for one wish to follow his lead. And I won't let you hold me back!"

Without another word, she lifted the latch, opened the door, and slipped out into the night. Tola covered his grizzled head with his hands and stalked off into the interior of the house, muttering to himself.

It was the opportunity Ezra had been waiting for. As soon as he could no longer hear the sounds of his father's frustrated fumings, he covered himself in a cloak of his own. It was dark gray, perfect for making himself as "invisible" as possible. Slipping through the door, he found himself in the gray-cobbled, high-walled canyon of the street, darting from shadow to shadow, his sandals slapping the stones.

He found Shub, just as they'd arranged, at the dark, arched corner at the end of Mishneh Street. He too was dressed in a dark cloak. One of his father's, to judge by the way it trailed along the ground. Shub's head was bare except for its natural covering of wild black hair. Cradled in the crook of his right arm, he carried his precious *kinnor*. It was a simple harp: a small, rectangular sounding box of cypress wood, two upward-curving arms of ash, a crossbeam of the same wood, and ten strings of dried gut. Apparently Shub was looking forward to a night of music and dancing.

"Hey!" said Shub as Ezra emerged from the shadows. "Where's your tambourine?"

"You know I don't have a tambourine," said Ezra impatiently. "Where's Hezekiah?"

"He'll be here," said Shub softly. As he spoke, he caressed the strings of the *kinnor* the way Ezra had sometimes seen his father caress his mother's hair—back when they were on better terms.

Hezekiah arrived shortly, draped in a very ragged and dirty piece of sackcloth. In compliance with Ezra's instructions, he had smeared his ruddy face with a handful of ashes so that he looked every inch the wild and homeless street urchin. Shub laughed when he saw him, but Ezra eyed Hezekiah up and down and nodded with solemn approval.

"Good," he said. "It wouldn't do for anyone to recognize you where we're going tonight."

"Where *are* we going, anyway?" asked the prince, looking up at the older boy with a frown and a wrinkled forehead.

"To a place I've always wanted to see at night," answered Ezra with a confident smile. "The *bamah*—the high place—in Ophel."

"Ophel? The high place?" said Shub. "You mean the pagan altar?"

"That's right. I told you there'd be music, didn't I? There's supposed to be a festival there tonight. It'll be fun!"

Without another word Ezra set off, leading the others southward along the winding lane that led to *Ha'iyr-David*, David's City, the most ancient part of Jerusalem, and beyond it to the Potsherd Gate and the Hinnom Valley. Above them loomed the dark and lofty grandeur of the temple, and beyond that the high roofs of the royal palace. They moved as silently as cats, keeping to the shadows.

Ezra was in high spirits, pleased as he could be with his own resourcefulness. He'd show them. He'd teach Hezekiah once and for all that a kid didn't need anything but his own brains. They'd visit the high place. They'd eat and dance and sing and have a great time. And nothing bad would happen to them. Then he'd be a bigger hero than ever. It was a good feeling.

For some reason the face of Shub's younger brother popped into Ezra's mind as he made his way down the street in the moonlight, thinking these pleasant thoughts. That pudgy, snotty face, topped with a bush of ridiculous black fuzz. Ezra was glad that he was so much wiser and cleverer than that insufferable bore of a mommy's boy. *Maher-Shalal-Hash-Baz*, he thought scornfully. *Give me a break*. He turned to Shub, who was walking at his side and said it aloud in a scornful tone. "Maher-Shalal-Hash-Baz. Quick to the Plunder, Swift to the Spoil! What's that supposed to mean, anyway?"

"It means," Shub answered carefully, "that if the people don't shape up, the Assyrian army will swoop down and make fish bait out of them. Just another way of saying that your sins catch up with you. My father's very fond of that kind of thing."

Tell me about it! thought Ezra, choosing to ignore the comment.

The moon went behind a blanket of cloud as they trudged forward. From that point on, the night seemed to grow darker with every step they took. They didn't dare carry a lamp for fear of attracting attention. Every so often they stopped and peered ahead as darker blobs of blackness loomed up or lunged out at them from the heart of shallower pools of murk. They would laugh at themselves nervously when they realized that the blob was nothing but a cat or the swaying limb of a stunted acacia tree. But Ezra couldn't help wishing that the moon would come out again. He'd never realized that Jerusalem could be so dark at night. He didn't *really* know the night side of the city at all.

On they walked, staying close to the wall. As they came around a bend in the lane, Ezra could see an orange glow rising beyond the dark shapes of the huddled houses and shops. The glow pulsed, fluttered, and reflected dully along the rough vertical edge of a tall structure of stone. The Tower of Ophel.

"That's it!" said Ezra excitedly. "See? There's a fire on the altar! The high place is just below the tower. There's an alley that turns to the left just before you get to David's City. It'll take us straight there. Not much farther now. Follow me!"

Quickening his pace, Ezra pushed on. But he was stopped in his tracks by a thud, a shout, and the jangling of harp strings behind him.

"*Ummpphh!* My *kinnor!*"

Oh no, thought Ezra. *Shub tripped again!* Wheeling around and peering through the darkness, he searched for Shub and found him lying on his back, the precious harp clutched tightly to his chest. His long legs were sprawled across another dark shape that lay beneath him on the ground. At first Ezra thought that Shub had fallen over Hezekiah. But no—Hezekiah was standing right beside him.

"What happened, Ezra?" asked the prince, staring down at the two prostrate figures.

"Oh, it's just that clumsy Shub again," he answered. "What did you trip over this time, Shub?"

Ezra bent down to get a closer look at the unlucky individual who lay squirming beneath Shub's long legs. It was hard to see anything now that the light of the moon was gone. He leaned closer . . . and closer. Then, with a gasp, he recognized the face at last.

It was Old Hephzibah!

"Help me," moaned Old Hephzibah in a pitiful voice, stretching out her hand to Ezra. "Help an old woman who has lost the use of her arm!"

Ezra stood and gaped. He pulled the hood of his cloak closer around his face. Old Hephzibah! Dressed in black, and with her arm in a sling. The very *last* person he'd expected to see. He felt he ought to speak to her, but didn't know what to say. He knew he should help her, but was afraid of being recognized. Instead of doing either, he reached down, took Shub by the hand, and pulled him to his feet.

"Come on!" he whispered fiercely. "Let's get out of here!"

Just then he felt a pair of strong hands seize him by the shoulder. They gripped him like a vise, so sharply that a bolt of fiery pain shot down his arm like a flash of lightning. Then they spun him around. Suddenly he found himself staring into a face that looked for all the world like a skull wrapped in a discolored sheepskin. The mouth opened, and a foul odor of red wine mixed with stale cheese invaded Ezra's nostrils.

"You heard her, boy," said a gruff voice. "The old lady needs help. How about it? A scrap of bread for her and a few coins for *me!* Eh?"

Suddenly the moon jumped out from behind the clouds again. In its silvery light, Ezra saw the flash of a dull blade before his face.

"Let me go!" he shouted, struggling to free himself from the man's grasp.

"Thief! Thief!" shouted Hezekiah. In the next instant he and Shub were at Ezra's side fighting furiously to rescue their friend. Ezra heard the man cry out as Hezekiah landed a solid punch on his bony jaw. The strings of the harp sounded in sympathy as Shub, too, got in a swift kick. It was too much for Ezra's assailant. Howling in pain, he released his grip on the boy and fled into the darkness, cursing as he went.

"Whoa!" muttered Shub, breathing heavily and checking his precious *kinnor* for damage. "You didn't tell us it would be like *this!* I thought we were going to have *fun* tonight."

"Don't worry," said Ezra shakily, dusting himself off, straightening his leather headband, and pulling his hood back up over his head. "We *will*."

Old Hephzibah twisted and turned, groveling upon the ground. *"Unnhhh!"* she groaned.

"Ezra," said Hezekiah, taking his friend by the arm, "what about *her?* Don't you think we should . . . ?"

"Yeah," put in Shub. "My father always says that poor widows deserve—"

"Not now, *hamor*," whispered Ezra, a little more vehemently than was necessary. "We're almost there!"

"Don't call me a donkey," said Shub.

"Well, then, don't preach a sermon. We've got to keep going or it'll be too late!" Without allowing his friends to say another word, he pulled them away from the old woman and in the direction of the orange glow. He was trembling inside more violently than he would have liked to admit.

They reached the dirty side alley Ezra had mentioned and turned into it. Here the blackness of the night was broken at intervals by the glow of lamps, glimpsed dimly through broken window lattices and torn curtains. There were torches too, and fires burning in clay pots, and bronze braziers under the cover of tattered awnings and low, arched doorways.

"Don't be scared," Ezra whispered nervously to Hezekiah, who walked hunched over at his side. "It's just one of those poor neighborhoods you're always hearing about. That's all." But inside his only thought was to get out of that alley as quickly as he could.

Around the fires huddled the dark shapes of strange, gaunt men and women, their faces hideous and unnatural in the blood-red light of the flames. A yellow-skinned, black-haired woman, her head bound with strands of gold coins, her face aglow with stripes of red paint, turned and beckoned to them with a crooked finger as they passed. Ezra pretended not to see her. A sallow-faced man with a pale, stringy beard studied them closely out of his single eye. Little boys shouted and assaulted them with handfuls of rotten dates. Soon they put all thought of dignity aside and began to run.

As the end of the alley came into sight, Ezra became aware of an odd fluttering sensation in the pit of his stomach. Not that he was afraid. There was nothing to be afraid of, he told himself. *He* was clever enough to get himself and his friends through *anything*. Even this.

They reached their goal under a juicy hail of some other kind of fruit—probably pomegranates, Ezra guessed—and emerged into a large, open square. Directly ahead of them, leaning menacingly over the scene in the reddish light, was the Tower of Ophel itself. The tower was a fortification of massive stone built for the city's defense by Hezekiah's grandfather, Jotham. At its base, in the exact center of the plaza—a space contained on one side by the city wall and on the three remaining sides by the surrounding shops and houses—was a sight that took their breath away.

"Hoi!" exclaimed the prince, leaning on Ezra's arm. "This *does* look fun!"

It did. The place was filled with people dressed in bright, multicolored clothing. Some of the women wore loosely wrapped, gauzy pastel robes such as Ezra had sometimes seen on foreigners from Ammon and Philistia. Headbands of shimmering gold dangled from their foreheads and down over their noses. Their feet and arms were bare, and many of them had painted the skin of their faces and legs.

Men dressed in the Assyrian or Egyptian style, bare-chested and in wraparound loincloths of embroidered wool, dashed here and there with torches and platters of food. Some of them wore masks of hideous or hilarious design. From what Ezra could see, the crowd was made up of people from every class in Jerusalem: wealthy officials and courtiers; well-to-do merchants; honest working folk; dirty, sunken-cheeked beggars. All of them were laughing and talking merrily.

Some of the people had spread blankets on the ground and were reclining in groups of threes or fours, dining eagerly on bunches of grapes and raisin cakes. Others were downing great silver cups of wine. Still others were dancing to the beat of the small *tabor* drum and the music of the pipes and flutes. The air was filled with smoke and cooking smells and the confused jangle of hundreds of talking and shouting voices.

Ranged around the square were ranks of wooden poles, ten to fifteen feet in height, each one carved from top to bottom with strange, intertwining shapes. Some of the poles had ribbons of white, purple, or scarlet cloth fluttering from their tips. It was like a forest of bright color and endless motion. *Asherah poles*, Ezra said to himself when he saw them. *So that's what they look like.*

"This is what I've been waiting for!" said Shub, gripping his *kinnor* tightly under his arm and heading for the nearest group of musicians. "I'll see you two a little later."

"What's *that?*" asked Hezekiah, tightening his grip on Ezra's arm and pointing, wide-eyed, to a pyramid of stone steps that culminated in a peak of curiously carved stone and a tongue of bright flame. The fire leaped and bowed, casting an eerie glow over the entire scene, illuminating the tower and even painting the distant walls of the temple a dusky orange.

"That's what we came for," answered Ezra in an excited whisper. "The high place! The altar of Baal and Asherah. And see what I told you? All of these people are having a great time. Nothing bad is happening to any of them."

"It *does* look like fun," Hezekiah said hesitantly. "Do you think we could get some food?"

"Why not?" laughed Ezra. "Come on! What are we waiting for?"

With that they plunged into the thick of the festive crowd. Ezra's spirits were high, his heart light. The evening *had* gotten off to a rough start, he told himself, but it was all going to be worth it now. This was the payoff. He laughed aloud as a bare-chested man in a satiny red turban slapped him on the back and offered him a hunk of roasted meat, still on the bone, sizzling and dripping with red juices.

"Straight from the sacrifice," the man said, his narrow black eyes sparkling. "Share it around, share it around!"

Ezra and Hezekiah sat down on a thick, striped rug of red-and-white strands of wool, holding the shank of meat between them. Greedily they bent into it, tearing the moist flesh from the bone, scattering spots of grease and blood down the fronts of their cloaks and over the carpet.

"Hey!" laughed Ezra. "Look at Shub!"

It was obvious that the prophet's son was in his glory. There he stood, in the middle of a group of prancing celebrants, plucking at the strings of his *kinnor* in a fit of pure pleasure. Through the rhythmic flash of the dancers' bare arms and legs, Ezra and Hezekiah could see him, a look of ecstasy on his long, high-cheekboned face, his hair wilder and more uncontrolled than they had ever seen it. *Yes*, thought Ezra, wiping his chin and licking his lips, *I'm really glad we came*.

That's when he saw a face—a face he hadn't expected to see in that wild place. He didn't recognize it at first, perhaps because it seemed so unlikely that the face would appear there. Or maybe it was the unusual way in which the face was framed—in a headdress curiously like that of an Egyptian nobleman, with a bold stripe of red paint across the forehead and eyes. But recognize it he did. When he did, so great was his shock that he dropped his end of the shank bone and grabbed Hezekiah by the shoulder.

"Hezekiah!" he said in a sharp whisper, pointing with his other hand. "Look! That man who was with your father at the dinner the other night—Hanun! Does *he* worship at the high place?"

"Why not?" said the prince with a shrug. "Just about everyone at court does."

For a moment Ezra feared that Hanun would recognize them. But he soon came to realize that there was no danger of that. The noble courtier's attention was absorbed, his eyes fixed upon the bright eyes of a veiled woman whom he was leading by the arm, a woman dressed in a cloak of midnight blue edged with Tyrian purple. Reeling and swaying in time with the music, the two of them passed very close to the spot where Ezra and Hezekiah were sitting. That was when Ezra heard a voice—a melodic voice and a silvery laugh.

"No, you silly man," the voice said with a giggle. "I certainly won't— not unless you ask me *nicely!*"

Then the two figures slipped away together, through the forest of Asherah poles and into the heart of the heaving, dancing crowd.

With a strange, sinking feeling in the pit of his stomach, Ezra released his grip on Hezekiah and dropped his hands to his sides.

"Hezekiah," he said flatly, "go get Shub. I think we'd better go home."

"Home?" said Hezekiah, looking up from the hunk of meat in surprise. "But why? We just got here."

"Don't be stupid!" said Ezra irritably, shaking himself and straightening his leather headband. "It's getting late. I don't want my father to find out that I've been here. Now go on!"

He got to his feet, wiping his greasy hands on his cloak as the bewildered Hezekiah scurried over to Shub. Ezra stared down at his fingers, sticky with blood and fat. He shook himself again and tried to believe that it must have been his imagination.

The woman's voice had sounded exactly like his mother's.

CHAPTER 5

Ezra awoke late the next morning to the sound of a raven complaining loudly in an almond tree just outside his window. "Get up! Get up!" the rude bird seemed to say.

Somewhere out in the street, children were shouting and playing a game of Wedding and Funeral. He could tell by the sound of one of them piping on a little wooden flute. Beyond them, from someplace even farther away, came the faint notes of a harp. *Shub's already up and at it*, he thought disgustedly.

He raised himself on one elbow and pushed the dark curls out of his eyes. Already the sun was high enough to dart sharp little javelins of light down through the spaces in the window lattice and straight into his face. Why did it have to be so bright? The light was offensive to him. It reflected off the ceiling and bounced off the walls. It revealed every crack, dip, and bump in the whitewashed mud plaster that covered the inside of his room. Ezra groaned and shoved his knuckles into his eye sockets. Then he lay down again and covered his head with his woolen blanket.

That's when he heard another sound—a sound smaller and softer than any of the others, and much closer. It was the curtain at his door swishing aside. This was followed by the pad of footsteps crossing the stone-flagged floor of the room. Then came a tug at the blanket.

"Ezra—are you going to sleep the day away?" His father's voice was gentle and quiet, but something about it made the boy jump inside. He threw off the blanket and sat straight up.

"I *am* up!" he said loudly. "I mean, I've *been* up for a while, only I just didn't want to *get* up—that's all."

The amused twinkle in Tola's eye was like a mirror in which Ezra was forced to look at the ridiculous image of his own confusion. There was the slightest hint of a smile playing at the corners of his father's mouth. That bothered Ezra. He hated it when his father shouted at him, but it was that ironic smile of his that made him *really* angry.

"Here," said Tola, reaching for Ezra's rough-spun yellow-and-golden-brown tunic where it lay on a stool next to the wall—just where Ezra had left it when he came in during the small hours of the morning. "Get dressed, and we'll have some breakfast."

Tola picked up the garment. Beneath it lay the gray, woolen cloak Ezra had worn to the high place, the smeared grease and blood from the roasted calf shank clearly evident down its front side. Seeing it, his father stopped and stared for a brief moment with parted lips and raised eyebrows. Then he simply tossed the tunic to his son, saying, "Come on. The food's waiting in the other room."

Compared with Ezra's cramped sleeping quarters, the main room of the house was spacious and airy. There were two arched windows looking out into the street. The floor was of stone and the walls were of white-washed plaster. Overhead, the roof was supported by six bare rafter poles of oak. In the center of the room, Ezra's father had spread out a mat of woven reeds. On the mat lay a wooden bowl of goat's milk, a platter of disk-shaped barley loaves, and another bowl of *leben*, or soft white cheese.

"Sit. Eat," said Tola. He himself sat cross-legged on the mat and reached for the platter of bread. Ezra followed his example, watching his father warily.

Then, with a sudden jolt, Ezra remembered something. "Where's mother?" he asked.

"Still asleep," his father answered, calmly breaking a circular loaf down the middle. "She came in even later than you did," he added without looking up.

"Me?" cried Ezra, dropping his own loaf in his lap. He'd taken every precaution to make sure that no one heard him come home. "What do you mean? Are you accusing me—?"

"Ezra," said Tola, looking straight at his son, "there's no need to shout. Let's reason together like men."

"That'll be the day," scoffed Ezra. "To you I'm still a baby. To you I've got no life of my own . . . and neither does Mother!"

Ezra thought he saw his father wince. But all Tola said was, "I've been thinking about what you said the other night. I think I understand how you feel."

"What *I* said?"

"Yes. About being yourself instead of an extension of me. And about your name. I know how hard it must be for you to . . . to be *my* son."

Ezra took a bite of bread and chewed it slowly, staring up at his father's bearded face. He didn't know what to say. He wasn't sure what was coming.

"The prophet feels very strongly . . ." Tola paused and then went on after a moment, "*I* feel very strongly, that we *must* raise up reminders for the coming generation . . . reminders that the Lord, *He* is God. Otherwise all is lost. We must *be* those reminders. Isaiah stated it so very clearly in one of the earliest speeches he ever gave in the temple courts. That was years and years ago, before you were born, but I remember it as if it were yesterday:

> Bind up the testimony
>> and seal up the law among my disciples.
> I will wait for the Lord,
>> who is hiding his face from the house of Jacob.
> I will put my trust in him.
>> Here am I, and the children the Lord has given me. We are signs
>>> and symbols in Israel from the Lord Almighty, who dwells on
>>> Mount Zion.

"That, you see," his father concluded, "is why we've given you names like 'A Remnant Shall Return' and 'A Help Is Our God.' We want the people to remember, every time they see you, that God is God and that He doesn't change from one generation to the next!"

"That's great for *you*, I guess," said Ezra bitterly. "But what about us? What about me and Shub? What if we don't want to be 'signs and symbols'?"

"Ezra, it isn't a question of what we want. As the prophet Isaiah says—"

"What do I care what Isaiah says?" shouted Ezra. "He's just an old fanatic, that's all! Remember when he walked around the city barefoot and in a loincloth for three years? Is that what you call sane?"

Tola laid the rest of his loaf on the mat and stared at it thoughtfully. After a pause he continued in an even quieter voice.

"A 'fanatic,' you say. Yes. Perhaps you have good reason to think so. But do you know what it is like for a man"—and at this he looked up and fixed his son with his calm, dark eyes—"to be owned by Another? To be no longer his own? Do you know what Isaiah saw in the temple while he was still a very young man?"

"How would I know?"

"It was the year King Uzziah died. Young Isaiah had gone in to pray before the altar. Suddenly the whole place was filled with wings and smoke and a living stream of blinding light. That light was like the flowing skirts of a great fiery royal robe, pouring, cascading down from the throne of God. Everything started shaking and trembling! And seraphim were shouting, 'Holy! Holy! Holy!'"

Ezra stopped chewing and stared. "So what did he do?"

"He didn't know what to do," answered Tola. "He just said, 'Woe to me! For I am a man of unclean lips!' That's how it made him feel. And then he saw one of the seraphs take a hot coal from the altar with a pair of tongs. The angel brought the coal over to Isaiah and reached out and touched his lips with it!"

"With a *hot* coal?"

"Yes! And the angel said, 'See, this has touched your lips; your guilt is taken away and your sin atoned for.' And then Isaiah heard the voice of the Lord Himself saying, 'Whom shall I send? And who will go for us?' So Isaiah said, 'Here am I. Send me!'

"So you see," Tola concluded slowly after another pause, "Isaiah has a good reason for being a 'fanatic,' as you call him. He's *seen* the Lord! He belongs to Him completely. And that's not always easy . . . when a man has to think about the needs of his wife and children. I know," he added, putting one hand to his forehead, "how difficult it can be."

Ezra gazed at his father as he continued to eat. He had never seen him quite like this before. He wondered if he had ever really known his father. What was it like to be a prophet, to experience such strange events? Ezra felt as if his brain were too small to wrap itself around the things he'd been hearing. Could this really be what his father had been talking about all these years? Not rules and regulations and religious ceremonies, but wings and light and smoke and burning coals and flying creatures? And a God who really comes down and talks to people?

"Father," he said after a moment, "where does Mother go when she . . . goes out?"

Again the lines in Tola's face deepened. He shut his eyes and pinched the bridge of his nose between the thumb and forefinger of his right hand. His mouth hardened into a straight line. Ezra wondered if he were about to cry. He thought his father looked very much as if he were fighting back tears. Then suddenly Tola braced himself, opened his eyes, and looked up.

"That," he said to his son, "is something you'll have to ask *her*. Only she can answer that. But I can tell you this: The matters we discussed the other night—Ahaz and his flirtation with the foreign gods—are very serious indeed. Believe me, my son, any man—or woman—who would play with strange fire must beware lest he—or she—be burned."

There it was again! That same old recurring refrain. Serious consequences. Strange fire. "Oh, come on, Father!" said Ezra. He could feel the hot flush rising in his cheeks. "You don't expect me to believe that about Mother, do you? What does it hurt if she goes out and has a little fun with . . . her friends?"

"I say nothing about your mother," answered Tola. "I only say this: The Lord is a jealous God! He will not accept second place. And as for the gods of the Syrians and the Assyrians—the Baals and Asherahs, and worst of all the Red King Molech . . ." He paused and shuddered. "Well, all I can tell you is that people do abominable things in their names. Abominable things as part of their worship."

"I don't believe it!" said Ezra. "King Ahaz may be an old grouch sometimes, and he does drink too much, but he's basically a good man. And he's done good things for the country. Mother says so. I can't picture him doing anything *abominable!*"

"Ezra," said Tola looking straight at his son, "has Hezekiah ever told you about his brothers?"

"Hezekiah doesn't have any brothers."

For a moment Tola bowed his head and held it between his hands. Then he looked up and said, "Ezra, the Red King is the bloody king of all the kings of the nations. Molech doesn't grant his favors for nothing. And so the kings of the earth make horrible offerings to him. Their own sons . . . they cause them to pass through the fire. Strange fire. Into the belly of the gruesome idol itself! I dare not speak of it further."

"No!" shouted Ezra jumping to his feet. "I don't believe any of that! King Ahaz wouldn't do such a thing. Mother wouldn't have anything to do with it. It's all just a story told by that fanatical prophet to turn people away from the new gods!"

And with that he threw down what was left of his bread and ran out into the street to look for Shub.

No sooner had Ezra left his father's house than he was obliged to pass the circle of children who were playing Wedding and Funeral in the street. It was a very large circle by this time, for more than twenty children had joined the game, and it covered the narrow street from one side to the other. Ezra realized at once that he couldn't pass the circle at all. He'd have to walk right through the middle of it to get to the place where he thought Shub must be sitting with his harp. That was the base of a narrow flight of stone steps that connected Ezra's street with Mishneh Street up the hill.

Ezra stopped, straightened his leather headband, and sighed. *Kids*, he thought. He would have preferred to avoid any contact with the neighborhood children this morning.

"Ezra!" shouted a round-faced little boy in a black-and-white-striped tunic. "Hey, it's Ezra! Come on, Ezra. Play with us."

Oh, great! thought Ezra. "Forget it, Jonathan," he yelled.

"Play us something, Gershom," called a petite girl in a brown robe.

Immediately an older boy in sheepskin began to play a tune on his wooden flute. It was a slow, sad air, set in a minor key and filled with the haunting, empty spaces of the Judean wilderness beyond the city walls.

"Funeral!" shouted a dark-haired girl, jumping up and clapping her hands with excitement. At once the smile on her face gave way to a grim and piteous frown. She covered her head with a black shawl and began to parade around the edge of the circle with heavy, weary steps, wringing her hands and wailing as she went. The music droned on, and one by one the other children got to their feet and followed her example.

Ezra stood with folded arms, shifting his weight from one foot to the other. *This is ridiculous,* he thought. *I've got no time for kids' games today!*

"Come on, Ezra," called the little girl in the brown robe. "Funeral! Funeral! Come on."

Ignoring her, Ezra shoved his way past several of the "mourners" and started across the circle. But just as he got to the center of the open space, the tune changed, suddenly jumping to a higher key, dropping its sad halftones, and shifting into a happy, bouncing dance rhythm. Most of the children caught the change immediately. The girls threw off their veils and began to spin and twirl on their toes. The boys lifted their hands into the air and hopped up and down.

"Wedding!" yelled several voices at once. "Wedding! Wedding!"

"You're out!" shouted the small boy in the black-and-white tunic, pointing at a pudgy, curly-headed girl who was still moving very slowly and had neglected to remove the shawl from her head. "You're out! Wedding! The funeral's over. You too, Ezra. You're out!"

Give me a break, thought Ezra in disgust. "Get out of my way," he snorted, glaring down at the boy and shoving him roughly aside. "I've got better things to do." Then he broke through the other side of the circle and took off running up the street.

He hadn't gone far—only a hundred paces or so to a narrow spot where the canyonlike street curved to the right—when another sound stopped him short. It was a sound that chilled him to the bone and made his hair stand on end, in spite of the bright morning light that streamed down over the tiled and wattled roofs of the houses. It was the sound of a voice. The voice of an old woman.

It was Old Hephzibah's voice.

"Alms! Alms!" cried white-haired Old Hephzibah from her seat on the stony gray doorstep of a house just beyond the bend in the street. Her arm was still in a sling of dirty brown wool, and she sat leaning on the end of a crooked walking staff of gnarled olivewood. "Alms for a poor old woman who can no longer work to support herself."

Ezra stood paralyzed. *This can't be happening. It's like I can't get away from the old witch!* A cold sweat broke out on his forehead. His hands and knees began to shake. He wasn't scared, he told himself. What was there to be scared of? But he *was* concerned about the success of his new strategy. He couldn't let her see him. It would spoil everything.

"Alms! Alms! Alms for a poor old widow with a broken arm!"

He had to get past her somehow. He had to link up with Shub and explain his plan for that night and get him to communicate it to Hezekiah. He looked around for some way of escape. The house on his right had an outdoor stairway. *That's it!* he thought.

Without a moment's hesitation, he turned and ran. Up the steps he dashed as if pursued by Death itself. Gaining the roof of the house, he rushed across to the low parapet at the other side, and from there he vaulted to the roof of the next house. *Lucky the houses are built so close together here*, he thought as he made his way across that roof as well and repeated the process.

At the fifth house he found another outdoor stairway and descended to the street just at the spot where the lane of narrow stairs climbed the hill to Mishneh Street. Shub was right where he had expected to find him, sitting on the first step. Ezra breathed a sigh of relief as he ran over to greet his friend.

"Shub!" he called. But Shub didn't hear him. There he sat, lost to the world, his precious *kinnor* cradled in the crook of his left arm. The fingers of his right hand flew back and forth over the ten gut strings, plucking out a stream of chords and bright single notes. It was clear that Shub was deaf to everything but his own music. His head was back, his eyes closed, his thick black hair flying in every conceivable direction as he swayed in time to the melody. Then, as Ezra watched, Shub opened his mouth and began to sing:

> I will sing for the one I love
>> a song about his vineyard:
> My loved one had a vineyard
>> on a fertile hillside.
> He dug it up and cleared it of stones
>> and planted it with the choicest vines.
> He built a watchtower in it
>> and cut out a winepress as well.
> Then he looked for a crop of good grapes,
>> but it yielded only bad fruit.

Ezra was entranced. He was no expert when it came to music, but somehow he felt that he'd never heard anything quite so lovely in all his life. The melody gripped him and held him. It was strong and sweet, distant and sad.

> Now I will tell you
>> what I am going to do to my vineyard:
> I will take away its hedge,
>> and it will be destroyed;
> I will break down its wall,
>> and it will be trampled.
> I will make it a wasteland.

Ezra had never heard Shub sing before—poor, clumsy Shub. He had always known that Shub played the *kinnor*, but . . . such music! He rubbed his eyes. He couldn't believe that these sounds were coming from his friend's fingers and mouth.

> The vineyard of the Lord Almighty
>> is the house of Israel,
> and the men of Judah

are the garden of his delight.
    And he looked for justice,
        but saw bloodshed;
    for righteousness,
        but heard cries of distress.

The song ended as abruptly as it had begun. Shub let his right hand drop to his side. His chin fell onto his chest, and he sat there for a moment, eyes closed. Stealthily, quietly, Ezra approached and laid a hand on his shoulder.

"Wedding!" said Ezra with a loud laugh.

Shub started violently and opened his eyes. Then, recognizing Ezra, he relaxed and smiled. "Actually," he said, "I'd say it's more funeral-like."

"But it's a love song—right?"

"Yes. About a lost love. It's a very sad song, really."

"Where'd you learn it? Is it yours?"

"Oh no!" said Shub with a little self-deprecating laugh. "My father wrote it."

Your father? thought Ezra. He pictured the towering, daunting figure of Isaiah, the stern face framed in curling side locks and a flowing, gray-streaked beard. *That stuffy old goat writes songs like that?*

"Well," Ezra said, straightening his headband and clearing his throat, "it was pretty good. Not bad at all, really."

"Thanks," said Shub, his cheeks coloring slightly.

"Yeah. But that's not why I came."

"Why, then?"

"Shub, your father knows about these things. Where do we go to find a . . . Molech festival?"

"Molech? Are you crazy?"

"No. This is important, Shub! I want you and Hezekiah and my father—especially my father—to see. We went to the high place last night, and nothing bad happened. We can go to the altar of Molech too. That'll really show 'em!"

"But Ezra, do you know what happens there?"

Ezra laughed. "Oh, sure. My father tried to scare me with all those stories. Now, do you know how to get there?"

"Well," Shub answered slowly, leaning his cheek against the curve of his harp and caressing the strings, "I've *heard* that it's outside the city. In the Hinnom Valley. South . . . through the Potsherd Gate, on a little rise of hilly ground under a big terebinth tree."

"Good. You get Hezekiah and meet me right here after dark. Bring your *kinnor* and be ready for a *really* good time!"

"But Ezra, I—"

"Listen, Shub. Are you my friend or not?"

"Of course I am."

"And are you as sick as I am of all this Remnant stuff—this business of keeping up our *fathers'* reputations at the expense of our own lives?"

"Well, sure. You know I am."

"All right, then. Bring Hezekiah. You'll see. They'll *all* see! Nothing bad will happen. And then they won't be able to say another word about it. Ever."

That afternoon Ezra fell asleep over his lessons. It could have happened to anyone. Mishael, the scribe who tutored Ezra and six other boys in one of the small priestly chambers off the temple courtyard, was about as dull as a teacher could possibly be. He was a thin little man with a gray beard and curling white earlocks. His long, pointed nose stuck out beyond the shadow of the blue-bordered shawl covering his head. His voice would drone on in a midrange monotone as he lectured at great length about the Levitical prescriptions for the cleansing of lepers or the proper way to write the letter *zayin*.

Under Mishael's hypnotic influence, in the dark coolness of the stone-walled chamber, Ezra could have easily dropped off almost anytime. And today he was seriously short on sleep as a result of the previous night's events. All through the first part of the lesson, his eyes drooped and the yawns came thick and fast. When the scribe's back was turned and the other boys were busy practicing their letters with stylus and clay palette, Ezra closed his eyes and rested his head in his hands—just for a moment or two.

But how strange! No sooner had he bowed his head, than it seemed to him that a thin, high string of harp notes floated into the room and began falling on the paving stones like sparkling drops of rain.

Shub? thought Ezra. But no, it couldn't be. Shub couldn't possibly be there. Shub's father gave him his lessons at home. And yet the sound of his friend's *kinnor* was unmistakable. Even more unmistakable was the clear tone of Shub's voice as the harp notes blended with the words of the song:

What more could have been done for my vineyard
    than I have done for it?
When I looked for good grapes,
    why did it yield only bad?

Ezra lifted his head and looked around the room for Shub. Nowhere could he see the tall, gangly form of his friend. But what he *did* see caused him to open his mouth and gape in disbelief.

Wings. The whole place was full of wings. Transparent wings. Transparent faces too: some smiling, some stern, some etched with pain, others flaming with fiery indignation. They all seemed to be made of billowing smoke and flowing, liquid light, so that Ezra could glimpse the forms of Mishael and his fellow students right through them. And up near the ceiling, in the right front corner of the room, was a blinding blaze like the eye of the sun. What looked like great folds of a large sheet of gold cloth poured down from the heart of it onto the schoolroom floor.

And he looked for justice,
    but saw bloodshed;
for righteousness,
    but heard cries of distress.

On and on the voice sang, changing gradually as the song progressed. Now it was the voice of his father, now of the prophet Isaiah. Now it was his mother's voice, sweet and melodic as a cooing dove's, but faint and fading into the distance. Then it became the voice of Shub's brother, Maher-Shalal-Hash-Baz, whose pudgy, fuzz-topped face leered down at Ezra from among the other faces and wings, taunting, accusing, warbling a tattletale singsong.

Ezra tore his eyes away from the face of the nine-year-old junior prophet and focused them on Mishael's back. As he did so, the music of the song slowly deteriorated and faded into the scribe's dry monotone.

Then, as he watched, his teacher turned and began walking straight toward him, his long-nosed face perfectly hidden within the shadow of his
scribal head covering.

"For righteousness," droned Mishael's voice. "For righteousness. He
looked for righteousness, but heard cries of distress."

Ezra cringed as the man drew near and bent over him. The spindly
little scribe stopped, drew back the veil from his face and—it was the face
of Old Hephzibah! She reached out with her one good arm and aimed a
bony finger straight at Ezra.

"Who will go?" she demanded in her high, creaking voice. "Whom
shall we send? Who will go for us? Is it you? You young ruffian! Is it you?
Is it *you*?"

"No!" shouted Ezra. "No! Not me!"

"Who will show us the correct way to write the letter *tsadhe*?" droned
the voice of his teacher. "Will you, Ezra?"

"No! No!" Ezra screamed, jumping up from the place where he had
been sitting on the cool stone floor. "Not me!"

Mishael leaned over him with a puzzled look in his eyes and a single
drop of sweat glistening on the end of his pointed nose. "Ezra! What in
the name of Zion is *wrong* with you?"

"N-nothing," answered Ezra. He glanced around and saw that the
other boys were all laughing at him. "I-I'm sick, teacher, that's all. Awful
sick!" He groaned to strengthen his case. "I think I'd better go home!"

"I suppose you'd better," said Mishael in a distressed tone, backing
away from his student with a look of alarm.

Ezra got up in a daze and stumbled out the door.

CHAPTER
8

Soon Tola learned of his son's strange and sudden sickness, for Mishael lost no time in reporting it to him. Tola confined Ezra to his room for the rest of the afternoon and evening, explaining that a boy so seriously ill should not leave his bed until a qualified physician or man of God had a chance to examine him.

Tola even hinted that he might ask the prophet Isaiah himself to make a house call. At this suggestion, Ezra perked up and insisted that he was feeling much better. But Tola was unrelenting. Ezra was not to leave his room until the hour of his lessons the following day at the earliest.

There was no supper to speak of that night—just more of the same round loaves and *leben* he had shared with his father that morning. Ezra's mother had gone out again.

Ezra ate his meager meal alone and in silence, sitting on his reed sleeping mat as the last slanting rays of the red sun faded from his window. Tola's measures were seriously complicating his plans to meet Shub and Hezekiah at the base of the stone stairway after dark. But he hadn't given up hope. This wasn't anything he couldn't handle. *I can still sneak out the door after Father goes to bed*, he told himself.

But then he found out that the door was going to be blocked that night—blocked in a most unexpected and frustrating way. Apparently Tola had invited a houseguest to come and sleep in the front entry hall— the last houseguest Ezra would *ever* have chosen to sleep under the same roof with him.

"Old Hephzibah," he whined when his father told him. "You can't be serious!"

"It's the least we can do for her, Ezra," Tola responded. "She's old. She's a widow. And now that she's hurt her arm, she can't possibly fend for herself. If there's one thing I've learned from the prophet, it's that the Lord wants us to look out for people like Old Hephzibah. Isaiah has said it many times:

> Defend the cause of the fatherless,
>   plead the case of the widow. . . .
> Provide the poor wanderer with shelter. . . .
> Then your light will break forth like the dawn. . . .
> Then your righteousness will go before you.

"I really don't think we have any choice except to take her in."

That absolutely settled it. Rendezvous or no rendezvous, there was no way Ezra was going to wait around that house for a confrontation with Old Hephzibah. He just *had* to get out. So as soon as his father left the room, he grabbed his cloak and took the only way of escape that was left to him.

Off came the window lattice. Up onto the sill went Ezra. Then, leaning out the window as far as he could, he laid hold of the nearest branch of the almond tree that grew outside and swung himself out. The scent of the almond blossoms invaded his nostrils. The gentle night breeze brushed his cheek. He was out; he was free! It was great to be alive.

He found the others waiting for him at the bottom of the stairway leading to Mishneh Street. Shub was there with his precious *kinnor*. Hezekiah had covered himself in the same ragged, ash-smeared sackcloth robe he had worn the previous evening. Overhead, the first stars were gleaming dully through a gauzy veil of gathering cloud and mist. Ezra took a deep breath and straightened his headband. This was going to be his night of nights. The making of a true hero.

"Well," he said, spreading his feet and folding his arms, "I'd say it's time we got going. What do you guys say?"

Hezekiah got up from the step where he was sitting, glanced at the sky, and drew his cloak closer around his shoulders. "Where are you taking us this time?"

"Didn't Shub tell you?"

Hezekiah looked at Shub. Shub shrugged his shoulders. "No, Shub didn't tell me. As a matter of fact, he's been acting pretty funny about the whole thing. I almost didn't come. I figured you must be up to something *really* bad this time. You're *going* to get caught one of these days, Ezra, and I don't know if I want to be around when it happens."

Ezra laughed. "So what if I do? What's it to you? And anyway, you *did* come—which shows that you *know* I'm right after all."

"I don't know about that." Hezekiah bit his lip, rubbed his right temple, and sat down on the step again. "I'm not sure *why* I came. I guess there are some things I have to find out for myself."

"Whatever," said Ezra impatiently. "So do you still want to know where we're going?"

Hezekiah looked up. "I've got an idea, but . . . go ahead and tell me."

"All right, then." Ezra drew himself up to his full height, pushed the dark curls out of his face, and smiled. "We're going to a *Molech* festival."

Shub shuddered at the name of the Red King. Hezekiah set his jaw, folded his hands in his lap, and stared down at them. "I had a feeling you'd say that," he said.

"So are you still coming?" Ezra asked.

Hezekiah didn't answer right away. He just bit his lip and kept staring down at his two thumbs where they lay locked in his lap. His face was pale and his eyes looked glassy. Ezra stared at him and shifted his weight from one foot to the other. He felt very uncomfortable for some reason. *That Hezekiah. Scared and worried again.* It was the same old story. And yet, somehow, there was something different about it this time. *Well, he can go on home if he wants to*, Ezra told himself. *I've had just about enough of his worrying anyhow.*

"I don't *want* to go," Hezekiah said at last. "But . . . but maybe I *should.*"

Shub perked up at this. "Should?" he said. "What do you mean *should?*"

"I need to know . . ." Hezekiah said slowly, "exactly what happened to them."

"Them?" Ezra shot a questioning glance at Shub. Shub looked down at his *kinnor.*

"I've only heard rumors," Hezekiah continued. "I asked my mother several times before she died. But she wouldn't talk to me about it. Sometimes I think that's what killed her—the grief and the shame . . . and the fear. Not that they were *her* sons. They were the children of other wives. But she was afraid.

"Shub's father says I'm under Yahweh's special protection. Otherwise, the same thing would have happened to *me.* Supposedly Isaiah made a big deal of it in his prophecies when I was born. There was an oracle or something."

"Yes," said Shub quietly, without looking up. "It went something like this:

> "For to us a child is born,
>> to us a son is given,
>> and the government will be on his shoulders. . . .
> He will reign on David's throne
>> and over his kingdom,
> establishing and upholding it
>> with justice and righteousness."

Ezra was confused. "What are you guys talking about?"

"I'm going to sit on my father's throne someday," Hezekiah went on, ignoring Ezra's question. His lip was beginning to tremble. "And yet, by right, it should have gone to one of *them*. I just have to find out what . . . *happened* to them. I don't really want to know, but I *need* to know." He looked up into Ezra's eyes. "Do you understand?"

"No," said Ezra angrily. "I *don't* understand! And I'm not going to take the time to try right now. You're wasting my time. If we don't get going soon, it'll be too late! Do you know the way, Shub?"

Shub stood up and gave him a sheepish look. "I think so," he said.

"Well, then—lead on!"

CHAPTER 9

This night's walk was even darker and more unsettling than the journey the boys had made to Ophel the night before. There was no moon—Ezra knew that it would rise a little later on—and clouds were rapidly blocking out what little light fell from the stars.

They encountered no one as they picked their way along through the somber alleys and lanes of Jerusalem, staying close to the walls of the shops and houses. Mishneh Street was quiet. Even the cramped and winding lane that led past Ophel, through *Ha'iyr-David*, and eventually to the Potsherd Gate was strangely empty: no beggars, no thieves, no painted women veiled in red. The air felt close and heavy, and a sense of unspoken threat hung in the atmosphere. Ezra and his friends barely said three words to one another until they were outside the city.

Luckily, they didn't need to get past a sentry to make their exit. Hezekiah knew how to get out without using the Potsherd Gate at all. He led them through a small, unwatched portal between the two walls near the King's Garden, a place known only to the royal family and its aides.

Once beyond the walls, the boys made a sharp turn to the right and began their descent into the Hinnom Valley. On this particular night, *Gey' Hinnom* looked every bit as deep and dark as its reputation. At least Ezra thought so. He had often heard about the mysterious, forbidden things that went on in this place during the hours after sunset: secret pagan rites, wild dances, unspeakable sacrifices. He shivered a little as he thought about it—not because he was afraid, he told himself, but out of excitement.

Hinnom's sides were steep and rocky. The boys didn't reach the bottom without stubbing their sandaled toes and falling and scraping their knees often. Shub, of course, fell at least five times as much as the other two. And yet, somehow, he managed to keep his precious harp from getting a single scratch.

Once at the bottom of the ravine, Ezra called a halt and looked around. The night had grown exceptionally dark. It was difficult to see their way. But down toward the west end of the valley, Ezra could see the reddish glow of a faint and eerie light. It throbbed and pulsed against the underside of the gathering clouds and what looked like a column of rising smoke.

"This way," he said, gathering his cloak around him with one hand and pointing at the glow with the other. "We're on the right track!"

"Are we?" asked Hezekiah in a doubtful tone, dragging his feet as the older boys led the way. Shub pulled his *kinnor* deeper into the folds of his cloak and trudged ahead beside Ezra.

Patiently, doggedly they followed the glowing column of smoke until they came to a place where the ground began to rise in a gentle upward slope. They paused at the base of a small, round-topped hill.

"What's this?" asked Hezekiah, squinting through the darkness and reaching out to touch the top of what appeared to be a leafy hedge.

"Grapevines," answered Shub. "It's a vineyard. Looks like there's a garden just beyond the rows too. Father says they always put these places in the middle of gardens and under big, spreading trees. Gardens are sacred—'holy'—to Molech worshippers."

Ezra could see that the reddish smoke was rising from the top of the hill. Obviously, this was another *bamah,* or high place. Faintly, through the darkness, he could hear the confused noise of jumbled voices and a few rumbling drums and tinkling bells. He straightened his headband and set his jaw. "What are we waiting for?" he said. "Let's get going!"

They pushed their way past the vines and up through terraced beds of flax, coriander, and rue—brightly-colored flowers that only gleamed dull and gray in the darkness. Up the slope they labored, breathing heavily, always keeping the forbidding vision of glowing smoke before their faces. Behind him, Ezra could hear Shub chanting lines of verse to himself in a low, thoughtful voice:

> "You will be disgraced because of the gardens
>   that you have chosen.
> You will be like an oak with fading leaves,
>   like a garden without water."

As for Ezra, the words of another song were pounding through *his* head. Try as he might, he simply couldn't get rid of them:

> Now I will tell you
>   what I am going to do to my vineyard:
> I will take away its hedge,
>   and it will be destroyed;
> I will break down its wall,
>   and it will be trampled.

Over and over those words sang to him. The farther up the slope he climbed, the more maddening it became. He felt that he must find some way to stop it. In a moment or two, he'd have no choice. He'd have to scream or throw something or turn and run back down the hill. Anything to banish that song from his thoughts!

That's when they reached the summit.

Ezra put out a hand and signaled the others to halt. Before them lay a wide circle of ruddy light. The boys stopped just beyond its margin and stared. The scene in front of them was similar to the one they had witnessed at Ophel the night before. And yet it was different too—different in some indefinably, chilling way, Ezra thought. He shivered again and told himself that the night air was growing colder.

In the center of the open space on the hilltop stood a terebinth tree. Ezra knew that it must be very old. He had never seen a terebinth so tall or with such thick and widely spreading branches. A flickering red-orange light played over the bark of its gnarled trunk and skipped through the open spaces in the overarching ceiling of its lance-shaped leaves.

Below the tree was the source of the pulsating light: a towering altar of baked brick standing at the top of a flight of ten wide steps. It was topped by a stone image of the Red King himself—the head of a bull on a grotesquely distorted human figure squatting on its haunches. Within its bowels danced the flames of a fierce and roaring fire. The idol's apelike arms were outstretched as if to receive the offerings of its worshippers. Even at this distance Ezra could tell that the statue was hollow and that any object placed in its arms would roll instantly down through its tube-like body and into the raging flames below.

"So," said Hezekiah quietly, almost to himself. "*That's* what he looks like."

Shub gave a low whistle.

"Let's see if we can get any closer," urged Ezra. He was surprised at the hoarse, dry sound of his own voice.

As the boys inched forward, they could see that the people gathered around the altar—a much smaller crowd than the one at Ophel—were divided into two groups.

On the left side stood the women. Some were veiled and solemn. Others looked wild and disheveled. A few were wailing and chanting in strange, high voices, their dark robes loose and open, their faces streaked with paint. Several of these robes were of a pattern strangely familiar to Ezra: midnight blue, with a stripe of Tyrian purple at the hem.

Suddenly a thought occurred to him: *Could Mother be here?* At once his heart began to pound. His eyes roved back and forth in search of her. What if she *were* here? With Hanun? But it was no use. In the throbbing half light, it was impossible to get a good look at any of the faces.

On the right side stood the men. Some were heavily cloaked, their faces covered. Others were bare-chested. A group of them held musical instruments—lyres, pipes, drums, or cymbals. And a few, oddly enough, carried babies in their arms. As the boys watched and listened, the drums took up a hypnotic beat. The infants started to scream.

"Babies!" whispered Hezekiah, gripping Ezra tightly by the arm. "It's what I was afraid of. I asked them, over and over, but no one would ever talk to me about it!"

"Quiet!" growled Ezra. He didn't want to think about Hezekiah's problems. The thought of his mother being there with Hanun was proving even harder to banish than the words to Shub's song. For the first time he asked himself whether it had been a good idea to come.

Between the men and the women, directly in front of the altar, stood a tall figure in a flowing scarlet robe. As the boys watched, this man walked over to a bronze pot that hung from a tripod over a small cooking fire. Leaning over the pot, he dipped a ladle into it and poured a measure of steaming red broth—what it was made of, Ezra couldn't guess—into a wooden bowl. Then, taking a step forward, he raised the bowl in both hands and called out in a loud voice: "Keep to yourselves! Do not come near me, for I am holier than you!" With that he put the bowl to his lips and drank deeply.

"Holier! Holier! Holier than we!" chanted the people. The cymbals chimed and the drums pounded.

"Let the circle be cast!" called the man in red. "Let the dance begin!"

At his words the entire group fanned out and formed itself into a wide ring. Instantly the beating of the drums grew louder. The pipes and lyres intoned a dark, alluring tune in a mysterious, ancient mode. Slowly the feet of the celebrants began moving in time to the music, at first with carefully measured steps, and then with increasing agitation as the melody line rose and dipped and rose again. The pounding of the drums grew more insistent. The drone of the pipes swelled.

Ezra shook himself. Was this, after all, just another dream? His foot was tapping to the rhythm of the music. He couldn't remember when it had started. It seemed to him that it had always been tapping. He felt that his mind was emptying itself, like a pitcher of water poured out on the sand. He pinched himself and fought to control his thoughts. "Mother," he whispered, casting his eyes around the moving circle. He *had* to know if she was there. Without thinking, he stepped into the light and made a move to join the dancers.

Shub was at his side in an instant, his *kinnor* nestled securely in the crook of his left arm, the fingers of his right hand already plucking the tune in unison with the other instruments. Ezra turned to look at his face and saw the red light of the flames reflected in his eyes.

"This is why I came!" said Shub in an excited tone of voice Ezra had never heard him use before. "To play. Maybe all night long. With real musicians!" And with that he broke away from his friends and ran to join the other lyrists and pipers.

Through the gathering fog in his mind, Ezra somehow became dimly aware that Shub was not acting like himself. Something, he felt, was wrong with Shub. He blinked and tried to swallow, but his throat was too dry. Something was wrong with this whole situation—dreadfully wrong. Dizziness threatened to overwhelm him, but he fought it off. *Dance,* he thought vaguely. *I've got to join the dance.*

He turned to Hezekiah, who was lagging behind and looking for a chance to slip away. "Come on," he said in a voice that sounded as if it belonged to someone else. "Let's go! Nothing bad will happen. You'll see." And then he grabbed Hezekiah by the arm and pulled him into the circle.

Why did I say that? The question drifted into his mind as if from a distance as he and Hezekiah were swept away with the furious beat of the drums, the swirl of the dancers' robes, and the high wail of the flutes and pipes and vibrating strings. *Why am I doing this? This isn't right. Something bad is going to happen, I just know it.* But it was too late to stop now. Ezra felt his brain relax and let go, like an overstrained muscle. He ceased to think.

How long they were caught in the churn of the circle, Ezra didn't know. On and on it turned, like the relentless spin of the starry sky-wheel, like an irresistible sucking whirlpool in the heart of the sea. The music swelled, and the red light of the flames flashed past his eyes over and over again.

And then—without warning—there was a face. A cry of distress, a dark hood thrown back, and a weary, bearded face, etched with deep lines, emerging from the swirling storm of light and dark and revolving colors. A face open-mouthed, staring-eyed, wearing an expression of confusion and fear. A face that was looking not at Ezra but at someone beside him.

"Hezekiah!" cried the voice that burst from the mouth in the face. "Hezekiah! What are *you* doing here?"

It was King Ahaz.

At that cry everything came to a halt. The circle slowed and stopped. The chanting ceased. The dancers turned and gaped at the king. The music dragged, hesitated, soured, and fell apart. The wailing infants grew quiet. From across the circle Ezra caught a glimpse of Shub's face, pale and wide-eyed as if he had just snapped out of a nightmare. Slowly the prophet's son lowered his harp and stared.

In the silence that followed, Ezra saw the man in red come striding across the open space toward them. Bells tinkled at the hem of his flowing robe, and bright rings flashed on his long fingers. The features of his face, as grim and severe as if they were chiseled from stone, lurked threateningly within the shadows of his scarlet head covering. On he came, with a slow and stately step, until he stood beside the king. There he stopped and smiled thinly down at Hezekiah.

"Your son?" he said, glancing sideways at the king. "Well! I think it's fairly clear what he is doing here. The Red King has drawn him. For a purpose."

Ezra could see that Ahaz was shaken. The great talker, the easy conversationalist, the social charmer, the persuasive leader—this is how Ezra had always thought of his king. Now he saw him as someone a lot like himself: small, shivering, frightened, vulnerable. Quickly his eyes moved from the king's face to the face of the man in red, and then to the dark, overclouded face of the sky above. From beyond Hinnom's western rim, the sound of distant thunder reached Ezra's ears.

"What are you saying, Tammuz . . . great priest?" asked Ahaz. He barely moved his cracked, dry lips as he spoke. Sweat ran in two trickling streams down his cheeks.

"I say nothing," answered the priest of Molech. "The great Red King speaks for himself. Can't you hear him? Isn't his will plain to all who have eyes to see and ears to hear?"

A low murmur ran around the circle. Ahaz turned a pale face upon his son and said nothing. Ezra saw the pleading look in Hezekiah's eyes as he returned his father's glance.

"Weren't we speaking of this very thing tonight, just before we called the circle together?" the priest persisted. "Haven't you confided to many of your advisors and closest friends your firm belief that only the power of Molech can remove the Assyrians' thumb from the small of Judah's back? As in the past, so it will be on this occasion. By the hand of the Red King we may yet fight fire with fire."

More voices. Another rumble in the sky. And close at hand, one of the Molech worshippers suddenly spoke. "He is right, Your Majesty. We discussed this subject at your dinner party the other night. You remember. We agreed then that Assyrian gods might very well be the key to ridding us of the Assyrians . . . and their tribute. You said so yourself."

That voice, thought Ezra. A sick thrill of recognition coursed through his brain and body as it rang in his ears. He turned to see the darkly handsome face, framed by a black beard. Hanun. *Him again!* If Hanun were there, could his mother be there too? Once more he scanned the circle in search of her face, but to no avail.

"It is true," King Ahaz was saying. Sweat poured down his face. His eyes were fixed on the ground. "I did say it. But *this,*" he added, looking up at the priest, "I never meant to go through *this* again!"

"Ahaz," said Tammuz in calm, measured tones, "it is clear to me that Meni, the Lord of Destiny, and Molech, the Red King, have joined counsel this night. The sacrifice has been provided. Yes! Provided by the hand of Molech, that the power of Molech might be released!"

With that the priest laid one hand on Hezekiah's shoulder. With the other he beckoned to two dark-robed men who stood several paces away, awaiting his orders.

"Bind the boy!" he called. "Let him be prepared. He goes to join his brothers. He goes to the great Red King. It is the will of Molech!"

"*Molech! Molech!*" chanted the circle of worshippers.

"Now stand away!" shouted Tammuz with a flourish as the men in the dark cloaks drew near. Just beyond them Ezra could see Shub, his *kinnor* under his arm and an alarmed expression on his face. In the next moment the prophet's son began to cross the open space at a run.

"Away! Keep to yourselves!" the priest shouted, his arms raised above his head, the huge sleeves of his red robe falling down around his shoulders. "Do not come near, for I am holier than you!"

"Holier! Holier! Holier than we!" echoed the crowd.

"And this boy—this prince of Judah—he is holier than all. He goes to the Red King!"

"The Red King!"

Shub ran up to Ezra, panic in his face. Ezra shot him a questioning glance and then looked over at Hezekiah, who was visibly trembling.

"Let the circle be extended!" cried the priest, his voice growing louder and more frenzied with every word. Each worshipper took three steps backward. "Wider and wider. Until there is room for all the gods and all the forces of the high and circling wheel of heaven. Sun and moon and stars. Call upon them, one and all, to attend us! Let there be no narrowing of the circle. Let their power be joined to the power of the Red King. Let them come and serve us in exchange for the sacrifice we offer!"

"Ezra," pleaded Shub in an urgent whisper, "you see what's happening! Do something!"

Ezra felt as if he were about to faint. "*Me?*" he said. "*Me* do something? What can *I* do?"

There was no time to think clearly. The dark-robed men were only a

few steps away. Already their sinewy arms were outstretched to lay hold of
Hezekiah. Hardly knowing what he was doing, Ezra grabbed the prince
by the edge of his sackcloth cloak.

"Run, Hezekiah!" he shouted.

Then, dragging his friend after him, Ezra turned and fled.

"I'm right behind you!" shouted Shub.

This bold move took the priest and his men by surprise. The boys
were several strides beyond the circle before they heard any noise of pursuit. Then a great outcry rose at their backs, followed by a flash of lightning and another peal of crackling thunder.

Ezra ran, conscious only of the wildly elongated and leaping shadows
that the altar's flames cast before him. Dimly, just ahead, he could discern
the gray patches and rows of the terraced garden beds along the descend-
ing slope. Behind him he could hear Shub's labored breathing and the
pounding of his heavy footsteps. It seemed to him that the noise of the
crowd and the shouts of their pursuers were fading. A thrill of hope shot
through him. *We're going to make it*, he thought. *We're going to make it!*

Then, just as it looked as if the rows of grapevines were within their
reach—*crash!*

"Mmmpphh!"

A burst of sounds just at Ezra's back: a sickening thud, a muffled cry,
the crunching of wood and the jangling of snapping strings. *Shub*, he
thought. *That clumsy Shub. He's tripped and fallen again!*

A nauseated feeling rising in the pit of his stomach, Ezra slowed his
steps and turned to look for his friend. Instantly pain shot down his arm
as strong hands grasped and held him. He heard Hezekiah cry out in
anguish.

"Ezra," whimpered Shub as two large men yanked him to his feet.
"My *kinnor!* It's ruined! Oh, we should never have come."

In a matter of moments, all three boys stood once again in the flickering light of the altar, facing the king and the priest.

Ahaz had no indulgent smile for them this time. He avoided their eyes. He drew his cloak around his shoulders and stared down at his feet. At last he muttered, "I am sorry . . . my son. It seems there is no other way. Apparently it is the god's will."

"Even so," assented Tammuz. "Now take him! Let him be brought near. The Red King calls!"

"No!" screamed Ezra, his eyes darkening with despair as two black-robed men stooped to bind the prince. "Hezekiah, I never meant for this to happen!"

Hezekiah turned to face his friend. He said nothing.

"It can't happen. Not to *you!*" cried Ezra as the men tightened the knots of the cords. Then a crazy idea popped into his head. It had worked before; maybe it would work again. "Take me!" he shouted. "Take me instead. It's my fault, Your Majesty. Let them take *me* instead!"

"I'm sorry," mumbled the king, still without looking up. "It cannot be."

"The Red King demands a king's son," said the priest, who stood beside Ahaz with folded arms. "No other will do."

Ezra's knees felt like rubber. His face was hot and feverish. *I've got to stop this somehow*, he thought. Suddenly he remembered something.

"But Hezekiah," he said, laying a hand on his friend's shoulder as the men began to pull the prince in the direction of the altar, "what about Isaiah's prophecy? What about the promise that Yahweh will protect you and make you sit on your father's throne?"

"I don't know," said the prince. "He must have been talking about someone else. There must be another."

Then the men dragged them apart. Ezra watched helplessly as his friend, in the company of the scarlet-robed priest, was led across the open circle to the base of the brick stairway that led to the altar.

CHAPTER 11

"Wait!" screamed Ezra, shocked at the sound of his own voice. So loud, so urgent was its tone that every eye in that horrible circle, every face, etched in flickering lines of black and red by the light of the flames, turned toward him.

The priest raised a hand and stopped the men on the bottom step of the great stone altar. The bells on the fringes of his long scarlet robe jangled. The gold and silver rings on his fingers flashed in the firelight as he turned, put his hands on his hips, and glared at Ezra. Ezra could see the whites of the man's eyes, shining like two milky crescent moons in the night of his dark and frowning face. They fixed the beam of their stare upon him through the smoky air. "*Another* interruption! What do you mean by it, impudent boy?" the priest demanded.

Ezra found himself striding boldly into the center of the circle. He straightened his headband, planted his feet, and raised his arms toward the sky. "In the name of all that is holy," he called out in a loud voice, "I ask leave to speak with the king!"

A murmur ran from one end of the open space to the other. It seemed to find an echo in the stirring of the leaves as the wind sighed through the branches of the great terebinth tree. From the lowering sky above came another rumble of thunder. The priest scowled. He was opening his mouth to say something when suddenly Ahaz stepped up to him.

"Let the boy speak, Tammuz," the king commanded. The priest of Molech hesitated, raised one hand, and opened his mouth. Then, as if thinking better of whatever he had planned to say, he folded his hands, bowed, and took a step backward.

Ezra was trembling violently. He felt sure everyone could see him shake. Any moment he feared his knees would begin knocking together uncontrollably, and his teeth would start chattering. His throat tightened, causing him to gasp for air. He was terribly afraid, and he knew it. But he also knew that, for just this once, he was doing the right thing and dared not stop.

"O King," he said, his voice quavering painfully, "I-I think you're making a terrible mistake."

The murmur rose again, louder this time. Ezra ignored it and pushed ahead. "Yes!" he said, gathering confidence. "A huge mistake. Don't you see? You're playing right into a trap!"

The murmur became an excited babble. The priest took a step toward Ahaz, his face twisted into an expression of outrage. The king put out a hand and held him off.

"Go on, boy," said Ahaz, moving closer to Ezra, his face pale and wet but strangely eager, his lip trembling. "What trap? What do you mean?"

"Well," answered Ezra, stretching the moment of advantage, "it's like this: You're asking a foreign god to help you get rid of the foreigners. Does that make sense?"

Ahaz said nothing, but an odd kind of light seemed to dawn in his haggard face.

"It seems to me," continued Ezra, "that once a god like this Molech sees you bowing down at his altar, he's got you right where he wants you. And that can't be good, because . . . well, after all, he's on *their* side—the Assyrians, I mean. What then? I'll tell you: *Wham! Bam!* He calls in his people to finish you off! Old Tiglath-Pileser, King of Assyria, couldn't have come up with a better plan himself."

More murmurs and another growl of thunder, but the king didn't seem to hear any of it. He was leaning closer and closer to Ezra, listening intently, his hands clasped tightly together.

"Besides," Ezra went on hesitantly, "Israel—and Judah—have their own God. Right? Isn't our own God strong enough to take care of us? Why do we need Molech?"

"*Aaaagggghh!*" shrieked a woman somewhere on the edge of the circle. "This boy is one of *them*! He violates all that is holy. He narrows the great circle!"

"Exactly!" shouted the priest, his red robe swirling menacingly in the dancing light as he put out a hand to lay hold of the king's cloak. But once again Ahaz waved him back.

"Let the boy speak, I say!" shouted the king.

Ezra did. "And that's not all," he said. His stomach was churning. The hair above his leather headband was dripping with sweat. He licked his lips and tasted salt. He felt that he was coming to the point—the point of everything. "Israel's God says that what you're doing here is *wrong!*" He spoke the words but could hardly believe they were coming out of his own mouth. The circle burst into a chaotic outcry.

Out of the corner of his eye, Ezra stole a glance at Shub. The tall boy's mouth had dropped open so that his chin almost rested on his chest.

"Yes!" shouted Ezra. "It's wrong of you to kill your own son like this, King Ahaz! Israel's God calls that murder. He's not like the other gods. He'd never even *dream* of asking you to do something like this. He calls it an *abomination!* That's what my father says—and Shub's father too, the prophet Isaiah. Israel's God promises to take care of you if you trust Him. But if you do this thing, you'll live to regret it. You'll have to face the consequences."

"Now he quotes Isaiah," laughed the woman in the circle. "The man no one believes!" Other voices mumbled assent.

Ezra looked straight at Ahaz, awaiting his response. He half expected the king to lash out at him in fury, to order his arrest, to cast him into the flames within the idol's belly along with Hezekiah. But Ahaz did none of those things.

What he *did* was something Ezra could never have predicted. He dropped to his knees, covered his face with his hands, and began to weep uncontrollably. Somehow the sight struck fear into Ezra's heart—a far greater fear than any threat of punishment could have inspired.

"Seize the unholy blasphemer!" shouted the priest of Molech pointing at Ezra, his dark countenance darker than ever with rage. But at that moment King Ahaz, in a sudden and rare burst of energy, jumped to his feet and faced the man. Another peal of thunder, louder than any that had preceded it, burst from the heavens.

"No!" cried Ahaz, his jaw set, his face still wet with tears. "The boy is right. I *have* lived to regret it! Night after night, in the dark watches of the early morning hours, their faces have passed before me in a ghastly parade. I have regretted it over and over again, I tell you. But this time I say *no!*" Then he turned and called to the men who were holding Hezekiah on the bottom step of the altar. "Release my son! Your king commands it!"

Immediately the two dark-robed figures obeyed. Ezra caught the glint of polished bronze as they drew long, bright knives from somewhere within their cloaks. Every face in the circle turned toward the three figures who stood silhouetted against the pulsing orange glow of the furnace. The knives flashed, the ropes fell, and Hezekiah came dashing over to Ezra and his father where they stood in the middle of the circle.

"Now go, my son!" said Ahaz hoarsely. The king's face was deathly pale and creased with deep lines and furrows. "All of you boys, go! Run! Back to the city as quickly as you can. And tell no one what you've seen!"

Ezra looked at Hezekiah. It seemed to him that his friend was too overwhelmed to move or speak. He stood staring up at his father out of great round eyes, as if seeing the man for the first time in his life. A few big drops of rain fell on the prince's forehead and dripped down his cheeks.

"Come on, Hezekiah!" said Ezra, grabbing his friend by the sleeve of his garment. "We'd better do as he says." He pulled the prince to the edge of the circle, where Shub stood waiting. The other celebrants parted ranks to let them pass. Then side by side, the boys, trembling from head to toe, slowly began walking out of the range of the firelight and out of the great circle. They made their way up the slope of the Hinnom Valley toward the lights of Jerusalem that twinkled faintly through the falling rain.

"Stop!" boomed the priest. So loud and powerful was his voice that Ezra felt he had no choice except to obey. He stopped, turned, and saw the man throw back the hood of his cloak. A wrinkled head was revealed, shaved in front and tattooed with dreadful symbols and signs—crescent moons, serpents, and spiderwebs. The priest grasped the king, who stood bent over and shaking, and cried out, "In the name of Molech, the great Red King, and of all that is holy, I tell you that you must complete the sacrifice or suffer destruction at the hands of the god. Seize the prince and bring him back!"

In answer to the priest's cry, several men broke from the circle and charged after the boys. At that very moment the rain began to pour from the sky in sheets. Then came a deafening crash of thunder and an explosion of lightning directly overhead. In the split second of brightness, Ezra saw the altar of Molech wrapped in clouds of white smoke and boiling steam. The pounding rain drenched the altar and put out the fire in the idol's belly. Terrified, the priest's servants fell to the ground or ran for their lives.

"What are we waiting for?" Ezra shouted to his two friends. "Let's get out of here!"

And then the three boys turned and ran toward the city with all their strength.

"**S**he isn't coming home."

Ezra winced at his father's words. He sat at the end of his sleeping pallet hugging his knees. In spite of his determination not to cry, his lower lip kept trembling, and there was a twitch under his right eye that he couldn't control. *Mother not coming home?* Ezra couldn't believe it. He rubbed his nose and reached up to straighten his leather headband.

Tola sat opposite him on a short three-legged stool, making no attempt to conceal his tears. "She says she doesn't belong here anymore. She's found someone who . . . *understands* her better . . . or believes as she does. More *open-minded*. Like King Ahaz. At least that's the message I got."

King Ahaz. Ezra would never again be able to think of King Ahaz in quite the same way. Banished forever was the image of the engaging, confident, persuasive leader of men. In its place was a picture of a shrunken, careworn, frightened child in an adult body, racked with anxiety and indecision, cowering before the horrible demands of the Red King.

"But Father, don't you even know where to find her?"

Tola raised an eyebrow and gave his son a piercing look. "I was hoping *you* might have an idea," he said significantly.

Ezra's face burned with shame. He bowed his head. "I'm sorry, Father," he said. "I told you she wasn't there. I saw Hanun but not Mother. Not once. I looked for her—I looked hard! But it was dark, and the light of the flames distorted everything, and most of the women had their faces covered."

Ezra paused. His vision blurred. Into his mind came a picture of the narrow alley off Mishneh Street, its striped awnings dirty and tattered and blowing in the night breeze. Distorted faces leered at him in the half light cast by oil lamps and charcoal grills. He saw baubled and bangled women stretching out their hands to him from shadowy nooks and stone arch-ways. Again, in his imagination, he stared up at the Tower of Ophel and gaped open-mouthed at the high place, the altar, and the forest of Ash-erah poles, bright with little fluttering banners. A sudden idea struck him.

"Father," he said, "I *might* know where to find her. I really might! Can I go out and look?"

"We've been over this," his father said sternly. "You're confined to this house for the next two weeks. No—make that a month! Do you under-stand me, young man? After last night's little escapade, I've a good mind to put an iron ring in the wall and tie you to it like a donkey. You simply have no idea, Ezra. No idea. Why, for a while there I thought I'd lost *both* of you!" He paused, and for a brief moment the bearded face flushed red. "I suppose you'll never know until you have children of your own."

"I said I was sorry, Father," Ezra replied, squeezing his eyes shut and pressing them against his knees until he saw stars. "You wouldn't believe how sorry I really am!"

Then the tears came, and he made no further attempt to hold them back. Why had he never realized before how much his father cared about him and his mother? He knew now that he was something much more to him than a prophetic sign or wonder. He knew—and felt—that his fa-ther, like Isaiah, was a man possessed—by love. A man who would sooner die than buy peace or prosperity or personal achievement by sacrificing his own son. Why couldn't he have recognized it sooner?

Tola got to his feet, wiping his face with the back of one hand. Then he reached down and ran his fingers through his son's tangled black locks. "Do you know what?" he said. "I believe you this time. Somehow or other, I believe you really *are* sorry. But we don't have time to mope about our troubles now. There's another meeting of the Remnant tonight. We'd better have some supper before the prophet and the others arrive. Looks like lots more stale loaves and sour *leben* for you and me. At least until Old Hephzibah's arm heals up. Oh, didn't I tell you? She's promised to stay and cook for us. For a while, anyway. Until your mother . . . changes her mind."

Ezra looked up and saw him smile sadly as he turned to leave the room.

By the time the members of the Remnant began to gather, Ezra was feeling more like himself again. *Maybe more like a new self,* he thought as he watched them file through the door.

First came the slight young Elisabeth, one of the king's servants, who blushed and smiled when Ezra caught her eye and then hurried in to sit beside Old Hephzibah. She was followed by Ira, the hunchbacked weaver. Then came Ben-Shimri, a hard-fisted, square-jawed silversmith who'd lost most of his business by refusing to make images of the Baals and Asherahs. Acsah, the round-faced wife of Ezra's tutor, Mishael, was there too, and Maacah the baker's daughter, and Pua, who served as a reserve member of the King's Guard.

They weren't the kind of people Ezra would have chosen as friends—not most of them, anyway. In the past he would have laughed at them and called them "losers" and "a bunch of nobodies." But tonight he seemed to see them with new eyes. Tonight they felt like family. Somehow, in his mind, they glowed with a soft, warm light that was altogether different from the leaping flames in the idol's belly. *Signs and wonders in Israel* were the words that popped into his head as members of the group passed him and went to find a place to sit on the floor of the main room.

Finally the prophet himself entered—stern-eyed, his dark brow furrowed with lines that reminded Ezra of the creases in his own father's forehead. He was followed by his wife, the lively little Abigail. She flitted through the door on tiptoe, directing a few words at Ezra's father before moving farther into the house. Trailing after her came fuzzy-haired, red-cheeked Maher-Shalal-Hash-Baz. He raised an eyebrow at Ezra and gave him a knowing smirk before sweeping past on the hem of his mother's skirts. Any other time Ezra would have felt like bashing him in the face. Tonight he just shook his head.

Last of all came a face Ezra hadn't expected to see. "Shub!" he said. "What are *you* doing here?"

Shub looked sheepish. He put a finger to his lips and shuffled his big feet. "I had to come," he said. "After last night, I . . . well, it's just that everything has . . . *changed* somehow."

Ezra nodded but said nothing.

"Besides," Shub went on, "without my harp I don't have anything to do at home. My father says the only way I'll ever get another *kinnor* is if I build it myself or earn the money to buy one. And neither one of those is easy." He bit his lip and frowned. "He's *really* mad, Ezra."

Ezra frowned too and nodded again.

"But mostly I came to talk to *you*. I keep thinking about last night. It still seems like some kind of weird dream. I keep remembering the things you said. Did you mean it?"

Ezra blushed and stared down at his feet. "Mean what?"

"You know. What you said to that priest in the big red robe and all those other people. About abominations and consequences and Yahweh, the God of Israel. You were like . . . like some kind of *hero*, Ezra! Like Moses or Joshua or Elijah. I couldn't believe it! Did you mean it? Or was it just another one of your tricks?"

Ezra looked his friend in the face. "I'm not sure if I meant it *then*," he said slowly. "But I think I do *now*."

He glanced at the plain, humble faces of the people who sat on the floor of his father's house. They spoke in low voices, waiting for the prophet to start the meeting. "I was wrong, Shub," Ezra continued. "Something bad *did* happen. And it would have been much worse, except that . . . I don't know . . . except that God, the *real* God, really *was* watching out for Hezekiah. Just like your father said He would. I was wrong, and Hezekiah was right. I should have known all along. I guess I'm just too stubborn."

"Well, I'm glad to hear you say so," said a voice at the door. Ezra and Shub wheeled around at the sound. There, draped in the same soiled and torn street-urchin's cloak he'd worn to the pagan high places on the two previous nights, stood the stocky little prince. He was breathing hard, his round, ruddy face glistening with sweat.

"I came to join the Remnant," said Hezekiah in answer to their blank stares. "Had to sneak out to do it too. Ran all the way here. You taught me well, Ezra," he added with a grin. "Not that it was all that hard. My father has been trying to avoid me all day."

From the inner room came the deep, melodic voice of the prophet, who had risen at last to address the gathering of the Remnant. "Comfort, comfort my people, says your God," he chanted in slow and soothing tones.

> Speak tenderly to Jerusalem,
>   and proclaim to her
> That her hard service has been completed,
>   That her sin has been paid for,
> That she has received from the Lord's hand
>   double for all her sins.

Ezra straightened his leather headband and smiled. Then he grabbed Hezekiah by the hand and pulled him into the house.

"Come on," he said. "We'll *all* join! And I've got a feeling that it'll be the biggest and best adventure we've ever had. *You'll* see!"

LETTERS FROM OUR READERS

This story is scary, especially the part about Molech worship and the strange parties the idol worshippers had. (Brent P., Indianapolis, Indiana)

Idol worship *is* scary! The boys shouldn't have gone to the high places at all. Sometimes, like Ezra, we think that we can get away with doing things we know are wrong. But there are consequences to dabbling in evil. Ezra found that out when his friend Hezekiah was almost sacrificed to the evil god Molech.

Unfortunately, people aren't very different today. They start out doing things they think are innocent, such as reading horoscopes, playing with Ouija boards, or developing a fascination with entertainment that makes the occult look fun. Once they get caught up in these things, it's easy to get deeper and deeper into it until they're hooked, just like the Molech worshippers. The Bible tells us to stay away from idols and evil practices (see Deuteronomy 18:10-12; 1 Corinthians 10:14, 20-21; Galatians 5:19-21).

Where can I find this story in the Bible, anyway? (Josh R., Cheyenne, Wyoming)

You'll find the basis for this story in the book of Isaiah, 2 Chronicles 28, and 2 Kings 16, all in the Old Testament. Isaiah was a prophet who wrote during the reigns of King Ahaz and King Hezekiah, when the Assyrian Empire was expanding into Canaan. Isaiah warned the people about worshipping the Assyrian gods, which didn't make him very popular. Isaiah had at least two sons, Shear-Jeshub (Isaiah 7:3) and Maher-Shalal-Hash-Baz (Isaiah 8:3).

You won't find any mention of Ezra or his dad, Tola, in the Bible, though. We imagined what it would be like to be a prophet's kid. What if this boy got tired of everyone expecting him to be supergood, like his father and the prophet Isaiah? What if he was just a bit too curious and wanted to find out if all those stories about idol worship were true? What if he thought nothing bad could happen to him? Maybe you know someone like that.

Did King Ahaz really sacrifice his children to a false god? (Danielle M., Greenville, South Carolina)

Unfortunately, yes. The Bible says, "He [Ahaz] walked in the ways of the kings of Israel and also made cast idols for worshiping the Baals. He burned sacrifices in the Valley of Ben Hinnom and sacrificed his sons in the fire, following the detestable ways of the nations the LORD had driven out before the Israelites" (2 Chronicles 28:2-3).

The boys mentioned the prophecy that says, "For to us a child is born, to us a son is given." They said it was about Hezekiah, but I thought that prophecy was about Jesus. (Justin M., Chicago, Illinois)

Many interpreters of Scripture think that Isaiah's immediate thoughts were focused on present-day events when he uttered those words. That he really was hoping and expecting that Ahaz's son would turn around the sad state of affairs that had developed under Ahaz. Many centuries later, we can look back and see that his words had a much larger meaning—a reference point that he himself was perhaps unaware of. Much of Old Testament prophecy is like that. For example, God tells David that his "son" will "build a house" to the Lord's name, and that his throne or dynasty will never end (2 Samuel 7). The obvious immediate reference is to Solomon and the temple. But in the long run, Solomon turned out to be a big disappointment, the temple was destroyed, Judah ceased to be a nation, and the line of her kings failed. So the prophecy must have had some larger reference—to Jesus and the "house" that He would build in the form of His church.

Did Bible-era kids really talk back to their parents the way Ezra did in this story? My parents wouldn't let me do that, and I don't even live in Bible times. (Matthew M., Anchorage, Alaska)

Since no one can say exactly how kids acted and spoke back in Bible times, authors have to use their imaginations and what they know about the culture to guess at what life might have been like. Kids tend to be the same in any time period, so maybe they disobeyed sometimes and talked back to their parents. No matter what culture or era we live in, though, God wants us to respect our parents and others. (See Leviticus 19:3; 1 Peter 2:17.)

It seems like many of the kings of Israel and Judah worshipped false gods. How about Hezekiah? What happened when he grew up? (Kyle H., Toledo, Ohio)

He's called "good King Hezekiah" for a reason. In 2 Kings 18:5-6, it says, "Hezekiah trusted in the LORD, the God of Israel. There was no one like him among all the kings of Judah, either before him or after him. He held fast to the LORD and did not cease to follow him; he kept the commands the LORD had given Moses." It also says that he removed the high places and the Asherah poles and broke up the sacred stones and the bronze snake Moses had made. You can read the story of Hezekiah's reign in 2 Kings 18–20 and 2 Chronicles 29–32.

ABOUT THE AUTHOR

JIM WARE is a graduate of Fuller Theological Seminary and the author of *God of the Fairy Tale* and *The Stone of Destiny*. He and his wife, Joni, have six kids—Alison, Megan, Bridget, Ian, Brittany, and Callum. Just for fun, Jim plays the guitar and the hammered dulcimer.

FOR PARENTS AND TEACHERS

TROUBLE TIMES TEN
▶ *Background*

Sometimes we learn a lot of Bible stories, but hardly give any thought as to how they might be connected. In many cases, that piece of information can help us understand the individual accounts.

For example, when *Trouble Times Ten* begins, the Israelites are slaves in Egypt. How did they get there? Let's back up to the story of Abraham. You may remember that God called him out of his homeland to a new country and promised to make him a great nation, but he went many years before he even had a child of his own. Then Isaac was finally born. Abraham was going to offer him as a sacrifice on the altar as God instructed, but an angel intervened just in time. You may remember the story of Isaac's twins, Jacob and Esau, and how Jacob conned Esau out of both his birthright and his father's blessing. And you may remember how Jacob had a whole slew of sons—twelve, to be exact. But he liked Joseph best and gave him a coat of many colors. (Don't doze off just yet. We're almost there.)

You may remember that Joseph's brothers despised him so much that they were ready to kill him, but sold him into slavery instead when the opportunity came along. Where did Joseph end up? That's right—in Egypt. He started as a servant until he was falsely accused of a crime, then spent several years in prison. But God had given him the ability to interpret dreams, and when Pharaoh had a dream that no one else could figure out, he called on Joseph. After Joseph prepared the nation for a seven-year famine and saved the day, he was promoted and given land in Egypt. His whole family migrated from the land where God had called Abraham and established homes in Egypt where they would be safe from the famine.

Weeks became years . . . then decades . . . then centuries. The family of seventy grew and grew and grew. By the time our story takes place, there were hundreds of thousands of Israelites. The new Pharaoh had no idea who Joseph was and didn't feel he owed the Israelites anything. In fact, he was afraid one of his enemies would strike an alliance with them to turn against Egypt. That's when he decided to enslave them.

About four hundred years after Joseph went to Egypt, Moses came along. *Trouble Times Ten* recalls how Moses' parents released him in a basket on the Nile, how he was adopted by Pharaoh's daughter and raised as royalty, and how he killed an Egyptian while trying to protect an Israelite. Moses fled and stayed away for forty years. What the people didn't know at the time was that God had called him back to Egypt from a burning bush (perhaps you remember that story too). It would be Moses' task to lead God's people out of slavery and back to the land God had promised Abraham centuries before.

As you can see, these are not random, individual stories, but a single, interconnected saga. The big story is about God's provision and deliverance, one that continues in your relationship with Him today.

TROUBLE TIMES TEN
▶ *Learning Activities*

If you'd like to get more out of *Trouble Times Ten*, consider these projects:
- Conduct a little research on phobias, the kind of fear Ben had about water. What's the number one fear people have? Are phobias rare or common? What are some unusual phobias?
- Find a Bible map and trace the route the Israelites would have taken to get from Egypt to the Promised Land. What challenges would you expect during such a journey?

- The author mentioned some Egyptian gods. See what you can find out about Hapi, Heket, Ra, and any other gods the Egyptians worshipped. In each case, how would one (or more) of the ten plagues have influenced the Egyptian perception of the god?

TROUBLE TIMES TEN
▶ *Discussion Questions*

1. At one point in the story, Enoch asks, "How does anyone know, while he's trying to live through it, whether the days of his life are the stuff of great stories and tales that will be told throughout all time?" Have you seen or done anything lately (either very exciting or quite ordinary) that you think you might tell your grandchildren about?

2. Some people suggest that God is mean because He continued to intensify the Egyptian plagues each time Pharaoh refused to respond. But God would not have needed to send the plagues if Pharaoh had responded the first time Moses asked nicely. Can you recall a time when you refused to respond to a polite request, and some authority (parent, teacher, etc.) had to get a bit harsh to grab your attention?

3. Do you have a friend or relative like Micah, who needs your special care and attention because of a disability? If so, how do you feel about trying to maintain that responsibility, especially when it limits what you get to do with your other friends?

4. When you sense God might be prompting you to do something a little scary, how do you respond? In the story, Enoch suggested that we should be more afraid *not* to do as God asks than to do whatever it is that scares us. Do you agree?

RULED OUT
▶ *Background*

Most of this story takes place while Moses is receiving God's Law on top of Mount Sinai. Today few figures in Jewish history are as revered as Moses. But Moses' success as a leader raises a big question: Just how did he get in that position?

Think about it. Sure, his parents risked a lot by putting him in a basket and floating him down the Nile River. And sure, anyone who is adopted by royalty has a good chance of success in life (see Exodus 2:1-10). But all that background was erased with one decision Moses made. One day he saw an Egyptian beating a Hebrew worker, and he killed the Egyptian. He thought he had gotten away with it, but no. Soon he had to flee into the desert (Exodus 2:11-15).

Overnight, his life changed. While a refugee from Egypt, he took a wife, had a couple of kids, and started tending the flocks of his father-in-law—a far cry from the pomp and comfort of the royal palace. No doubt he'd resigned himself to remaining a country bumpkin for the rest of his life. But that's when he had his encounter with God at the burning bush. Again his life changed with one decision.

It was at the burning bush where God spelled out the plan He had for Moses (Exodus 3–4). That's where Moses learned he'd been chosen to deliver the Israelites. He was told in advance that Pharaoh would not listen to him—but he was supposed to go ask that his people leave, anyway. At the burning bush God also showed Moses he could throw his staff on the ground and have it become a snake. (He also could give himself leprosy, but apparently never needed to demonstrate that sign.) Moses learned that when Israel left Egypt, the Egyptians would actually give them silver, gold, and clothing. And God promised that after Moses had led his people out of Israel they would all worship Him on that very same mountain (Exodus 3:12).

Even though Moses was reluctant to step up and become the leader of the people, God answered his every concern. Moses decided to respond, accepting his calling and returning to Egypt. It must have helped to know everything God had told him in advance. After Moses connected with God, it didn't matter that Pharaoh wouldn't listen to him at first. It didn't matter that the people grew resentful and impatient. He knew what he had to do, and he did it.

By the time this story takes place, the Israelites had witnessed the plagues on Egypt, their official release from slavery, crossing the Red Sea, being miraculously fed every day while on the move, receiving water from a solid rock, and an underdog battle victory over a powerful enemy. God's presence was with them—literally—through a pillar of cloud by day and a pillar of fire by night. God's promise to Moses was fulfilled as they gathered together to worship on the mountain. They should never have doubted God or Moses.

However . . . Moses and God told the people to abide by a few simple rules, and the people didn't want to. That's where complications arose, as you discover in this story. The people created headaches for Moses, but worse, they severed the relationship between themselves and God. That was a *real* problem.

RULED OUT
▶ *Learning Activities*

You might want to dig a little deeper into the background of *Ruled Out* by doing one or more of these projects:

- The golden calf was an idol—a "pretend god." List at least a dozen modern-day "idols" that people allow to take their attention away from the true God. Consider people, possessions, activities, and anything else you think qualifies. Then brainstorm how, with all those options, you can maintain a strong relationship with God.

- God's laws are scattered throughout the books of Exodus, Leviticus, Numbers, and Deuteronomy. After careful examination, the Jewish leaders had eventually come up with 248 dos and 365 don'ts. Skim through those books and write down at least a dozen of the laws you think are most important. (The Ten Commandments are listed in Exodus 20:1-17 and Deuteronomy 5:6-21.) Then see which laws Jesus singled out (Matthew 22:34-40; Deuteronomy 6:5).

- It seems that a lot of important stuff in the Bible took place on top of mountains. This story reminds us how Moses received the Law on top of Mount Sinai. What other mountainous events can you think of (or look up)? Start with Genesis 8:1-4; Deuteronomy 34:1-6; 1 Kings 18:20-40; and Matthew 17:1-13.

RULED OUT
▶ Discussion Questions

1. Who in this story are you most like: Ethan, Leah, or Melki? Why?

2. When you know your friends are watching you, are you more likely to follow rules or break rules? When you know your parents are watching you, are you more likely to follow rules or break rules? Why do people your age sometimes have different responses to these two questions? What does that suggest about them?

3. Have you ever had to move away from a place where you liked to live? If so, what were your regrets? What were the positive results of the move?

4. It's natural to resist rules sometimes. But what would happen if, say, everyone decided to ignore traffic rules? How about rules for basketball? Or rules for building skyscrapers? What's the problem with everyone doing what he or she wants to do?

GALEN AND GOLIATH
▶ *Background*

By the time David faced off with Goliath, the Israelites had experienced a long and turbulent history with the Philistines. Even way back when Moses led Israel out of Egypt and Joshua took them into the Promised Land, the Philistines were already there to give them trouble (Joshua 13:1-3).

You might remember the story of Samson and how the Philistines were in control of Israel at the time. They could do little to control Samson, of course, until he fell in love with Delilah. So they hired her to get close to the strongman and betray him. Yet even in his dying efforts, Samson took out thousands of Philistines (Judges 13–16).

The Philistines weren't finished with Israel. When Eli was priest and had begun to take care of the young Samuel, the Philistines again went to war with Israel. In the battle, they stole the Ark of the Covenant and killed both of Eli's sons. When Eli heard the tragic news, he fell over backward, broke his neck, and died (1 Samuel 4:1-18). But God did not allow the Ark to remain in Philistine possession for long. He sent a plague among their people, and they gladly returned it to Israel (1 Samuel 5–6). (By the way, this passage contains a fascinating story about what happened when the Ark of God was placed in the same temple with the Philistine god, Dagon.)

As Samuel grew he had his own confrontation with the Philistines, but Samuel realized that the problem was a spiritual one. He had the people rid themselves of other gods, confess their sins, and pray for deliverance.

The Philistines were approaching, ready for another war, but God sent loud thunder that rattled them so much that the Israelites had no trouble defeating them (1 Samuel 7). And we are told, "Throughout Samuel's lifetime, the hand of the Lord was against the Philistines" (verse 13).

At that point in history, the people demanded a king in spite of Samuel's objections. Saul was chosen and took over leadership of the nation. Samuel died soon thereafter, and it turned out that Saul didn't have sufficient faith and courage to lead. Before long the Philistines were a problem again. Saul (and even more, his son Jonathan) had some success against them (1 Samuel 14). But in contrast to the peace that Samuel had achieved, "All the days of Saul there was bitter war with the Philistines" (1 Samuel 14:52).

All this had taken place prior to David's one-on-one with Goliath. But even afterward, when Saul was attempting to capture or kill David, the young leader and his followers hid out in Philistine territory. Saul didn't dare look for him there, and David even negotiated for a city where he and his men could stay. They were there for a year and four months (1 Samuel 27:1-6).

When David became king, no enemy was a match for his armies. But the Philistines were still lurking in the area. Many years later, when Hezekiah was king, he was still battling Philistines (2 Kings 18:8). Amos prophesied the ultimate demise of the Philistines (Amos 1:8), and they eventually fell to Nebuchadnezzar and the Babylonians.

But even today when someone is being rude and uncouth, he or she might be referred to as a "philistine."

GALEN AND GOLIATH
▶ *Learning Activities*

If you want to get a little more out of the story of Galen and Goliath, here are some projects you might want to try:

- Do some research on armor and weapons of the era. (For example, Goliath wore something called *greaves*. Do you know what they are?) Try to get a size and weight estimate for Goliath's battle gear (see 1 Samuel 17:4-7).

- In contrast, learn more about David's weapon of choice by looking up the biblical version of a sling. (It's not like most of the slingshots you might see in toy stores.) Read Judges 20:16 to get an idea of how accurate a sling could be.

- Find a tape measure. Go out when the sun gets low in the sky and shadows get long. When your shadow gets between nine and ten feet long, have a friend trace your outline on the ground. Then try to imagine someone that big, fully armed, coming after you. With that in mind, what kind of person do you think David must have been?

GALEN AND GOLIATH
▶ *Discussion Questions*

1. Have you ever really wanted to do something, but were prevented because of some physical limitation (height, weight, health, etc.)? How did you handle your disappointment?

2. If you were over nine feet tall, what are some things you'd want to do? Would your life be better or worse? Why?

3. Galen's image of the god Dagon was little more than a good-luck charm for him. Do you know anyone who thinks an object or habit will bring him or her good luck? How do you think God feels about good-luck charms? Why?

4. What do you do when you're around mean people who are bigger and stronger than you and are bossing you around?

What can you learn from this story to inspire you the next time you're bullied by someone? Do you think this story teaches us to strike back at bullies? Why or why not?

THE PROPHET'S KID
▶ *Background*

This story is set during one of the more depressing eras in the history of the Jewish people. When God gave Moses the Ten Commandments (many centuries before this story takes place), the first two commands on the list warned against putting other gods before the true God, and making or worshipping idols (Exodus 20:3-5).

A lot had happened since the Israelites received those laws. They'd entered the Promised Land, but failed to run out the residents as they'd been instructed. In time, they defied God and adopted many of the gods and religious practices of their neighbors. During the time of the judges God allowed enemy after enemy to overpower His people. Each time they'd repent, and God would send a judge to deliver them. But then they'd go right back to their idolatry.

After the people demanded a king, David fully trusted God and united the twelve tribes. His son, Solomon, had been faithful for a while, but then allowed his many wives to turn his heart away from the true God in pursuit of many other gods. The kingdom that David had united soon split after Solomon's reign. The southern kingdom of Judah contained Jerusalem and the temple—a special place that most people visited several times a year. So the king of the northern kingdom, Israel, decided to create his own attraction for worshippers. He set up golden calves in two prominent cities and established shrines and priests at various other "high places" (locations where pagan peoples had held their religious rites).

The spiritual status of Israel and Judah had spiraled downward from there. Very few of the kings after Solomon had any redeemable qualities.

Devotion to God was forgotten in pursuit of political power. King Ahaz was among the worst of the kings. But as the story reminds us, his son Hezekiah was one of a faithful few.

Isaiah was a steadfast prophet during this time. He had a lot to say about the idolatry of his people and how foolish it was to worship figures of wood and stone. He pointed out that a guy could cut down a tree, use half of it to heat his dinner, and then carve the other half to worship as a god (Isaiah 44:9-20). Did that make any sense? Even more telling, people had to nail down their idols to keep them from toppling over (Isaiah 41:7). What kind of power could someone expect from an object that couldn't even stand up on its own?

Still, idol worship wasn't just ridiculous. It was dangerous. The sacrifices to Molech described in this story are no exaggeration of what was involved with worship of that particular god. Perhaps that's one reason we're told to watch out for the "powers of this dark world" and the "spiritual forces of evil" that oppose God (Ephesians 6:12).

THE PROPHET'S KID
▶ *Learning Activities*

If you want to learn a little more about the time period of *The Prophet's Kid* or respond to what you've read, here are some suggested projects to get you started:

- Find a concordance, Bible dictionary, or similar reference and see what else you can discover about the following figures and items mentioned in the story:

    High places

    Baal

    Asherah poles

    Molech

    Strange or "unauthorized" fire (see Leviticus 10:1-2)

- Read the story of Isaiah's vision of God (Isaiah 6). How would you like to experience God in that way? How does God tend to communicate with people these days?
- Think of positive ways that your parents have influenced you so far in life, and come up with a creative way to tell them and thank them (a handmade card, preparing a meal, an original song, etc.).

THE PROPHET'S KID
▶ *Discussion Questions*

1. Do you have a treasured possession like Shub's *kinnor* (harp)? If so, why is it special to you?
2. Have you ever done something dangerous or stupid primarily to impress someone else? Did you accomplish your goal, or did your attempt backfire?
3. When was the last time you had to suffer consequences for something you'd done? What did you learn from the experience?
4. Did you ever display or express a level of faith in God that surprised even yourself? What typically prevents you from speaking up for God as much as you might want to?

Start an adventure!
with Focus on the Family

Whether you're looking for new ways to teach young children about God's Word, entertain active imaginations with exciting adventures or help teenagers understand and defend their faith, we can help. For trusted resources to help your kids thrive, visit our online Family Store at: